Red hats, purple dre

and applause for Haywoo

THE RED HAT CLUB

"A gossipy, engaging read, full of witty Southern characters readers will be unable to resist the urge to cheer on."
—*Florida Times-Union*

"Smith's celebration of comradeship is a loving tribute to those lifelong relationships that may defy logic . . . a joyous, joyful ode."
—*Booklist*

"Rowdy Southern feminist fantasy."
—*Kirkus Reviews*

"*The Red Hat Club* ladies are just Bridget, older, wiser, and with husbands who may or may not be faithful."
—*Toronto Sun*

"A fine, confiding . . . voice, which makes for a fast, easy read. Her dialogue is true to life. She has a wicked sense of humor."
—Bookreporter.com

"Inspiring . . . fun to read."
—*Romantic Times*

"A humorous, cathartic coming-of-middle-age story of five feisty women who refuse to throw in the towel—or the hat."
—*Tennessean*

"A hoot . . . A delightful read that shows that even 'mature' women can be full of surprises to themselves and others."
—*Chattanooga Times*

"A great story with many fond memories for anyone who had a group of ladies in their high school."
—*Book Review Café*

"An engaging tale that welcomes readers as if they were sharing wine with the heroines . . . fans of women's fiction will appreciate Haywood Smith's fine homage to the Southern female."
—*Harriet's Book Reviews*

And praise for Haywood Smith's previous book

QUEEN BEE OF MIMOSA BRANCH

"Strong characters and . . . irrepressible wit . . . snapshots of Southern living will charm the hardest-hearted Yankee."
—*Publishers Weekly*

"Smith is on to something good here in Mimosa Branch . . . where the Ya-Ya Sisterhood would feel right at home . . . this one just shouts 'sequel!'"
—*Booklist*

"With wit, style, and charm, Haywood Smith creates a vivid picture of small-town Southern life. Here's a heroine you'll root for and a wonderful book you'll want to talk about!"
—Jill Conner Browne, author of
The Sweet Potato Queens' Book of Love

"A witty look at a woman struggling to find herself . . . fans of small-town Southern living will gain plenty of delectation from Haywood Smith's hilarious slice of life."
—*Midwest Book Review*

"A portrait of lasting relationships between family and friends in the small-town South. [Smith's] colorful cast of characters is unforgettable."
—*Southern Living*

"Linwood Breedlove Scott is a Southern belle with a plate of problems so hilarious, overwhelming, and relatable you will root for her from start to finish . . . an original character with pathos and pluck, a real woman with heart."
—Adriana Trigiani, author of *Milk Glass Moon*

"Don't miss this fabulous feel-good book. It's laugh-aloud funny, outrageous, deeply touching, but most of all, wonderfully uplifting."
—Deborah Smith, author of *The Stone Flower Garden*

Also by Haywood Smith

Queen Bee of Mimosa Branch

The Red Hat Club

Haywood Smith

 ST. MARTIN'S GRIFFIN ☙ NEW YORK

This novel is a work of fiction about a group of women who belong to a group like The Red Hat Society. It has not been authorized or endorsed by The Red Hat Society. All the characters and events portrayed in this book are either products of the author's imagination or are used fictitiously.

Cover photography by Herman Estevez

www.stmartins.com

Library of Congress Cataloging Number: 2003009124

ISBN 0-312-34130-X

First St. Martin's Griffin Edition: October 2004

10 9 8 7 6 5 4 3 2 1

This book is dedicated to my wonderful son,

James Lofton Smith, Jr.,

our living miracle who has given us so much joy, excitement, and pride.

Thanks for always taking up for your mama

and loving me anyway. It's mutual, doc.

Warning BY JENNY JOSEPH

When I am an old woman I shall wear purple
With a red hat which doesn't go and doesn't suit me.
And I shall spend my pension on brandy and summer gloves
And satin sandals, and say we've no money for butter.
I shall sit down on the pavement when I'm tired
And gobble up samples in shops and press alarm bells
And run my stick along the public railings
And make up for the sobriety of my youth.
I shall go out in my slippers in the rain
And pick flowers in other people's gardens.

You can wear terrible shirts and grow more fat
And eat three pounds of sausages at a go
Or only bread and pickle for a week
And hoard pens and pencils and beermats and things in boxes

But now we must have clothes that keep us dry
And pay our rent and not swear in the street
And set a good example to the children.
We must have friends to dinner and read the papers.

But maybe I ought to practise a little now?
So people who know me are not too shocked and surprised
When suddenly I am old, and start to wear purple.

Author's Note

I've often wondered if Jenny Joseph had any idea what she was starting when she wrote her wonderful poem "Warning." Her free-spirited declaration has become a joyous hymn for millions of baby boomers like me. Red Hat clubs have sprung up all over the world, a grassroots insurgence of women who have lived long enough to savor the simple act of having fun with the girls. Espousing no lofty sociological aims, these Red Hats thumb their noses at fashion and convention. They get together and have tea parties, do lunch, or browse to their hearts' content at swap meets and garage sales. They go to Vegas, take in Barry Manilow concerts, check out the outlet malls, cry without fear of ridicule in great chick flicks, get tipsy on wine and do one another's colors, or hide out from their responsibilities at the lake for a long weekend. The only restriction on their activities is that a good time be had by all.

Red Hats are a happy antidote to a culture that conditions women to tear each other down personally and professionally, and trains us to "fix" everybody and everything, including our friends. Having fun with them is so much less frustrating and destructive.

Inspired by "Warning" and the experiences of two brave and wonderful friends, I wrote this book to add my voice to those of all the world's women who help each other rise from the ashes and go on to sing—and laugh—even stronger than before. I hope you have fun with it and come out feeling better about yourself and the other women in your life. After all, that's the point.

The Red Hats

WE DIDN'T START OUT AS RED HATS. WE STARTED OUT IN the late sixties as Mademoiselles, self-proclaimed crème de la crème of Atlanta's Northside High, Dykes High, Westminster, and Lovett, full of ourselves and drunk with the power of our blooming sexuality and good looks. Coming together from different schools, different religions, and different backgrounds, lifelong friendships were forged as Mademoiselles.

That was back when there were still rules to be broken, and Atlanta was an overgrown, provincial small town despite its booming commerce and lofty proclamations of being the city too busy to hate.

God, did we have some fun—intensified by lots of luscious teenaged angst. Everything in our cloistered world seemed so *important*. Boys. Grades. Clothes. Sneaking out to the Varsity. Pep rallies. Dances. Hiding our coveted little harlequin-mask sorority pins during school, then flaunting them as we cruised Lenox Square or gathered at Wender & Roberts soda fountain.

We didn't realize then that we were the last of our kind.

With rare exceptions, our mothers had stayed home to take care of us. They might not have been June Cleaver, but they did their best to give that impression. Still, they urged us to go to college so we would have the choices they hadn't.

Yet, despite the feminist sea change within our generation, we Buckhead girls had been shaped by an older, more subtle imperative: to marry well and live happily ever after. It was a dream born as we played with our bride dolls, solidified by *Father Knows Best* and *Leave It to Beaver*, and secured by our bridge-playing, PTA-ing, dinner-on-the-table-every-night mamas. Those were our models, regardless of what our mothers told us about becoming lawyers and doctors and executives.

We Mademoiselles never imagined we would end up as the Jilted Generation. And we never dreamed that thirty-five years later we would still be friends. Well, most of us.

Nor did we ever suspect what secrets—and hidden strengths—those lifelong friendships might conceal.

Swan Coach House. Wednesday, January 9, 2002. 11:00 A.M.
After a brief, nonproductive swing through the gift shop and gallery in search of some "thinking of you" trinket to brighten up my son Jack's bachelor apartment or my daughter Callie's dorm room, I went downstairs to the sunny main restaurant, cheered by the familiarity of its dark wood floors, chintz tablecloths, and padded walls bright with tastefully garish tulips. As usual, I was the first to arrive, still clinging to the illusion that punctuality was possible with the Red Hats despite more than three decades of evidence to the contrary. But that was just me—always expecting things, and people, to be better than they really were.

"Table for five, please," I said to the lone waitress, a plump, nondescript woman I didn't recognize.

She didn't blink at my red fedora, ancient sable car coat, and tailored dark purple pantsuit. The Red Hats were such a fixture here that our eccentricities had become part of the basic orientation for the staff. "Sorry, mah-dahm," the waitress said in a thick Slavic accent, "must wait for all here to be seated." Clearly, she had no idea she was dealing with a Buckhead institution, one that was allowed to bend the Coach House's ironclad edict. With the exception of private parties, mere mortals were never seated until everyone in their party had arrived. But owing to our long-standing presence, the Red Hats were the exception that proved the rule—provided we were discreet about it. Clearly, this new waitress hadn't gotten the message.

I looked for her name badge, hoping the personal touch would thaw her out a little. She wasn't wearing one, but I tried anyway. "My name is Georgia," I said in my most pleasant manner. "What's yours?"

She arched an eyebrow in disdain. "You could not say it. Too hard."

Serious attitude.

My master's in Southern Bitch kicked in, smoothing my voice to honeyed ice. "What a lovely accent. Where are you from?"

"Where're y'all from?" the belle asked the Yankee couple.

"From a place in which we know better than to end a sentence with a preposition," the haughty Northern woman answered with a sneer.

"Oh, I'm sorry," the belle cooed sweetly. "Where're y'all from, bitch?"

"Romania," the waitress answered with a defensive shrug.

Great. This was going to be a challenge for both of us.

"Please get the manager," I said distinctly. "Tell her it's the Red Hats."

She scowled again.

I pointed to my red fedora. "Tell the manager that the Red Hats are here, and I want to be seated."

She disappeared into the back, then returned with the apologetic manager du jour. "Sorry," the young woman whose name tag identified her as JOSIE said in her most appeasing manner. "We were shorthanded, so we pressed Vashkenushka into service from the kitchen. I forgot to tell her about y'all. Please forgive us." Despite the fact that we were the only ones in the cheery yellow foyer, she glanced about, her expression clouded with concern as she lowered her voice. "I really appreciate your continuing discretion about this arrangement, though. We'd have mutiny if the other customers found out."

"Trust me," I reassured her. "No one will ever hear it from us." As if everybody who was anybody didn't already know.

The manager's brow eased. She motioned the waitress toward our regular banquette in the back corner near the kitchen door. "Seat the ladies in red hats as soon as they come in. Just this one group, no one else," she instructed, "and treat them well. They're very special guests."

"Yes, madam," Miss Romania said, but her manner bristled with contempt as she led the way across brilliant slashes of winter sunshine that slanted through the white plantation shutters.

I sat down in the shady corner, but kept my coat on. The room was chilly, and I hadn't been warm between November and April since 1989.

When our little group had first started meeting here—long before we were Red Hats—the waitresses had been Junior Leaguers working their required service placements. Back then, the bigger the diamond, the worse the waitress, and Atlanta's well-to-do young matrons were seriously solitaired. The League had eventually hired paid staff, but the joke was on everybody for a while: the quality of service hadn't improved for a long time. For the past decade, things had been much better, though still a little slow from the kitchen. But that was an accepted part of the mystique, along with the limited tearoom menu.

The Red Hats didn't come for the service, anyway, or for the food. We came because the Coach House was an Atlanta institution, a link to our past with a great tea party quotient. I couldn't count the bridal showers, baby showers, luncheons, and receptions we'd all attended there.

"To drink today?" the waitress asked with a decidedly aggressive note.

"I'll have unsweetened tea, please," I said. "No lemon." I like iced tea, and I like lemon, but nowhere near each other.

"No coffee?" she challenged. "Isss cold today. Maybe hot tea?"

"No, thank you." I suppressed a blip of irritation. She would learn. "Just plain iced tea, please, no lemon." It's a Southern thing, drinking iced tea at lunch even in the winter. Shrimp salad just doesn't taste right with coffee. "And I'll need lots of refills," I said, smiling in an effort to lighten things up. "I'm a heavy drinker."

Not a flicker of amusement crossed her broad face, prompting me to wonder if she didn't understand, or if total lack of humor was one of the main requirements for working there, as I had long suspected.

"My friends will be here soon," I told her. "We usually stay until closing. If you'll keep our glasses filled, we'll give you a *big* tip." It was only fair, since she wouldn't be able to turn the table.

"Big tip." She seemed to understand, but she didn't break a smile. "I get your tea."

A Romanian waitress at the Coach House. What next?

I still wasn't accustomed to Atlanta's being crowded with people from other countries. Who'da thunk it? Atlanta *G-A*, buzzing with Mexican domestics and laborers, Vietnamese manicurists, polite Ethiopians, religious fugitives from the Baltics and Russia, Koreans, elegant Sudanese, Central American refugees, well-to-do Japanese, Haitians, plus hordes of Indians and Pakistanis in the fast-food and convenience store business, to name a few.

Outwardly, I had met the onslaught with resolute enlightenment and Southern hospitality, but inwardly, a lingering part of me wanted to circle the wagons. Gone were the narrow social boundaries of my childhood—Crackers, Blacks, Catholics, and Jews, Mainlines, and Pentecostals—erased by this new invasion that made unlikely allies of anybody who'd grown up here.

And then there were the Yankees, a group that has expanded to include anybody from anywhere but the South. We were overrun with them, including the ones from Florida who considered themselves Southern but weren't. Not that the changes they brought with them were all bad, but Southern accents had become a rarity, and you never saw a soul you knew shopping at Phipps Plaza or Lenox Square anymore.

Maybe that was why we Red Hats clung even tighter to our

little group as we grew older. It was the one solid connection to our past.

"George!" Diane called to me from across the room. She must have just had her hair colored, because her white roots were not in evidence below her red beret. She'd worn contacts since she was nine, but today the thick glasses I hadn't seen in years contorted her attractive face into a peanut shape, reminding me of the momentous day we'd met so long ago.

Lord, I'd forgotten how blind she was without her contacts.

"I lost a lens and almost didn't even come." Even more flustered than usual, she muddled her way between the tables, poking through her enormous Vuitton shoulder bag as she bumped the chairs. "Dad-gum it. I put that paperback you loaned me in here somewhere, but now I can't find it."

Considering the shape the paperback would probably be in, I quickly reassured her, "Well, don't worry if you can't." She was notorious for loving whatever she read nigh unto death—breaking the spines, slopping coffee on the pages, sometimes even baptizing them in the tub with her—so I only loaned her the ones I could live without.

I changed the subject. "Did you remember your joke? It's your turn, you know."

She flopped dramatically into the seat beside me. "Yes. But it's getting harder and harder since Sally"—her good ole girl hairdresser—"had that stroke. She was my only source."

"What about the new girl?"

Diane grimaced. "She weighs eighty-seven pounds, has black lips, piercings, and a fuchsia streak in her 'bedhead' hair. I don't think she would know a joke if it bit her."

I laughed. Diane was naturally a stitch, but she could not tell a proper joke for beans. "How many times have I told you?" I said, "You need to get e-mail. People send me jokes all the time. You should try it. Lee's been dying to set it up for you." Her only son, Lee, had graduated in business with a minor in Japanese from Harvard and a master's from Wharton. Now he made big bucks consulting for a major Japanese company in Asia.

"Lee?" she scoffed. "From Tokyo?"

Diane and I had been playing this little game about the computer for at least five years. I never got anywhere with her, but she took such satisfaction from resisting that I hated to give it up.

"He comes home every three months, and you know it." We baby boomers might be dragged kicking and screaming into the Age of the Internet, but not our grown sons and daughters; they were all computer savvy.

Diane, on the other hand, seemed to consider it a matter of honor to hold out. Very passive-aggressive, which was definitely her style. I loved her, but you had to be careful or she'd store up hurts, then bite you on the ankle when you least expected it.

"I swear," I harped, "once you get on-line, you'll love it. Instant gossip, honey. And Lee would probably e-mail you every few days from Tokyo, instead of just calling once a month."

"Right. And what about spam and viruses and upgrades and expense?" She adjusted her thick glasses.

I stifled the urge to laugh.

She peered at me earnestly from the depths of distortion. "I haven't got time or energy for one more thing in my life. But since you're so hot about the Internet, why don't you just find me some jokes next time it's my turn?"

"No. That defeats the purpose."

Diane straightened the rich purple-and-red paisley of her challis skirt. "I thought the purpose of bringing a joke was for us to laugh," she grumped.

"It is. But it's also important for us to have to *find* the joke," I reminded her. "Finding the joke requires positive personal interaction outside the group. It's good for you. For all of us."

"Lord." Flat-mouthed, she sagged. "Like I said, I have enough to do without having to prod people for jokes."

Game called on account of pain.

We both knew the secret sorrow she was talking about, but Sacred Red Hat Tradition Five (Mind your own business) kept me from prodding. If she ever decided to talk about it, she would. Frankly, if John had done to me what Harold was doing to her—after she'd put him through law school and remodeled their houses and been the perfect corporate wife for a quarter of a century—I'd have jumped off the top of Stone Mountain long since.

But then, I was the only one of us who hadn't finished college and hadn't worked. I'd met John my junior year and taken the June Cleaver track.

Diane deflected the pregnant silence that had fallen between us by scanning the Ladies Who Lunch now filling the room. "Where's our waitress? Are you sure we have one?" she asked, reminding both of us of the long-ago meeting when we'd finally realized that nobody wanted to wait on us because they couldn't turn the table. We'd triple-tipped ever since, and a good time was had by all.

I wasn't so sure about today, though; Miss Romania had a chip the size of Bucharest on her shoulder. "I don't see her. She's new—Romanian, doesn't speak much English. She took my drink order and promptly disappeared completely."

Diane opened her napkin, then snagged another waitress on her way to the kitchen. "Excuse me, miss. Could you get our server, please? We need drinks and muffins and rolls and lots of plain butter."

We didn't *need* the rolls and butter, of course, but some of us wanted them.

"Right away, ma'am."

I looked past her to the entry, saw a small red pillbox hat bobbing through the waiting patrons, and waved. "Oh, good. There's Teeny."

Teeny nodded in acknowledgment, doing her best not to attract attention in her tasteful black reefer coat and impeccable purple wool sheath as she skirted the room in our direction. When she reached us, she slipped gracefully into a chair, her blue eyes less shadowed than they'd been in a long time.

"M-wah, m-wah." Hats grazing, Diane did that fake Euro kissy thing on either side of Teeny's delicate features. "Look at you, Teeny girl, gorgeous as Audrey Hepburn in that new dress. I swear, you don't look a day over twenty in that outfit."

As always, Teeny responded to the compliment with awkward pleasure. "Thanks." She shrugged off her coat, revealing tapered sleeves in a rich bouclé wool. "I made it."

"You are joking." I reassessed the simple, elegant creation. The cut was sophisticated and beautifully tailored. "I'm gabberflasted. It looks like you paid a fortune for it." Teeny hadn't sewn since our boys were in T-ball, but her rotten, rich husband kept her on such a short leash financially that she might have been forced to take it up again. The possibility annoyed the poo out of me, but no way would I let on. Teeny was allergic to conflict of any kind. "That tailoring. I can't believe you actually made it."

Teeny's eyes glowed as she looked down and to the right. "Thanks."

Diane gave her a sideways hug. "Worthy of Old Miz Boatwright's Home Ec class."

"Miz Boatwright," I mused. "Now there's a blast from the past. How in this world did you remember *her*? You didn't even go to Northside."

"SuSu and Linda bitched about her enough." Diane mimicked Linda's dead-on imitation of the woman we had tortured for trying to teach us to cook and sew. "No spiders, ladies. Tie and trim those loose threads, or it's ten points off for every one of 'em."

Teeny giggled behind her hand, prompting me to wonder yet again if she ever let loose and laughed aloud like she used to. Our monthly jokes were no way to tell. She never "got" them. And she was even worse than Diane at telling them.

"Miz Boatwright," I repeated, nostalgic. "Ruling duenna of Northside's domestic arts." Her image sprang vividly from three decades ago, surrounded by cutting tables, arcane kitchen appliances, and sewing kits in the Home Ec lab. I could still remember the faint underscent of sewing machine oil mingled with the aroma of the muffins she baked every morning for her friends on the staff. "A blast from the past," I repeated.

"Who's a blast from the past?" Linda approached from behind a group settling at the table beside us. Her wide face was framed by soft, shiny silver curls that only she, among us, had the courage to wear. She looked ten years older than we did, but didn't care, secure in her doting husband's love. Her red knit waif-hat and bulky purple sweater earned a few curious glances before she plunked into her usual chair.

"Miz Boatwright in Home Ec," I informed her. "Diane actually remembered her name."

"Ah." Linda nodded. "The poor soul who tried unsuccessfully to make proper homemakers of us." She looked to Diane. "Thank your lucky stars you didn't have to suffer such nonsense at Westminster."

"I'm sure they assumed you'd hire all that out," I said without malice. It was true.

Linda looked at me. "Miz Boatwright succeeded with you, George. You can cook like Julia Child and sew almost as well as Teeny."

"My sewing days are long gone. The last thing I made was a Nehru jacket for John." Then a sobering thought struck me. "Oh, gross. Do you realize that when we were in her class, Miz Boatwright was probably younger than we are now?"

Linda groaned. "Thanks a lot for that cheerful little observation."

Teeny jumped in with a prim, "Perhaps you'd like to follow it up by counting crow's feet. If so, I suggest you start in the mirror."

"Teeny!" I perked up, hoping she'd intended the zinger. But she simply blinked back at me with her usual wide-eyed innocence. Teeny didn't have a hostile bone in her body; she just said whatever she thought without considering how it might sound.

Uncomfortable at the mere hint of conflict between Teeny and me, Diane invoked the first of our Sacred Red Hat Traditions: "Do over."

Tradition One (Do over): Any one of us, at any time, can simply ask for a fresh start and get it. Change of subject, change of attitude—no matter how bad we might have screwed things up (in which case, immediate apologies are in order).

Diane peered in her best ex-schoolteacher manner at both of us. "I'm in no mood to be reminded of my middle-aged shortcomings, even by Teeny."

"Oh, for cryin' out loud, Di," Linda chimed in, "Teeny didn't mean anything by it." She never did.

Frankly, any one of us would have been delighted if she had. She hadn't stuck up for herself since 1974, the one and only time. (More about that later.) We all longed to see her stand up to that sorry, good-looking, good-for-nothing husband of hers. But Teeny would steadfastly keep up appearances, hanging quietly on her discreet, tasteful martyr's cross until the day she died, and we'd love her anyway.

"So." Linda steered to a topic we could all safely complain about. "Where's the waitress? Don't tell me you've scared her off already, George."

Did I mention that George is my nickname? It's short for Georgia, but not my native state. That would be *too* redneck. My mama was very artistic and forward-thinking, so she'd named me after the infamously liberated artist Georgia O'Keeffe, a fact that has always given me a clandestine sense of scandalous satisfaction. But only the Red Hats and my husband are allowed to call me George.

Miss Romania finally appeared with my tea—*with* lemon despite my request otherwise, dad-gum it—and a small basket of bread with strawberry butter balls.

I removed the wedge from the side of my glass, then wiped the rim with my napkin, but the damage had been done. That first glass would taste faintly of disinfectant to me, even with plenty of Sweet 'n Low.

Typically straightforward, Linda took charge of the bread basket and assessed its skimpy contents. "I'm afraid we're going to need lots more than this."

When the waitress frowned, clearly confused, Linda clarified, pointing to the tiny muffins and fat rolls. "More bread, please. Now. And much plain butter. Plain butter."

Still scowling, Miss Romania disappeared—without taking the drink orders.

Linda helped herself to a muffin. "Yum. Poppy seed."

"Well, keep 'em down there by you," I grumbled. "Don't tempt me. I have to save my calories for the main course."

"Tradition Twelve," Linda invoked. (No mention of weight or diets.) Passing the rolls to Teeny—whose metabolism, unlike the rest of ours, kept her rail thin no matter what—she promptly shattered the same tradition. And Tradition Five. "I'm tellin' you, George, as long as you walk at least four times a week and give up on trying to look thirty again, fat's like dust: it reaches maximum thickness pretty quickly. Then you can eat whatever you want within reason without gaining any more."

Easy for her to say. Her devoted little urologist husband was as barrel-bodied as she was. But my husband had grown increasingly thinner and more distant in recent years, working out and working late with driven compulsion. I dared not risk letting myself go.

Of course, I was still operating then under the illusion that if you "did it right," your marriage would be safe from the plague of infidelity that had wiped out most couples we knew. It had started slowly with our parents, then spread like some immoral Ebola through our own generation, with Bill Clinton as its poster boy.

At the sound of a familiar smoker's cough over the polite din of female conversation, we all turned to see SuSu hurrying in, her freckled face overtanned and her once-red hair a strangely greenish hue. She never wore a hat, red or otherwise; flatly refused.

She could have used one, though. One look at her hair, and I didn't have to see the others' reactions. I knew that another of our sacred traditions was on its way as soon as she got settled in.

"Hey, y'all," she said in her husky smoker's voice as she shucked her jacket, revealing the khakis, sweater, and white shirt that were her flight uniform. "I've gotta leave early to work the six o'clock to Houston, so let's get this show on the road."

Essence of SuSu: arrive at least half an hour late, then cause a scene trying to hustle everybody up.

None of us wasted any emotional energy being annoyed by it anymore. We did, however, compensate by teasing her about being the world's oldest stewardess.

"You manage to get to the airport on time," Linda chastened. "So we know you *can* teach an old dog new tricks. How 'bout spendin' some of that newfound punctuality on your best friends for a change? Don't we deserve it?"

"Punctuality is precious," SuSu shot back. "What little I can muster up, I have to save for matters involving money."

Still, I kept hoping she might eventually apply some of it to her social engagements.

"Where's the waitress?" SuSu asked with a familiar, dangerous glint in her eye, scanning the menu as if she actually might order something besides her usual. "I've gotta be out of her by two."

She closed her menu decisively, rose, and headed for the foyer. "I'm gonna tell the manager we need some service."

"Our poor waitress," Teeny murmured, her gentle soul always pained by confrontation. "She doesn't seem to understand much English. I don't think it was very wise of them to assign her to us."

Linda cackled. "God, no. We're something you work up to."

"Yeah," I chimed in, "like waitress boot camp: a shared ordeal that bonds the staff together."

Diane let out her throaty chuckle. "Somebody gets to be the Princess and the Pea. It might as well be us."

"Princess? Hah," I said with more than a hint of bitterness. Princesses, indeed. We had all had our tantalizing tastes of happily-ever-after, but only Linda's had lasted. The rest of us were living in denial or running scared. SuSu had lost everything, forced to support herself after two decades of wife-and-mothering.

"Oh, dear." Teeny peered toward Josie, who, standing beside a haughty SuSu, was searching the room for our invisible server. "I hope SuSu doesn't get snippy this time."

There was a heartbeat of silence; then the four of us—even Teeny—burst out laughing, loud enough to draw stares and muffle the herd-of-birds roar in the room.

Of course SuSu would get snippy. She always did, but we loved her anyway, just as we overlooked her chain-smoking (thank God, the restaurant was smoke-free), her drinking, her stubbornly disastrous taste in men, and her persistent failure to wake up and smell the coffee.

Diane motioned her back over. Before SuSu reached the table, our favorite waitress, Maria, emerged from the kitchen with warm rolls, plain butter, and her pad. "Sorry about the hang-up, ladies. Seems Vashkenushka just up and left without telling anybody."

"Oh, gosh." Teeny grimaced, quick to take responsibility and drag us along with her. "Now see what we did. We ran that poor woman off."

"Well, good riddance if you did," Maria said matter-of-factly. "The devil owed this place a debt, and he paid it with that woman." She lowered her voice conspiratorially. "The manager only put her out front because the cook threatened to quit if she didn't get her out of the kitchen." She poised her pen. "How about drinks? Water for everybody, plus the usual?"

Linda considered, buttering a roll. "Could you make us some more of that hot lemonade you did the last time, Maria? It was so-o-o good."

"Certainly. How about a couple of pots for the table?"

The room was still cool, and the hot lemonade sounded wonderful. "Good with me."

The others nodded.

"All right, then." She knew without being asked to take our orders right away. "The soup of the day is clam chowder, and the fish is pan-seared tilapia with a lemon-butter sauce." She patiently endured the cosmic compulsion that causes Ladies Who Lunch to complain about the delay while waiting to order, then dither like they've never even seen a menu when the waitress finally arrives with pen in hand.

I won't even discuss the thing about splitting checks and the havoc wreaked by to-the-penny purists. In the interest of time and global tranquillity, Maria also knew without being asked to do separate checks.

After allowing a decent interval for consideration, I went first, as usual. "I'll have the shrimp salad plate, please."

Maria scribbled away, flipped the page, then waited through the lengthy passive-aggressive pause of indecision that followed.

I kept myself from getting annoyed at the others' dithering by checking for familiar faces across the room, but found none. An office luncheon of twelve, six Talbotsy, white-haired quads, lots of upscale duos, and a corner table with three women in tennis sweats, which was *so* not done these days.

Not a soul I knew. It just wasn't our town anymore.

Finally, Diane got things rolling again by ordering her usual. "I'll have the Favorite, no pineapple, please."

"Same here," Teeny followed on cue. "But pineapple's okay for mine."

Linda muttered over the hot entrées, then ordered what she always did. "I'll have the French onion soup and chicken salad croissant."

"Very good." Maria removed their menus, waiting for SuSu to make up her mind.

"A glass of Chablis and the combination plate," SuSu finally declared. "But bring me regular coffee, too, please." She turned to us. "I need the caffeine. The flight goes on to Arizona, then Salt Lake City, so it'll be morning before we make the layover."

Coming from SuSu's mouth, the term *layover* was a double entendre of galactic proportions, but the four of us managed to keep straight faces.

We waited until Maria was gone before we all leaned in toward SuSu and whispered, "MO! Big-time."

Red Hat Sacred Tradition Two: Anybody can call a makeover (MO) when it's warranted.

"What is *with* that hair color? Shades of senior green," I said sotto voce, referring to the summer I'd worked as a lifeguard in high school and ended up with olive drab instead of bleached blond hair.

"The color's not nearly as awful as George's was that time," Teeny was quick to soothe, "but it definitely has a cast of that same green."

"You didn't resort to drugstore hair color, did you?" Linda asked, aghast. " 'Cause that's what happened to my cousin's friend. The salon color interacted with the cheap stuff, and she went bald within a week. Had to wear an Eva Gabor wig for more than six months while her hair grew back out." Sounded like an urban myth to me, but Linda clearly believed it.

"Of course I didn't use that junk," SuSu said, indignant to be accused of one of the most alarming signs of impending poverty or personal neglect in a Buckhead girl. "Charles still does my color, just like always." She clearly wasn't taking the MO in the spirit of sisterhood. "Granted, I'm a little late getting to him this month. I had to cover for a flight on my regular appointment day. But I haven't sunk to shampoo-in."

Diane peered at her uncovered coiffure. "Kinda that pool-green color we got as kids."

"Pool." SuSu's eyes sharpened as the truth sank in. "Shit."

"Ha. Mystery solved." I drove the point home. "Those layovers in Cancún and Arizona and New Mexico. Pool hair."

At least SuSu had the good grace to look sheepish. "I've been swimming laps." She pulled a thick shock of her stylish bob toward the front for a closer look. "Double shit. It is green." She flicked it back into place. "Oh, well. Charles'll fix it next week."

The rest of us exchanged glances.

"Speaking of Charles, Suse," Diane ventured, "maybe this might be a good time to try somebody else. He hasn't done you any favors for the last few months."

SuSu scanned our faces for confirmation and got it. "Why didn't you say something sooner?"

Ever the peacemaker, Teeny leaned forward, sympathetic. "It just happened sort of gradually. Today's the first time it's rated an MO."

"Okay. I'll consider it, but next month. I don't have time to go hunting."

"Try Joanna, at Athena on Buckhead Avenue," three of us said in unison.

"You can have my appointment next Tuesday," Linda volunteered. "You'll love her, and she can fit me in anytime."

"Okay. Enough. I'll go." Uncomfortable, SuSu glanced toward the kitchen. "Where's my wine?" She turned back. "Enough about me. I call a do over. Who's got the joke?"

Diane raised her hand. "Me, but remember, joke-telling is not my forte."

"We live in hope, Di," Linda said as always. "Go for it."

Diane pulled out a paper from her purse and unfolded it to reveal her loopy, inflated handwriting. "A Buckhead housewife and her husband were having an argument about sex," she read, dropping her voice on the last. " 'You never tell me when you're having an orgasm!' the guy yelled.

" 'How can I?' she yelled back. 'You're never here!' "

Linda and SuSu laughed. I'd heard it ages ago, but laughed anyway.

"Good one," SuSu ruled.

"I second that." Linda.

Teeny smiled politely, a quizzical expression on her face. We'd long ago given up on trying to explain the jokes to her. We loved her as much because of her naïveté as in spite of it.

Suddenly Diane looked as if she might burst into tears. "Okay, now that that's out of the way," she said, leaning in to keep anyone beyond the table from hearing, "I've got major trouble, and I need y'all to help me."

That got our attention, pronto. Spring-loaded with concern, four red hats and one green head huddled up as she reached into her pocket and produced a tidy little note that she smoothed out next to the bud vase where all of us could see it.

"Buy sheets—310 thread count. Paint the kitchen," it said in a precise male hand.

"I found that in the pocket of Harold's suit last night."

"So?" Linda asked.

"We don't need any sheets," Diane growled in a tone I'd never heard her use before. "And he sure as hell isn't painting any kitchens at *my* house!"

At last. She'd finally acknowledged the truth that we had long since known. The question was, what was she going to do about it?

My mind swirled with possibilities. I was great at analyzing my friends' problems—almost as great as I was at denying my own.

Another One Down

"OHMIGOSH," TEENY BREATHED OUT, WIDE-EYED. "YOU DON'T think—"

"Of course she thinks," SuSu said. "She'd be a fool not to."

"God, Diane, I'm so sorry." I was shattered for her. We all were, despite the fact that Harold was a selfish brat, never worthy of her devotion.

The chorus of a golden oldie echoed through my brain yet another time: *Another one bites the dust. Ungh!* So many in the past few years. As the toll mounted, so did the gnawing fear that kept me from looking below the surface of my own lackluster marriage.

Before I could get my next thought out, Linda spoke it for me: "What are you gonna do, honey? Whatever you want, we're with you all the way."

Diane's usually placid features hardened, but the gravity of her expression was counteracted by the distortion from Coke-bottle glasses. "I'm counting on that." She exhaled heavily. "We made a killing on the house in Nashville"—thanks to her; she'd restored the place on a shoestring, with no help from him—"I couldn't understand why Harold wanted to put so little into the house we bought here, but it all makes sense now." She shook her head. "He had this planned all along. Five'll get you ten, he has a condo 'with' somewhere. He had me sign a boatload of financial stuff last summer when we moved." She grimaced. "I've got a sinking feeling he's already plundered our joint assets."

We'd always teased Diane for their "traditional" financial arrangement. (She didn't even balance her own checking account.) Harold was the banker, the financial whiz. Suddenly, it was no laughing matter that she'd trusted him with the assets she'd worked as hard as he to save.

Fatal choice.

She'd trusted him, just as I still trusted John. A salty wash of fear diluted my righteous anger. But John was a straight arrow, always had been. Totally different from cut-the-corners Harold.

Teeny's compassionate eyes looked huge as a sugarbaby's. (That's a flying squirrel, for all you non-Southerners.) "Well, shit. Just shit."

We all looked at her in amazement. She *never* cussed.

"Judas priest!" You could see a lightbulb going on in Linda's brain. "Those Friday nights at the sailboat."

"I know." Pain and shame ravaged Diane's all-American face. "Y'all told me it was stupid to believe him when he said he just needed some time alone. You were right." She hid behind perfectly manicured hands. "God knows what else I let him get away with."

"Tradition Eight! Do not waste one second beating yourself up about this, Di," SuSu chided, aiming a swift kick at Linda under the table, but hitting me instead.

Linda, contrite, shifted her shins safely out of range. "She's right. This is *not* your fault. Harold must have lost his mind. You're the best wife any man could want—cute, fit, smart, interesting, superthrifty, a great hostess, and the best mother ever. Hell, you even do electrical and plumbing."

"Yeah, well," Diane said, "somehow that's cold comfort at this point."

With the exception of SuSu, we were an endangered species:

well-educated women who didn't work outside the home. Despite mounting evidence to the contrary, we'd all believed that if we "did it right," we'd be safe from the midlife male epidemic of self-indulgence, betrayal, and irresponsibility. But that hope was a lie, a huge, cruel, soul-eating, razor-edged booby trap.

"Yeah," Linda added. "The only crime you ever committed was knowing him, warts and all."

"The cardinal sin," SuSu said with biting sarcasm. "God forbid they might have to face somebody who knows their faults. The idiot probably thinks he's perfectly justified in getting some dumb, adoring little bimbo with a father fixation."

"Wait a minute," Teeny cautioned us. "Y'all might be jumping to conclusions, you know." She pointed to the note. "I know that's disturbing, but it won't do anybody any good to let your imagination run wild."

Cold resolution turned Diane's wounded hazel eyes to steel. "No. And that's where y'all come in." She plucked a muffin from the bread tray. "Harold handles all our accounts, so I don't have access to the funds for hiring a private detective without tipping him off. But I need to find out exactly what's going on before I confront him." She scooped up a chunk of strawberry butter with her knife, then brandished it as she spoke. "Y'all know Harold; he's learned a lot of dirty tricks working for the bank all these years. He's a shark, especially when it comes to assets." One by one, she met our eyes, rock solid. "I'll have to have hard evidence before he finds out I'm on to him. Otherwise, I'll get nothing. Hell, he may have already hidden everything away somewhere." Terrible as this was, she seemed to have found a backbone in it.

"You can do this. *We* can do this," I encouraged, seconded by the others, all of whom brightened except Teeny.

"I assume this means you wouldn't want him back," Teeny said, agonized, as always, by conflict of any kind. "Even if he came to his senses?"

"If he's done what I think he's done to me, hell no," Diane responded without hesitation. "But I have no intention of letting him get away with it. The bastard will pay, and pay big." She hunched closer to whisper, "He's leaked enough about the monkey-business at the bank for me to know there are plenty of bodies buried. I'm talkin' prison, ladies, and a shipload of trouble for the bank. With y'all's help, we ought to be able to dig up enough to give me some serious leverage."

God, I love a woman who means business.

A fierce and deadly estrogen heightened the adrenaline in our veins.

"Who needs a private eye?" SuSu rubbed her hands in anticipation. "Hand me my shovel, honey. Let's dig us up a stink." I hadn't seen her so excited since she'd gotten that first contempt citation against her ex.

"Yeah." Happily married Linda took a slug of SuSu's wine. "It's about time one of us got the drop on a no-good husband instead of the other way around." She looked like Betty Crocker playing Michael Corleone, which made me laugh.

"Okay." Teeny got on board. "What should we do first?"

"Eat some serious chocolate," Linda proposed. "Not here—*way* too tea party. I'm talkin' nuclear grade: Henri's Bakery for éclairs."

"The gravity of the situation clearly merits it," I confirmed.

"But then we need a battle plan," Teeny said. She could always be counted on to reduce the most daunting task into manageable bites, a skill that made her one of Atlanta's favorite hostesses and committee members. "And we need to do it somewhere private."

"Yeah," I said. Too many gossips here, poised for a tidbit. We were already taking a chance just talking about this. "Where and when?" I looked to the others. "This *is* a drop-everything proposition, is it not?"

"Absolutely." SuSu reverted to her pledge-chairman, head-cheerleader persona. She fixed on Teeny. "Your place is practically in Diane's backyard. How about it? What's Reid up to these days?"

The rest of us ignored the blatant double entendre in *that* question.

An odd look crossed Teeny's face before she shook her head. "Better not my house. Reid's too nosy. Trust me."

News to me. I'd been under the impression that he never gave his family a second thought. But seeing her expression, I wondered for just an instant what secrets might be hiding in their perfect Buckhead mansion. Whatever they were, Teeny would never dig them up. It might shatter the careful illusion of stability she stubbornly clung to.

"Okay." SuSu looked to me. "How 'bout Georgia's, then?"

"Fine with me," I said brightly despite the strange unease I felt about it, maybe because my house had its own secrets, as did I, though only Teeny knew. "The kids aren't coming home from school, and John's leaving tomorrow for a long weekend at Calloway." The words weren't out of my mouth before a cutting suspicion made me wonder if John's frequent teaching seminars were his personal "sailboat." Did the others wonder the same thing? "A physics seminar," I added to reassure myself, but it didn't work. "We'll have the house to ourselves."

"My flight back won't get in till tomorrow afternoon," SuSu said. "And I'll be wasted. Can we wait till Friday? It's just one more day."

Diane nodded. "Sure."

"Oooh!" Again, the lightbulb went on over Linda. "I've got an even better idea." She motioned us into a huddle, and four red hats and one green head again drew together. "Why don't we tell the guys we're having a spur-of-the-moment girls-only slumber party up at our lake place this weekend? Then I can get a couple of rooms at the Ritz"—Brooks's practice had made them rich, so we gladly accepted her generosity—"under an assumed name, of course. We don't want anybody to know we're here—and rent a car and follow Harold. If he thinks Diane's out of town, he's bound to be up to no good."

The resulting pulse of silence resonated surprise and admiration.

"It's short notice." For some reason, I considered it my sacred duty to point out all the possible complications in any given situation. SuSu called it pessimism, but I considered it good planning. "I mean, don't y'all have stuff to do this weekend?"

We looked at each other, holding our breaths. SuSu shook her head, her eyes alight with an unholy glow.

Smiling, Teeny shrugged. "Nothing I can't postpone." There was the subtlest hint of "cat that ate the canary" in her expression, or was I just imagining it?

We were really going to do this! "Dang." I couldn't remember the last time I'd been spontaneous about anything, much less something as risky and reckless as this. My heart beat fast with excitement—a sensation I hadn't felt in far too long.

You'd think we were planning a celebration instead of the funeral for Diane's twenty-eight-year marriage.

Diane brightened, her chin high. "Sounds like a plan to me."

Linda clapped her hands. "This is going to be *so* great! I'll make the reservations and get the car. I saw on TV about a rental place that doesn't require a credit card, so nobody can trace us. Then I'll check into the rooms. Adjoining, of course." She literally bounced in her chair. "It'll be my treat." Plots and plans sent her eyes out of focus. "Let's see. I'll need to pay cash for the rooms, too, and sign in with a bogus name." Her vision cleared. "Spy stuff. Goodie. Brooks won't believe this when I finally tell him what"—when we all opened our mouths to warn her against telling our husbands, she raised a staying hand and finished without missing a beat—"after it's all said and done, of course, and not a word before."

"Good. Absolute secrecy," Diane cautioned. "No husbands." She looked at me. "And no sisters." Normally, Southern sisters talk about *everything*, and I do mean everything, but she had a point. "I'm not even telling my own. There's too much at stake."

We nodded gravely, resolute.

"Okay. Check-in's at three. Y'all can come any time after that."

"Why don't we make it three?" Teeny said, clearly afraid that an open-ended rendezvous would be all the excuse SuSu would need to roll in at midnight.

My sentiments exactly. "Good. Three's good. Especially since we have to get settled and make it downtown at rush hour to catch up with Harold."

"Three, on the dot," SuSu said in all sincerity. We managed not to roll our eyes. "I'll bring the wine," she volunteered, "and the munchies." Which meant a jug of yeasty white zin from the grocery store, bottled salsa, and, yuk, plain old Fritos, not even the restaurant kind.

Teeny came to the rescue. "I'll bring some, too. And some sweets and sandwiches from Henri's."

"Oh, y'all." Diane scanned our little gathering, radiant for the first time in a long time. "How did I ever manage all those years in Nashville without y'all? What would I ever do without you?"

Teeny hugged her. "You'll never have to find out. You're home, and we're *not* letting you leave again."

SuSu lifted her empty wineglass to signal a refill to our wait-ress, then turned back to us, smug as a Buckhead housewife who's finally found somebody to do her ironing. "We are gonna have fun nailing Harold's ass, ladies. The kind of fun we haven't had since Mademoiselles." She raised her water. "To Diane. And justice."

"To Diane, and justice!"

Friday night, April 16, 1965
Rumor had it that pledge pickups for the Mademoiselles would be tonight, so I stayed home, trying to act casual but wanting with every molecule of my being to hear the "big sisters" pull into our modest driveway.

Nervous and pacing, I waited up until ten. My mother had tried to calm me with ice cream—even though she knew I was on a diet—but I didn't hold it against her, because she meant well. The truth was, she acted more nervous than I was, which seemed odd after all the noises she'd made against sub rosa sororities. But my teenaged self-absorption quickly pushed aside any questions that might have raised.

As the minutes dragged into hours, I passed the time on the phone with SuSu in front of our black-and-white TV, obsessively mulling over our chances.

"You'll get in," she assured me. "You're good-looking, built like a brick shithouse, and smart as hell. And you're on everything—Student Council, Honor Council, all those clubs."

"Which is why Mama doesn't want me in. If I get caught, they could kick me out of everything. I'd never get a scholarship." But we both knew perfectly well I'd gladly risk it. "Same for you. You could get kicked off cheerleading."

"Phoo," SuSu dismissed with a snort. "They don't give cheerleading scholarships." They didn't, back then. "And nobody's ever been caught for being in an illegal sorority, and you know it."

"Well, you'll get in for sure," I reciprocated. "You're gorgeous, which is something rare in a redhead, and you're the most popular girl in school. Of course they'll take you."

"But my folks run a diner." It surprised me to hear her say it. We never talked about her silent, paranoid parents who toiled long hours feeding Tech students at their little greasy spoon on Hemphill, leaving SuSu and her big sister to fend for themselves. Just like we never mentioned the burglar bars or sparse furnishings of her tiny little Jim Walters home three houses up from ours on College Circle.

"So what?" I countered, ever loyal. "They're getting you, not your parents. Look at you—only a sophomore, and captain of the cheerleaders. That's unheard of. And you're not just popular with the guys, but with the girls, too." It was only the truth. "And anyway, Mademoiselle has plenty of influential parents already."

"Okay," she conceded. "So maybe I have a chance, but it's a long shot. You, though, you're a shoo-in. Y'all belong to Brookwood Hills and go to the Cathedral, and your parents are in that

Great Books group with the governor and the mayor."

"Brookwood's not a club. It's only a pool and tennis courts," I deflected. "And we're not rich." In the mid-1960s, Atlanta was a New Money town, and all we had was old debts. My father earned a good living managing the Southern Trust branch in Buckhead, but the six of us kids (so much for the effectiveness of condoms and diaphragms) outstripped his income, leaving us crammed into our three-bedroom starter home forever.

We might go to church and swim with some of Atlanta's movers and shakers, but we were only one step ahead of the finance company the whole way. Other families started on College Circle then moved up and out to Brookwood Hills or Hanover West or the good side of Dellwood, but only SuSu's and my families remained.

I did "come from people," though. Both my parents were Old Atlanta, and for what it was worth, my great-grandmother had been a Life Regent in the Atlanta DAR, a fact that my grandmother considered crucial, as she mentioned it often. But old-line ancestors wouldn't help with the Mademoiselles. It was nothing if not nouveau.

"I told you," SuSu reminded me, "I heard Pam Bowden talking to Dee Dee Thomas in art class today about how a lot of their parents were coming down on them for their elitist, party-hardy reputation. Pam said they'd decided to pledge some smart, responsible girls to improve their image."

"Maybe we can get in on affirmative action," I offered, tongue in cheek. "It's the least they can do for the civil rights movement."

Like many of the baby boom's educated middle classes, my family was staunchly liberal, in word if not in deed. But our personal involvement extended only to the narrowest applications: signing petitions, supporting fund-raisers, having earnest dinner discussions, even being nice to the few token blacks in our school, but never asking them home. The most painful sacrifice we ever made was boycotting Lester Maddox's Pickrick restaurant. (The fried chicken there was *really* good.)

So if the Mademoiselles, in the spirit of the Camelot we all still mourned, decided to broaden their pledge base, it would probably only be to a select few, slightly less-advantaged, gorgeous, white girls. They'd already stretched the boundaries by including several schools and making no distinctions about religion.

The rest of the South might have been anti-Semitic, but forward-thinking North Atlantans (with the exception of their clubs) eschewed such prejudices, and we never considered the small, concentrated population of well-to-do Catholics who lived near Christ The King any different from the rest of us. Since Buckhead's excellent public schools were substantially Jewish, we'd grown up together and merely envied our non-Christian friends the Jewish holidays they got in addition to the Christian ones, and their eight days of presents at Hanukkah to our one with Santa. And as we'd entered adolescence, we coveted the Catholics' fast-track to a clean conscience provided by the confessional.

"Hello-o-o." SuSu exaggerated a debutante drawl. "Welcome to our little fête. Please enjoy the champagne and hummingbirds' tongues. And you'll want to meet our token real people, Georgia and SuSu. They go to public school. Georgia's brilliant, and SuSu's the first sophomore captain of the cheerleaders."

"Are you sure we still want to do this?" I joked, though both of us were consumed with a scorching hunger to join the in crowd.

All my life, I'd hovered on the fringes of that golden circle, going to church and school with girls who had the best of everything: fine homes; sleek English bikes; frilly bedrooms with French Provincial furniture, canopy beds, and tons of Madam Alexander dolls; expensive designer clothes; houses at Rabun or Sea Island or Hilton Head; and shiny new cars when they turned sixteen. I'd watched them, befriended those I could—usually by helping them with their schoolwork—emulated their manner, copied their clothes on my mother's old sewing machine. I don't know what spawned my overriding hunger to be like them, but

I would have done almost anything to enter their ranks.

Maybe that was why SuSu and I had always been so close: we'd shared that burning compulsion to be more, have more, than life had handed us.

We just *had* to get in; that was all there was to it.

As the night deepened, we did our best to convince ourselves that we were just the last ones to be picked up, but when midnight came and went, we gave up and said good night in voices thickened by tears. Too depressed even to roll my hair, I scrubbed off my makeup, brushed the teasing out of my perfect blond "flip," and collapsed to cry myself to sleep with a depth of self-pity only a teenaged girl can plumb. When I finally slept, exhausted, I dreamed of being naked in the middle of a pep rally, but nobody seemed to have noticed yet, so I spent the rest of the dream frantically trying to hide under the bleachers and find some clothes before I was discovered.

By seven the next morning I was out stone cold when the covers were ripped off me to a screeching female chorus dominated by, "Get up, maggot, and get dressed! Your ass is ours!"

I opened tear-swollen eyes to behold a circle of girls wearing senior rings, black harlequin masks, and black T-shirts that showed off the little mask pins gleaming on their chests.

Mademoiselles! Sweet Lord in heaven, they'd come for me after all!

"Get up!" They grinned with varying degrees of joy or malice. "Don't make us tell you anything twice!" one snarled with all-too-convincing animosity. "We said, 'Get dressed!' "

Sitting up, I saw no sign of my little sister. Her bed was tousled but empty.

Elated and terrified, I stumbled out of bed and tugged up my jeans underneath my nightgown. "Yes, ma'am."

Mistake number one.

"That's 'big sister' to you, pledge!" the bitchy brunette roared. (That was back when the term *bitch* had impact and meaning, unlike its tattered, overused counterpart of today.)

"Yes, big sisters." She could be the queen of all bitches if she wanted. She held my future in her hands.

When I found my bra, Miss Bitch snatched it away. She poked her face close to mine, magnifying the pale freckles of her flawless skin, her close-set blue eyes dark with menace. "No bras."

No bras? What kind of an initiation *was* this? Only hippies went without their bras! Certainly no decent Southern girl bigger than an A cup would, and I was an abundant C. "Yes, big sister."

Embarrassed that they were watching, I grabbed a T-shirt and hastily ducked inside my gown to put it on, then shucked the gown. To my horror, the mirror reflected my nipples clearly through the fabric, so I pulled on yesterday's blue oxford-cloth button-down boy shirt for modesty.

When I went for my shoes, Miss Bitch intercepted me again. "No shoes, either."

Grabbing my elbows, they hustled me toward the front door.

On my way, I caught a glimpse of my mother peeking down the hall from her room, her face wreathed in smiles. She waved at me, then disappeared.

She'd been in on it! How else would they have gotten in? And after all the fuss she'd made about high school sororities being illegal! She must have known they were coming all along! A surge of affection for her welled up as I was escorted outside into the cool spring morning.

The grass was cold beneath my bare feet, so I danced gingerly toward the waiting white Cadillac, a rich mother's car if ever there was one.

"Eyes down, pledge!" Miss Bitch ordered, but even when I obeyed, I could still see inside the car through the open windows as we approached.

Three pledges huddled in the backseat, their eyes obediently to the floorboard. I looked, praying, for SuSu, but saw only one familiar face: Linda Bondurant, a friend of SuSu's from the squad, a walking oxymoron—a Jewish varsity cheerleader who was a

math and science whiz—and very rich. Her daddy was a gyne-
cological surgeon at Emory. The other two, I'd never seen. One
was as tiny as a dark-haired Twiggy, but a lot prettier, with slender feet and hands, and sleek dark hair drawn to her nape with
a classic bow. She stole a glance at me, and I thought of Jackie
Kennedy. They shared the same wide face and huge doe eyes,
only hers were a brilliant azure.

Then she hiccupped, her tiny body wrenching with the muffled *skwerk*, momentarily shattering the Jackie thing. Jackie would
never hiccup. Ever. But the poor girl looked so miserable and
embarrassed, my heart went out to her.

The third one, from what I could tell from her profile, would
have been pretty, too, except for glasses thick as Coke bottles.

Miss Bitch opened the back door. "Get in. And no talking."

When I slid across the maroon velvet upholstery, the glasses
girl looked over, and I had to bite my lip to keep from reacting.
Her lenses squeezed up her face so badly you could practically
see clean around behind her.

I must have betrayed my feelings, because she quickly looked
away in shame. Chastened, I vowed to make it up to her. After
all, we were going to be sisters.

Poor Jackie hiccupped again.

"Cut that out!" Miss Bitch ordered. "I told you, it's gettin' on
my nerves." She opened the driver's door and got in.

So there we were, four pledges in the backseat. Two of the
other big sisters piled into the front seat. The last one leaned
inside and nudged me. "Move over," she said in a pleasant tone.
"I've gotta sit back here with y'all. Do 'up and back' so we can
fit."

I squeezed in behind Linda's fanny, and the big sister managed
to get the door shut.

The Jackie look-alike erupted with another stifled hiccup.

The car was packed. No room for SuSu.

"Back to Beanie's!" Miss Bitch started the car, then gunned the
engine and laid rubber up our quiet little street, right past SuSu's.

Eyes welling, I peered at her little house. She'd be waking up later, hurt, but secure that we still had each other since we'd both been passed over. But I hadn't, and she had.

What would this do to us? We'd been best friends since we were four.

For a fleeting instant I actually considered depledging, but the impulse was abruptly overridden by my own compulsion to belong. We'd stay friends, I vowed. I'd see to it. And maybe I could get her in next fall. The Mademoiselles had a mini-rush after school started if anybody had moved away or dropped out over the summer.

Miss Bitch lit up a Salem, and her seatmates followed suit. Ignoring us, they started yakking about the dance they were throwing in June at the PDC. (That's the Piedmont Driving Club to all you non-Atlantans.) Driving way too fast, she headed back toward the high-rent enclaves from whence she had come, our progress punctuated by stifled hiccups.

But I paid little attention, too upset about SuSu. How could they take me and not her? She was much more popular.

And poorer, with no "people"—only her paranoid, antisocial parents and a mother who worked. Not an in-crowd thing for a mother to do. The other Mademoiselles' moms spent their days playing bridge or tennis or doing charity instead of earning a paycheck.

Our mothers might have encouraged us to go to college and aim for the stars, but we'd learned a far more powerful imperative from their example: marry, to a man who can provide well for his family. Find someone who can take care of you. Ozzie and Harriet, *I Love Lucy*, and a zillion perky housewife commercials cinched the job. SuSu's mother was a living warning to what might happen if you didn't marry well.

I'd never consciously considered it, but deep down, I knew that being a Mademoiselle would significantly improve my prospects by giving me access to Atlanta's privileged sons.

Me, but not SuSu. I forced myself to accept the fact that my best friend really hadn't been picked up.

Self-interest battled loyalty all the way up Northside Drive, then onto West Wesley Road past Howell Mill and under I-75. That's when my bladder piped up so urgently that tears welled in my eyes again, this time from exquisite agony. Wetting the posh upholstery would hardly get me off on the right foot, but when we bombed across the bumpy intersection at Moore's Mill, I truly feared I would.

Please, please let us get there in one piece. And dry!

We passed Margaret Mitchell Drive, then careered down the long hill, slowing only a little to take a screeching left onto West Nancy Creek. Half a block from the corner, we turned between two ivy-covered brick pillars onto a winding driveway.

Thank God, my bladder decreed. Almost there.

After meandering through oaks and azaleas to a sprawling gray-shingled house like something from the cover of *Southern Homes of Distinction*, we drove down around the side to a large, crowded parking area between the pool and the house's lower level.

"Okay," Miss Bitch instructed, "Out of the car. Eyes down. Mouths shut. Follow me."

A full-blown hiccup popped loose from "Jackie" as she emerged, otherwise impeccable.

Miss Bitch's close-set eyes narrowed. "I told you, cut that out!"

Her fellow big sisters let loose a reassuring giggle that went a long way to ease my tension, but their reaction only sharpened the edge Miss Bitch's voice. "Don't get the idea that this is a joke. One false move, just one, and I'll blackball your sorry asses back to the band members and majorettes."

A fate worse than death. Looking back, though, I realize that the band members and majorettes were probably happier and better adjusted than the in crowd ever was.

We piled out of the Cadillac, eyes downcast, and filed obediently into the large rumpus room crowded with somber big sisters who overlooked two rows of pledges kneeling on the yellow shag carpet.

Jackie's hiccups intensified, attracting unwelcome attention from big sisters and pledges alike.

Poor kid.

Miss Bitch went over to the big sister in the middle of the room who held a three-ring binder and wore a pin with a tiny gavel hanging from its chain. The president, it had to be. Miss Bitch whispered something to her, then nodded and headed up the stairs.

Only then did I dare risk asking the big sister who had sat beside me in the car, "Please, big sister, may I go to the bathroom? It's very urgent."

She glanced furtively after Miss Bitch, then pulled me by the arm toward what looked like a maid's bath. "Okay, but make it quick. Carolyn'll never let you hear the end of it if she catches you."

So Miss Bitch had a name: Carolyn.

As luck had it, I relieved myself, then made it back to kneel between Jackie Kennedy and the dark-haired glasses girl well before the dreaded Carolyn returned bearing a shoe box full of small spiral-bound notebooks.

We all remained kneeling on the carpet for what seemed like eons, but was probably only a few minutes. Only Carolyn and a few of her pals seemed annoyed at the delay. The rest, I sensed, seemed to be waiting in heightened anticipation as if something unexpected was about to happen.

Boy, did it.

We heard another car pull down and park.

"At last," one of the bitch bunch muttered. "Typical Nancy. Late as usual."

I saw a lot of significant glances exchanged as car doors slammed outside; then footsteps approached.

"Eyes down, pledges," Carolyn ordered. I sincerely hoped she wasn't Pledge Mistress, but she sure acted like it.

We heard the door open and another group file in to kneel behind us.

As the last of them entered, I heard Carolyn gasp, then saw her legs march over to the president. In a furious whisper we could hear all the way across the room, she blasted, "What the hell is *she* doing here? I balled her, and you know it."

A tense buzz erupted among the big sisters, but the president remained smugly undisturbed.

Without lifting our heads, the first three rows of pledges strained to see the poor unfortunate who had set Carolyn off. She was definitely in that last batch, but every one of them had gone stone-still behind us, and I didn't dare risk turning around.

A sickening fizz of adrenaline shot through me when I thought about what the doomed pledge must be feeling right now. God, how awful it would be to be in her shoes. Better to be passed over entirely, like SuSu. At least she'd been spared public humiliation.

The president faced Carolyn squarely. "Gee, Carolyn," she oozed with the cold confidence of a duchess. "I don't know what you're talking about. You signed off on the final list just like everybody else." She produced a list of names, addresses, phone numbers, and signatures.

By now we were all watching openly as the drama unfolded before us.

Carolyn snatched the list, scanned both sides, then thrust it back in scorn. "You changed it after I signed."

The president's features hardened. "I did not. Perhaps you don't remember because you were so full of daiquiris. I'll have to insist that you drop this until we can discuss it in private."

By now, every eye in the room was on them, including ours. Carolyn looked like she might haul off and sock the president right in her pert, gently upturned nose. "Now!"

The president dragged her aside, and the next salvo was in more discreet whispers.

The agitated hum among the sisters escalated. It was easy to pick out the few who sided with Carolyn, but the rest of the Mademoiselles seemed to be enjoying her comeuppance.

Jackie's hiccups got closer together. I decided they must be some bizarre stress indicator.

The glasses girl covered a chuckle with a fake cough, then leaned over to whisper, "Oh, boy, what fun. Beanie's finally gotten even with Carolyn for snaking her boyfriend."

"Beanie?" I whispered back.

"Beanie Johnson, the president. She's great." She leaned even closer so we couldn't be overheard. Not that anybody was watching us with the confrontation going on. "Carolyn, though," she murmured, "as I'm sure you've noticed, is a witch with a capital *B*. Just plain mean. I've never done anything to her, but she made me wear these glasses instead of my contacts. How cruel is that?"

Our common enemy made us fast friends and allies from that moment.

I stuck out my hand. "I'm Georgia Peyton from Northside."

She shook it, unself-conscious for the first time since we'd met. "Diane Culpepper, Westminster." A preppie, but clearly not stuck-up. I liked her immediately. Without the glasses, she would have been attractive with her short, brown "bubble" cut, slim build, even features, and clear complexion. But with them, she made me think of that little bookworm played by Burgess Meredith on *The Twilight Zone*.

Meanwhile, Miss Bitch escalated back to a roar. "I mean it, Beanie. We settle this now, before it goes any further."

Beanie shook her head with a condescending sigh. "If you insist. But upstairs, in private. We've embarrassed these girls enough." She handed her notebook to a sweet-looking blonde beside her. "Pam, as vice president, you're in charge until I get back. Everything's written down on the agenda. Introduce them to their big sisters, and get them started with their pledge books." She aimed a cool glare at Carolyn. "This shouldn't take long."

Pam looked like she'd rather be road-tripped naked at the Varsity than take over amid such conflict, but she did as instructed.

Properly terrified, we pledges were left to contemplate the fact that one of the girls in that last batch was headed for a hideous humiliation. It took the fun right out of things.

Another truncated hiccup drew a scathing glare from Miss Bitch that clearly put Jackie on Carolyn's shit list in indelible ink.

Dead silence fell as everybody in the room watched Carolyn stomp up the stairs in Beanie's wake, followed by two more of Beanie's minions. Blessedly, the tension seemed to leave with them.

Pam invited us all to sit instead of kneel, then began reading the welcome.

A concerned big sister took Jackie to the little kitchen for some water and a teaspoon of sugar to cure her hiccups. When she rejoined us, I was happy to note that it was working.

Since things seemed to have relaxed, I ventured a look behind me and saw good news and bad news.

The good news was, SuSu was there! My prayers had been answered.

The bad news was, she sat last in line, her face ashen.

Her haunted gaze met mine, and my stomach lurched.

God, no! Please! She couldn't be the unwanted one. It wasn't fair. Nobody deserved what Carolyn was about to do, but SuSu least of all. She didn't have a mean bone in her body. And before today, she'd never even heard of Carolyn.

Be careful what you wish for. . . .

"Bitch alert." Diane grabbed my arm and pulled me back around. "One of Carolyn's toadies was lookin' daggers at you."

I tried to focus on the vice president's speech, but it wasn't until she started announcing the big sister assignments that I was able to summon body and soul together. "Mary Lane Adams," Pam read out, "your big sister will be DeeDee Thomas." A petite blonde emerged to escort her little sister into the pack as Pam read on. "Linda Bondurant, Catherine Nichols." Linda gave a little clap of joy as a tall brunette came to collect her.

"The big sisters list their top three choices," Diane whispered, "and the president cross-references them, so hopefully everybody will get a big sister who wants her."

"Tina Chandler, Lissa Cooper." Jackie Kennedy raised big, timid eyes to see a kind-looking strawberry blonde approach her with a smile. I silently repeated her name in an effort to remember it: Tina Chandler, Tina Chandler, Tina Chandler.

"Pru Bonner, Pam Bowden." Pru and I were friends from school. Flashy and popular with the boys, she was neither wealthy nor connected, but she had special qualifications. More about those later.

Several names later, Pam called Diane's name and big sister; then said she was upstairs and would be down to get her later. The list went on without event until SuSu's name was called. "SuSu McIntyre, Beanie Johnson."

The bitch bunch gasped while the rest of the sisters buzzed with approval.

Beanie! I felt like I could breathe again. Twisting around, I saw SuSu's expression reflect shock, then hope. I shot her a thumbs-up.

"All right." Diane grinned, rubbing her hands with alacrity. "How exciting," she whispered. "Seriously juicy."

Regardless of the power play going on between Beanie and Miss Bitch, SuSu had a formidable protector.

"Georgia Peyton." Pam looked at me with a satisfied smile. "I'm your big sister. And I'm told you can help me with my French."

"*Mais oui, ma grande soeur. Certainement,*" I gushed, then froze because I realized—too late, as usual—that I'd been too eager and too eggheaded. The nonacademics rolled their eyes in derision, but I was comforted to know that a bunch of the others went to Westminster and Lovett. You had to be a good student to make it at those schools, so I wouldn't be the only egghead in the group.

"We'll talk after I've finished," Pam said, then resumed her duties.

Pam was a good scout—smart, confident, sweet, and easygoing. We'd gotten to know each other at student government meetings. She'd make a perfect big sister.

When she reached the end of the big sister assignments, only SuSu, Diane, Carolyn's little sister, and one other pledge remained unclaimed, waiting for their big sisters to come back from upstairs. I sat beside them while Pam completed her duties.

She picked up the box of little notebooks and announced, "Everybody gets one of these pledge books. I recommend that you put your name and phone number on the front immediately. Pick any one in the box, but treat it like your dearest treasure, ladies, 'cause if you lose it, you're sunk." She took one, then passed the box on. "To insure fairness, we do the pledge assignments in advance, generically, so nobody can get catty with any individual pledges." Clearly relieved to have completed the orientation, she concluded with, "Party starts up in the den as soon as Beanie gets back."

She approached me, glancing briefly up the stairs with a frown. "Good thing these pledge assignments *were* made out ahead," she confided as she motioned for me to rise. "Lord knows what Carolyn would have given poor SuSu to do."

Diane and SuSu and the two others waited awkwardly while all the other pledge–big sister pairings filled the room with animated chatter. Pam hastened to reassure the big-sisterless. "Sorry about the delay, ladies. Why don't y'all just grab a pledge book and start looking it over? Your big sisters will be down shortly."

Sure enough, Beanie and her cohorts entered right on cue. The room electrified when everyone saw that Carolyn wasn't with them, but Beanie remained unfazed. Her pleasant expression completely opaque, she went straight to the bitch bunch and whispered to one of them. The girl frowned but nodded.

Next, Beanie singled out Carolyn's little sister, a tall, country-club natural blonde. "Something came up, and Carolyn had to leave unexpectedly, Lisa, but Martha will get you started off, then take you home after the party."

The girl nodded, clearly uncomfortable to be the only one whose big sister wasn't present.

Beanie's smile was dazzling and appeared genuine. "Don't worry. Everything's perfectly fine." The ideal corporate hostess in the making, smoothing over the rough spots and easing difficulties. "Carolyn hated to leave, but it couldn't be helped. She told me you and Martha were friends."

"Yes." The girl—Lisa, I prompted myself—relaxed a little. "She's great. Swims for Cherokee, same as me."

"She'll take good care of you. Just call Carolyn when you get home," Beanie instructed. "Her number's in your pledge guide."

She steered her toward her foster big sister, then turned that same dazzling smile on SuSu. "Hey there, little sister. Sorry to take so long."

Conversation dulled as everyone, including me, listened to see what SuSu would say next. She colored and dropped her voice. "I was beginning to think I was gonna get kicked off the squad before tryouts got started."

Beanie waved her hand with a melodious laugh. "Oh, don't let Carolyn bother you. She's forever gettin' things mixed up and popping off, but it doesn't mean anything. She's a sister, so we love her anyway." She sobered, speaking clearly for the benefit of eavesdroppers. "Take it from me, SuSu, Mademoiselle needs and wants every girl we picked up today. You're in." An impish grin broke across her face. "As long as you complete your pledge assignments on time and pass initiation."

SuSu cocked a halfhearted smile, clearly unconvinced. I wondered, as she must, how she could pass initiation if Carolyn didn't want her in.

"Come on," Beanie coaxed, pointing to the pledge book. "Let's see what the sisters have given you to do in the next four weeks."

"Good idea," Pam said beside me. "Let's do the same."

Absorbed in SuSu's drama, I'd completely forgotten that my own big sister was standing right beside me. I opened my pledge book to the first page and read that I had to call each big sister in the list and get a comprehensive biography—birthday, school, hobbies, boyfriends, family information, favorite foods, brand of cigarettes, and so forth—then commit it all to memory. I'd be quizzed at initiation. I had to do the same for my fellow pledges, whose names and phone numbers were listed on a separate page.

"The biographies were the hardest part for me," Pam confessed. "I'm not very good at memorizing."

Luckily, I was.

Looking over the pledge list, I was relieved to see SuSu's name right where it belonged, in the *M*'s. Maybe Carolyn had only been blowing smoke. Maybe it was all an act, a show, just to scare us.

No. Carolyn's anger was all too real, before and after she'd seen SuSu.

"The individual assignments are listed next." Pam flipped past the lists to pages that each bore a name, phone number, and appointed task. "Nothing awful. The pledge duties are supposed to be fun. We just pass the books around and think up stuff we'd like."

I searched for hers and found it. "Bake me chocolate chip cookies every Monday." As sweet, simple, and straightforward as Pam herself.

She dimpled. "I don't need 'em, but I sure do love 'em." She raised her brows. "I meant that about helping me with my French."

"*Vraiment. C'est mon plaisir,*" I gushed.

"I hope that means yes."

Beanie marshaled the troops. "Come on, everybody. Let's get this party goin'!" She led the way up the stairs.

Watching the tide of laughing, yakking young women who followed, I got my first taste of life above the clouds.

But all was not perfect in paradise. The Mademoiselles had a bitch dragon, SuSu was her prey, and Beanie was Saint George.

And I already had a headache from trying to remember names.

3

The Best-Laid Schemes

Muscogee Drive. Thursday, January 10, 2002. 9:45 P.M.

ALONE AT HOME, I HAD JUST SETTLED IN BED TO WATCH *A New Leaf* on DVD when an alarming thought jolted me to my toes.

Disaster, unless I could get hold of Linda tonight! She'd told me earlier that she planned to leave the house about 6:00 A.M. to take care of a bunch of errands (whatever the heck errands you can do at six in the morning) before she checked into the hotel, and I couldn't trust reaching her on her cell phone. Half the time, she didn't turn it on.

I snatched up the receiver and hit eight on the speed dial. (Number 1 was John's cell, 2 was his office, 3 and 4 were the kids' cells at school. The rest were Red Hats, starting with SuSu. My own mother got relegated to the double digits.)

Linda's phone rang three times. Asleep already?

I glanced at the clock and saw it was already half after nine. Rats. She might be in bed. Linda—convinced that it's crucial for a husband and wife to start and end each day together—turned in early with Brooks every night and got up at five every morning to fix him a hot breakfast before he made hospital rounds. Bad as it made the rest of us look, who could argue? They were still as close as newlyweds, and Brooks even came home for a midday quickie every now and then.

Ring five. One more, and I'd get the service.

My personal Chicken Little ran shrieking circles in my brain. *What shall we do? What shall we do? Disaster! Disaster!*

Thank goodness, she picked up. "Hello?" Alert, not groggy.

"You're still up," I said, relieved, though adrenaline kept my pulse hammering. "Something monumental just occurred to me."

"Oh, hey, George," she responded with just a hint of an un-natural edge that tipped me off that Brooks was within earshot, but she didn't miss a beat. "Don't tell me you've already forgotten what food you're supposed to bring to the lake."

We'd used this subtle code for years when our husbands might be listening. Ordinarily, our men zoned out the instant they re-alized it was one of the group on the phone, but leave it to a man to decide to get nosy just when he shouldn't.

I dropped my voice so he couldn't hear me through the re-ceiver. "Is he right there?"

"Yep. If I remember, it was your sausage casserole and a tossed salad," she said smoothly. "Think of anything else we might need?" Dead-bone honest though she was, Linda certainly managed to be convincing in our little deceptions.

"Hell yes, I thought of something else," I hissed. "You forgot to tell us what name to ask for at the hotel!" *Shriek, shriek.* "I had this vision of us lurking behind the potted palms in the lobby with all our luggage, trying not to be noticed, while you waited for us upstairs, wondering where we all were."

Linda laughed out loud. "Holy crow, we did forget! It never even occurred to me." Then she added for Brooks's sake, "Of course we'll need another breakfast casserole. Why don't you bring a quiche?"

"So what's the name?"

She paused. "Um-hmmm." I knew she was having trouble coming up with something on the spot. Linda's one of those people who needs to chew on things for a while, consider all the alternatives. Trying to rush her was like trying to stuff a cat into a hole; the harder you pushed, the more she balked. But this time her precious, passive-aggressive subconscious coughed up a doozie. "Oh, you'll never guess who I ran into after all these years: Nadine Bonner, of all people."

It was my turn to laugh. "Bonner? Holy moley." Now there was a rabbit out of a very old hat. "What made you come up with Bonner?" She must have been thinking about Pru.

"I don't know," she said, clearly annoyed by the criticism implicit in my question. "She said very kind things about you."

Pru Bonner held the title of Black Sheep of the Mademoiselles, hands down. We were thick as thieves through high school, but our relationship had been strained after she'd married spoiled, gorgeous Tyson Fouché and started smoking pot—and worse. "I'm not into the June Cleaver scene," she used to say.

Then, in the mid-seventies, we'd all watched WSB's first televised cocaine bust on the eleven-o'clock news, and the camera had showed the axing of the very door John and I had gone through only weeks before when we'd had dinner with Pru and Tyson (at my insistence; John couldn't stand them).

Remembering that broadcast dredged up the surreal, indelible image of the girl who had kept the bride's book at my wedding reception being shoved into a patrol car in handcuffs while a policewoman handed her three-year-old son to a social worker.

Poor Ty Junior. Little wonder he'd grown up to be a Deadhead.

We'd done our best to reach out to her after the arrest. I'd called her several times, only to be brushed off, so I'd driven over to offer help in person, but she'd been distant and unreceptive. Then she'd gone back to the bathroom for only a minute and returned positively manic. Naïve as I was, even I knew she must have taken something. She said her daddy was a Shriner, and he'd had her case transferred to a circuit where all the judges were Shriners, and she'd never serve a day.

She was right. She got a speedy trial, probation, and a divorce. With that, she'd moved and left no forwarding address. We knew she was somewhere within her probation's jurisdiction, but even back then, Atlanta was big enough to swallow up somebody who wanted to disappear.

Rumor had it, she'd eventually taken her son to a commune out west. I'd run into her—overweight and hard—Christmas shopping one night in the mid-eighties. She was living in an expensive apartment, sleeping all day and "working" all night for her male "business associate" who paid the rent. Her body language told me she was ashamed and embarrassed when I asked her what kind of work. She didn't answer, just shifted the conversation abruptly to her son, the Deadhead. It was clear she didn't want to resume old ties.

"Are you sure you want to use Bonner?" I asked Linda, serious as a positive on a home pregnancy test. "I mean, for all we know, Pru might be on the Ten Most Wanted List, with Nadine as an alias."

"Must you always project everything to the direst, most ridiculous conclusion?" Linda fussed, digging in as she always did when challenged. "It's all I could think of." For Brooks's benefit, she tacked on an unconvincing, "in the way of food." A pause. "Will you make sure all the others are clear about it for me?"

"Okay, okay. Nadine Bonner it is, then. I'll call the others; I'm sure they're still up. You're the only one who goes to bed with the chickens."

So she could get up at five every day to have breakfast with Brooks. Now, *that* was love.

"See you tomorrow, sometime after three," she concluded.

"Okay." I flashed the call, then hit 9 on the speed dial for Diane.

Pru Bonner. A tug of sadness dampened my excitement about tomorrow.

The next afternoon at the Buckhead Ritz.
I had half expected to run into Linda at the desk when I walked in cleverly disguised in my fur hat, black gloves, full-length mink, and Jackie O. sunglasses—trailed by a bellman and a cart holding my two huge suitcases, a cooler, a hanging bag, and four stuffed shopping bags filled with thermoses and food. But Linda was nowhere to be seen. I hesitated, not wanting to draw any further attention to myself by jumping the gun. I tipped the bellman, then found an inconspicuous chair to sit in, but I was too nervous to stay there long (plus, my furs quickly got too warm).

I hadn't planned on having to wait around. I looked at my gold watch. 3:01 P.M. Friday, January 11. Why I always felt compelled to be so punctual remained a mystery to everyone, including me.

Anxious, I looked to the front desk and saw it was empty of customers. Might as well ask. The worst they could say was that Nadine Bonner hadn't checked in yet. I approached the pretty, young Middle Eastern clerk.

"Good afternoon, madam," she said with professional deference. "How may I help you?"

"I'm meeting Nadine Bonner. Has she checked in yet?"

She discreetly eyed my getup, then checked her records. "Ah, yes. Ms. Bonner has booked an executive suite with an adjoining room on the twenty-first floor for your group."

Twenty-first floor? Holy cow! Teeny would crepe a brick (our ladylike alternative to "crap a brick"). The only thing she hated worse than elevators was heights. We might have to send somebody down with sedatives to collect her.

And those tandem suites went for seven hundred dollars a night! This was some treat Linda was providing, especially since we might end up spending the night in a rental car surveilling Harold instead of snug in the pillow-topped beds of the suite.

Before she gave me the key folder, the clerk slipped a pen and registration card across the polished counter. "If Madam will please fill this out."

Okay, Mata Hari, do your stuff.

I wrote down the first thing that came to mind: Myrna Loy, 10689 E. 78th Street, New York, NY 10010 (the only New York zip code I knew). "May I have my key, please."

"Oh, yes, of course." She handed it over. "Your room number is written inside the folder. Just show it to the bell captain on your way to the elevator, and he'll have your luggage sent up right away."

I did as instructed, and sure enough, the cart and another person to tip were waiting for me when I reached my floor. I preceded him to our suite, then inserted the keycard into the slot. No green light. I tried again.

"Here, ma'am, let me try," he offered, reaching for my key, but before he could get past the luggage, Linda opened the door.

"Crap, George!" she all but shouted. "You look like *Sunset Boulevard* moving in for a month! We were supposed to be inconspicuous." She eyed the overloaded cart. "What the hell's in there, for cryin' out loud? We're only here for two nights."

I heard the door across the hall open behind me, then close abruptly. Probably checking to see what the ruckus was about.

I turned so the bellman couldn't see me and made a silencing grimace. "Speaking of calling attention to ourselves," I bit out, "may we please come in?"

"Oh." Only a smidgen abashed, Linda stepped aside. "Sure."

After he'd unloaded everything, I tipped the guy ten dollars, then closed the door behind him as he left. "That was brilliant." I shed my prescription shades, then my gloves. "You were so loud, the people across the hall came out to see what was up. Hell, the whole floor probably heard you."

Linda tried to look serious, but she ended up laughing and pointing as I took off my fur coat, revealing my warmest sweats underneath, which just happened to be pink. "First Natasha, now the Energizer bunny!" She collapsed onto the sofa. "What were you *thinking* with that getup?" she hooted.

I felt a defensive flush, welcoming its heat in spite of my embarrassment. "I think it's a good disguise. If anybody noticed me, it'll be what I had on they remember, not what *I* look like."

Clearly, she didn't see the logic. On a roll, she wiped helpless tears from her cheeks as she crossed her legs. A good belly laugh has its perils at our age.

"And anyway," I protested, "I didn't want to freeze on stakeout. It's going down into the twenties tonight."

The laughter subsided a bit, but after a glance at the mountain of stuff in the corner, her tickle box tumped over again. "What the hell is *in* there?" she managed.

"It's mostly blankets and pillows for the stakeout." I remained aloof. "I knew none of y'all would bring any." I am all about my creature comforts and always have been.

She rubbed her face. "And those shopping bags?"

"Stuff from Henri's, chips, salsa, cashews, homemade guacamole, Diet Coke, plus some hot Arabica coffee in thermoses and a bottle of dark rum for toddies."

Brightened by the prospect of a marathon snack-in, she finally got hold of herself, huffing to relax her cheeks.

"I brought six of those apple tarts you love so much," I offered by way of justification.

"Oooh." As I'd hoped, that was all it took to distract her. Linda did love her French apple tarts. "Where? I want one. I haven't had a thing since five thirty this morning."

"How come?" Linda rarely missed a meal.

"You'll see," she said with uncharacteristic obliqueness.

I laid a box of pastries on the table and broke out two Diet Cokes.

Tradition Ten, which applies to all of us but (for obvious reasons) Teeny: we use artificial sweeteners and drink diet sodas with our calorie-laden treats, a fact that baffles men but makes perfect sense to women.

We had just sat down when there was a polite knock on the door. Linda jumped up to answer it. "Oh, boy. Another operative for Operation Stick It to Him." I swear, she was as excited as a kid.

Diane entered dragging a single rolling suitcase, too thrifty even to consider a bellman.

"Is that it?" I asked, amazed that anyone could pack so light for a whole weekend.

"No. My cooler's out in the hall," she said as Linda pulled it in behind her. The thing was huge, with wheels and a drag-along handle. "I did low-carb chicken salad, fresh plums and nectarines, and veggies with diet dips. I mean, why should we pay an arm and a leg to eat hotel food?"

Because the dining room here is celestial, I thought but didn't say. I'd known we'd have trouble with her about the prices. "I appreciate all that healthy food you fixed, sweetie, but I was hoping we could eat downstairs together at least once."

I appealed to Diane's sense of justice. "Heck, if I were you, I'd be maxing out Harold's credit cards on any whim that struck me. Live a little." The flush in her neck darkened. "When I think about what he's probably been up to while you were home squeezin' the life out of every penny, strippin' quarter-round to refinish when you redid that whole kitchen and den all by yourself . . . Well, it makes my blood boil."

Her reply was as flat-footed and practical as she was. "The credit cards are all joint, so I'd only be shooting myself in the foot."

So much for financial revenge. I once secretly envied Diane's lack of fiscal responsibilities, but now I realized how it opened the way for disaster.

I made a mental note to review our own accounts, never dreaming that I might find something amiss.

Diane pulled a diet ginger ale out of the cooler, then sat opposite me. "I've been doing some detective work on the phone since Wednesday. I used Harold's social security number to access all our accounts—at least the ones I know about: brokerage, savings, CDs, mutual funds—and I was right. Even after adjusting for market shifts, we're down about two hundred thousand."

Linda and I froze, appalled.

"Damn." I went queasy in sympathy. The amount was staggering. John and I had managed to save only thirty thousand in the savings account we'd started back in 1969. Could it really have been that long ago? "Oh, Diane, I am so sorry."

"At least I know where we stand." She jabbed at the corner of the bakery box. "Since he's plundered our joint assets, it can hardly improve matters for me to squander what's left. No fifty-dollar dinners for me."

I quoted my favorite motto: "So you get to the poorhouse a few days sooner. Might as well have some fun along the way."

"I swear, George," she said, "with that attitude, it's a wonder you have two nickels left to rub together."

We did, but not much more. John's professor's salary couldn't hold a candle to Harold's income. The mortgage would be paid off in another six years, and then we could think about selling the house, buying something smaller, and retiring.

John, home all day. What would we say to each other? I stuffed the errant thought into a mental hole and shut it away.

"So this is no little fling," Diane confided. "Harold is positioning himself to leave." She absently helped herself to an éclair. "Thank God I found that note. If we can just get the goods on him before he suspects anything, I may stand a chance." We watched in amazement as she ate half the forbidden treat in a bite—Diane, who considered sugar on a par with rat poison.

"Diane, honey," Linda ventured. "Are you aware that you've just eaten half an éclair?"

Clearly, she wasn't. "Shit!" She grabbed a paper napkin to swipe what was left out of her mouth. "Why didn't you *tell* me?"

"Under the circumstances," I answered, "I considered it an understandable lapse. Beats getting plastered or taking barbiturates." I proffered the pastries. "Heck, have another."

She glared at me. "Get thee behind me, Satan. The last thing I need is to be jilted, poor, *and* fat."

My twenty pounds of cellulite and I didn't take it personally. There had to be tremendous anger in her, and we were the only safe ones she could spend it on.

Teeny arrived, providing a welcome diversion. "Hey, y'all." Even in a simple black coat, slacks, and V-neck sweater over her white turtleneck, she looked like somebody who should be surrounded by paparazzi. And she seemed none the worse for her elevator trip, though she did take the chair with its back to the window. "Oooh, goody," she exclaimed. "Napoleons from Henri's." She helped herself with alacrity.

I checked my watch—3:45. "I hope SuSu gets here before too much longer," I worried aloud, compelled, as usual, to anticipate complications. The trouble with that is, though, it's never what you expect that nails you. "If we're going to tail Harold from the bank, we need to be in place by at least four thirty."

"Or five," Diane corrected. "His secretary said he had a meeting with the board at three. Those never break up before five thirty. Harold says the board members schedule for Friday afternoons because they enjoy keeping the hirelings there as late as possible, just because they can."

"Let's hope this isn't the first time they break up early," I fretted.

"What kind of car did you rent?" Diane asked as she rummaged up some crudités.

Linda fairly glowed. "A nice big conversion van with a raised roof and tinted windows. It has a TV, two pull-out beds, and a little refrigerator. Even a little chemical toilet." She was so proud of herself.

"Sounds great." So much for my fears of us crammed into a regular car in the cold.

"Oh, and wait until you see these." Linda retreated into the bedroom, then came back with a bulging gym bag and some headphones connected to a small portable antenna dish mounted on what looked like the muzzle of a gun, complete with trigger. "This is *so* cool. The guy from the electronic surveillance store swears you can hear a whispered conversation outside up to two thousand feet away. If you come in close, he says you can even hear indoor conversations from outside. You just aim it at a window. And it has this little jack, so you can plug it in any tape recorder."

She drew a mini–tape recorder from the bag. One of its wires ended in a small suction cup; the other, a tiny jack. "If you hook this up with the jack, it records whatever the dish picks up. Or you can stick the sucker dealie to the phone receiver and record conversations. Up to ninety minutes per tape, but he said the sixty-minute ones were better," she informed us. "The ninety-minute ones are so thin, they break a lot."

The three of us peered at her in amazement.

"Is that legal?" Teeny asked.

"Who cares?" Linda shot back, grinning wide as a Junior League Sustainer after her sixth face-lift. "I can't wait for Diane to call Harold 'from the lake' and record what he says." She lifted a finger. "Oh, and I also brought our video camera to tape Harold when we catch him."

"Linda," Diane chided. "I appreciate this, I really do, but all this stuff, and the rooms—this must be costing you a fortune."

Teeny nodded, her brow furrowed with concern.

"Shush." Linda actually giggled. "This is a whole lot cheaper than that week I spent at The Golden Door, and a helluva lot more fun." She neatly coiled the cord to the headphones. "There's more great stuff, binoculars that snap digital photos—got that at the Discover Store—and a cell phone scanner, but we can play with everything later in the van."

She'd always had more money than sense, and loved sharing her "toys."

"Who'da thunk it?" Diane shook her head as she looked at her old friend as if really seeing her for the first time. "Our own little

Linda, a spy at heart. Remind me never to try to keep any secrets from *you*, sweetie."

Teeny's smile glazed at the mention of secrets, which triggered a gaspingly vivid memory of my own deep, dark adolescent secret I had shared with only her—the one I'd wrapped in the pain of desertion and packed away forever. It speared me like a laser, but I mentally stuffed it back into its crypt and shifted my focus back to matters at hand.

I looked at my watch. Almost four. I'd resolved to give SuSu an hour before I called her, so her time was up. After retrieving my cell phone from my purse, I hit the speed dial for hers.

"I'm almost there," she said in that disconcerting way of people with caller ID. "I just have to pick up a Black Russian cake from Wright Gourmet."

"Don't bother. We've already got enough sugar here to send the lot of us into diabetic comas. Just come on in, or the van's leaving without you."

"You don't mean that," she whined with more than a note of unattractive petulance. "Wait for me. Y'all always wait. I'm coming as fast as I can." Never mind that she knew as well as we did that Atlanta's Friday afternoon rush hour started before one.

I did my best to be convincing. "We can't wait long this time. We have to catch Harold leaving the office, which means we've gotta hit the road soon."

I heard the sound of a horn and brakes squealing in the background as SuSu hollered, "That's what you get for riding my butt, asshole!" She resumed the conversation as if nothing had transpired. "*Pleeze* don't leave me. Just give me fifteen minutes. I'll be there. Four hundred's a parking lot, so I just whipped a U on the Glenridge connector and I'm heading back to Peachtree Dunwoody." That explained the sound effects. "Do not leave me."

"Okay, but get valet parking and come right up. It's room twelve thirty-six. I'm not kiddin', SuSu, we have to walk out of here within twenty minutes. If you miss us, call my cell and we'll arrange a rendezvous." Realizing she was sure to forget the room number because I'd said something after it, I added hastily, "Room twelve thirty-six. Say it."

"Room twelve thirty-six." She hung up.

"Would you really leave without her?" Teeny asked, brow furrowed. *Conflict. Conflict. Run away!*

"If she doesn't get here in the next twenty minutes, I just might."

"It would serve her right," Diane said. "Just once, we ought to do it."

"Yeah." This, from Linda. "If we don't get the goods on Harold, Diane will be in the same boat as SuSu, only Diane doesn't deserve it. SuSu, on the other hand, ignored our warnings and insisted on hooking up with that shyster Jackson despite the fact he was engaged to somebody else the whole time he was engaged to her"—more about that later—"and then she hooked back up with him after he married and divorced! How self-destructive can one woman be?"

"Hey!" As always, I took up for my lifelong friend. "Tradition Three!" (We do not beat ourselves or each other up, no matter how stupid the mistake.) "Why jump on SuSu's case? Don't you think she's paid enough already for letting Jackson sucker her in?"

The greasy-haired sleazeball had conned her out of all the insurance from her first husband's death, plus the house she'd renovated on West Paces Ferry. Now all SuSu lived for was collecting the $750,000 settlement the judge had awarded her after Jackson skipped out to Florida on the arm of the bimbo into whose name he'd transferred all his assets. But unless Jackson came back into Georgia, the law wouldn't lift a finger to arrest him or enforce the judgment. Can we say, "gross miscarriage of justice"?

Heck, if I'd been reduced to working as a waitress without tips on a flying Greyhound, I'd be obsessed with getting that money, too.

Diane sighed, chastened. "Point taken. Tradition Three." She looked at the bag of surveillance equipment. "But we really do need to leave by four twenty. We can't let Harold get away."

"Yeah." Linda gloated over the cache of equipment. "Who knows? If we pull this off, we could help other people. Start an agency. Wouldn't that be fun?"

Fun? From the looks the rest of us exchanged, I could tell that one of us would have reminded her this was serious business rooted in Diane's heartbreak, not some *I Love Lucy* caper, but then Linda would put on her hair shirt for the rest of the weekend—boring, boring—so we let it slide.

"You seem confident we'll catch him doing something to-night," I told her.

"We will," she said with a steely-eyed squint that would do Sam Spade proud. "We have to."

"Even if we catch him in the act," Teeny said, "will that be enough? I mean, these days, that kind of stuff seems almost ex-pected. Nobody turns a hair." She looked to Diane. "What if Har-old just tells you to go ahead and blow the whistle on his affair? Where does that leave you?"

Damn. She was probably right.

"I considered that," Diane admitted. "But the stuff about the accounts . . . If I can document what he did with our joint assets, get the exact dates and reconstruct a pattern of fraud, that might cause him enough trouble with the bank to give me some lever-age."

Teeny arched a perfect eyebrow. "The bank . . . now *there's* an idea." Her innocent face went shrewd. "Remember that time at the beach when we were all down at the surf watching the sunset, and Harold's sunburn sent his whiskey straight to his head? Didn't he say something that night about some monkey business at the bank? Holding transfer funds longer than they were sup-posed to, to inflate their cash assets."

"He's always saying something about the monkey business at the bank," Diane confirmed, her own features sharp. "Work is the only thing he ever talks to me about anymore. But what good would that do us? He's told me plenty, but it comes down to my word against his. I'd have no proof."

"Maybe you could tape him," Linda suggested.

"Great idea," I said. Then another, even more brilliant notion struck me. "Better still . . ." I flashed on the alligator briefcase Harold always kept with him, even at the beach. "What's in that briefcase of his? He guards it like the Crown Jewels."

"Nothing so exotic. Just work stuff. He keeps it locked, but I know the combination," Diane said. "But he doesn't know I know it." She shrugged. "He usually puts in a couple of hours in his study after dinner—on-line and at his desk."

Teeny scanned us with an evil smile. "Are you thinking what I'm thinking?"

I jumped in eagerly. "Two things—first, we need to find out what's in that briefcase. Second, we need to get hold of a serious hacker who can retrieve information off y'all's computer." I searched my brain, growing more brilliant by the second. Of course. "John's best friend chairs the computer department at Tech. I'll tell him it's to help a friend who erased some important material by mistake and wants to retrieve it before her husband comes back from his business trip and finds out." Were we cookin', or what? "That should get you your proof. Assuming Harold's crossed over to the dark side of the force."

Diane glowed with anticipation. "Oh, he's been there since his first job out of law school." She hugged herself, eyes alight at the prospect of nailing him with his own crimes. "Now, *that's* what I call leverage."

"Too brilliant." Teeny grinned. "I just love it. Honest-to-God blackmail." She took her third éclair and used it as a pointer. "We'll need copies of the briefcase stuff."

"Oh, *I* know," Linda chimed in. "We can get you one of those little cameras like in the movies, and you can photograph every-thing."

"Down girl," I said. The spy thing had gone to her head. "That would mean having the film developed. We don't want anybody seeing this stuff but us." I had a better idea. "There's an all-night Copy World only a few blocks from y'all." I nodded to Diane. "How about if you snuck out the papers after Harold went to sleep every night; then I could take them over and copy them and bring back the originals, with Harold none the wiser."

"But what if John wakes up and misses you?" Diane asked.

"A 747 could crash next door, and it wouldn't wake John up after he takes his sleeping pills," I said in a tone that sounded harsh even to my own ears. "Anyway, the way he's been lately, I'd have to be gone for a week before he'd even notice."

The others looked away, giving me the privacy of that bleak acknowledgment.

Teeny erased the awkwardness with a laugh. "Shades of *The Firm*. Y'all are makin' this *way* too complicated." She looked to Diane. "Why don't you just buy a personal copier and hide it somewhere he won't look?"

We stilled, impressed by the simple logic of her suggestion.

"Now, why didn't I think of that?" Linda asked. "I'm supposed to be the practical one."

Diane wasn't as thrilled as we were. "That would be perfect, but don't those things cost about a thousand dollars?"

"They used to," I said, "but they've come down."

"You can use mine," Teeny volunteered. Too careful of Diane's pride to offer one as a gift, she'd probably just buy another for herself and never mention it again. "I'll tell Reid it quit working and I had to get another one. He never balks about office supplies."

Diane's confidence returned. "Perfect." She checked the clock. "We probably ought to call valet parking and start rounding up our stuff." She stood, closing the pastry box.

"I didn't use valet parking," Linda explained. "I was afraid the van would attract too much attention, so I parked over at Phipps." We all failed to pick up on the phrase "attract too much attention." She went on, "I can walk over and bring it to the back entrance."

"Great," Diane said. "We'll take everything down there and meet you."

I donned my mink hat and coat. "I'll wait for SuSu at the front, then bring her around."

"Not in that outfit, you won't," Linda ruled. "Let Teeny do it. At least she looks normal."

I gave in without a fight. "Okay."

We watched Linda leave dragging the cooler full of drinks and low-carb concoctions behind her.

I grabbed my shopping bags of pastry, booze, and junk food. The game was afoot.

We all stood silent in the elevator as it stopped at almost every floor on the way down. I looked at Diane's resolute expression and was glad she had decided to strip away her rose-colored glasses and face the truth.

For a fleeting moment, I found myself wondering what would happen if I took a long, hard look at my own marriage. Everything in me told me John was safe, but then, half my divorced friends had thought the same thing.

It was silly to suspect John of having an affair just because everybody else was. Everybody but Brooks. He and Linda still *saw* each other and really talked and couldn't wait to touch each other. But they were the exception that proves the rule.

Still, it was hardly realistic for me to suspect John. He was nothing if not safe. It was why I'd chosen him. Our marriage was solid, dependable. There never had been fireworks for me, but I had wanted it that way because I had still been aching from the agony of what had happened with my first love.

Brad Olson. All the old emotions sprang, vivid and dangerous despite the years, full to mind, and I inhaled sharply with a surprising "little O."

I hadn't had one in so long, I almost didn't recognize it.

Why would he rise up to haunt me now? I wondered, shaken.

How had he escaped the muffled tomb to which I'd long since consigned him?

A less pragmatic person than I—SuSu—would have called it a premonition, but in looking back, I'm more inclined to think that dredging up Harold's dark secrets had awakened my own.

But there I stood in the elevator, ambushed by a tide of brilliant emotion, lust and longing, exhilaration and loss. The year Brad and I had been together—he at Georgia, I a high school junior—exploded in Technicolor amid my black-and-white, middle-aged universe.

I had loved Brad so obsessively, so blindly, that I had ignored all my upbringing and willingly offered him my virginity, telling myself that we were married in God's eyes from that moment on.

That was the deep, dark secret only Teeny knew.

And then he'd disappeared. No warning, no note, no word to me or his parents. He was just gone, leaving me sundered, maimed, and frantic. All the color, all the passion of my adolescent dreams departed with him, compounding his loss with the agony of uncertainty and, ultimately, a lingering anguish born of the notion that my own obsession had somehow brought down the wrath of a jealous God, not on me, where it belonged, but on the one I loved.

That loss had wounded me so deeply, I had wanted life to end. Only the hope that he might come back had kept me going. And only Teeny had known how deeply I grieved, and why.

As the years had passed with no word, she alone had understood why I avoided any relationships that even hinted of intensity—and risk. She alone had comprehended why I'd chosen to "settle for" John, a good and gentle man I valued and respected, but did not love.

I had loved Brad too much, so much that now the mere echo down the decades was enough to awaken another jolting shard of passion, even stronger than the last one.

Linda peered at me as the elevator doors opened on the lobby.

"Lord, Georgia, you've gone red as a beet. Hot flash?"

Several of the other passengers turned to gawk, deepening my flush of embarrassment.

I grabbed Linda's arm, bumping shopping bags of goodies, and said, "It was a hot flash, all right, but not the kind you think."

Let her chew on *that*.

4

Prudence "Pru" Ellen Bonner Fouché

P RU BONNER WAS THE FIRST PERSON WHO TOOK PITY ON ME when I went from being a big fish at E. Rivers Elementary to a big zero at Northside High. Those were tender years, when joys were all too often scribed in disappearing ink, and anguishes, however trivial, etched themselves into the rudiments of the women we would one day be. Between sixth and seventh grades, puberty had rearranged my baby fat into an hourglass figure, leaving me twelve going on thirty, which had the seventh grade boys buzzin' in circles. Intoxicated by the power it gave me, I'd played my nubile sexuality for all it was worth—in a most proper way, of course.

But once we, along with the students from Margaret Mitchell and Morris Brandon Elementaries, were funneled into Northside High, those same boys took one look at the fresh crop of high-powered flirts from Morris Brandon and promptly made a beeline for new faces. Unfortunately, the Morris Brandon and Margaret Mitchell boys didn't reciprocate and give us the rush.

But Pru, out of the kindness of her heart, took me under her wing. She helped me work my way into the fringe of the in crowd and generously shared her steady stream of castoff beaux.

And what was Pru's claim to fame?

She wasn't "to the manor born," as my nana would have said.

In an era when few mothers worked, Pru's mama—who had a beehive way taller than any of my mother's friends'—had worked as a teller for the C&S Bank since 1943. She'd been widowed in the Big One, leaving her with Pru's half brother Carl to support. Then she met and married Mr. Bonner, Pru's daddy, a plumber who suffered ill health and terrible flashbacks from two years in a Japanese POW camp, so Mrs. Bonner had had to keep working.

The weird thing was, none of us realized he was an alcoholic. We just thought he was sickly and overly grumpy on occasion. If Pru knew, she kept it to herself. But we liked Mr. Bonner because he let us drink his homemade muscadine wine (great, with a serious kick) and borrow his truck for midnight outings. It had once been an Atlanta Police Department paddy wagon, and you could still see the emblems through the black spray paint on the sides.

Pru wasn't beautiful, either. A tall, lanky, Clairol blonde who had more fun, she wore her trendy mod clothes like a runway model, yet she had no class or sense of personal style.

The boys didn't care; they were drawn to her Goldie Hawn giggle and overt sexuality. They stuck around because underneath her flashy exterior, she was truly kind and uncomplicated.

As for the girls, Pru's claim to fame was her permissive parents. Allowed to smoke at home, she had no curfew in an era when the rest of us had to be in by midnight. Even more exciting, Pru's lack of restrictions extended to sleepover guests, and her mama never ratted anyone out. Miz Bonner had told more than one suspicious parent calling to check on a daughter that the girl was in the shower, when in fact she hadn't darkened the doorstep. We could smoke the air blue, come in plastered, or not come in at all, and the Bonners wouldn't tell on us. Instant popularity: teen freedom on the cusp of the sexual revolution.

Now that I'm a parent, it makes my glands go sour just to think of it. But back then, it was Nirvana. The popular set flocked there in batches of three to ten, undaunted by the lack of accom-

modations and the Bohemian sleeping arrangements that re-
sulted.

Date night at Pru's was a teenaged boy's wet dream, high-
lighted by the line of naked girls waiting our turn at the shower
head in the combo bathtub. (Of course, our boyfriends' fantasies
would have left out our big brush rollers protected by giant plastic shower caps with terry-cloth linings.)

We ended up in the shower at the same time because everybody had to be ready by seven o'clock, when our dates always
came to pick us up. Earlier, and they'd have to buy us dinner, an
event reserved for special occasions only. Later than seven thirty,
and they broke the unspoken rule that decreed such tardiness
showed a disrespect the belles of Buckhead simply would not
tolerate—unless the offender was a steady who had to work late
or eat supper with his grandparents, in which case occasional
allowances were made.

Bohler Road. Friday, April 29, 1966. 6:00 P.M.
We had none of today's quick shower, blow-dry, blush, lipstick,
and go for us back then. On date night, we tampered with nature
in rituals that made a matador's preparations seem slapdash.

Third in line behind SuSu and Pru in the hall bathroom's
combo shower, I waited my turn for water, then lathered up my
body, rinsed, and got out to dry off, leaving Candy Thompson
alone to enjoy the scant few minutes of tepid water left. It was
always first-come, first-served for the hot water.

I entered Pru's room to Beatles blaring in the usual cloud of
menthol smoke and Aqua Net hairspray. Probably just as well,
since the Jungle Gardenia I sprayed between my breasts and legs
might have choked the others had their noses not already been
deadened. I added even more cloying gardenia by dusting with
scented powder before wriggling into my panty girdle and French
bra. The scent would subside to maximum male-bait by the time
I was clothed and seven rolled around.

Next came makeup, then hair. I set my mirror on the bookcase and sat cross-legged on the floor before it. Candy arrived, lit up, then perched her mirror on the open windowsill. Not wanting to be the odd one out, I lit a Salem. Can you imagine? Four people smoking in an eleven-foot-square room? Makes me wheeze just to think about it. But cigarettes were readily available at only a quarter a pack back then, and everybody cool smoked, including our parents.

Wincing against the plume that invariably drifted into my eye while my hands were busy, I smoothed pale Silk Fashion foundation over my entire face—lids, lashes, lips, and slightly pimply skin. That stuff could cover *anything!* The result was a pale, featureless canvas to work with, almost Kabuki-looking. Janis Joplin might have been going around barefaced, looking like a Gila monster, but we Georgia peaches were always artfully made up.

After covering the ever-present dark circles under my eyes (milk allergy, but who knew?) first with white Max Factor concealer, then medium beige, I blushed my cheeks, powdered the whole thing down with loose translucent, then wet my eyeliner cake and started to give myself eyes.

As she always did, Miz Bonner shed her pumps and joined us, ashtray and cigarette in hand, for a rejuvenating dose of gossip and youthful anticipation. She moved Pru's robe aside on the bed, then propped herself up with pillows against the brass headboard. "Georgia, honey," she asked me, "are your parents still down on that sweet Brad of yours?"

"Unfortunately, yes." I finished the perfect point at the artfully uplifted outside tip of my black eyeliner (just like Sophia Loren's). "They won't let any of us steady till we're seniors." I spoke in the collective for myself and my three sisters.

Looking back, I can hardly blame my parents for resorting to hard-and-fast Boy Rules with No Exceptions. Who wouldn't, with four headstrong teenaged girls who had long since mastered gang tactics? I must have scared them half to death, reeking of hormones and Jungle Gardenia.

Kids come in two kinds: watchers and tryers. I was no watcher, and they knew it.

It wasn't until I turned forty that I discovered both my parents had known I was seeing Brad exclusively—well, not quite exclusively—but neither of them had ever told the other, probably because I didn't end up pregnant (despite plenty of opportunities), and Brad had conveniently (to their minds) disappeared, dropping out of college, never to be heard from again.

I took a drag of my Salem, sizing up Miz Bonner's towering brown beehive in my makeup mirror. She'd set a new altitude record. "But if Mama should call and ask, I'm out with Bob Araka," I told her. As it happened, I would be. I occasionally used my parents' suspicions as an excuse to go out with somebody else, just to keep Brad from getting too complacent.

"Right," SuSu said with uncharacteristic sarcasm. "And Lee Harvey Oswald was a lone assassin."

"Mama does *not* know Brad and I are steadies," I argued for the fifty-seventh time. "We've been too careful. Even Beth"—my tattletale big sister—"doesn't know."

"Well," Miz Bonner interjected, "nobody'll hear it from me. I'm always on the side of true love, and Brad is a darling boy. Lord, that kid could charm the tail off a peacock."

How I'd wished then that my own mother would be so cool.

Pru gave her a big hug. "Mama, you're the best."

We all envied Pru for the fact that she never had to lie to her parents, and they trusted her to make the right decisions—almost as much as we envied her for the 1958 DeSoto Fireflite convertible she'd gotten for her sweet sixteenth in January. Its huge white fins and push-button transmission were so uncool, they were cool.

As I said, we never realized that Mr. Bonner was a hopeless alcoholic, or that Miz Bonner was desperate for Pru to be popular with the "right" kids so she could marry "up" and have a better life than Miz Bonner had endured.

The irony of her mother's hope still makes me shake my head.

Pru married her prince, all right. (Well, not exactly a prince, but Tyson Fouché's social-climbing mother told anybody who'd listen that he was a direct descendant of a French count.) Yet look what marrying "up" had gotten Pru: addiction, public humiliation, and degradation that made her mother's struggles seem mundane.

But back on that April evening, our dreams were still wide open. It was Friday night, and we had dates—all it took to make us queens of the universe.

When we resumed our din of gossip and anticipation, though, Mr. Bonner hollered from behind their bedroom door, "Goddammit, Nadine, knock it down in there! My leg's killin' me! My head's killin' me! Are y'all tryin' to finish me off?"

Miz Bonner checked her watch. "Uh-oh. I forgot to give him his pill." She tossed Pru's bathrobe to me. "Georgia, honey, would you mind gettin' J. D. some water from the kitchen and takin' him his pill?" She fished a prescription bottle from her skirt pocket and meted out a hefty-size white pill with the number *512* etched into it. "He's cross as an old b'ar with us lately, but he won't be with you."

Something inside me didn't want to go into that room alone with Mr. Bonner, but I had no reason to feel that way. He'd always been a perfect gentleman. Yet I could hardly refuse to take him his medicine. It was the first time Miz Bonner had asked anything of me.

"Sure." I donned the robe, cinching it tightly closed, collected the pill, then got the water. When I opened the master bedroom door, I found Mr. Bonner stretched out in stained sweats on top of the covers with his leg propped up on pillows, his forearm across his eyes. The darkened room smelled sour, increasing my misgivings.

"It's about time," he complained.

"Here's your medicine."

When he heard it was me, he uncovered pain-reddened eyes and propped himself up on his elbows. "Sorry, sugar. I thought it was Deenie."

"That's okay." Wondering why they didn't keep his medicine on the bedside table where he could get it when he needed it, I handed him the water and his pill. "What's wrong with your leg?"

"Flea-*bite*-iss." He took the pill, then flopped back down to his pillow. "Damn stuff hurts as bad as anything they did to me in that Japanese prison camp."

"Flea bitis?" Mr. Bonner was always joking, making up funny words even in the direst situations. I chuckled. "Flea bitis, that's a good one. I didn't even know you *had* fleas."

He glowered at me. "I ain't kiddin', girlie. It's a real disease, and it hurts like fuckin' hell."

Appalled to hear a parent—even one as coarse as Pru's father—use the F-word, I backed toward the door. "Gosh, I'm sorry, Mr. B. It sounded like a made-up thing, so I thought you were kidding. I'm sorry. Really."

Cheeks smarting, I escaped to safe haven in Pru's room. "What's flea bitis, Miz Bonner?" I asked as I settled to take out my curlers.

Her focus glazed into the middle distance. "An inflammation of the blood vessels," she recited just the way the VA doctors must have said it. "Very painful."

"Gosh. Poor Mr. Bonner." I brushed through my shoulder-length hair before ratting it into a blond umbrella, the first step for a perfect flip.

"Poor Bonners, period," she said with uncharacteristic sharpness. "He hasn't been able to work all week." Sensing our sudden discomfort, she forced a smile and changed the subject. "So, what's up for this weekend, girls?"

"Ted Parks is having everybody over to his place after the show," Pru volunteered. His house on Tuxedo Road practically backed up to the new governor's mansion.

"Ummm." Miz Bonner's smile became genuine as she drew on her Newport. "I guess that means his parents are out of town."

Candy, Ted's date, piped up with, "Well, yes, but there won't be any trouble, Miz Bonner, I can assure you of that. I'll call the police myself if anybody tries to get out of line." Only her third date with him, and she was acting like Ted's official hostess. "He's promised to have everybody out by one."

"Including you?" Miz Bonner asked with every semblance of innocence.

We all laughed and threw rollers at Candy, who went red to the roots of her naturally platinum hair.

"Why, of course," she blustered. Candy was too smart and ambitious to stay overnight. This was, after all, the era of "Why buy the cow? . . ."

I flushed with tantalizing guilt at my own secret love life, half-afraid it would somehow show out and betray me.

The sexual revolution was just getting going on the West Coast. It hadn't made it to Atlanta, progressive though we claimed to be, and wasn't welcome when it did. So any girl who went past third base with one of the privileged cadets from Marist (a Jesuit military school) was instantly and irrevocably demoted to the status of slut—girls who were used, traded like baseball cards, then dumped when the novelty wore off, but never invited to real parties or brought home to Mama.

Brad and I had burned so hot, I had risked even that to have him, convinced that he would never tell, and he hadn't.

"It's no big deal," Pru explained to Miz Bonner. "Just a regular late-night thing. Some dancing, some discreet necking, some polite drinking, a few lovers' quarrels. The usual guys: Mike Morris and Barty Marchman and Rhode and Alex Mills and their dates."

"I been lovin' you-u-u-u, too lo-o-ong to stop now," SuSu sang into her hairbrush in a passable imitation of Otis Redding. The Marist boys were big into Otis Redding; they'd even booked his revue for their big dinner dance on Sponsor Day. I got to go as sponsor for Will Candler.

Even now, I cannot hear Otis or the Four Tops without remembering the feel of a close-cropped military haircut beneath my hand, the scent of Canoe or English Leather, and the heady sensations aroused by kissing boys who tasted of bourbon.

"Pru, who's your date tonight?" Candy asked with more than a hint of malice, undoubtedly in retaliation for Miz Bonner's embarrassing her. She knew perfectly well who it was, just as she knew Miz Bonner didn't like the boy because he was rapidly squandering the huge inheritance he'd gotten when his parents were killed in that horrible crash at Orly Airport in Paris.

"Drew Bailey," Pru said without a hint of defiance or anger. "We're doubling to the movies with Georgia and Bob Araka."

Candy pivoted on me in surprise. "I thought you and Brad were steady!"

"We are." I kept applying thick mascara to my lashes. "But I still have to go out with other people occasionally, or my parents really will get suspicious."

"So Georgia gets to play the field," my so-called best friend SuSu chided, "but is Brad allowed to date other people? No-o-o-o!"

SuSu was so right—I couldn't defend it. I did want to shop around, at least a little. The depth and scope of my obsession with Brad frightened even me. I just wanted to make sure we were right for each other, and the only way to do that was to kiss at least a few other people.

But when I thought of Brad's doing the same thing, I panicked, far too jealous and insecure about my hold on him.

Miz Bonner shook her head. "Georgia, you may act like the primmest little pre-deb on earth, but God help the boy who believes it. You're a shrewd one, sugar, and good for you."

"Thanks, Miz B." Now why couldn't my own mother see things that way?

"What movie are y'all gonna see?" Candy asked.

"*The Loved One.*" I'd made the choice when Bob had asked me out.

"Maybe we might want to change our minds," Pru said. "I heard it was *too* weird."

"About death and everything." Candy shivered. "Gross."

"Then George'll love it," SuSu ruled. "The weirder they are, the more she likes 'em. Take that awful *Dr. Strangelove*."

"*Dr. Strangelove* was great," I defended. "Funny, too."

"Only if you think doomsday is funny," SuSu retorted.

"So shoot me. I did think it was funny. And I'll probably love this one, too"—I turned to Pru—"but you have my permission to hate it."

She made that pouty face that worked so well on the boys. "Do we *have* to go to that one? *The Rare Breed* is playing at the drive-in. Couldn't we go there instead? I just love Maureen O'Sullivan."

"O'Hara," I corrected. "And I am *not* going to the drive-in with Bob Araka. This is only our second date. But I'll make you a deal. We can single if you'd rather, then meet up at the party later."

Pru brightened. "Great. Now why didn't I think of that?"

"Because you didn't want to leave me alone with the infamous Bob Araka?" I guessed. "But you don't have to worry. I've fended off far worse than him."

All but SuSu laughed, sure I was kidding. The truth was, since I'd started working at sixteen, answering the phones at a local car dealership, I'd already had to rebuff two overeager, married department managers, plus almost half a dozen grabby salesmen. Only SuSu knew. I hadn't told my parents; they'd have made me quit, and I needed the money to dress like the popular girls.

Pru must really have been against seeing *The Loved One*, because she agreed without hesitation. "Okay, we'll go our separate ways. If the guys agree."

Like all true Southern girls of our generation, we deferred to our men. Makes me gag when I think of it now.

"I'll call Drew and see," Pru said as if it were no big deal. The rest of us would never dream of calling a boy, but she pooh-poohed such impractical restrictions with an artless charm that allowed her to get away with it.

After talking with Drew, she announced that our dates would be delighted to single.

Unfortunately, though, my evening got off on the wrong foot and stayed there. Bob arrived in his parents' enormous new Cadillac, impeccably dressed but reeking of the scent Brad wore so subtly that until that moment, I had thought it was his own natural aroma.

"What's that cologne you're wearing?" I asked with guarded composure despite the surge of irrational anger I felt.

"Jade East."

Not only had he stolen my boyfriend's scent, but he also had on way too much of it. The nerve! It was all I could do to remain civil, but then, I always overreact when someone strips me of my illusions.

Strike one for Bob.

Strike two followed at the movie: He didn't like it, but I loved it in spite of the hate vibes he was putting out.

Strike three (times ten!) happened at the party, where he pulled a truly scummy trick on me.

I never drank with people I didn't know well—too risky—so I brushed off Bob's insistence that I join him in the steady consumption that seemed to have no effect on him. I held out till midnight, when I headed to the bar for yet another Tab.

Bob came up behind me and put his arms around me. "Come on, Georgia. Give in. Have at least one drink with me. We're not leaving here until you do."

I wriggled free of him. "I told you, Bob," I said, not bothering to conceal the annoyance I felt, "lay off. I said no and I mean it." I'd had enough. "It's late. I want to go back to Pru's."

If I didn't get there before the others, I might end up sharing a twin bed with another girl in Carl's room, a fate worse than death. Pru's half brother hated the lot of us, farted monumentally in his sleep (probably on purpose because we had invaded his room), and whenever we made so much as a peep, he sat up and threatened noisily and profanely to take us home.

You never knew how many girls Pru might have invited to join us. I wanted first dibs on an outside berth in Pru's sagging brass bed, despite the fact that I had to sleep with my forearm tucked under the foam mattress to keep from rolling on top of whatever unlucky soul ended up in the middle.

Seriously peeved at Bob's manipulation, I decided to try Pru's methods on him. "Come on, big boy." Bat, bat went my *That Girl* eyelashes. "Don't make me change my mind about kissin' you good night."

He wasn't buying. "Just one drink, and you're on your way home, but not before." His classic features hardened. No way was he going to relent.

I scanned the den. Pru had already left. And Candy. Not wanting to make a scene, I decided to employ the ultimate threat one could use on a true Buckhead boy. "Take me back to Pru's, Bob," I said, grim, "or I'll call your mother and tell her what you tried to pull."

He laughed, delighted. He wasn't supposed to be delighted. "No, you won't. She's in Sea Island for a month. With an unlisted number." He traced an elegant finger along my eyebrow. "But you sure are cute when you're mad. Those big brown eyes just sparkle." Believe it or not, back then, that crass deflection would have mollified most girls, especially coming from a college junior, but I was too angry to see it as anything but patronizing.

His handsome face congealed again. I didn't dare ask for help from the others, not after that boast I'd made at Pru's. And I couldn't call my parents to come get me. They'd ground me until I was twenty-one!

For the first time, I felt uneasy.

"How 'bout it?" His dark eyes were sly as a snake's. He knew he had me.

"Okay." Better to just get it over with. How much damage could one drink do, after all?

I found out when he returned with a jelly glass filled to the brim. "Rum and Coke, just like you like," Bob the jerk said.

"All right, dammit, but I think you are a royal A-hole for doing this." Strong words from Miss Honor Council and Class Secretary, and I didn't care who heard me.

A tentative sip sent a shudder of revulsion through me. I love champagne and sweet wines, but I do not like the taste of hard liquor of any kind or concentration. So I held my nose and drank down that tumbler in a few huge gulps, then set the glass aside, dabbed my lips with a napkin, and grabbed my purse. "Okay. One drink. Now take me home."

Everybody in the room burst out laughing, and not at me.

His ears and neck flushed, Bob led me to the car, put me in, then drove us toward the street at about five miles an hour. He only sped up to about fifteen when we reached the pavement.

I figured he was going so slow because he was drunk. It never occurred to me that he was waiting for my atomic cocktail to go off.

By the grace of God, nothing happened. He slowed to ten miles an hour when we finally got to Bohler Road, but I just sat there, steady as a rock and royally pissed off that I had wasted one of my non-Brad excursions on such a jerk.

When we pulled into Pru's driveway at last, I barely waited for the car to stop before letting myself out. I bent to face him. "Don't bother getting out, Bob. And don't bother calling me, ever. That was a dirty trick you tried on me, but it didn't work. Good night." Glaring at him, I slammed the door.

Even by the faint light of the dashboard, I could see the consternation in his face. He'd made the drink, and made it strong. Why hadn't it worked?

Clearly, I was a Goody Two-shoes who could hold her liquor like a man.

I was beginning to believe that I'd sprung from a hollow limb of the old family tree, myself.

Bob gunned his Cadillac, slammed it into reverse down to the street, then laid rubber for half a block. With a lard-ass Caddie!

I entered Pru's kitchen in triumph, then pivoted to head for bed.

It must have been the pivot that did it, because the next thing I knew, I was flat on my face on the linoleum. I rolled over with a moan. Everything was spinning, the lights too bright.

The crash brought Miz Bonner at a run, an apocalyptic vision in her pink chenille robe, silver-clipped spit curls, and beehive wrapped in toilet paper and nylon net. She loomed over me. "Lord, child, what have you done?"

"That rotten Bob tricked me," I managed despite the wave of nausea that lurched through me. "Jus' one drink, he said. Musta put a half a pint of rum innit." She helped me sit up. My liver turned over. "Oh, God. I think I'm gonna throw up."

"Hang on till I can get you to the bathroom." Carl must not have been there, because she pulled me to my feet and into the bathroom without help. Once there, she held my waist until I'd lost everything and then some. The room smelled like a distillery gone terribly awry.

"Whew! Mercy, child, I think you were right about that rum." She cleaned me up with a cold cloth then made me brush my teeth before leading me to Carl's room. "You just stay in here, honey. There's clean sheets on the spare bed, and Carl's gone for the weekend, so you'll have the room to yourself." After tucking me in, she turned on the little bedside lamp printed with sepia cowboys roping and riding around the shade.

When I looked at them, they started galloping. Bad idea.

"Just keep one foot on the floor, and everything will settle down. But in case it doesn't . . ." She set the plastic wastebasket beside the bed. "You can use this."

I grabbed her voluminous sleeve. "Please, Miz Bonner, don't tell anybody 'bout this. Please. Bob wouldn' take me home till I had a drink, so I finally gave in, but thank God it didn' hit till he was gone. If anybody finds out what it did to me, they'll never let me live it down."

She stroked my hair away from my forehead. "Don't you worry, honey. It'll be our little secret. I'll never tell a soul."

And she didn't.

I was sound asleep by the time the others got home, and a legend was born. From that day on, nobody ever tried to ply me with drink. I was the Goody Two-shoes with the hollow leg, the one who had gotten the best of sophisticated Bob Araka, then dumped him.

I was *in*.

5

Mission Impossible

AITING AT THE HOTEL'S BACK ENTRANCE FOR LINDA AND
the van, Diane and I had given up on SuSu when we
spotted her Miata—top down despite the cold—zoom
under the viaduct to Phipps Plaza. We stepped out into the side
driveway to see her screech off the Buckhead Loop into the cob-
bled hotel driveway and roar toward the main entrance.

"Damn." As she disappeared past the corner of the building,
I couldn't hide my consternation. "I *really* wanted to leave her,
just this once."

"Me, too." Diane shook her head. "It would have done us all
a lot of good, including her."

I raised my eyes to the heavens. "Someday. Some sweet day."

Who were we kidding? We had let her get away with it for
thirty years, and we'd probably put up with it for thirty more.

We both chuckled, resuming our stations at the rear entrance.
At Linda's insistence ("Anonymity!"), we'd refused the help of
the bellman who now waited discreetly inside, allowing us our
privacy as we guarded our ragtag mound of stuff. You'd have
thought we were going camping for a week.

Three minutes later, SuSu emerged dramatically from the
lobby doors, a study in chaos. Flushed and disheveled, arms
loaded, she pulled a drag-along and dripped belongings that

Teeny elegantly scooped up behind her with the regal aplomb of a lady in waiting.

"See?" SuSu panted out. "I told you I'd make it."

I didn't attempt to hide my disappointment that she had. "Lord, SuSu, you wear me out doin' this to us. Rude and a half."

She opened her mouth for her usual excuses, but was cut off by an automotive racket and cloud of smoke from the parking lot behind Saks Fifth Avenue. "What the *hell*"—only she said it like *hail*—"was *that?*"

We heard the battered DOT-yellow conversion van before we saw it belch its way toward us across the viaduct. Only the strong late-afternoon sun enabled us to see Linda through the heavily tinted windows when she turned into the back entrance.

"Holy mother of God," Diane wheezed out.

"Where'd she get that thing?" SuSu demanded. "Steal it from the parking lot of a poultry plant?" Pure SuSu, politically incorrect as always.

"No. Rent A Reck," Teeny said, "way down on Stewart Avenue, near the airport. I took her to pick it up this morning."

"What's the matter with Hertz or Avis?" Diane asked.

Teeny smiled. "Linda's convinced somebody might trace us if she used her credit card. It was the only place in town that didn't require one."

"Trace us?" SuSu shot back. "The place sounds like terrorist central. She's probably on FBI video renting the thing."

"Oh, now, SuSu." As always, Teeny did her best to smooth things over. "Don't you dare mention a word of that FBI terrorist nonsense to Linda. She'll go completely paranoid, and she's having so much fun."

As if in confirmation, Linda rolled down the window and twiddled a cheery wave from the far side of the drive as she passed by on her way to making a U-turn to collect us.

Everybody within a half a block peered toward the rumble and clatter.

Susu's face broke up. "Great," she managed as her tickle box turned over. "We'll blend right in at Harold's office."

It was contagious. By the time Linda rolled to a noisy stop beside us, we were all in helpless hysterics, attracting even more unwelcome attention with hilarious conjectures about what might happen when we arrived at the bank's corporate headquarters in that rattletrap.

SuSu wrenched open the side door with a bloodcurdling *skreek* and started heaving things into the fake fur interior (leopard, with bright yellow ball fringe). "Hurry up, y'all. Get in, before I wet myself laughing."

"I think this was originally fitted out to be a camper," Linda said with endearing sincerity. "It has a potty."

Diane took one look at the small chemical toilet peeking from behind a draped enclosure at the back corner and hooted. "Not unless it comes equipped with Clorox or a blowtorch," she barely managed to say as we tumbled inside in a tangle of food, coolers, pillows, bags, and bodies.

Clearly embarrassed by the spectacle we were making of ourselves, Teeny sought refuge up front.

Diane closed the panel doors behind us, chuffed, then wiped the tears of mirth from her eyes. "Oh, God, y'all. It feels so good to laugh. So good."

"Okay. We're off." Linda launched us in a clatter and billow of smoke, followed by a monumental backfire as we passed the main entrance on our way to Peachtree Street. Three people dropped in their tracks, and at least six others ducked, looking for the sniper.

That set us all off again.

All but Teeny, who swiveled in genuine concern. "Oh, y'all. We really scared those poor people."

Beyond the pale, we laughed even harder.

The good news was, inbound traffic on Peachtree had already cleared, and we caught only a few of the jillion red lights between us and the bank's main office downtown. The bad news was, we attracted unwelcome attention every foot of the way.

Can we say, "Security alert! This vehicle does not belong in Buckhead!"

Fortunately, by the time we used one of Harold's employee access cards to enter the bank's main office parking garage, we'd gotten a grip on ourselves and stowed everything away with some semblance of order.

Our presence echoed through the concrete tiers as Linda climbed the levels to the executive parking spaces. Late as it was, we had our choice of several spots a discreet distance from Harold's Jag. She selected a slot with a clear view and easy exit, and we settled in to watch and wait in dense, anticipating silence.

SuSu lasted only thirty minutes before she had a nicotine fit and begged to slip out for a smoke, but we all said no. Sulking, she suggested we break out the booze to "calm her nerves."

"Hell no," Linda ruled in blithe denial of SuSu's self-destructive cravings. "I'm glad to be the designated driver, but if y'all start drinkin' now, you'll be useless when I need you."

Women like us never applied the term *alcoholic* to those we knew, no matter how many times they'd had to be "hospitalized." Alcoholics were skid row bums, and addicts lurked in dark alleys or under bridges, not in the shaded enclaves along Paces Ferry Road. People in Buckhead simply "had a problem."

SuSu wadded herself up in the back and pouted, her bad temper snuffing out the lingering effervescence of our hilarious launch. Though the others sensed her anger, they had no idea how deep it ran. Nor did they suspect the clawing fear that lurked beneath her stubborn denial.

I was the only one she'd told about the snowballing panic that had stalked her since she'd started working smokeless flights after the divorce. She'd also confessed—with an edgy laugh that dismissed the serious implications—to drinking before and after the shorter runs and sneaking a few discreet snorts during the longer ones. Everything in me had wanted to fix her, to shake her until she admitted she had a problem, to drag her to a twelve-step program, or arrange an intervention or do *something* before she lost her job and her self-respect. Only Sacred Red Hat Tradition Five (MYOB) had held me in check.

Fortunately, none of SuSu's moods ever lasted for long, so within the hour, we were all back to yakking. Only Linda remained on the alert.

"Y'all go ahead, but keep it down," she said. "I'll take the first shift. We can swap out at hour intervals."

"Sounds like a plan to me," Diane responded.

In the brief silence that followed, I suddenly remembered I had big news to share. "Oh, y'all! Did y'all hear about KiKi Abrams?"

"The divorce?" Diane waved her practical American manicure in dismissal. "Leo screwed her over horribly, but isn't that the way it goes these days? That's old news."

"No, not that. This is *so* rich." I had their attention, even Linda's, though she kept her eyes on Harold's car. "I was having lunch with John at Chops the other day when nature called, bigtime, so I ended up in the stall and—"

"God, I hate when that happens," SuSu interrupted. "There ought to be some way to train your insides not to take a dump when you're—"

"Gross!" Diane's sneaker shoved at SuSu's leg. "Must you always be so crass? Shut up, and let her finish."

I kept on going despite the sidebars. (We'd tried a Tradition against interruptions, but it had failed so miserably that we'd repealed it.) "Okay, so I'm sittin' in the stall when—"

"*Sittin'*?" Teeny snapped around, aghast. I'd forgotten her toilet seat phobia. "What is wrong with you, woman? Lord, when I think of the *germs* . . . I mean, Chops is a nice place, but . . . Do you have a death wish?"

"Not all of us," I snapped, "still have the ability to hover."

"Oh, honey." Crestfallen, she retracted immediately. "How could I have forgotten about your poor knees. I'm so sorry."

"Could we please get back to KiKi?" Linda requested. "You were in the stall—"

Grateful, I went on. "And, lo and behold, who should I hear

coming in but KiKi and Jill Goldstein, and they weren't there to use the facilities. So, of course, I lifted my feet so they wouldn't know I was there. I mean, it's so embarrassing to get caught fouling the atmosphere—"

"Whoa, girl," Linda herded. "We've had enough of the gross details. Why were they there?"

"KiKi was *too* smug," I revealed. "She told Jill she'd gotten these Polaroids in the mail that morning, and when she started showin' them to Jill, Jill shrieked so loud KiKi actually had to cover her mouth to keep somebody from calling 911."

"Did you get a look at the pictures?" SuSu demanded.

"Yes, but I had to stand up onto the seat without making any noise and peek through the slot."

Teeny curled away from us, no doubt mortally offended by my shameless, shabby bathroom espionage.

Gossip was like cussing to me: I had enough of my straight-laced Presbyterian mother in me to make me feel guilty about doing it, but not quite enough to make me stop. So I continued with guilty alacrity. "You will *not* believe what was in those pictures." I paused for dramatic impact. "Leo Abrams, butt naked, beer gut and all, trussed up like a Thanksgiving turkey in black leather and chains, with a *very* tight leash on his pitiful little hard-on, cryin' like a baby or mad as hell, depending on the picture."

"Eeyew." They grimaced collectively. Not an image anybody would want to see. Leo had started out cute enough, but the older and richer he'd gotten, the fatter, hairier, and toadier he looked.

"Obviously, S and M gone seriously awry." I couldn't help grinning. "You should have seen the gleam of vengeance in KiKi's eye. Somebody had finally stuck it to Leo."

"Who?" Diane asked.

"Maybe KiKi hired somebody to set him up," Diane offered.

"That's exactly what Jill asked, but KiKi said no. Anyway, after what Leo did to her in court, I doubt she could afford anything like that."

"Ohmygod." Linda's mouth fell open. "I bet it was that woman!"

"What woman?" What the hell would Linda know about S&M?

She glowed with wicked discovery. "This is serious Tradition Four, y'all." (No telling.)

"You've gotta swear not to repeat this to a soul," she reiterated. "Not even talk about it among yourselves. If word got out, Brooks could lose his practice."

Brooks? We didn't make the tenuous but logical connection between S&M and urology.

"What the hell are you talkin' about?" SuSu demanded.

"For the last few years, Brooks has been getting these patients, all of them divorced men, with whip marks on their butts and minor injuries to their wankers. Seems there's some mystery woman seducing guys into S and M with the promise of giving them head." Well-turned-out Southern ladies are historically against giving oral sex. Except me, but that was one little secret I had no intention of sharing.

Teeny went deathly still, properly horrified, but then, it was her job to be properly horrified for the rest of us. She wasn't being superior. True class and her genteel upbringing had convinced her that intimate matters and bodily functions had no place in conversation, even among dear friends. "I'll take over as lookout," she said, providing herself an acceptable excuse not to roll around in the mud with us.

"None of them know who this woman is," Linda went on. "Two of the guys told Brooks she contacts them by e-mail or letter with provocative notes. When they get to her hotel room, she's there waiting in a black mask, erotic leather, and an elaborate wig—blond, black, redhead. Different color every time." She lowered her voice for dramatic emphasis. "She has black eyes. Not brown. Black."

"Contacts, I bet," SuSu decreed. She was always jumping to conclusions then hanging on to them as if they were holy writ.

Diane hugged her knees in lurid anticipation. "Why haven't we heard about this?"

SuSu poked her. "If you were a middle-aged-crazy male, would *you* want anybody to know some mystery seductress had suckered you into being shamed and punished on camera?"

She had a point. Unlike us women, who are compelled to share our humiliations, most men would rather have their tongues cut out than expose their own stupidity. Except to their urologists.

SuSu nodded, eyes narrowing. "She's probably blackmailing them."

"Nobody said anything about blackmail," Linda cautioned.

Diane frowned. "Who in his right mind would want to be tied up and tortured?"

"I told you, she offered them head." Linda.

"They'll do anything for head," Diane said, bitter. As if she knew. Her experience with men began and ended with Harold, and head was definitely not a part of the deal.

"Quit interrupting me," Linda groused. "Do y'all want the gory details or not?"

The yeses were unanimous—Teeny excepted, of course.

Linda resumed. "First, she has them service her with dildos, but she never lets them kiss her on the mouth. Then she trusses them up, promising to keep her end of the deal, but she only follows through with the good-lookin' ones."

"Can you get AIDS from oral sex?" I wondered aloud.

"No," said SuSu just a little too quickly, almost on top of Linda's decisive "Yes!"

"Y'all are sick," Teeny said from the front seat. "Sick, sick, sick."

Refusing to be distracted, Linda continued. "That's when things get mean for these guys. She never does them any permanent harm, just hurts them good and proper while she tapes the whole thing on video and takes snapshots with a digital camera."

"You knew about this," Diane accused, "and did not tell us?"

Linda invoked the Red Hat Rules. "Sacred Tradition Three clearly states that I do not have to tell y'all everything, especially when it would betray a confidence." She sobered. "I meant what I said about Brooks losing his practice. This cannot get out. Not from us. He never mentioned any names, of course, but still . . . The only reason *he* knows is because of the damage to their tallywhackers."

"Shouldn't he have reported it to somebody? The police?" Diane asked.

"That was up to the guys, not him. And anyway, there was no crime," Linda defended. "It was consensual, and no money changed hands. Heck, in Clinton terms, they didn't really even have sex."

"Oooh." My mind took another left turn to a revelation. "I'll bet Brooks knows who's got what STD for half of Buckhead. Does he tell you about those, too?"

"No, he doesn't," Linda snapped, genuinely affronted. "And I can't believe you'd ask."

Sensing we had pushed her too far, SuSu, of all people, directed the conversation back to safer ground. "How many of her victims has Brooks seen?"

Linda calmed, considering. "At least ten or eleven."

"Wow." SuSu's eyes glazed. "If Brooks had that many, think how many other divorced dickheads there might be out there who went to other doctors or were too embarrassed to get treated." She grinned. "Buckhead boys who dumped their wives only to be stalked and humiliated by a sexual vigilante. Kinda restores your faith in justice."

"Not Buckhead," Linda corrected. "She always meets them in Dunwoody. Brooks calls her the Dunwoody Dominatrix."

Even Teeny chortled at that one.

"I'll drink a toast to *that*," SuSu proposed.

"Nice try," Diane responded, "but it's still too early to break out the booze."

"I wonder who this Dunwoody Dominatrix really is," I mused. "Clearly, a woman with an agenda."

"A woman scorned," SuSu said with her usual deductive conviction. "Her victims are all divorced. Betcha a hundred dollars, she's somebody who got the short end of the stick, like KiKi."

"That's a pretty huge sorority." Diane's tone was grim. "One I'm determined not to join."

"That's why we're here, sugar," Teeny said quietly from the front.

Speaking of which, Harold chose just that moment to emerge from the stairway and head for the car.

"Oooh!" Teeny jumped as if she'd been hit with a cattle prod. "There he is."

"Get down," Linda whispered as if he weren't a hundred feet away. "He's coming."

Adrenaline shot through me, ending with a sparkle at my toes and fingertips. "Oh, y'all. This really might work."

"Of course it's gonna work," Linda hissed. "We are the Red Hats. Failure is not an option."

We watched Harold, who looked impeccable in his tasteful cream silk muffler and black alpaca overcoat, stride under the dim lights with his cell phone to his ear, a wide smile on his face.

"Look at that leer," Diane ground out while peeking between the front seats. "He hasn't looked at me that way in decades. He's talking to *her*. I know it." Her words were harsh with raw pain.

Linda tensed, her hand on the ignition. "Turn on the cell phone scanner. And the tape."

With great whispered hullabaloo, SuSu and I retrieved the thing and cranked it up, but all we got was disjointed fragments of conversations. I located the instruction book and started reading frantically.

Harold backed out of his slot and headed for the exit.

Amid Diane's and Teeny's conflicting advice about how long to wait before following him, Linda cranked the van, then eased it out, and shifted into forward. We each held our breath until we were underway without backfires. Fortunately, the smoke and racket weren't quite so bad as before.

"Maybe you just have to baby this thing," Teeny said, relieved.

SuSu and I managed to get the scanner working, but it kept picking up bits and pieces of dozens of conversations. Maybe when we got out of the garage, we'd be able to lock in on Harold.

Linda kept just far enough back so he wouldn't see us when he made the turns down the ramps toward the exit. At ground level, we were relieved to note that late as it was, the exit swing-arm had been left up, so we were able to glide through about ten car-lengths behind Harold, who by then was signaling a west turn toward Phillips Arena.

"Damn," Diane said. "I'll bet he's going to the damned Hawks game."

"If he does, it'll take a miracle to keep from losing him," Linda said with open frustration.

"Ah-ah-ah," SuSu chided. "Don't start dumpin' bad karma on us."

"Karma?" Diane turned on her. "Since when do you know anything about bad karma?"

"Since I've been dating this really interesting New Age guy I met on the Houston run." Translate, "sleeping with him."

"This is your captain speaking," Linda interrupted. "Could you two try to stay focused, please. I've gotta drive this thing, so I need y'all to keep Harold in your sights and warn me when to turn."

Sure enough, he went straight to one of the outrageously expensive surface lots near the arena.

Linda halted, blocking traffic, beside the lot. "Teeny and SuSu," she ordered, "y'all get out and follow him as soon as he gets to the sidewalk. Be sure to take your cell phones. Call mine when you find out where he's sitting, and I'll bring my camera. George and Diane can guard the van." The woman should have been a general.

Teeny jumped right out onto the sidewalk, but SuSu had trouble finding her purse. "How can we follow him?" she complained as she rummaged for it. "We don't have tickets."

"Buy some!" Linda snapped, exasperated.

"But what if there aren't any left?" SuSu insisted, purse finally in hand.

"There are always Hawks tickets left," the rest of us said in unison, ready to choke her.

Careful to stay out of Harold's sight line, Diane opened the side panel. "For God's sakes, SuSu, he's already at the crosswalk. Go, go, go." She unceremoniously shoved her out.

While Linda pulled into the lot (twenty dollars) and parked the van as close to the exit as possible, we watched Teeny and SuSu trail Harold across the street at the back of the crowd. Ignition off, Linda climbed back for her digital camera and dropped it into her shoulder bag.

"You know, they're really picky about what they'll let you take in these days," Diane warned her. "They may confiscate that."

Linda gave her a "Xena, Warrior Princess" look. "Then I'll just have to use my secret weapon." She made a benign face. "My Ultimate Mommy Persona. I've had total strangers ask me to hold their children while they ran inside a store."

I could believe it. Linda was nothing if not innocuous looking.

Happy as Nancy Drew hot on the trail of a crime, she reminded us to keep the doors locked, handed over the keys, then headed after the others.

For a few long seconds, Diane and I savored the pulse of silence that followed. Then she exhaled heavily. "I leave him alone, and he goes to the damn basketball game."

"Maybe he's meeting her there," I ventured by way of consolation. "She might like basketball."

"Naaah," we said in unison.

Diane opened the cooler and pulled out the chilled Chablis. "I think it's time for that drink."

"And then some."

She poured two generous servings, then handed me mine before stretching out on the other seat. After a healthy slug of wine, she shook her head. "The damn basketball game." She took another swig. "I hate basketball."

I nodded, picking up the scanner instructions. "Me, too."

6

Tina Elizabeth Chandler Witherspoon

Swan Coach House. Wednesday, September 11, 1974.

I'VE ALWAYS LIKED OUR SEPTEMBER MEETINGS. THE WHOLE world seems to heave a collective, cleansing sigh when school starts back. Along with the cricket-song that promises an end to the oppressive heat, the subtle aura of order and expectation has always provided a much-needed pick-me-up after the August wilts.

There would be only three of us at the Coach House that day. As I explained earlier, Pru had dropped off the world after her recent televised arrest. SuSu and Diane had moved away (traitors!)—Diane and Harold to a fixer-upper carriage house in Nashville's Bellemeade. SuSu was in Beaufort, South Carolina, happily gestating her son, with a daughter soon to follow, and a slew of cats, Irish setters, and Labrador retrievers to keep her company while her adorable veterinarian husband ran his clinic. We'd had to console ourselves that at least they'd stayed South, within a day's drive.

This September, though, Linda and I were both out of sorts as we waited for Teeny, who was late for the first time ever. Our faded tans too harsh, our cuticles destroyed, and my come-hither tresses long since clipped short in deference to the demands of motherhood, we waited impatiently in wrinkled shifts that only partly concealed my lingering baby weight. (Linda wouldn't birth her own little Jewish Princess until after Brooks's residency, so her figure was still compact.) For the first time ever, I weighed more than she did. I didn't like it one little bit, but I certainly didn't hold it against *her*.

Maybe it was the heat, or maybe we had somehow picked up on the grievous injury suffered by one of our own, but the two of us we were definitely crabby.

Eleven fifteen came and went, then eleven thirty. Linda scowled. "I'm gonna call her. Something's wrong. She's never this late. Ever."

"Maybe she had a wreck." My overactive imagination conjured dramatic, film-at-eleven carnage.

But just as Linda rose to head for the pay phone, I saw Teeny, almost furtive, slip into the empty lobby. "Oh, look. There she is." Wearing long sleeves despite the heat, she had on her usual enormous Jackie O. sunglasses but did not take them off, and her hair was swathed in a gorgeous Liberty scarf beneath her red straw hat. Totally Garbo.

Linda shot her a relieved glance before resuming her seat. "Thank God she's all right."

I wasn't so sure.

Never one to pick up on subtleties, Linda turned her attention to the menu. "I have made myself a promise. I am *going* to order something different today, even if it kills me."

As Teeny approached, her hand went protectively to the rim of her glasses, shielding the left side of her face. My lungs turned into corkscrews even as my mind stubbornly resisted what was all too obvious. Close up, I could see her left eye swollen shut beneath the glasses.

I felt like I'd just opened my bathroom door and stepped off the top of Stone Mountain at midnight.

Keeping her back to the curious glances that trailed her, Teeny reached Linda's chair and gave her a not-so-gentle shove. "Scoot over. I want to face the window."

"So now she wants to change seats," Linda groused good-naturedly without looking up. "Never mind that this has been my seat from the beginning." She collected her stuff and slid into the chair facing the lobby. "Since it's Teeny, I'll do it. Just this once. But don't get the idea that this is perma—" She saw my welling eyes and stopped in midword, following my line of sight to Teeny's carefully made-up face.

Even Silk Fashion foundation has its limitations. It couldn't erase the bruises on her swollen cheek or the ones that ringed her neck and wrists.

Teeny shrank in her seat, pulling her hands back into her sleeves.

"Oh, my God, Teeny." Linda covered her mouth in alarm.

For the first time in my life, I understood why people do murder. A blind and mindless hatred erased my staunch pacifism. I wanted to kill Reid Witherspoon with my bare hands. Annihilate him. Cut off his protruding parts and throw them to the dogs.

Voice shaking, I leaned forward to whisper. "When did he do this to you?"

"Night before last." Teeny's voice was hard as steel. "It doesn't matter."

Conscious of the attention we were attracting, I forced myself to remain seated and speak softly. "Of course it matters." Murder. Mayhem.

"Where is he?" Linda demanded in a tight hiss. "I'll kill 'im. He needs to *die*." She said the word with a broad, flat *I* that conjured images of white-sheeted mobs with torches glaring.

Teeny leaned forward. "Tradition Five, y'all. I mean it. This is mine to deal with, and I have."

"Tradition Five, my ass," I ground out, so angry I could hurl cars. "You want help, Teeny, or you wouldn't have come here. Admit that much, at least."

Linda glared at me. "Easy, George. I can guarantee she didn't come here to get fussed at."

I didn't care. Traditions or no traditions, this awful thing could not be repeated.

"I came because I needed to see y'all," Teeny said, her whole manner softening. "To be with you. To start putting my life back to rights."

"Back to rights?" Linda tucked her chin in alarm. "Jesus, Teeny"—the most offensive profanity a Jew could utter in the presence of Christians, one she'd never used before—"tell me you're not going to let him get away with this."

"You can't go back to him," I insisted. "Not after this." Rage and frustration escaped in silent sheets of tears. "If you go back, he'll only wheedle his way out of this like he has with everything else." The "everything else" Teeny never allowed us to discuss; I covered her small hand with mine. "Take some time away to sort things out."

I felt sick. Sick.

All-too-vivid memories of my Junior League placement at the women's shelter sprang full-blooded to my mind. I had thought us safe from the sad, sordid realities of the shelter, our pretty world above that sort of thing. I'd never questioned our ability to make a decent life by staying busy and employing the Southern woman's time-honored tools of feminine manipulation, ego-massaging, "keepin' ourselves up," hard work, and good cooking. But now, seeing Teeny, I realized it could happen to anybody.

Teeny epitomized the true Southern lady. She had more grace and goodness in her baby finger than the rest of us had put together. He had no cause to hurt her. Nothing *any* woman did, short of attempting murder, justified being hit.

"Bring the boys to our house," Linda urged. "We've got room, and I promise not to try to convert you." It was a running joke—Linda was a nonreligious Jew—but the joke fell flat.

Teeny motioned for her to lower her voice. "I told you, I've taken care of it."

I was unconvinced. "He'll do it again. They always say they won't do it again, but they always do."

"Please, Teeny," Linda begged. "Just visit us for a little while."

"I told you, that won't be necessary. I will not take my boys from their home." (Chandler was two, and Dalton only a few months old.) She pried my too-tight fingers from her own. "I know y'all mean well, but no." Her hands returned demurely to her lap, and cold-blooded resolution restored her perfect posture. "It will not happen again."

Linda groaned. "That's what they all say—"

"No," Teeny interrupted, which she never did. "That's what *I* say."

"And how, pray tell, do you intend to accomplish that?" I demanded, ashamed that my anger was spilling over onto the one person who deserved it least.

She took a leveling breath. "The same way we always have with our Buckhead boys. Only Reid's mama is dead, so that leaves Big Dalton." (He'd become *Big* Dalton four months ago when Reid and Teeny had named their second son after him.)

"His daddy?" Linda exclaimed, causing a pregnant pulse of alert silence at the surrounding tables. The waitress heading our way with water did a one-eighty. Crimson, Linda dropped her voice to a bitter whisper. "That ol' sorry-ass, whorin', thievin', drug-takin', alcoholic bastard?" The madder she got, the broader and trashier her accent. Definitely not what you'd expect to hear from a surgeon's daughter who belonged to Hadassah. "Why do you think Reid's mama drank herself to death? Everybody in the *state* knew he beat her—and Reid. What in God's name makes you think the old fart'll help you?" She let out a most unladylike snort. "Hell, he'll probably buy Reid a beer!"

"No," Teeny said with grim assurance. "He'll put the fear of God into Reid."

"Oh, really." I eyed her in challenge. "And why would he do that?"

"Because he's addicted to his image as the New South's God Developer," she said quietly, "and phobic about bad publicity— especially now, with that huge Singapore deal in all the papers and magazines. So the morning after Reid did this . . ." She paused to get her bearings. "Yesterday, I wrote down everything that happened and had Alvaline take Polaroids of my bruises." Alvaline was their live-in maid and nanny.

Linda and I stared at her in amazement. Such calculating precision from our passive little Teeny!

She might have merely been mapping out a charity project for all the emotion in her voice as she continued smoothly, "Then we put the boys in the car and headed for Tom Atchison's office. He's that shark divorce lawyer who lost so much money on that shady land pool Reid cooked up." Reid had sold shares to purchase land, then promptly drained off huge sums for "management fees." It was immoral but not illegal, so he'd gotten away with it, but he'd also made some serious enemies, Tom Atchison among them.

Teeny's tight little smile was lopsided from the swelling. "We didn't have an appointment, but Mr. Atchison saw us right away and made up sworn statements for Alvaline to sign. After I showed him the bruises, he even dictated and signed his own statements." She straightened, proud. "And I didn't even hiccup once. Haven't since. Maybe this knocked them out of me."

"What have you done with our timid Teeny," Linda whispered in awe, "and who is this warrior goddess in her place?"

"I will not let Reid hurt my children," Teeny responded, transformed from long-suffering saint to a primal force of controlled maternal fury. "And I will not let them grow up thinking it's permissible to hit a woman. You see what that did to Reid."

I was dead impressed. Finally, Teeny had stood up for herself. How tragic that it had taken something like this to make her do it.

"So what happened next with the lawyer?" Linda prodded.

"We copied and notarized two sets of everything," Teeny continued. "I left one, along with half the pictures, in his safekeeping, with instructions that if anything happens to me or my children, he's to go to the police and the papers immediately."

We blinked at her in astonishment.

"Then I took my set and the rest of the pictures to a safe deposit box I got at Trust Company"—not Reid's bank—"in your names." She dug into her purse. "The keys are in here somewhere."

"How could you get one in our names?" Linda asked with more than a hint of reverence. "The signature card . . ."

Another lopsided smile. "I told them y'all were watchin' the kids in the car, and I went back out to the parking lot and copied your signatures from a couple of notes y'all had sent me."

I peered at the swollen, mottled side of her face. If John had done that to me, I probably wouldn't have been able to put two sentences together for a week. But Teeny must have lain awake all night, planning this thing with a mastery worthy of James Bond.

It made me wonder if I'd ever really known her at all.

Locating the safe deposit keys at last, she handed them over. "Here. Guard these with your lives. It's at the Buckhead branch." Mission accomplished, she sat back and let out a relieved sigh. "As long as those papers are safe, I'll be safe. But if Reid or his daddy should ever get hold of them . . ."

Reid was a coward, but Big Dalton was ruthless, and we all knew it.

"Damn, Teeny." I sank back into my chair, staring at her as if she'd turned into an alien. "Just damn."

Linda did the same. "I didn't know you had it in you."

"Why is it," Teeny asked in mild exasperation, "y'all never give me credit for being able to take care of myself?" Her one good eye blinked behind her sunglasses. "I know y'all didn't want me to marry Reid." It made me wince to hear her say it out loud. "But I knew what I was getting into. I knew he was wild and spoiled rotten, but I loved him, and believe it or not, I love him still. Even after everything."

"How could you?" Linda asked, knowing it wouldn't do any good. "Especially now?"

One perfect eyebrow peaked above her oversize tortoiseshell frames. "Because he can still make me feel like a queen. And because he's my children's father and my husband. I know he's flawed, but the bad in him doesn't erase the good. My boys need a father, and I am bound for life to my husband." The Catholic thing. "So I do what I can to make a decent life for my family." Where had this new, candid resolution come from? "I know y'all disapprove, but it's my life, and I'm doing the best I can." She peered at us. "Tradition Five, y'all." MYOB. "And I mean it."

How could I condemn her?

I, too, had loved not wisely but too well, and the reckless passion Brad Olson and I had shared had ended in the abiding tragedy of my life when he'd disappeared. The mere thought of him awakened an all-too-familiar throb of loss that went straight to the marrow. Over the years, I'd had to block away all memories of him to stop the agony that permeated every thought, every image. I blocked them still, along with any dangerously strong emotion.

But looking at Teeny, it occurred to me that perhaps I was the fortunate one. For me, Brad would always be the dashing fairy-tale prince of my adolescent dreams. Teeny's dreams of happiness had been eaten away by a corrosive, relentless reality. Yet here she was, gathering the pieces of her life without flinching.

Until that moment, I had always harbored a secret disdain for her "look the other way" approach to her marriage, thinking she got some sick payoff from being the perpetual victim. But the strength I saw in her now replaced all that with genuine sympathy. "When will you see Big Dalton?"

"I already did." She spread her napkin in her lap, looking down. "First thing this morning. That's why I was late."

Linda leaned forward. "Man, would I have loved to be a fly on the wall. Tell, tell."

Another lopsided but larger smile from Teeny. "It was pretty rich, I must admit."

"We want all the gory details," I said.

Smiling even wider, Teeny winced, then covered the side of her face with her hand. "Fortunately, he was in the office. His secretary said he was on the phone with Singapore, but I just went right past her. He had his back to me, so I unplugged the phone and cut him off."

We were rapt in admiration.

The waitress chose just that moment to bring our water, so Teeny clammed up until she was gone. The moment she was out of earshot, Linda and I leaned forward. "So you flushed the call."

Teeny nodded. "He turned around, cussin' a blue streak, then stopped short when he saw it was me." The power of that confrontation still radiated from her. "I took off my scarf and glasses so he could see what his son had done to me, but I didn't raise my voice. I just said very quietly that I wasn't like Dalton's wives, and money or no money, I had no intention of ever letting Reid abuse me or the boys. The curse of the generations would stop here and now. I wouldn't let my sons grow up with violence the way Reid had."

"Ohmygod." Linda's jaw dropped. "You dared to say that to him?"

"It's only the truth," Teeny said. "Then I told him about the lawyer—not by name, of course—and the pictures. I told him I meant business, and he believed me."

I was loving this, wishing even as I heard it that we could suspend Tradition Four. (No telling.) "Did he go ape-shit, or what?"

"I expected him to," she said, "but he didn't. He just narrowed his eyes at me for a few seconds, then leaned back into his big, black leather chair and laughed and laughed and laughed."

"Laughed?" Linda was outraged. "How dare he? I—"

"He wasn't laughing *at* me," Teeny hastened to correct. "It was . . . Well, after he quieted down, he looked at me with respect for the first time since I'd met him." She shook her head, obviously still amazed by his reaction. "Then he said Reid was a fool and promised I'd never have any more trouble if *he* had anything to say about it. He swore that if I did, he'd beat Reid to a pulp himself."

"The acorn never falls far from the tree," I commented dryly.

"My point exactly. I can't have my boys acting like that." Purged, she took a self-satisfied breath, then looked around. "Where'd that waitress get to? Suddenly I'm starving." And just like that, all was right with the world again.

"No wonder you're hungry," Linda said in awe. "Bearding the lion in his den works up an appetite."

Suddenly I was ravenous, too. I raised my glass of water. "Here's to Teeny. Long may she reign."

Linda joined me. "Amen and amen."

It was a glorious moment.

Reid never laid a hand on Teeny again. Over the years, he broke things or put his fist through the Sheetrock on occasion, but he never hurt her or touched the boys.

Yet sadly, that September day was the only time Teeny ever stood up for herself. After we finished our celebratory swan meringues filled with chocolate mousse, she quietly climbed right back up on her tasteful Miss Melly cross. Why she did, I cannot say, but she turned all her energies to making a happy home for her sons, who—despite her best efforts—grew up to be harddrinking hellions.

But they never hit their women, and they dearly loved their mama.

That's something.

It wouldn't be enough for me. I could only hope it was enough for her.

7

Condo, With

*T*HE HAWKS GAME MUST NOT HAVE BEEN GOING WELL (SO what else is new?), because after less than an hour, we monitored a steady stream of disgruntled fans leaving. By the time we spotted Linda and SuSu and Teeny, they were part of a massive premature evacuation.

Linda and SuSu rushed through the throng to open the van doors and pile in with much dramatic clatter. Only Teeny had kept her cool, but even she was a bit flushed and winded when she reclaimed shotgun.

"I don't know how far behind us he is," Linda panted out from the driver's seat, "but there was no bimbo at the game."

"Damn." This from Diane. "I don't know whether to be glad or disappointed."

"The evening is young," SuSu said, maintaining her role as cynic. "I mean, if a guy can't go to a basketball game when he wants, what's a mistress for?"

"SuSu!" I glared at her, along with the others. "Could you be a little more crass and insensitive?"

"Oh, get real, George," she snapped. "It's true, and you know it."

"No, I don't know it," I deigned.

She narrowed her eyes at me. "Not *yet*, anyway. Your turn will come."

"Whoa!" Linda sliced a hand between us. "Tradition One"—Do Over—"big-time! We are here to barbecue Harold, not each other."

"Sorry, Diane," SuSu offered with fairly convincing sincerity. "I guess that was pretty harsh."

"Uhp!" Teeny interrupted. "Harold alert. Here he comes."

We followed her pointing finger to find him back on his cell phone with that same leering grin.

Linda cranked the engine. "Cell scanner!" As Harold opened his Jag and slid inside, she turned the wheels, ready to bull her way into traffic.

I turned on the scanner and adjusted it, but all we got was a blizzard of static mixed with what sounded like the entire Mormon Tabernacle Choir speaking in tongues at once.

Harold backed into the aisle, then started inching his way toward the exit behind half a dozen cars.

Slowly, so as not to attract the SWAT Team with a backfire, Linda wedged us into traffic, then eased around the corner, where we waited to the anemic beat of the van's right-turn signal. When Harold exited the parking lot onto Marietta Street, we were only three cars behind him. "Okay, y'all," she ordered, "no distractions. Keep your eyes peeled, and sing out when he makes a move."

Tense as troops in a transport behind enemy lines, we stared at the low silhouette of his car. Still on the phone, he drove with surprising caution for a male.

"Ever since he got that damn Jag," Diane spat out with a goodly measure of pent-up venom, "he's driven like an Eagle Scout. Hell, he even signals." Signaling turns was the ultimate sacrifice for a Southern male. "Never mind all those years he terrorized me and Lee, ignoring our pleas, risking our lives with his speeding and zigzagging and tailgating, acting like he was on a race course every time he hit the pavement. Forget that. He gets a Jag, and suddenly he's driving like he had newborn babies strapped to the doors and bumpers."

Can we say, "Bitter, bitter, bitter?"

As we followed him onto the northbound Connector, I considered Diane's abrupt shift in attitude from doting wife to wounded shrew. Maybe it's a defense mechanism, but once our illusions about our men are shattered, all those things we've overlooked for so long suddenly become overwhelming and we get mad, mad, mad. And sad, sad, sad.

Of course, this works both ways, but with different results. Once a man decides his wife is no longer the apple of his eye, he doesn't get mad and he doesn't get sad. He gets restless.

Does he try to fix things? No-o-o-o-o. That might mean facing life honestly and—horror of horrors—making a few changes.

Instead, he just gets himself another woman who doesn't know about all his faults—usually a bimbo: no experience in a perfect package. But after a while, even bimbos want the top put back on the toothpaste and the garbage taken out, so when accountability enters the picture, the man trades her in faster than a set of bald tires, for yet another misguided member of our sex who's willing to keep the whole sick cycle going.

If I sound cynical, it's only because I'd seen this happen over and over since we'd joined the forty-somethings.

No wonder Diane was bitter. As my mama has always said, we're all flawed, so if you make up your mind to stop overlooking the ordinary irritants of life, you can end up hating the person you love most within twenty-four hours. Which is why I never got analytical when it comes to me and John.

A sudden flash of Brad and me erupted into my consciousness, resurrecting a jolt of adolescent passion so intense, I died the little death, right on the spot.

Where had *that* come from?

"He's headed toward Cobb County," Diane announced when

Harold passed the Paces Ferry exit and crossed the Chattahoochee. "I might have known his bimbo would be from Cobb County."

When we were teenagers, we city kids believed only hayseeds and low-rents came from Cobb County, and none of them knew how to drive. Since then, East Cobb's new money had elevated things considerably, but old prejudices have a way of lingering.

"He's getting off at Aker's Mill!" SuSu alerted.

Keeping a reasonable distance behind him, we followed him to Aker's Mill, passed Cumberland Mall on the right, then took a left into Mondo Condo Land between Vinings and the mall.

"Oh, gosh," Linda piped up as we passed apartments and condos galore. "What if it's a gated complex?"

"We'll park on the curb and climb the fence if we have to," SuSu decreed.

We didn't have to. Harold turned in at an older town-house development, then parked half a block down on the main drive.

Linda pulled over, cut the lights and motor, then rummaged in the stealth equipment for her digital and video cameras, the Mega Mike listening device, and the minirecorder.

The rest of us watched Harold let himself into the condo.

"Bastard," Diane hissed. "He has his own key!"

"Did you see anybody at the door?" Linda whispered.

"No. The angle was wrong," SuSu whispered back.

"Why are we whispering?" Teeny asked in a normal voice. "He's inside, half a block away."

"Because we have to be quiet when we get out," Linda decreed. "I do not want y'all blowing this by yakkin' once we deploy to the bushes."

I looked at the condo in question. "No bushes there, my deario."

"You know what I mean." She handed the Mega Mike and recorder to Teeny. "Take these over to those trees across the street and see if you can pick up anything. Just aim the receiver at the glass, pull the trigger, and press that button on the tape to make it record. Take SuSu with you. George and I will go around back with the cameras to see what we can see."

"What about me?" Diane asked, indignant.

"Stay here and look after the van." Seeing Diane's resistance, Linda softened. "Honey, if he should see one of us, it probably wouldn't even register, but if he sees you, we're blown before we start."

"She has a point," I added, more than ready to get out of the van and into the action. I couldn't blame Diane for being frustrated, though.

Teeny laid a consoling hand on Diane's arm. "Anyway, do you really want to see what's going on in there? You'd never be able to erase it from your mind." Which may very well have been the reason Teeny had never confronted Reid about the other women in his life. The empathy in her eyes wasn't lost on Diane.

"Oh, all right," Diane conceded. "I'll stay."

"Why don't you turn on the cell scanner and see what you can find?" Linda suggested by way of conciliation. "He might make some more calls." Then she turned to us. "Okay, out you go, but remember, keep a low profile." She pinned SuSu with a trenchant stare. "And no talking. We want to be as inconspicuous as possible."

About as inconspicuous as the Marx Brothers with our spy equipment, we exited the "Call security!" van and split up.

Separated by ten-by-twenty-foot segments of solid fencing, each unit had a sliding door onto a small terrace and garden area that opened onto a common lawn, beyond which a thick stand of magnolias and rhododendrons provided a privacy screen from the next complex.

"The condo's fifth from the corner. I counted," Linda whispered. "We can use that hedge for cover until we get there. Then we can work our way back through to the edge and see what we can see."

It seemed like a good idea at the time. The only trouble was, we sounded like a herd of rhinoceroses as we shoved through the branches and stepped on dried rhododendron and magnolia leaves.

So much for stealth. But it must not have sounded as loud in the condos as it did to us, because nary a light went on. At last, we hovered just behind the last veil of curling green leaves at condo number five.

No need to guess if we had the right one. The kitchen/dining area opened onto the patio, giving a clear view into the living room, where Harold's floozy had thrown down with him on the sofa and was tearing off his clothes without even bothering to draw the drapes or shut the lights.

"Oh, God. Yuck." I closed my eyes in revulsion as she mounted him astride and rode him, her nails dug into his chest. Despite her gyrations, her boobs stayed high and hard, damn her. Harold arched his back to meet her, his mouth stretched wide in feral grimace. *Not* a visual image of Harold Williams (or anybody else's husband) I had ever wanted to have. "Gag me with a shovel."

For a brief, shattering instant, I saw myself and Brad, both of us young and hard-bodied, in their place. Ignoring the shocking twist in my twat, I shook the image off in horror.

"Bingo." Linda deployed the camera's built-in monopod, zoomed to the max, and then started shooting. She snapped away for several minutes, checking the shots for clarity on the tiny monitor, until I heard a furtive noise at the corner of the building and made out the shapes of SuSu and Teeny skulking across the lawn beside the rhododendrons. Right out where anybody could see them! Teeny was trying valiantly to get SuSu to take cover, but there was no holding her back. Mega Mike aimed and ready, SuSu crouched along in plain view of anybody who might look out their windows.

"Uh-oh." I tugged at Linda's jacket. "Look."

Her eyes turned to where I was pointing. "Oh, Lord." She exhaled abruptly in exasperation. "SuSu's a loose cannon. That's why I put her out front in the common areas. Go get her before somebody calls the cops."

I slithered out, feeling as exposed as if I were Harold's naked bimbo in Linda's lens. Six long strides brought me within reach of SuSu's arm. "Get out of sight," I rasped, dragging her into the vegetation. Teeny melted into the thicket so thoroughly and quietly, it gave me the creeps. But then, disappearing had always been her forte, especially when it came to conflict.

"I was only trying to hear what they were saying," SuSu explained in a stage whisper that carried all the way to the sliding glass doors and back again. Her breath reeked of rum.

Spiking adrenaline with every crunch and crack, I shepherded her over to Linda. SuSu took one look at our best friend's husband (who had a death grip on the bimbo's obviously fake boobs and looked for all the world like she'd ridden him into a grand mal seizure) and blurted out, "Oh, shit. Wash my eyes out with soap."

Linda stifled her with a firm hand over the mouth and whispered threats of evisceration.

I couldn't believe Harold was still at it. I was lucky if John lasted five minutes, but then, I was just the wife. And my genuine size D bustline had taken on the configuration of an Olympic ski jump, as genuine size Ds will. (Unless you have them surgically lifted, in which case your nipples run the risk of looking like Munch's *Scream* in stereo.)

Lurking there, spying on Harold's sordid liaison, my conscience kicked in and doled out a heavy dose of good, old-fashioned shame at my brief, errant fantasy of Brad. So I looked away, searching the shadowed darkness for Teeny. I found her not with eyes averted, as I would have imagined, but staring intently at the scenario.

Maybe she was in shock. Or calling down avenging angels in Diane's behalf, but it surprised me how unflinching her gaze remained.

It occurred to me that there might be a bit of voyeur in her, too, but I quickly dismissed the unworthy thought. Maybe she was seeing Reid's face instead of Harold's. Would this be the thing that finally opened her eyes to reality?

"Give me that." Linda wrested the listening device from SuSu and aimed it at the patio doors. She pushed the trigger, and amplified sounds bled from the headphones in tinny coherence.

"Ooooh, baby, give it to me," the bimbo crowed so loud, I was sure the neighbors were getting an earful. "So big. So big, it hurts, my huge Harold. Hurt me, big boy, hurt me. Harder, harder. Ride that Viagra express."

"So that's how he's stayed so long," SuSu whispered. "I bet he never took it for Diane."

"He didn't," Linda said flatly. "Diane asked me for some of Brooks's samples, but said Harold was all offended and refused to take them."

The bimbo ranted on, "Oh, yes. Like that. Fuck me till I die," et cetera, et cetera.

"Listen to that garbage," SuSu said. "She's a pro, a hooker if I've ever seen one."

"Oh, really?" Linda challenged in a prissy whisper. "And how many hookers have you seen in action, exactly?"

SuSu bowed up, but her confidence faltered. "Well, anybody in their right mind could tell. And look at those boobs. Fake. No real boob that big ever stood out at ninety degrees. Fake, fake, fake."

Perverse curiosity drew my unwilling eyes back. "Harold doesn't seem to mind," I observed dryly. He still had a death grip on them, his eyes rolled back into his head.

There are some things a Christian just shouldn't see, Mama's voice chided sternly, *because once you see them, they're with you forever, dirtying things up.*

Again, the vivid image of me and Brad transposed with that of Harold.

Why was my mind *doing* this to me? Maybe Mama was right.

Sin begets sin, and Brad and I had been as deliciously sinful as you could get. A tidal wave of mother guilt set my stomach queasy. "Oh, y'all, let's get out of here. We're not much better than they are, sitting here and watching this."

"We got what we came for," Teeny seconded quietly. "I'm freezing. Let's head to the hotel for a hot bath and some Kahlúa cocoa." She led the way, and the rest of us followed.

Halfway back through the thicket, I paused, struck by the sad reality of what we had just seen and done. We'd all known for years that Harold was a selfish shit, but Diane had really loved him. "Poor Diane."

The others halted in a moment of silent sympathy. Then we followed Teeny back to the van.

"Well?" Diane asked when we were safe inside, Chablis heavy on her breath.

Suddenly, we were all at a loss for words. Linda cranked the engine before she responded. "I'm so sorry, honey, but you were right. It is a condo *with*."

"The bastard." Diane's voice was thick with hurt. "Knowing him, he probably paid cash for it with our retirement money."

"Ouch." SuSu topped up Diane's cup with Chablis. "Here, honey, you deserve it."

As usual, it was Linda who mapped out the next move. "There's plenty of time for us to find out who she is and what's up with the condo," she soothed. "We got what we needed for now."

"Pictures?" Diane shuddered and took another hefty swig of wine. "You got pictures of them, together?"

"In flagrante delicto," SuSu piped up before anybody could stop her. "Up close and personal, in living color. When we get through with Harold, he's gonna be *under* the jail. Not like that sorry, two-timing shyster who shafted me. You are gonna stick it to him, baby." Her smug smile faded when she realized we were glaring at her, and she hunched down in apology. "Uh-oh. Do Over, big-time. Sorry. Sorry."

"Damn, Suse," I told her. "Do you think you could put your mind in gear before your mouth, for once?"

Diane gave a spasmodic shudder, then burst into tears.

"Great." Linda smacked the steering wheel with both hands, glaring at SuSu in the rearview mirror. "Now look what you've done."

SuSu promptly started wailing, too, doubtless prompted by equal measures of booze and true contrition.

Teeny retreated into her seat, hugging her knees to her chest.

At this rate, it was going to be a long night. Somebody had to do something. "Damn," I interjected. "This is worse than that night the paddy wagon broke down at the Varsity."

"Ohmygod." Ever reliable, Linda caught the conversational ball and tossed it back. "I had forgotten all about that. When was that? Ninth grade? Tenth?"

"Spring of our junior year," I said. "Don't you remember? God, what a night. The six of us sittin' on five-gallon containers of plumbing parts, chuffing down onion rings and drowning our sorrows in Frosted Orange because you and I had made C's on Mrs. Colley's Algebra II exam, and SuSu and Pru had flunked it."

As I had hoped, the tears abated. Despite Diane's very real tragedy, neither she nor SuSu could stand to be left out of a conversation.

"I told you we should have stayed home the night before that test and studied instead of going to Lake Spivey with the guys," Linda chided with definite recrimination.

"Cripes, Linda," I said, genuinely wounded. Was she still blaming me for the only C she'd ever made? "That was, what— thirty-five years ago? Can we say, 'Let it go'?"

"Thirty-six years ago," Teeny corrected politely from the front seat.

I felt the black cloud begin to dissipate.

SuSu dragged a long sniff, then dabbed at her eyes with a cocktail napkin. "*I* was the one who talked y'all into going to

Spivey. And I still think it was worth it. We had a blast." She crossed her legs. "So I made an F on the test. Big deal. I passed the course with a solid C. And Pru couldn't have passed even if she'd made a hundred."

"Whad aboud Spivey?" Nose stopped up, Diane made a truncated honking sound when she tried to blow, then smeared mascara as she rubbed the last of her tears away. "Which tibe?"

"Not Spivey," Linda corrected brightly. "The night after that, when the paddy wagon broke down at the Varsity."

"Oh, yeah." Diane relaxed, her swollen features easing. "I'd forgodden all aboud that."

"Erased it, more than likely," Linda commented. "Way too scary."

"Man." SuSu took another swig of her wine. "I thought Tim Whitlock was gonna kill Pru for real."

"That's what happens when you get out of your car at the Varsity," Teeny, our etiquette expert from day one, ruled, just as she had a dozen times that night.

"Well, we couldn't very well have walked home," SuSu responded as she had then.

We'd committed the cardinal sin: we'd not only gotten out of our vehicle at the Varsity after curfew, but we'd gotten into cars with the Marist guys, as well. They'd promised to take us straight back to Pru's, but instead had conspired to rendezvous at the Witch's Cave at Chastain Park, where things had gotten truly ugly.

"That was a dirty trick they played on us," Teeny said. "No real gentleman would have done something like that, especially to decent girls like us." She hadn't given a one of them, boy to man, the time of day since, but that night, the rest of us hadn't felt entitled to raise too much of a stink. After all, they were all from nice families. And we were out long past every *decent* Buckhead belle's curfew—plus, we'd compounded things by allowing ourselves to be picked up.

I, for one, had been appalled and piqued in equal measure.

My thrill at crossing the lines of decent behavior had only been intensified by the possibility of dire consequences. But that was fun only until things got nasty. Then I was just scared witless. "What made Tim go off the deep end like that?" I mused aloud.

"Try a six-pack of beer in thirty minutes," Linda said, "plus God knows how many before that."

"Nah," Diane countered. "We'd all seen him drunker than that, plenty of times. And he and Pru had been broken up for six months."

Something had made him decide that if he couldn't have Pru, nobody would. "She didn't provoke him," I confirmed. "She was just talking to Bob Araka about his girlfriend and the fraternity stuff at Georgia. Strictly platonic. And the next thing you know, Tim's got a tire iron and is chasing her through the trees."

At first, it had seemed like a game. I mean, Tim was pretty wild, but decent enough. But somewhere in the chase, things had gotten scary. Hyped on adrenaline, Tim had run like a demon, feeding on his anger. His shouts took on a homicidal edge that jarred us out of our halfhearted efforts to intervene and put us in earnest pursuit.

Teeny had gotten the hiccups so bad, you could hear her for blocks as we'd chased him.

It was all we could do to catch him. And it had taken every one of us but Pru—who'd sensibly locked herself into Bob's Caddy—to subdue him.

"God," Linda recollected. "Remember how strong he was?"

"Hell, yes." Diane blew her nose again, this time with more success. "I was siddin' on one of his legs with all my weight, and he just lifted me right off the ground." Four strapping boys and five girls atop him, yet still he'd fought with supernatural strength.

"What would we have done if he hadn't passed out?" I shivered at the memory of my own panic.

"Bob Araka had that pistol," Teeny reminded us, her eyes huge as a sugarbaby's. "Don't you remember? He shot it over

Tim's head when we were chasin' him, but Tim didn't flinch." She shivered. "I guess he could have held Tim at gunpoint until we got help."

I'd forgotten all about the gun—more accurately, erased it—a Walther PPK that Bob kept in his glove compartment to impress his dates. (He had this James Bond thing going.) When we'd realized Tim really meant to do murder, Bob had fetched the pistol.

I shuddered, remembering the sound of those shots and Pru's winded screams. Good thing she had those long, strong legs.

"Did we realize," Diane asked, "how close we came to something that could have ruined, even ended, some of our lives?"

"I did." Just like my mama always said: *Things have a way of gettin' out of hand when you break the rules, Georgia. One sin always leads to another.* "That was the scaredest I think I've ever been."

"I seriously thought I was gonna hiccup my lungs slap out of my chest," Teeny confessed. "I was terrified."

The others concurred. It had been a chilling initiation into life's perils. The sense of perspective that came with that memory wasn't lost on any of the others. We'd survived that crisis. Diane would survive this one. As I'd hoped, the memory had the power to get us over the hump.

Diane took a cleansing breath, then reached for the wine. "Okay. Who's got a joke?"

"I do," SuSu volunteered.

"Let's have it."

"Okay. After forty years of putting up with her cheapskate husband, a woman finds out he's croaked of a heart attack on the golf course. After the memorial service, she picks up his ashes and goes straight to the lawyer's for her insurance check and the reading of the will. He's left everything to her. She's a multimillionaire. On the way home, she deposits the check, stops at the car dealership, the jeweler's, and the furrier's. When she gets home, she pours the ashes out on the kitchen table and sits down to face them.

" 'Ralph,' she says, jangling a set of Mercedes keys. 'You know that convertible I always wanted? I bought it today. Wrote a check for it. Didn't even haggle.

"'And Ralph, you know that diamond ring I always wanted?' She wiggles a two-carat solitaire. 'I bought it today. Wrote a check for it.'

"She smoothes the collar of her full-length mink. 'And Ralph, you know that fur coat I always wanted? I bought it today, not even on sale. Wrote a check for it.' She snuggles in up to her ears. 'All female skins, fully pelted.'

"Then she leans in close. 'And Ralph, you know that blow job you always wanted?'" After a dramatic pause, SuSu blew as hard as she could, sending us all into delighted laughter. Even Teeny.

Linda took her eyes off the road. "Ohmygod! Teeny got it! Alert the media!"

"The Day of the Lord is upon us," SuSu declared.

We were still chuckling, well purged of Harold's black cloud, when we rolled into the hotel parking lot. This time Linda handed over the keys to valet parking, but not before she'd gathered up all the spy equipment for safekeeping. When we, laden with our goodies, reached the deserted lobby inside, she hurried toward the elevator. "Last one in has to get the ice!"

And that would be . . . *SuSu*, of course. We had to hold the doors open for her.

Linda grinned as they finally closed. "Dibs on the chocolate Häagen-Dazs."

"Dibs on peach," I chipped in, adding a smug, "Bring on the Red Hats, baby. We don't need no stinkin' detective," I said in imitation of a line from an old western.

"Hell no," Teeny seconded. "We had the cameras, the Mighty Mike, the tape recorder, and the cell scanner."

"So." Diane faced her. "What do we do next?"

"Tonight, we play. Tomorrow, we track some more. But first thing Monday, I'll go through the photos and print them out on photographic paper. They'll probably be a bit grainy, but clear enough to ID Harold." She looked to Diane "And you, my love, are going to go with George to the Cobb County deeds room to see who owns that condo. What you find may help us trace his hidden assets."

"And *I*," Teeny volunteered, "am going to get the condo's phone number."

Whatever secrets Harold was hiding, we would find them. Maybe *somebody* would get justice, after all.

8

The Twelve Sacred Red Hat Traditions

EFORE I GO TOO MUCH FURTHER WITH MY STORY, I SHOULD probably acquaint you with the tried-and-true backbone of our lifelong friendships: our Red Hat Rules (the Red Hat designation is recent, the rules are not), otherwise known as the Twelve Sacred Traditions.

TRADITION 1: DO OVER

Any one of us, at any time, can ask for a fresh start and get it: change of subject, change of attitude—no matter how bad we might have screwed things up (in which case, immediate apologies are in order). No grudges allowed.

Even as Mademoiselles, we realized that guys had the right idea about getting past conflicts with their friends. They get physical and then get past it, unlike women, whose extra leg on that X chromosome seems to contain a grudge box gene. So we adapted the guys' methods, eliminating the need for schoolyard fistfights or contact sports, and adding a verbal element (of course). A simple "DO" or "Do Over" is all it takes to make us retract our claws, whether we like it or not.

This works amazingly well, by the way.

TRADITION 2: MAKEOVER

Anybody can call a makeover (MO), provided there's a consensus and immediate improvement can ensue, which excludes weight, physical deficiencies, and cosmetic surgery. Clothes, jewelry, makeup, accessories, hair color (especially hair color), nails, and hairstyles are fair game.

Usually, the worse it's needed, the more resistant the makee, but experience has taught us to pay attention for our own good.

TRADITION 3: NO LIES

We must be able to trust each other for the truth.

But that does *not* mean we have to tell everything we know, especially if it would betray a confidence or cause senseless hurt. Thus, if one of us asks a question better left unanswered, we are obligated *not* to tell what we know. In such instances, "I'm sorry. I really couldn't say," is the preferred phrasing. (We rehearsed it over and over as Mademoiselles.) It took me *years* to master those words, and to this day, they are never my first inclination.

So if one of us doesn't really want to hear how those new white slacks look from behind, she shouldn't ask, or she's liable to hear, "I'm sorry. I really couldn't say." Which is *ouch* enough.

TRADITION 4: NO TELLING

Never, ever, ever will we rat out one of the group, even anonymously to the IRS when there's a huge contingency fink-fee involved. Our shared secrets are to be kept secret. We do not pass them on—even to blood sisters, therapists, priests, ministers, rabbis, the police, the FBI, grand juries, Congressional committees, lawyers, husbands, or mothers. *Especially* not lawyers, husbands, or mothers!

The penalties for breaking this tradition are immediate banishment from the group and eternal damnation featuring perpetual upper-lip electrolysis, freezing feet, and zero-carb diet.

TRADITION 5: MYOB (MIND YOUR OWN BUSINESS)

If a Red Hat doesn't want to talk about something, she doesn't have to, and that's that.

Further, a Red Hat has a perfect right to be wrong without being judged or bullied.

This tradition is the hardest one to keep, since we care so much. Well, and because we're all "fixers" at heart. Mainly this tradition binds us in a solemn covenant *not* to try to fix each other. (Another guy thing we have borrowed.) Impossible for many women, but it's the ideal we strive for.

With two notable exceptions, we've committed only minor and well-intentioned—though frequent—lapses of this tradition:

The first major lapse occurred that time when Teeny's boys were both still in diapers and her sorry-ass, drunken husband Reid gave her that black eye. I've already discussed how we tried to intervene.

The second time we blew Tradition Five was when Jackson Cates showed back up on SuSu's doorstep three months after marrying his *other* fiancée. Divorce in hand and elopement on his mind, he made a huge play for her. Despite our horrified objections, SuSu fell hook, line, and sinker for his impassioned declaration that he'd married the other woman only to honor the "sacred commitment" (spare me) he'd made before he met SuSu and discovered what *real* love was. (Retch, retch, but she bought it.) Further, he claimed that when his new wife had discovered he really loved SuSu instead of her, she'd set him free.

I mean, how deep can the ca-ca get?

We'd begged, bullied, and cajoled SuSu to let us hire a private detective to check him out—or at the very least, contact his ex-wife for her side of things—before they eloped. But Jackson's ardent attentions blinded SuSu to the truth. And I do mean blinded; the man looked like a redneck Aristotle Onassis with Dippity-Do in his slicked-back, yellowing gray hair. Perfect for Branson, Atlantic City, or Vegas, but Jackson Cates was not someone you'd want to be seen with at the opera or a Chastain dinner concert.

The idea of SuSu in bed with him was enough to make us have a collective seizure.

Yet in spite of our pleas to wait, she'd stubbornly invoked Tradition Five, only to suffer the dire consequences three years later when she discovered he'd transferred every penny out of state and was having an affair with "the trailer-trash slut" who managed his sleazy nursing homes in north Florida. We'd had to suffer along with SuSu through her rude awakening—worse, loyalty had demanded we be sympathetic without so much as a single "I told you so"—just like we now had to live with her obsessive efforts to get the $750,000 settlement the judge had ordered. Which bleeds over to Tradition Six.

TRADITION 6: GF (GIRLS FIRST)

No male, including husbands, lovers, sons, fathers, brothers, bosses, or pals, shall come between us. The Jackson affair had sorely strained this one, but in the end, Tradition Six had stood the test.

TRADITION 7: NO SECRET AFFAIRS

Despite the fact that it seems to contradict Tradition Five, this tradition is the exception that proves the rule. If one of us is contemplating a fling, she doesn't have to tell everybody in the group, but she *must* tell at least *one* of us. Affairs are far too dangerous to be waged without backup and advice, especially these days. I mean, you never know where his thing has *been*.

SuSu has kept this tradition's motor hot single-handed, since the rest of us are either too happily married (Linda), too moral (Teeny), too traditional (me), or too content (Diane) to even look at another man.

TRADITION 8: NO BEATING OURSELVES OR EACH OTHER UP WHEN WE BLOW IT

Pretty self-explanatory. The second part is fairly easy. The first is hard, hard, hard, since it seems to be our curse to feel responsible for everything that happens. With the notable exception of SuSu, who hasn't felt responsible for anything since her first husband was killed in a car wreck.

TRADITION 9: NO GENERAL DISCUSSIONS ABOUT RELIGION, ABORTION, OR POLITICS

When it comes to religion, our little group ranges from angry ex-Baptist atheist (SuSu) to guilt-driven Catholic (Teeny) to non-practicing Jew (Linda) to born-again Protestants (Diane and me). This never mattered much until ten years ago, when Teeny and I, along with six hundred other Buckhead matrons, got involved in this great interdenominational Bible study and started having sidebar discussions about the Scriptures at Red Hat luncheons. Diane ignored us, but Jewish Linda and atheist SuSu took umbrage, so we agreed to cool it, content to leave the dispensation of each other's souls to the Lord God Almighty, where it belongs. Brief mention of church activities is allowed for planning purposes only.

As for abortion (RU-Whatever included), we cover the board on that topic, too, but our convictions have always been too deeply held and polarizing to make discussion anything but anguish for us all. So we agreed to disagree and let it lie.

Well, most of us let it lie. The pro-abortion camp occasionally can't resist slipping in a little "enlightenment" in sheep's clothing, for which they are promptly slapped down and forced to pay for everybody's lunch. (This and Traditions Four and Eleven are the only three that involve a penalty, and there is no appeal.)

Teeny and I just keep her Catholic and my fundamental pro-life sentiments to ourselves and pray for the others behind their backs. So there.

Regarding politics, we span the spectrum from right-wing reactionary (SuSu) to active Republican (Diane) to middle-of-the-road apolitical (me and Teeny) to yellow-dog Democrat, bleeding heart tree-hugger (Linda). When the Clinton Administration put an end to our ability to have polite, objective political discussions, we decided, in the interest of harmony and mutual respect, to add a political ban to the religious and abortion restrictions. The only exception regards local elections and referenda, provided comments are based on recorded fact or issues, not editorials or image.

TRADITION 10: WITH THE EXCEPTION OF ALCOHOLIC BEVERAGES, ALL CALORIES SHALL BE IN CHEWABLE FORM

Our artificial sweetener rule restricts real sugar to foods we can actually chew. Hence the diet sodas with our ice cream sundaes, artificially sweetened iced tea with our chocolate éclairs or coffee with our pancakes. This tradition is not observed by Teeny (who would probably shrivel up and blow away without the sugar in her sweet tea) and Linda (who is fluffy but doesn't care), but we outnumbered them and voted it in on principle anyway.

TRADITION 11: NO "I TOLD YOU SO'S"

Simple to say, but maybe our biggest challenge to obey. This extends beyond words to gestures and facial expressions. Infractions are punishable by having to pick up the tab for the entire table or take everybody to whatever movie the victim wants to see, at the victim's choice.

TRADITION 12: THE SUBJECT OF WEIGHT WILL NEVER BE
MENTIONED OR EVEN IMPLIED

In our group, "my body, my choice" means no pointed looks
when fried foods, junk foods, heavy sauces, second desserts, or
alcoholic beverages are consumed or abstained from in our presence. We are not responsible for what any of the others chooses
to put into her body—our obligation extends only to taking the
car keys if it's drugs or alcohol. But as an extension of that individual responsibility, those of us who've let ourselves go are
banned from whining about tight clothes and resulting health
problems, or obsessing about diets. Bor-*ring!* If and when one of
us does decide to lose weight, she must let the results alone speak
for themselves.

Conversely, our well-meaning slender sisters are prohibited
from offering us helpful hints or harboring secret feelings of su-
periority. Nor shall the fluffy resent the svelte for their self-
discipline and/or enviable genes.

CODICIL: EXERCISE AND WORKOUT FADS MAY ONLY BE
MENTIONED ONCE

Once is informational. Any more is duress. And boring, boring,
boring. As with diets, let the results speak for themselves. (This
restriction does not extend, though, to details about hunky in-
structors or good gossip gleaned in a health and fitness setting.)

*I*n summation, these Red Hat Twelve Sacred Traditions have
kept us together and interested through three decades of trag-
edies, triumphs, pregnancies, out-of-state moves, toddlers, kiddie
sports, teenagers, hysterectomies, unfaithful husbands, disillu-
sionment, cancer, menopause, and, most of all, change.

9

Diane Elizabeth Culpepper Williams

Bohler Road. August 30, 1966. 8:30 P.M.

G OD, I'M BORED." ODDLY RESTLESS, DIANE ROLLED ACROSS
Pru's bed, closer to the fan that stirred the haze of menthol
cigarette smoke.

The sun had set, but it must have been over ninety in there. The four of us were sheened with perspiration, an old man's dream in our shorts and tees.

It was a Tuesday night late in August, the summer before our senior year, a dry time both literally and figuratively since our college beaux had already departed for football camp or fraternity preparations. My true love, Brad, had already left for school, but wouldn't disappear—taking my heart with him—for another month. The rest of the Buckhead boys had also dispersed to Georgia or any one of a dozen socially acceptable Southern colleges that welcomed them in hopes of future fat alumni endowments. And we Mademoiselles had already made our annual pilgrimage to the Queen's Court Motel in Saint Simons.

So we were on our own, at loose ends until after Labor Day, when school started and we could bask in our senior status. Despite the growing surge of feminism elsewhere in the country, we Southern girls, like our mamas, still defined ourselves by the men in our lives. Without them, we rattled around, anxious and out of sorts.

Not that Atlanta didn't have college boys. There were plenty, but it's true what they say about familiarity. The guys who went to State or Oglethorpe didn't rate, and Tech boys qualified only if they were football stars. Emory was out of the question, chock full of egg-headed Yankees—liberal know-it-alls, every one, who disdained everything we held dear and equated a Southern accent with stupidity, particularly when it came in a pretty package. And junior college was way below the scale, derisively referred to as "grade thirteen," a netherworld reserved for dweebs and those who'd been bounced out of *real* schools. So in our arrogant prejudice, we'd eliminated a lot of doubtlessly very fine, geographically convenient young men.

It never occurred to us—the same enlightened daughters of the New South who had embraced integration—to challenge our own silly social standards when it came to boys. When a thing wasn't done, it just wasn't done. We didn't call boys or ask them out. Ever. We didn't date dweebs. And we never, ever snaked another Mademoiselle's steady. (Well, it had been known to happen, but not in our little clique.)

"When's Teeny gettin' back from Saint Thomas?" SuSu drawled, her speech slowed by the heat as she painted her toenails fire-engine red. (Teeny's family had a house on the island.)

"Not till the thirtieth," Pru answered. For somebody who couldn't remember three sentences from a textbook, she did an amazing job of keeping up with who was where and what they were doing. And she knew every phone number in the Mademoiselles by heart.

Diane stood and arched her back, her usual pleasant expression unconvincing. Something was definitely up, but Tradition Five (MYOB) kept me from asking her what. She would tell us when she was ready. "And where's Linda?" she asked.

"Still at Lakemont," Pru reported.

"Man, that was a great Fourth of July party the Bondurants threw for us," SuSu reminisced. After a huge seafood buffet for the whole sorority and their dates, Linda's parents had hosted the five of us for two whole weeks—fourteen lazy, timeless days of swimming, water-skiing, eating (they had a great cook), and cool nights spent at supper parties or buck-dancing to the jukebox at Rabun Boat House with all the other Lakies.

If you can't be rich yourself, the next best thing is having rich friends. I'd barely been able to stand my crowded, run-down home afterwards. That taste of the good life had left me with an abiding hunger for more.

"If I had a place like that," SuSu pined, "I wouldn't come home until I had to, either."

Pru shook her head. "Linda says August is a bust up there, too, that the only thing to do is read—which, as we all know, she'd rather do than anything else." Levelheaded Linda was hopeless, preferring a good book to a lackluster date any day.

"Y'all," SuSu dictated for the ninety-leventh time, "We have *got* to get that girl a steady."

Pru burbled her infectious laugh. "Aaah, she'll find herself some bookworm in college. Let her be." Until that happened, we had enough moxie to get her dates whenever she needed one.

"Well, if Linda's bored up there, she can trade places with me anytime," I volunteered, getting smoke in my eye as I twisted my hair up off my neck. "She's always complaining about being an only child. She can have my sisters and brothers, and welcome to 'em."

"I'll take 'em if she won't." Diane's tone and expression were serious, concealing some huge, unspoken hurt. "You can't imagine how lonely it gets in a big old, cold, empty house with nobody else to take the blame." We all knew her mama drank too much behind closed drapes, something no one ever discussed, and Mr. Culpepper traveled all the time.

Had Mrs. Culpepper been on Diane's case again? She never gave Diane any credit, much less affection.

"I swear," Diane said, "if I stepped out of line even once, I think my mother would truly expire. And my father . . ." She was the only one among us who referred to her parents as Mother and Father instead of Mama and Daddy.

The grass is always greener, I guess, but mother or no mother, I would have been happy to give her life a try. "Too bad we can't really trade places. I'd take you up on it in a heartbeat."

SuSu giggled. "I'd give Diane fifteen minutes at dinner with the eight of y'all, and she'd sell her soul to get back to the peace and quiet of her lonely mansion."

Pru picked up the newspaper, deliberately shifting the conversation. "We need to decide on something to do tonight. Just because the guys are gone doesn't mean we can't have fun."

Heresy.

"How about a movie?" she suggested.

Yay! Air-conditioning. "Great," I said. "What's playing?"

She read off the list, but we'd seen everything in the theaters. August was a dry time for movies, too.

"It's just as well. I haven't got any money," SuSu said with a thin veneer of bravado to cover her embarrassment over the predicament Teeny and Diane never suffered.

"Actually," Diane responded, "neither do I. Not much, anyway. I bought those Weejuns this afternoon."

"Okay," Pru directed, "everybody get out their wallets so we can see how much we've got to work with."

Altogether, we had only $7.56. Not enough for a regular show, much less refreshments. (We had our priorities. Movies equaled popcorn, and not homemade, either. It had to be the artery-clogging, commercial coconut-oil variety.)

Pru cocked her head, fixing me with a pointed glance. "Looks like the drive-in for us, then."

SuSu groaned and so did I. That meant the *trunk* for us. Even with the convertible top, the Fireflite had room for both of us in its enormous trunk.

"Awww, Pru," I whined. "It's too hot. We'll die."

"Oh, suck it up," she said sweetly, deep dimples punctuating her cheeks. "It's only for a block. Y'all can have the Coke in there with you."

Diane, herself, had come up with our fallback cheap night out. For somebody so rich, she had an uncanny ability to pinch pennies. A thirty-nine-cent Coke from the Zesto on Piedmont Road got us a free pass to the drive-in movie across the street. That, with two of us in the trunk, would leave enough money for another ticket and refreshments. The trouble was, since Diane had major claustrophobia and we always took Pru's convertible, SuSu or Linda and I invariably ended up in the trunk.

"Tell you what," I said to Pru. "How about I drive this time? Just this once?"

Pru giggled. "Silly, you know Daddy'd kill me if he found out I let anybody else drive my car." Maybe because she had so few restrictions, she faithfully kept the few she did, and that one was first and foremost.

I slumped. It's impossible to argue with somebody so cheerful. "He won't find out. I just can't face the trunk."

"Oh, come on." SuSu stood up to her lithe five feet nine inches. "We can do it. We can always do it." That was our role in the group. Linda was our sanity. Diane was our bankroll. Pru was our alibi. Teeny was our conscience and etiquette expert. I was the brain, and SuSu was our cheerleader and fearless doer.

"Oh, all right," I groused. "I'll do it, but I resent being the one in the trunk every time."

"We appreciate it." Diane's classic features clouded with guilt. "I would if I could, George. Truly."

I hadn't intended to make her feel bad. (Southern women of our ilk had been trained from the cradle not to hurt anybody's feelings.) Abashed, I gave her a hug. "I know it. I'm just bitchin' in general." Diane was the last person I'd want to hurt, except maybe Teeny.

We gathered our cigs and empty Coke bottles.

"Cheer up," Pru said, not the least bit guilty about consigning SuSu and me to the Inner Darkness. "*The Pink Panther*'s playing. You'll love it."

I sulked. "I've seen it."

"And you loved it," SuSu reminded me, then blew a perfect smoke ring into my face.

"We all did," Pru contributed with her usual childlike enthusiasm. "I like the good ones even better the second time. You know what to expect." She looked out into the deepening twilight. "C'mon, y'all. Let's get this show on the road." Timing mattered. If we got there before it was dark, we might get caught sneaking out of the trunk. But if we waited too late, we'd miss the start of the movie.

Top down, we zoomed along West Wesley like Valkyries brimming with hubris and hormones. Buckhead *was* Atlanta, as far as we were concerned, and we owned it. We were Mademoiselles, and we were rising seniors. It was almost enough to make up for being stuck at home and manless.

Once safely inside the drive-in, we discovered that several other small groups of Mademoiselles had had the same inspiration, so we joined their noisy cluster of cars near the back of the vast and humpy forest of microphones.

"Oh, look," Diane said, pointing to a beige Ford Falcon. "There's Carolyn Marks." (Not to be confused with the bitchy Carolyn Watts.) Her usually open expression shuttered. "I'll be right back. I need to ask a her a favor."

Something was definitely up.

Piqued, I waited about a minute, then followed to find Diane and Carolyn huddled out of earshot from the others. My gossip alert went off the scale. I didn't actually sneak up on them, but I must confess to taking very careful steps as I approached.

I caught the name Johnny Jordan (pronounced *Jer*den) and saw Diane flash a look of hopeful longing that told me everything I needed to know. That did it.

Johnny was captain of Grady's football team. His good looks, intelligence, shy charm, and impressive physique made him the exception to the Mademoiselles' "no Grady guys" rule. (Grady was an inner-city school with some tough customers. We played them in football, but rarely mixed.)

"Diane Culpepper," I interrupted in discreet tones. "Are you thinkin' about dumping Nat Taylor"—her SAE gorgeous college sophomore steady—"for a *high school* boy?" Heresy, indeed.

I could see her blush even in the pale yellow light from the street lamp illuminating the exit. "Hush up, George," she snapped with uncharacteristic severity. "Somebody might hear you."

Carolyn handed her the keys to her Ford Falcon. "Just don't let anything happen to it," she pleaded. Everybody in Mademoiselle had followed the saga of Carolyn's three wrecks and two tickets. "Daddy said he'd take it away for good if anything else happened or he caught me letting anybody else drive it."

"I'll be careful," Diane promised, giving her a hug.

"And be sure to be back before ten thirty," Carolyn cautioned as she turned toward Pru's convertible. "I have to be home by eleven." A lingering consequence of the last ticket.

I circled the car, then got into the passenger seat.

Diane slid behind the wheel. "And what do you think you're doing?" she asked.

"Going with you. If you're gonna humiliate yourself by doing this, at least you won't be alone." Visiting a Grady boy! "Are we expected?"

"Oh, God, no," she said as if premeditation would make it even worse (an attitude responsible for many an unwanted pregnancy among proper Southern girls who "succumbed" to premarital sex). "I just found out he liked me this afternoon when Carolyn called. He told her at Christ the King youth group."

His Catholicism wasn't an issue, but his midtown neighborhood was.

"Why are you messin' with Johnny Jordan when you've got Nat?"

Eyes averted, she cranked up the dinky rear engine before experimenting with the three-on-the column gearshift. "I don't have Nat. He dumped me," she announced without emotion. "He waited until I was saying good-bye, then calmly informed me it was over."

She backed out of the space, but had trouble getting the car into forward gear. "Dammit." Her anger focused on the errant transmission. "This thing never has run right since Carolyn rear-ended that police car." Compared with mine, Diane's tantrums sounded like tea-party chitchat. She had never trusted herself to uncork her pent-up fury at life's betrayals. I wondered even then if she ever would.

"Well, screw Nat Taylor, then," I said in as close to a big "F———him!" as my genteel upbringing would allow. "I hope he catches VD."

She shot me a grateful little smile. "I hope his pecker falls off and he flunks out of school."

"Even better."

Cheered, she coaxed the transmission into drive at last, but didn't turn on the lights until we turned left onto Lindbergh. After a right onto Piedmont, we headed south toward Monroe Drive and Morningside, where Johnny lived—a trendy spot now, but then, a crumbling, transitional area.

Diane's quiet humiliation thickened the silence between us for the first few blocks, but by the time we crossed Cheshire Bridge, we had managed a crank up a casual conversation. Mademoiselles knew the value of safe, reassuring small talk in the face of embarrassment.

We chatted about upcoming football games, school dances, fall pickups and initiation—all the good things we had to look forward to. By the time we reached Johnny's tree-shaded street, Diane was brittle with anticipation.

"Okay," I said as she pulled into the driveway at a tasteful metal lawn marker that said JORDAN above the house number. She braked at the walkway to the tidy bungalow.

"I'll go to the door," I volunteered. "That way, if his parents answer, they'll think I'm the brazen hussy, not you."

"You *are* the brazen hussy," she said with affection and gratitude.

"Yeah, well, there's hope for you yet."

I went to the door and knocked. No response.

I rang. Waited. Then rang again.

Diane gripped the steering wheel, sinking lower in the seat with each passing minute.

There were lights on inside, but people often left lights burning when they went away. People did not, though, refuse to answer the door when they were home—that would have been an unthinkable breach of Southern hospitality back then. So I returned to the car.

"God has decided to save you from yourself," I told her. "There's nobody home."

Relief and disappointment competed in her face. "Oh, well."

She backed into the street with a little more speed than was prudent, then tried to shift into forward. The transmission made a horrible grinding, whining noise.

"Aaagh!" She jerked her hand from the shifter and slammed on the clutch and the brake.

"You have to ease off the clutch as you put on the gas," I, the fixer, said. "Just let your heel do the gas as your toe releases the brake and you ease out the clutch."

"I know how to drive a straight shift," she bit out, but numerous tries yielded only more alarming noises. Wild-eyed, Diane scanned the quiet, tree-shaded street. We were angled across both lanes. "Oh, no. What if somebody comes? What if Johnny comes."

"Nobody's going to come," I said, not even convincing myself. "It's almost nine thirty on a Thursday night. All these good people have gone to bed."

"Not the Jordans," Diane wailed. "I'll die of he sees us stuck here like the Beverly Hillbillies."

I petted her shoulder. "It's gonna be okay. Just keep trying. We'll do fine."

She backed across the street and down the block a safe distance from the Jordan's, but after fifteen minutes of jiggling and finiggling, coaxing and jamming, the car still refused to go into first or second gear.

Diane dropped her forehead to the steering wheel. "Shit. Triple shit!" Strong language for gentle, proper Diane.

We were in a real pickle—Carolyn in an even worse one. If her father found out she'd loaned us the car, she was sunk. And if she was late, she was sunk. Even if we could get to a phone, there was no way to alert the others. The concession stand would be closed by now.

"Here." I got out and circled to the driver's door. "Let me try it."

Diane paced the sidewalk, smoking, while I stubbornly refused to give up. Only after another fifteen minutes did I face the inevitable. "This car isn't going anywhere. We are all screwed."

Diane slumped like an abandoned scarecrow for a few seconds, then straightened resolutely. "It won't go forward, but it'll go." She jerked open the door. "Scoot over. I'm taking this heap back to the drive-in."

"Backwards?" Diane could hardly back out of her own driveway! "It has to be more than five miles! We'll never make it!"

"Oh, yes, we will," she ground out, bracing her arm across the seat as she pivoted to face the rear. "We have to."

"Wait, wait, wait." Shy Diane was really going to do this crazy, reckless thing! "What side of the street should we be on? The right one or the wrong one?"

And they say there are no stupid questions.

"The wrong one," Diane reasoned, picking up speed. "At least the people in our lane will be going the same way we are."

I couldn't argue the logic. "Ohpleez, ohpleez, ohpleez, dear God," I said as we made our somewhat serpentine way toward

Monroe Drive, "don't let there be any traffic between here and there. Especially not any cops."

To my vast relief, my prayer was granted for the first few blocks it took Diane to get a feel for going backwards. By the time the intersection with Piedmont road loomed ahead, we hardly wandered at all, and she'd begun to relax a little. "Check it out. Anybody coming?"

"Thanks be to God, no." Not a soul.

It would have made me think that God was looking after us, but for the fact that He'd allowed the transmission to screw up in the first place. "Do you think God does stuff like this for the entertainment?" I ventured. "I mean, this has got to be *too* funny from where He's sitting."

"There you go with that personal, Baptist crap," Diane said without rancor. "If God wants funny, I guarantee He can do better than this."

"I don't know," I said, sobering as I spotted an oncoming car round the curve at Rock Springs Presbyterian. I pointed to the headlights. "Alert, alert. Danger, Will Robinson. Incoming."

"No danger, silly." Diane sounded downright amused. "They can get by me." She stopped at the curb and put on her blinker.

"Speak of the devil." Headlights reflected in the windshield.

"Okay. Just stay calm. I'll motion them past." She did, and the driver stared as he rode by, well before the guy on the other side passed us.

The next hurdle was the intersection where Cheshire Bridge, Piedmont Circle, and Piedmont collided at Twelve Oaks Barbecue. We both watched in horror as the light turned red.

We pulled to a stop and tried to act casual when a man with a garbage bag stepped out of the restaurant and started picking up trash. He never even gave us a first look, much less a second.

"Surely he must see us," I said.

"Of course he sees us," Diane said with a chuckle. "How could he miss us?"

Maybe it was the tension, but a hysterical little laugh escaped me. "Hey. What if going backwards makes you invisible?"

The bug was catching. "Oh, God, George, don't make me laugh. I have to go to the bathroom. And I have to concentrate."

I started laughing in earnest. "Drive, then. Drive. But don't wet Carolyn's upholstery. Bad enough that we've got to tell her we drove this thing backwards all the way across town. Let's not add insult to injury."

The light changed, and we forged ahead. Or behind, as the case may be.

By the time we backed into the drive-in's exit, we were almost helpless with laughter and relief. Diane backed up next to the shielding underbrush, cut the engine, and leapt out. "I'll never make it to the concession stand." Ignoring the wave of Mademoiselles who approached us, she hied it to the honeysuckle, then returned, once more our composed, serene friend.

Carolyn reached her first. "What happened? I was frantic. Five more minutes, and I'd have had to get Pru to take me home."

"The car got stuck in reverse." I wasn't about to tell the others where. Carolyn knew, and that was enough.

"Yeah, well, I know it's a little tricky sometimes," Carolyn said. "You just have to baby it."

"We did," Diane said calmly. "We babied, and we bullied, and we tried jumping it into first. And second. But nothing worked. So we drove it home"—she cut her eyes at me—"from the Driving Club." A perfect cover, since her family belonged there.

Carolyn blanched. "Are you telling me you drove all the way back here in reverse?"

"Yep."

The others hooted and hollered. Another Mademoiselle legend was born.

"We had to," Diane explained. "I'd have pushed the thing, if I'd had to. I couldn't get you in trouble."

"Sweetie." Carolyn gave her a big hug. "You are so precious."

"Come on," Pru said. "We'll drop you off on our way home.

Your dad can't get mad if the thing broke on you, can he?"

"No." Carolyn smiled. "I guess he can't. Not really mad, anyway."

Adjusting our story to the Driving Club, we regaled the others with a modified blow-by-blow account. It was the happiest I could remember Diane's being in a long time. We were singing along to the Shirelles when Diane opened her cigarette case for another smoke. "Damn. I'm out of cigs." She leaned forward to Pru. "Can we swing by my place after we drop Carolyn off? I want to pick up a carton of weeds."

"Okey-dokey," Pru agreed. Ten minutes later, we pulled into the three-car garage at Diane's Georgian mansion on Cherokee (one of Atlanta architect Neil Reid's smaller but no less coveted masterpieces).

"I'll be right back." She bounced out and headed for the servants' entrance. Long minutes stretched before she reappeared, ashen. "Y'all go on," she said, grim. "I need to stay here." She hurried back inside.

"Diane!" I tried to go after her, but Pru stopped me. "Let her go. Tradition Five."

Diane had almost gotten the door shut when we heard her wail, "No, Mother. Please." With a jerk, it swung wide, revealing Mrs. Culpepper, her stained housecoat unbuttoned, exposing all her sagging glory, her makeup smeared, hair askew, and an almost-empty fifth of bourbon in her hand. A horrifyingly unforgettable image.

We all died for Diane.

"Holy shit," SuSu whispered.

Miz Culpepper lurched over to the car. "Come on in, girls." The smell of whiskey all but knocked us down. "Diane loves you girls. Why doncha come on in and spen' the night? A reg'lar slumber party." She laughed at her own nonjoke, then abruptly glared at Diane. "Whassa matter? Are you 'shamed of your poor old mother?"

Any one of us would have paid good money for the earth to open up and swallow us.

Gripping the steering wheel, Pru laid down her forehead in despair. I know now that she was all too familiar with such humiliations, but Miz Bonner had kept Mr. Bonner from embarrassing her in front of her friends.

I opened the car door and got out. "Okay, Miz Culpepper. Let's have a slumber party."

She beamed a sloppy smile. "Oh, good."

"Come on, y'all. Let's have a slumber party." Knowing it would only hurt Diane worse to be the object of our pity, I met her gaze with quiet resolution. "We're all going to come help get your mother to bed, and then we'll have our slumber party."

"Yeah." Pru put on her best dimpled grin. "Come on, Miz Culpepper. Let's get you into something a little more comfortable." She took her arm.

Miz Culpepper looked down, her expression clouded. "This is a dream idn't it? I dream I'm naked in all the wrong places all the time."

Pru giggled. "That's it. A dream. So you don't have to worry. I'll take you to bed, and when you wake up in the morning, everything will be all right."

SuSu stayed in the kitchen with Diane while Pru and I got Miz Culpepper into a nightgown, then into bed. She was asleep—or passed out—the minute her head hit the pillow.

Mission accomplished, we returned to find Diane weeping onto the breakfast table.

I squatted beside her and spoke with quiet resolution devoid of pity. "Diane, look at me."

"I can't," she sobbed. "I can never face any of y'all again."

"Oh, bullshit." I grabbed her hair and lifted, leveling our gazes. "Tradition Four! This is us. As far as anybody outside this room goes, what we just saw never happened."

I let go of her hair. "Hold up your head, woman. You're beautiful and smart and proud and brave. You are *not* responsible for your mother's behavior, so none of us feels sorry for you. Got it?"

"Amen," SuSu seconded.

Pru beamed as if she, too, had been redeemed. "We are *not* responsible for our parents' sicknesses."

"Now get your weeds, and we're heading back to Pru's. All of us."

Diane blew her nose on a paper napkin from the dispenser on the table. "I'll do better than that," she declared with heartening determination. She headed back to her mother's room, then returned with four twenty-dollar bills. "Let's go to the Varsity first. Mama's treat." She cocked a wry half-smile. "It's the least she can do after exposing herself to you."

Relieved laughter exploded from us all. And in that moment, I knew Diane Culpepper was going to be all right no matter what curve balls life might throw her. If she could come up smiling after getting dumped, driving backwards for seven miles, and having her mother greet her best friends half-naked and snockered, all in one day, she could survive anything.

10

Progress Reports

Swan Coach House. Wednesday, February 13, 2002. 11:04 A.M.

I LOOKED UP FROM OUR REGULAR TABLE AND COULDN'T BELIEVE my eyes.

SuSu! Desperately in need of a haircut and still stubbornly without hat or purple, but looking wonderfully well rested. And on time!

"Uh-oh," I teased as she approached across the empty dining room, "the end of the world is nigh. SuSu is on time. I'm gabberflasted."

She sashayed to her chair, far too smug for this hour that amounted to the crack of dawn to her. "I haven't been home yet."

That explained it. "Somebody new?"

"No, no." She spread her napkin and reached for a mini muffin. "You remember Ted Albertson?"

"Aw, SuSu." My spirits curdled with judgment and frustration. "The *married* Ted Albertson you swore off as a Christmas present to yourself?"

She ignored my question. "We spent the night in his penthouse." Facing me in challenge, she bit into the muffin. "M-m-m-m-m-m. Yummy." She wasn't talking about the muffin.

"Spare me." Why did she *do* this, not just to herself, but to

Ted's wife? Never mind that Deenie Albertson was a heinous bitch maniac, and Ted had bedded half of Buckhead long before he got around to SuSu. It was the principle of the thing. I hated for SuSu to settle for what amounted to mutual masturbation. It was so seedy. "I hope your next stop is the Any Test lab for a full STD screen."

The sex must have been *really* good, because she refused to rise to the bait. "Mercy. Somebody got up on the wrong side of the bed this morning." She scanned for our waitress, singing out, "Maria" in *West Side Story* style. "Maria. Maria, Maria."

The scattered patrons who were filtering in watched her with expressions ranging from distaste to amusement.

Maria emerged from the kitchen with a smile. "Ah, my favorite ladies."

"Maria." SuSu greeted her like a long-lost friend. "Coffee, darling, for both of us," she chirped out, repulsively cheerful. "And hot muffins, lots of them, with gobs of plain butter. Put it on my tab. And ice water all around."

"Right away."

"Okay," I conceded, catching her good mood. "Maybe there is something to be said for cheap, tawdry sex."

The vision of me and Brad shot heat where the sun never shined.

I was baffled by these sudden flashbacks, deviled that my mind had just up and decided to torment me with hard-buried memories so late in life.

I racked my brain to make sense of it. Some anniversary, maybe, that triggered my subconscious? But all our firsts had been in the fall or spring or summer. Brad hadn't ever observed Valentine's, finding it "gauche."

The whole thing was most disturbing.

SuSu arched her eyebrow, smug. "Oh, this has nothing to do with last night."

I shifted my focus back to her. "Spill it." I hadn't seen her this happy since Jackson had absconded with the funds.

"You'll have to wait for the others. I want you all to hear at once."

As usual, I leapt to conclusions. "Don't tell me you got the money?"

She soured instantly. "Of course I didn't get the money. Would I keep that from any of you for even an instant? No, I did not get the money." She slumped, deflated, in her chair.

"Oh, God, SuSu. I'm sorry." I gave myself a monumental meta-physical kick in the ass. "Here you were, happy as a kid in cotton candy, and I not only fuss at you, but I totally pop your balloon. I am *so* sorry."

"Oh, quit that," she grumbled, somewhat mollified. "I hate when you roll over on your back and wet all over yourself that way. Tradition Eight." (No beating ourselves or each other up when we blow it.)

"Only if you'll give me a Tradition One."

"Okay. Abject apology accepted. Do Over granted, on the con-dition that you not say another negative word about my choice in men."

I raised my middle three fingers in the Girl Scout salute. "Not for a whole month."

"Six," she countered, regaining her sass.

"Two."

"Done." We had to be realistic, after all.

"Two what?" Teeny asked as she joined us, wearing a red cashmere beret and matching sweater dress set off by a triangle of luscious purple, gold, and red paisley silk draped artistically across her shoulders.

"Two months," SuSu clarified. "That's how long she's prom-ised not to say anything negative about my choice in men."

Teeny eyed me indulgently. "I'll believe that when I see it." Folding gracefully into her seat, she scanned past the lobby. "Where's Linda?" She turned to SuSu. "I can't believe you beat her here. Good job, Suse. Keep it up."

I leaned in close. "She hasn't been home yet."

Teeny nodded without a smidgen of condemnation. "Whatever the cause, I'm proud of you, SuSu." Maria arrived with the water, and Teeny lifted her glass. "Here's to punctuality."

Diane came in at 11:15, brisk with resolution. After her past few years of encroaching unhappiness, it was great to see the old spark of determination in her eye.

"Hey," SuSu greeted. "How's Mission Impossible going?" We had abandoned our initial paranoia in favor of reasonable discretion, so the topic was back on the table at our regular meetings.

Diane absolutely preened. "I'll give a full report as soon as everybody's here." She halted, suddenly realizing who was there and who was not. "Wait a minute. SuSu? No Linda?" She checked her watch, then toodled the theme from *The Twilight Zone*.

"I'll call her." I whipped out my cell phone, but got Linda's message service before her mobile number rang even once. "Rats. She hasn't got hers on."

Maria arrived with our coffee and muffins, brought hot tea for Diane and coffee for Teeny, then left us to eat, drink, and dish. As the next half hour of trivial talk wore on, my impatience to hear SuSu's and Diane's news battled with growing apprehension about Linda. She was never this late.

"I hope she hasn't had a wreck," I worried aloud at 11:35, fulfilling my Chicken Little role. I stood up for another search of the crowded foyer and was rewarded with a brief glimpse of a swollen-eyed, red-nosed Linda coming in from the parking lot. "Thank goodness." I reclaimed my seat. "She's here, but something is definitely wrong. She's either got a bad cold or she's been crying."

"Oh, dear." Teeny's brow furrowed. "Maybe she did have a wreck."

Linda bulled her way to our banquette and sat down with an angry plop. "Sorry, y'all."

We stared at her in silent anticipation.

"Can I at least get some coffee before I explain?"

Teeny handed hers over. They both drank it sweet and black. Linda took a long swig, then sighed. "Okay. I'll tell you. But anybody who laughs will be on my permanent hate list."

"Oh, sweetie," Teeny offered. "Did you have a wreck?"

"No," she snapped with uncharacteristic venom. "Three guesses who."

It had to be her daughter, Abby, the sole difficulty in Linda's idyllic life. In December when she'd come home for winter break from her junior year, Abby had announced that she'd quit Agnes Scott (too many lesbians), decided to become a hairdresser (this, from a girl who made 1510 on her SATs and had a 4.0), and moved in with an Iranian tattoo artist in Little Five Points.

Happy Hanukkah.

"Abby came by this morning." Eyes welling, Linda struggled to maintain her composure. "She's gone and gotten a tattoo. Not a little, discreet one, but a hateful, honkin' big nasty, right out where everybody can see it."

"Oh, god." SuSu slumped with relief. "I thought you were gonna say she was pregnant by that scary lookin' Muslim she's livin' with."

"This is worse," Linda snapped. "If she was pregnant, at least I'd get a grandchild out of it. This is just humiliation, an endless slap in the face."

"Where's the tattoo?" Teeny gripped Linda's hand in sympathy. "What kind?"

"On her upper arm." Linda's voice thickened with frustration. "Right where anybody can see it. A band of twisted barbed wire. Navy blue, I think." A tear escaped. "Worse than Angelina fuckin' Jolie." Linda *never* said the F-word! "Pure redneck white trash."

Could it *be* any tackier? Linda's precious princess, permanently branded with gangbanger chic. A Jewish mother's worst nightmare.

Well, maybe not the worst, but way up there, just below terminal illness, drug addiction, or becoming a nun.

"Oh, sweetie." Teeny's big blue eyes welled in empathy. "At least it's a conservative color," she consoled, determined as always to find some bright spot in everything.

We all rolled our eyes. Nobody ever wants to hear "it could be worse," but Teeny meant well. She always meant well.

"She was actually proud of it." Linda shivered. "I haven't told Brooks. He'll poop his pants when he finds out."

"Oh, honey." SuSu flagged Maria down. "Mimosas for everybody." She pointed to Linda. "And make hers a double." SuSu's answer to everything: anesthesia.

Teeny and I demurred. A drink at that time of day would have put both of us under the table before the chicken salad ever arrived.

Once we'd ordered lunch and the others had gotten a start on their drinks, I shifted the subject. "Okay, Suse. We're all here. What's your big news?"

She grinned, and suddenly I got a flash of SuSu as a Mademoiselle, captain of the cheerleaders and not scared of any damn thing or any damn body.

She pulled a folded piece of flowered wrapping paper out of her purse. "As you know, I had another contempt hearing yesterday." Her fourth.

"And?" Diane dutifully asked.

"And I won, of course, as if it makes a difference, which it doesn't. But before I went, I had a brilliant revelation." She started unfolding the paper, keeping the flowered side to us. "Since the friggin' legal system won't cross state lines to bring Jackson to justice, I decided to turn up the heat myself." More dramatic unfolding. "I drew this up and showed it to the judge to see if it was legal." She turned the paper around to reveal a wanted poster with WANTED ON FOUR WARRANTS, Jackson's name, a stick figure where his photo would be, and a five-thousand-dollar contingency reward. "I'm gonna do this as a full-page ad in the Ocala paper and another in the national nursing home owners' professional publication. All I need is a graphic artist to put it together for me, and Mignon"—her daughter—"said she knows some-body." She handed the poster to Teeny.

"This is brilliant!" Teeny scanned it, then passed it on.

"Perfect!" Diane clapped like a little girl who'd just gotten a new My Little Pony.

"Too rich." Linda laughed, her humiliation exorcised. "SuSu, you are a genius."

"Amen." I was impressed. "What did the judge say?"

She grinned so hard, her eyes went narrow. "He said that if more women had the means and the wherewithal to do things like this, maybe more deadbeat husbands would pay up."

All this, and a judicial seal of approval. Maybe her self-imposed role as Jackson's victim was about to change.

"That is *so* great." No wonder she'd been so smug. And so punctual.

After she'd basked sufficiently in our praise, SuSu turned to Diane. "Okay. Enough about me. Progress-report time."

Diane looked askance to make sure the attention generated by SuSu's poster and our reactions had died away. Then she took a long, satisfied breath and huddled our red hats together. "It's going great, just like we planned. I've been getting up at three every morning and copying the contents of his briefcase. Then every few days, I duplicate everything and take one set to my attorney and the other to our new safe deposit box."

SuSu chuckled. "*Too* perfect."

"And he doesn't suspect?" Teeny asked, wide-eyed with ad-miration.

"No. Why should he?" Bitterness harshened Diane's face and voice. "He's put so much over on me for so long."

Linda propped on her forearms. "Find anything incriminating yet?"

Diane's features cleared. "Tons. I've gotten so familiar with everything, I could probably tell him a thing or two about those trust accounts." She smiled. "But the best news is, I've found all his passwords, not just to the computer at home, but his on-line links to the bank's mainframe. I've been accessing his files and copying those to disks and floppies."

"What?" SuSu straightened, chin tucked. "Mainframe? Floppies? Disks? The last time I looked, you didn't even know how to turn the damn thing on."

Diane blushed. "Well, I figured I'd damn well better learn, so I called Lee in Tokyo and asked him who I could hire for computer lessons so I could e-mail him, and he gave me the name of a teaching assistant at Tech. Such a sweet boy: the younger brother of one of Lee's buddies, nerdy, but so patient with me. He comes right to the house Monday, Tuesday, and Thursday mornings. And he takes MasterCard." She was so proud of herself. "Just to make sure he doesn't bail out on me, I always fix him homemade blueberry pancakes and bacon and fresh-squeezed orange juice."

"I cannot believe my ears," I said. "You go, girl."

"I actually like it," she confessed. "And as it turns out, I have a real knack with the thing."

I couldn't resist. "I told you you would."

She could have invoked Tradition Eleven (No "I told you so's"), but she was magnanimous. "Well, you were right, as usual." She straightened. "When I told Harold I was takin' e-mail lessons, he all but patted me on the head," she said. "Won't he be surprised when he finds out what I was really doing?"

"We all have to be there when you tell him," Linda decreed. "Swear."

"We'll see," Diane deflected, which meant *No, but I don't want to argue about it now*. She shifted back to Mission Impossible. "But the best stuff I've gotten so far is on tape. SuSu, you were dead right about that."

"Great," SuSu answered. "So tell."

"Every evening when Harold gets home—when he bothers to come home for supper—I've got the table set, his favorite foods cooked, cocktails and hors d'oeuvres waiting, and I greet him with enough wifely deference and concern to gag June Cleaver."

"Yuck," Linda said with gruesome alacrity.

"I sit him in the den with his paper, serve him a double, then give him about thirty minutes to scan through his satellite stations while I get the last of supper going. Then I bring in my glass of wine and another double for him"—she dropped her voice— "and discreetly turn on the tape machine in the flower arrangement on the coffee table. Once it's going, I ask if he minds if I put the tape on. He always says okay, because he thinks I mean the stereo. I made up a few cassettes of all his favorites and play those."

"So you have him on record giving permission to turn on the tape," Teeny said with a piercing look. "Very clever."

Diane smiled. "Then I click off the TV, turn on the music, settle into my chair with my wine, and ask about his day." Her features hardened. "Work is the only thing he'll talk to me about anymore, but aren't we glad he does?"

"And?" Teeny asked, very much "with it" for Teeny.

"And I've got enough on tape to send the bastard to jail for a long, long time," Diane whispered. "Not to mention the bank. Harold isn't alone in crossing the line. I could make big trouble with the feds for the entire trust department."

"Damn," SuSu said in awe. "I should have hired *you* to go after Jackson instead of all those private investigators and contingency lawyers."

Linda raised her mimosa. "Here's to Diane, and the first of many victories to come."

We all reared back into our seats, feeling expansive and optimistic. "To Diane, and victories to come."

Diane waited until we had sipped our tea and coffee and drinks to answer with her own bittersweet pronouncement. "And here's to friendship, the only love that lasts."

We drank, solemn.

SuSu rubbed her hands together. "Okay. Bring on the shrimp salad. I'm starvin'."

Speak of the devil, Marie exited the kitchen with our lunches.

After she handed them out and left us, Diane held up a finger. "Oh, I almost forgot. I need y'all, big-time."

Cheese stick poised, Linda said, "You got it. When and what?"

"A week from Saturday, the bank and Ted Turner are throwin' that big charity thing at the PDC to raise money for Save the City. Silent auction, great food, good orchestra, free booze, all on the bank's tab. I have to do my corporate wifey thing while Harold schmoozes four tables of his heavy-duty clients." She cocked her head. "Please say y'all will come. We'll have our own table, and it'll save me from havin' to sit with the philanthropic good-as-dead."

"Dates and husbands?" SuSu asked about the charity event.

Diane sighed. "Unfortunately." We'd long since abandoned the hope that we could all be friends as couples. My John and Linda's Brooks were the only two who got along, bound by a common aversion to the other husbands, but they saw each other only for an occasional dawn or twilight tennis game. It was enough to qualify their acquaintance as a friendship in masculine terms, but not enough to keep them from being dragged, heels dug in, to Red Hat couples events.

"Saturday week?" We went for the little two-year purse calendars Linda had supplied us all with since we were in high school.

Teeny checked her schedule. "Okay with me. My retreat's not till the week after that." Every February and October for the last decade, she'd taken two weeks at some Catholic women's retreat in Florida. Not my idea of a vacation, but at least she came home tanned and revived.

My kids, Jack and Callie, were scheduled to be home that weekend, but they always had their own plans for the evenings. As long as we fed them and did their laundry, they wouldn't miss us.

After much consulting and shuffling of previous commitments, we all agreed to be there for her.

"I knew I could count on you guys."

"Sure," Linda said, "but it won't be easy facing Harold as if nothing's wrong when Brooks and I would like to choke his eyes out."

"If Diane can bring him his pipe and slippers every evening and never utter a peep when he doesn't even show up," Teeny said, "the least we can do is act civil with the man."

She had a point. I said a silent prayer that none of us—mainly, me—would let the cat out of the bag. I was notoriously transparent but vowed, for Diane's sake, to be Mata Hari.

"Hell, yes, we can do it," SuSu declared. She gave Diane a sideways shoulder hug. "Whatever you need, kid."

That resolved, we attacked our lady lunches with a vengeance. Intrigue has a definite salutary effect on the appetite.

But everything has a salutary effect on my appetite.

11

You Can't Judge a Jerk by the Cut of His Tuxedo

Piedmont Driving Club. Saturday, February 23, 2002. 8:30 P.M.

WE WERE DIFFERENT PEOPLE WITH OUR MEN PRESENT. IT shouldn't have been that way, but it was. Along with their public Buckhead boy charms came a brier patch of tensions and booby traps. Little wonder we Red Hats no longer looked forward to charity functions like this one, but we were there for Diane, not for ourselves. Unfortunately, with the exception of sweet Brooks, our spouses lacked such a noble sense of sacrifice.

There had been a time when we'd all enjoyed the food, the free booze, the great music, and the electricity of seeing and being seen among Atlanta's movers and shakers, but those days had passed with the advent of trophy wives and the inevitable familiarity that bred contempt. I don't know when big bashes had stopped being fun. Maybe when we saw how many of Atlanta's moguls used and discarded wives like toilet paper and put millions up their noses. Not to mention the privileged princesses' fawning over Elton John, the city's most notable transplant, and his musical cronies as if they were the second coming.

Nevertheless, I'd dusted off my ancient Albert Nippon Great Little Black Dress, forced John—sullen as a twelve-year-old at a distant cousin's wedding—into his tux, and then dragged him here with me to Atlanta's sole surviving shrine to Old South society.

The theme was Broadway, and the ballroom had been transformed with chaser lights, huge show posters, and enough Mylar to carpet Rhode Island. A very good orchestra played a medley from *The Lion King* at a bearable volume. Maybe it wouldn't be so bad, after all. We hadn't danced in ages.

"Oh, look." I pointed across the sea of supersparkly tables to one in the far corner. "Linda's holding our spot." Along with Brooks, Teeny, and what had to be a new stud puppy for SuSu, who was nowhere to be seen. "See, back there?"

"Yeah," John said, still sulking. Despite dealing with fundraisers for more than two decades at Tech, John had no tolerance for schmoozing.

I squeezed his arm. "You go on ahead. I need to make a pit stop."

He stopped me with a firm grip on my elbow. "Georgia"—the only time he called me by name was when I was in trouble—"do not ask me to go in there by myself."

I smiled to conceal my irritation that even after all these years, he wouldn't suck it up to approach our oldest friends alone. "Wait for me, then, and we'll go in together. I won't be long."

"Yeah. I've heard that one before." His flat-mouthed sigh was as close as he ever came to a temper fit.

I entered the tastefully decorated soft-green bathroom to find SuSu at the mirror, compulsively fluffing a wretched new bedhead haircut with her long, scarlet nails as if there were some elusive arrangement (and I use the term advisedly) that would make it look like something besides your five-year-old sister's butcher job.

At least she'd gotten the color back to a subtle, believable red.

SuSu was definitely on the hunt tonight. Her floaty little red cocktail dress and stiletto slides showed off her long legs to great advantage. For a woman our age, she looked great and oozed sex appeal.

"Hey," she said without so much as a glance at me. "Are you ready for this?"

"No. I'm terrified he'll see right through us. Me." My internal Chicken Little was telling me Harold would take one look at me and know everything. How's that for megalomania? "I'll die if we blow this."

I dared not speak too specifically. Fresh gossip had always been Buckhead's most precious commodity, and rumor had it, these charity functions were bugged by the "Peach Buzz," our local gossip column.

SuSu turned her attention to applying more bright red, kiss-proof lipstick. "Did you see my date?"

"I think so. About thirty, buff?"

"Bingo." I scanned her image in the mirror along with her. She'd kept her figure and stayed trendy, but nothing could erase the hardness wrought by booze and cigarettes and years of trying to get what Jackson owed her. Her refusal to let go and move on had stolen the light from her eyes, and her Giorgio bore a deadly undernote of desperation that most men could smell a mile away.

It made me so sad for her, I wanted to cry.

But what the hell. Tonight she looked better than I'd seen her look in years.

"Do you thank God daily for those genes your mama gave you?" I teased.

"God?" she said mildly. "Why should I? He doesn't exist."

Smiling at her image across the marble sinks, I suddenly *saw* her—the way you do when you're riding down a familiar street and have a flash of new-eyed perspective that shows you what it must look like to someone who's never been there before—and realized with stunning surety that she'd had a face-lift.

Just like that, the subtle, irrefutable evidence glared out at me. "SuSu!" When? How?

She must have been able to read my mind. (I told you I was transparent.) "Georgia Peyton Baker," she warned, "do not say another word. Tradition Four"—no telling—"I mean it."

"Tradition Three!" I countered. No lies. Gabberflasted, I bent down to check the stalls, saw no feet, and then popped erect. "How could you do this without telling us?" Besides man-stealing, the most heinous of crimes among female friends is keeping major secrets, especially surgical ones. We women are so greedy and demanding in our relationships; it's one of our greatest flaws.

An appalling thought occurred to me. "Or *did* you tell the others?"

"Of course I didn't tell the others," she snipped out, redeeming herself somewhat. "If I'd told anybody, it would have been you."

I stared at her. How could we have missed it? Now that I knew, it was perfectly obvious. Gone were the bags under her eyes, the subtle fold on her lids, the crow's feet. But she wasn't pulled. She just looked incredibly well rested, despite the effects of sun and cigarettes on her skin. "Damn. I think it's the best one I've ever seen. Or not seen."

She grinned. "Only the best for this girl."

"When?" I demanded.

"Last fall when I went to see my sister in Seattle for two weeks. Remember? Then I had back-to-back runs for another two weeks."

More than three months ago!

"Well, I didn't have any runs," she confessed. "I was waiting for the swelling and bruises to go away. So technically, I guess I did break Tradition Three."

"Why didn't you tell us?" I searched her eyes in the mirror. "Why didn't you tell *me*?"

She squared off with my image. "I didn't need the hassle. Or the financial lecture."

My hurt feelings shifted instantly to guilt. There would defi-nitely have been a financial lecture. And a hassle. "Sorry." To make up for it, I resolved to spare her any recriminations. "Well, you look terrific."

She lit up like a spotlight. "Thanks. Now let's go rescue the others. John's probably catatonic by now, and God knows how Brooks and Linda are handling Harold's usual arrogant little put-downs."

"John!" I'd forgotten he was waiting. I hurried toward the door, but stopped short. I took her arm to whisper, "Suse, we really need to be careful tonight. One slip, and you-know-who could lose everything. If you-know-he gets even a whiff of what we're up to, he'll hide everything where she'll never find it. How 'bout we don't drink? Just till after the party."

She stiffened, defensive.

SuSu had a problem, but she was still the most loyal of us all. I appealed to that. "Too much is at stake," I said softly. "Can we do this? For her?"

She hid her hurt behind bravado, as she always had. "Hell, yes, we can."

I knew she meant it when she said it, and I hoped that just this once, she'd be able to do it. But as I've said before, I'm always making people better than they are.

She shot me a wry smile. "But it's cruel and unusual to subject anybody to one of these things without the benefit of booze. All those ass-pinchin' good ole boys and social climbers out there are not a pretty sight." Figuratively speaking.

I pushed the door open. "Well, you're a pretty sight, honey, and that's all that matters. For tonight, anyway." The others would never hear about her face-lift from me.

We headed for my fuming husband. The noise level in the ballroom had escalated to a genteel roar that echoed off the marble floors and elegantly plastered walls of the entrance.

"I might have known you'd get waylaid by one of your clones," he said with deceptive mildness as we approached. "Y'all always find each other. What is it? Telepathy?"

"Nice to see you, too, John," SuSu answered, undaunted.

I patted his arm. "Lighten up, honey. You'll end up having a good time. You always do."

We found Diane and Teeny chatting beside each other while

their spouses circulated, as usual—Harold to his corporate guests, and Reid to the developer crowd or whatever attractive young thing might seem the slightest bit willing. SuSu's stud looked relieved to see her return. Brooks and Linda sat like adorable Hummel figurines, doing their best not to look as tense as they were about enduring Harold, but not succeeding.

Ever gracious, Brooks stood when we reached our places. He and John exchanged greetings and shook hands.

Still deep in conversation, Teeny and Diane waved. I heard a mention of football. They must be talking about the boys. Teeny's youngest had been starting quarterback for Furman last fall, a fact that almost made up for Reid's disappointment that he hadn't gotten a bid from Tech.

A glare and a motion from SuSu brought her date halfheartedly to his feet.

"That's the trouble with the younger generation," she quipped as she pulled out her own chair and sat beside him. "Nobody ever taught them any manners." Stud Puppy gave no sign of being offended. He had that marijuana-mellow expression.

"Georgia and John Baker," she introduced, "this is my friend Jason Wilcox." I made no effort to remember his name. None of her stud puppies lasted past the discovery that her obsession with getting that $750,000 settlement from Jackson was hopeless. "We met when he did my newspaper ad. He's a genius with computer graphics," she purred. Her voice dropped to a stage whisper. "And in the sack."

Making no move to shake hands, Jason settled beside her with an indulgent chuckle. "She's just using me, but I don't mind. She's a genius, herself."

We all knew he wasn't talking about computers.

Only a deep flush betrayed the fact that Teeny had heard him.

"Careful," I warned. "Any more talk like that, and Teeny will get the vapors for sure."

Scarcely in his seat, John popped up again. He detested "blue" conversations and openly disapproved of SuSu's scandalous behavior, so in typical only-child form, opted to absent himself. He really was a stuffed shirt, but he was my stuffed shirt, and underneath it all, I loved him. "I think I'll get a drink." He bent to ask me, "What can I bring you?"

"Diet tonic and lime for me, please." I whispered the next. "I'm trying to set a good example for SuSu."

"God knows, she needs one," he whispered back, then straightened. "I'm off to the bar," he announced to the others. "Can I get anything for y'all?"

"I'll go with you." Brooks shot up, clearly unwilling to be left with the stud puppy and the women again.

Even the stud puppy had his limits. He drew SuSu to her feet. "Come on, my lady in red. Let's show 'em how to boogie." He steered her toward the dance floor. I waited till they were out of earshot to sit between Linda and Diane.

"How's it going so far?" I asked Diane. "Has he picked up on anything from any of us?"

"What do you think?" She cut her chin in Harold's direction. He was schmoozing at his most unctuous. "He's 'on.' I doubt he'd notice anything unless one of his precious clients got pissy." The bitterness in her voice was becoming a permanent addition.

Linda leaned over, speaking through a fake grin. "He may not suspect anything now, but five'll get you ten, half a dozen people in this room have filed away that hate look you're givin' him right now. Knock it off."

A brief blip of chagrin was followed by Diane's amazingly swift transformation to doting corporate wife.

"Man," I said to nobody in particular. "That was quick." I never dreamed she had it in her.

Diane got up. "Y'all talk among yourselves. I need to sing for my supper for a while." She glided off, the perfect picture of an executive wife: gracious, quietly personable, building bridges and egos by remembering the names of children or grandchildren or pampered pets, just deferential enough without being fawning.

"Look at her," I marveled. "On the way home, they'll all say,

'Isn't Harold's wife a lovely woman? Isn't he lucky to have her?' "

"He is, the bastard," Linda muttered, "but he won't have her long."

"Hush." Teeny gave her hand a gentle whack—violence in the extreme for her. "No more talk about you-know-what. Not a peep," she ordered. "God knows what might slip out, so zip it."

"Sorry," Linda said, but none of us believed it. When we settled back, chastened, she peered across the room. "I wonder what the guys are talkin' about."

We followed her line of sight to see Brooks and John chatting amiably in the long line for the open bar. Three places behind them, Reid—already florid and disheveled with drink—was putting the make on some silicon-busted chickie-boom wearing what amounted to two big, black Lycra Band-Aids, right there in plain sight of Teeny. Bad form, even for Reid.

Stung, Linda and I averted our eyes, but Teeny scanned past him as if he were a complete stranger. It never ceased to amaze me how she managed to clothe herself in a dignity he could no longer touch. I couldn't have done it, but I was quite fond of John and expected monogamy, at the very least, from our marriage.

Teeny hadn't loved Reid since he'd hit her. From that moment on, she'd cared only about her boys and keeping her family "whole" for their sakes. I felt sorry for her—we all did—but it was her choice, and we supported her in it. That didn't keep us, though, from secretly praying he would get AIDS or kill himself—and no one else—on one of his drunken tears in his Lamborghini Diablo, making Teeny a very wealthy widow. (At our insistence, she made sure the life insurance premiums were paid on time.)

Teeny shifted the subject. "So," she asked Linda, "what did Brooks say about Abby's tattoo?"

Linda sagged. "I haven't told him. How could I? You know, he and Josh have always been close, but Abby has always been her daddy's darling. Bad enough, she's dropped out of college to live in sin with a *Muslim*, for God's sake, but this could be the last straw. It'll break his heart. I just couldn't bring myself."

"You shouldn't be the one to tell him, anyway," Teeny said with uncharacteristic firmness. "Abby should. She's the one who's marked her body like the heathens. Let *her* tell him. If you do it, he'll only turn all his anger and frustration on you."

My mouth dropped open to hear her come out with something so eminently practical. "Where is Teeny, and who put Dr. Laura in her place?"

She sighed, flat-mouthed. "Y'all just never give me a lick of credit. I'm not an idiot, you know."

"Of course you're not an idiot," I backpedaled. "But pithy advice has always been Linda's department."

Teeny beamed at Linda. "Clearly, she's in no position to handle this situation objectively. She and Brooks have spoiled Abby too much for that." She said it as if she were bestowing a glorious compliment.

"Teeny," Linda gasped out.

"Well, it's true," I seconded, glad somebody had finally dared to "speak the truth in love," as the Bible put it. "Y'all do let her get away with murder." To prove my point, I asked, "Are you still supporting her?"

Linda colored. "Well, we couldn't very well have cut her off. Where would she live? How would she manage?"

"Maybe if she didn't have an income, her tattoo artist boyfriend might not be quite so interested," I dared to say. I hated psycho-pop, but only one phrase applied. "You're enabling her, Linda. Admit it."

"So you've said," Linda snapped, "at least half a dozen times. I would remind you of Tradition Five."

That was the trouble with passive-aggressives. They just wouldn't listen.

"Harold alert," Teeny murmured as the jerk in question headed our way, his impeccable tux accessorized by a big fake smile.

"Goodness, ladies." Butter wouldn't melt in his mouth. "Have all your menfolk deserted you?"

It was a definite dis.

Linda, usually our bulldog, squirmed and averted her eyes.

"John and Brooks went to get us drinks," I said with as much civility as I could muster. "The line's halfway to Stone Mountain."

Nobody mentioned Reid. Nobody ever mentioned Reid, even when he put in a rare appearance. Taking our cue from Teeny, we all basically ignored him, unless the guys were talking golf or hunting, in which case, they included him in their conversation.

Teeny's eyes narrowed with surprising savvy as Harold came up behind her. "Aren't you sweet to be concerned about us, Harold," she said without turning around to face him, "but you'd be amazed how well we can do on our own." No ditz, just grit, sugar-coated and bold as you please.

I cocked a grin at her, but Harold had no intention of letting her have the last word. He gripped her shoulders, and Teeny grimaced at his controlling touch. "Y'all have fun, now," he oozed. "Be sure to hit the buffet while there's still plenty of lobster left." Harold didn't invite you to do things; he gave orders, just like he'd been giving Diane orders for thirty years. His hands remained on Teeny's shoulders. "Where's Reid? I want us to bid on the Highlands golf weekend."

He'd deliberately mentioned the unmentionable, the louse.

Teeny pulled away from him on the pretense of searching for her errant husband. "The last time I saw him, he was swappin' war stories with Jack Portman." Not hardly, unless Jack had had a sex change.

Harold reclaimed her shoulder in a patent show of dominance. "If Diane swings by, tell her I want to dance with her."

I'd had enough. I could not remain silent. "Lucky Diane. You're a prince," I said through a stiff, narrow smile, fangs engaging. Teeny kicked me under the table.

"You're not the only one who thinks so," he shot back. Satisfied he'd won the encounter, he let go of Teeny's shoulders with a dismissive pat and went back to his clients.

True to Teeny's admonition, we didn't say a word about him, but watched the dancing in fuming silence.

SuSu's resolution to stay sober didn't last beyond the introduction of free-flowing champagne designed to loosen everybody's purse strings. With every flute, her expert dancing got a little wilder, attracting leers from the men, glares from the women, and pride from the stud puppy, who did a damn good tango, albeit a bit lewd. I rolled my eyes and prayed she'd keep her mouth shut about Harold.

John and Brooks finally came back. John set my drink in front of me. "What's the matter?" he asked. "You look like Princess Thundercloud," he said, resurrecting the persona of a kiddie show puppet from our sons' childhood. We still spoke the shorthand of parents who had reared children together, a private language peppered with references from those precious times that no one else could ever understand. It was one of the things that made the idea of life without each other impossible.

I clung to the brief connection, wishing we could go back and somehow do it better so we wouldn't end up so distant from each other now.

I took a sip of sweet-tart tonic. "My Harold threshold is a little low tonight. He gets on my nerves."

John stiffened. "Harold's all right." Men always take up for each other. "What'd he ever do to you?"

This was getting dangerous. "Nothing." I stood up and took his hand. "Come on. Let's check out the silent auction, then get some supper."

He exhaled heavily as he rose. "Well, okay. But only to browse. You know we can't afford to bid anything."

Maybe it was what had happened earlier with SuSu, but I stopped and looked at him, really seeing him for the first time in a long time. "When did we stop dreaming together?" I asked him.

"What?" His expression was the same one he used with bothersome students or parents—wary yet controlled.

When had I been relegated to an annoyance? "There was a time when we looked at every silent auction getaway and dreamed of being together in exotic places," I explained, feeling as if I were abruptly trapped in a choking mist. "When did we stop? Why did we stop?"

He frowned, impatient. "What's gotten into you? I thought those estrogen implants were supposed to take care of all that hormone stuff."

Hormones? I asked him a serious question, and he relegated it to hormones?

"Babe?" Annoyance. "Come on." He tugged at my hand. "Let's window-shop like we used to, then."

I should have been pleased. But the gesture was one of appeasement, not of caring. I realized it the same way I'd realized about SuSu's face-lift. That part of us was deader than a possum on Peachtree—not dead in me, but definitely in us.

Be grateful for what you've got, my Protestant conscience scolded in my mother's voice. *John's a good man. A decent man, a good provider. Don't repay him with childish expectations.*

But the void between us loomed so large and frightening that I slammed the door on it in a hurry, exchanging my tonic for the first of several flutes of champagne.

I knew perfectly well that small steps toward closeness would be far more helpful than projecting things to extremes, but I couldn't help wondering if our marriage was really as stale as it seemed in that moment.

John cocked a wry half-smile, his gaze really connecting, if only briefly. Then he drew me close to his side. "Maybe we ought to go away together. It's been a long time."

Hope rekindled. "Too long." I matched his gaze with one that saw the sweet, gentle man he'd been when we courted. "I miss you."

He sighed. "I miss you, too."

It was a start. What we would do next, I didn't know, but it was a start.

Two hours later, the buffet was stripped of seafood, SuSu was smashed, the rest of us were feeling no pain, and the live auction droned on and on from the dais. When SuSu started talking back to the emcee, I hustled her into the bathroom.

Once there, she collapsed on the john in the stall. "Sorry, George. I know I got a little tipsy. Sorry," she said as she struggled to pull down her pantyhose. "But I haven't said anything about you-know-who." She stood, got them down, and then flopped unceremoniously onto the seat. I held the door of the stall closed while she peed like a horse.

"That's good, sugar. Ye done good, then."

Linda appeared and mouthed, "Is she okay?"

"Yes and no." I mouthed back, "I think she should go home. Get Stud Puppy."

Linda was no good at reading lips. She frowned, flummoxed.

I motioned her close and whispered into her ear, "Get Brandon or Jason or whatever-the-hell his name is. She needs to go home."

"I hear y'all talkin' about me out there," SuSu warned. The toilet flushed; then she jerked open the door. "I'm perfectly fine." A wave of green washed across her face. "Whoops. Maybe not."

"I'll stay with her," Linda said. "John wants you out there for the live auction. He said something about a dream weekend."

Bless his heart. I went giddy. "Are you sure you can manage?"

"Go, go, go."

Against my better judgment, I left them.

John was bidding for a long weekend in Martha's Vineyard when I heard a subtle disturbance near the hallway and turned around to see SuSu weaving back toward our table, head high, trailing what must have been five yards of toilet paper from the pantyhose into which she'd tucked her dress, exposing her bare right cheek.

Everything went into agonizing slow motion.

Linda was doing her best to catch up and stop her, but SuSu had escaped with too much of a lead.

"I knew I shouldn't have left them," I groaned, assuming guilty responsibility as usual.

"Jesus God," Teeny gasped out.

Diane excused herself from a nearby table of clients and moved to intercept, while at the next table, Harold went livid, humiliated that SuSu was his guest—the one consolation in the whole horrid incident.

Reid, who had decided to put in his requisite brief appearance at Teeny's side, guffawed. "Well, it's sure not the first time somebody showed their ass at the PDC," he said to the table in his booming good ole boy voice, "but it may be the first time literally."

John and Brooks tried desperately to pretend nothing was happening.

Before SuSu got too far into the room, a merciful gentleman rose, took her arm, and bent close to apprise her of the situation. By then, everyone was watching, including the emcee. You could cut the tension with a knife.

Surveying the ass comet, SuSu let out a cackle followed by, "Well, shit!" Laughing, she freed her dress and cut herself loose, then took a bow to the broken laughter and applause that erupted from the braver or coarser guests around her. Linda almost caught up with her, but her way was blocked by the waiters who hastened to remove the toilet paper. SuSu strode ahead like a model on the runway, brassing it out.

For a heartbeat, none of us breathed. Then we did the only thing we could do. We laughed along with SuSu to cover the shame. But Teeny and Diane were crying when they did.

Stud Puppy thought it was a gas. "Whatta woman." He stood. "Wait'll the guys at the bar hear about this. At the fuckin' Drivin' Club." He nodded to the table. "Now, if you good people will excuse me, I think it's time to take Cinderella home while she can still make magic." He intercepted her and attempted a big, nasty soap-opera kiss.

SuSu might have shown her ass, but drunk or sober, nobody, and I mean nobody, got away with pawing her in public. She reared back like a duchess, abruptly—if only briefly—in command of herself. "Toss me my bag, Linda, honey," she said, crisp as you please. "We're leavin'. I have to be up early for church."

It was an old joke that had served as a code since Mademoiselles, one that meant we should call her later at her place.

Right or wrong, we would be there for her.

As she left on Stud Puppy's arm, Reid blared with the hubris his daddy's name allowed him, "Way to go, SuSu." He *would* think it was funny. He swiveled to whack Harold on the back. "Shit, Harold. Usually these things are dull as dirt, but that, ma boy, was worth the price of admission." (Three hundred dollars a couple that we hadn't had to pay.)

Harold glared at Diane, his cheeks mottled as he compulsively smoothed his bib and tucker and leaned over to hiss, "I *told* you we shouldn't have invited her. She's not our kind, and she never was."

For once, thank God, Diane refused to take the blame. It must have taken all her self-control to keep from slugging him for what he'd said about SuSu, but she managed to maintain her corporate façade. "Well, thank goodness she's gone then, huh, sugar?"

A waiter just happened to pass by with a tray full of dirty dishes at just that moment, and wouldn't you know it, he tripped on something suspiciously in the vicinity of Teeny's little foot, losing his balance with a truncated gasp. Teeny shrieked a warning to Harold even as she deftly deflected the avalanche smack onto his head.

God, it was beautiful. Time suspended as dish after dish ricocheted off him. The clients gasped in horror. The proceedings came to a standstill.

Plates were still rolling on the carpet when Harold stood up at last, so red he looked like he was ready to stroke out on the spot. Diane grabbed the waiter's arm and shoved him toward the service door. "Go. Now." She motioned two others to come clean up.

The emcee blew it off with, "Sorry, folks. You just can't get decent help these days."

Harold managed a grim smile for his clients that didn't convince anybody. "As the Presbyterian minister said after he fell down the stairs," he said through rigid lips, " 'Boy, I'm glad *that's* over with.' " Amid the nervous laughter that followed, he excused himself to go repair the wreckage, which was far less than it should have been, darn it.

We looked to Diane in sympathy. He would blame her as he always did whenever anything went wrong.

Her careful smile was rigid. "Thanks for warning him, Teeny," she said with perfect irony. "Nice job." So she'd seen it, too.

The men were clueless, of course, but the rest of us assessed our timid Teeny with a new respect.

It was a night that would live in infamy—and in the annals of Red Hat lore. There was more to Teeny than we had given her credit for. Little did we know.

12

Linda Leigh Bondurant Murray

Friday, May 14, 1965. 3:15 P.M.

CIVIL DEFENSE COULD TAKE NOTES FROM THE STUDENTS OF Northside High on how to evacuate an area in record time. By the time Linda, SuSu, and I met up at Pru's big white convertible in the school parking lot, we were virtually alone on the blacktop under the soft blue, cloudless May sky. We'd changed into the cutoffs and man-shirts required for initiation, but no way would we surrender our bras until we absolutely had to.

How does a D-cup commit suicide?

She runs downstairs without her bra.

Linda scanned the parking lot. "Typical," she drawled, unruffled. "I warned y'all we shouldn't have said Pru could drive. She's always late."

"And on the most important day of our lives," SuSu—Miss Punctuality—complained. Initiation started at Beanie's promptly at four.

"Crap." It was as close as I came to cussing back then, before I went away to college and contracted gutter gums. "The last thing we need is to be tardy." I turned to Linda, hoping she'd parked in the upper lot. "Did you bring your car?"

She shook her head. "No. I was counting on Pru. Daddy didn't want me to leave mine here overnight, so he dropped me off this mornin'.'" She didn't seem disturbed that we might be late, but then, she had no reason to worry—unlike SuSu and me, who had lived the past month in fear of accumulating even the slightest black mark with the big sisters, Linda was a shoo-in. Her father was a rich doctor, and her mother was president of the League of Women Voters. And of course, Linda had completed all her assignments without a hitch.

I had done all mine, too, but with a few bumps and close calls. "Have you got your pledge book?" I asked SuSu.

"Yes." She scowled at me, but when a green-eyed colleen like SuSu scowls, it's never very convincing. "That's the fourth time today you've asked me."

"I just wanted to make sure you didn't leave it in your locker."

"How about you?" Linda asked. "Have you got yours?"

"Of course I do." I opened my large straw bag and rummaged past the can of hair spray, my almost-empty wallet, the pocket calendar where I chronicled the events of every day in teensy print, my crib notes about the Mademoiselles' bios, a full-size hairbrush, Binaca, and a sack of makeup, all without finding my pledge book.

Adrenaline tightened my lungs and shot to the tips of my fingers. "Oh, Lord. Don't tell me I've lost it." A sinister suspicion bloomed. Could somebody have stolen it? "Oh, Lord."

SuSu shook her head, smiling. "Look in your calendar. Whenever you lose something in there, it's always stuck in your calendar."

I rooted my pocket calendar out and, sure enough, found it fattened by the little spiral notebook sandwiched between its pages. "Thank goodness." I laid a dramatic hand over my thumping heart. "It *had* to be in there."

I flipped open the pages and made sure—for the jillionth time—that everything was checked off.

√ 10' *Love Chain (made with gum wrappers)*—*Dianne Lummus*

✓ *Big Bag of Benson & Hedges — Adeline*
✓ *Theme: "Why I like the Hula" — Cheryl Cox*
✓ *Portrait (I was a fair artist) — Booky Allen*
✓ *700 Pine Needles in bundles of 10 — Patsie Hall*
✓ *Brush the pills off all of Bob Araka's sweaters — Penny Meyers*
✓ *Bring Lula's Lunch Every Day*
✓ *2 Cakes for Nancy M.*
✓ *My Height in Newspapers delivered to Beanie's paper drive at Westminster*
✓ *Theme: Why Lovett is Better Than Northside — Dee Dee Thomas*
✓ *Don't shave legs or pits for last pledge week — Carolyn (Leave it to witch-with-a-B Carolyn to be the most sadistic. She'd rescinded the humiliating restriction for all but the public school pledges — pubes, she called us with coarse vulgarity only a really rich Buckhead princess could get away with.)*
✓ *Bake Chocolate Chip Cookies Every Monday for Pam (my big sister, truly a good egg)*

The more conscientious sisters had filled out the list with such mundane items as writing the sorority constitution, memorizing the song, reciting the bios for all the members and pledges, and so on. I closed the book and placed it in clear view inside my purse.

"Do y'all know your bios?" Linda asked, mothering those of us who lacked her photographic memory.

"I think so." I glanced at my watch, then scanned the parking lot—3:25, and still no sign of Pru.

"I sorta know 'em," SuSu said. She smiled at me. "I figured you could help me in the car." Like I had with all her other tests since she'd moved to our street thirteen years ago.

At last, the metal doors beside the cafeteria swung open, and Pru exited—miniskirted as high as the law allowed above white leather boots—just ahead of the salivating vice principal, Mr. Howard, a man whose title suited his fixation with sexy, nubile female students. Pru was batting her eyelashes and swaying to beat the band.

When they reached the parking lot, she twiddled him a good-bye, then sashayed over to the car.

"What was *that* all about?" SuSu demanded. "I was afraid you'd hitched a ride to initiation with somebody else and left us."

Pru beamed her sunny smile. "Of course not, silly. I would never leave y'all in the lurch." She opened the trunk and tossed in her spare clothes. "Ole Miz Ballard, the witch, caught me smoking in the bathroom. It took some major mojo to talk Mr. H. into lettin' me off with a slap on the wrist."

"Long as that was all you let him have," Linda warned.

Pru dismissed her concern with a giggle. "Oh, honey, old men like him are so easy to control, it's not even funny." She opened the door and tipped the front seat forward. "Whose turn is it to be in back?"

I pointed to SuSu, but she and Linda both pointed to me, sentencing me to be lashed to within an inch of my life by my own hair and arrive with an indelible part down the back, not to mention getting hit by bugs.

"Come on, George," Pru chided with a smile. "Own up and take your turn."

Grumbling, I got in, then fished an eyelet babushka and my cheap Jackie O. ripoff sunglasses from my purse while the others piled in front.

Once we were under way, Linda turned back and hollered, "At least it isn't far."

I held my blond "flip" as best I could while we picked up speed on West Wesley past Moore's Mill. All of a sudden, Pru's car started to buck.

"What's that?" we all demanded.

We were already cutting it close on time. The last thing we needed was to break down. Mr. Bonner was always tinkering with the DeSoto to keep it running. I sent up a fervent prayer that we'd make it to Beanie's.

"Don't worry," Pru hollered. "It only does this over fifty. Daddy says it's something with the fuel filter. He's gonna pick one up on his way home from work and fix it tomorrow."

The three of us exchanged ominous looks. We definitely should have let Linda drive. The towering fins behind me, I tripled my prayers for divine healing of the DeSoto. My family might be scraping the bottom of middle class, but at least we took our cars to a real mechanic.

Fortunately, bucking seemed to be the full extent of the problem, so we made it to Beanie's with twelve minutes to spare. As always, we hunted up Teeny and Diane right away. Ever since pickups, the six of us had gravitated together, drawn by our common sense of barely belonging. Once united, we got as far from the dreaded Carolyn as possible.

Teeny gave me a big hug, looking more like Audrey Hepburn than ever in her precisely cut-off jeans and starched white manshirt. "Are you ready?"

"I don't know." I was pretty sure I'd nailed down the bios, but had cotton mouth anyway.

Teeny must have really been prepared, because she didn't even have the hiccups.

"You'll do fine," Diane said to me. "You're the smartest one of all of us."

"Book-smart, maybe," I admitted, "but without a lick of common sense."

SuSu let out a nervous laugh. "Well, luckily, we have Linda for that."

"Pledges," Beanie summoned. "Sisters! May we come to order?"

The group settled in, stepping over each other like so many spiders.

Beanie didn't wait for the last conversations to die away. With that many women in a room, they never did on their own. "Okay.

Quiet, please. Welcome to initiation. I am happy to say that all the pledges are present and accounted for." We clapped. "Unfortunately, Lane Freeman and Penny Meyers have the stomach bug, so Pam and I will be doubling up with their little sisters for tonight."

In the murmur that followed, I whispered to SuSu, "Too bad it wasn't Carolyn." We shared a subdued chuckle.

"Pledges," Beanie continued, "please pass your notebooks to Pam so she can verify their completion."

"Wup!" Cigarette in hand and clearly feeling no pain, Carolyn rose. "I still have to inspect all the pubes." The contempt with which she said it made the word even more repulsive.

Beanie laughed. "Okay, but make it snappy. We're on a tight schedule."

"Rise, you sorry pubes!" Carolyn ordered.

Seven of us stood, we four from Northside and three from Dykes High. "Take off your shirts," she said. "I want to see those hairy pits."

Teeny went crimson, and her hiccups caught up with her—with a vengeance. Not good, considering that Carolyn took them personally.

I blushed to my toes, too. The Saturday-night group bathing at Pru's was one thing; we were all best friends. But apart from that, only my blood sisters had seen me in my bra; I'd always changed in the stalls at P.E. and never used the cruddy showers in the locker room. So I was appalled to expose myself so publicly.

You could tell that a lot of the big sisters were almost as embarrassed as we were, but nobody dared cross Carolyn at this stage, so we dutifully unbuttoned. Only SuSu had the courage to brazen it out, determined not to give her nemesis the satisfaction of seeing her cringe. She tied her shirt around her hips and preened like a lingerie model. The rest of us held ours over our fronts, humiliated.

"Arms up!" Carolyn ordered.

SuSu boldly raised both of hers, the rest of us, only one.

Dripping ashes from her Benson & Hedges, Carolyn inspected the week's growth on our legs and pits. Teeny's was dark, fine, and straight; mine, coarse as a lumberjack's; SuSu's, like infinitesimal copper wires; and Linda's, thick, dark, and curly. Yuck, on all counts. The Dykes girls', all blondes, barely showed.

"Okay." Carolyn gave SuSu a parting sneer on her way back to her seat. "Let the games begin."

"Listen up, pledges." Beanie raised a fishbowl filled with folded pieces of paper. "These are your stunts, the first phase of initiation. Every pledge must draw one, complete it in the presence of her monitor, and be back here by seven. Your stunt will be marked either Lenox or downtown." That was back when security born of repression kept it perfectly safe for a gaggle of Buckhead belles to roam downtown Atlanta. "Once you've drawn, we'll sort you into groups of four and assign a big sister as monitor for each group. The rest of the sisters will stay here for the Seniors' farewell pool party. Remember, now—everybody has to be back by seven o'clock sharp. Are we all clear on that?"

"Yes, Beanie," we answered in grammar school singsong.

She set the bowl in motion. A buzz of speculation swelled, punctuated by shrieks of humor or consternation as the pledges read their assignments.

The bowl came to Teeny. She hiccupped, drew, passed it on to the rest of us, then opened her stunt. All the color drained from her already-pale face. "Oh, shit." The S-word, from our royal princess! "I have to apply for a job at a strip club downtown." The hiccups came closer and harder.

Of all people to get that one! Fate was cruel, indeed.

Pru opened hers. "I got Lenox. I have to try on every hat in the Paris Hat shop." She giggled. "That'll be a breeze." Her life was charmed, as ever.

SuSu opened hers, then laughed. "I have to tap dance and sing for five minutes on a bench at the bus station downtown." She looked to Teeny. "That means I can go with you for moral support. There are plenty of strip clubs near the bus station."

In our sheltered world, only the dregs of the earth traveled by bus. I shuddered to think what the strip clubs' clientele would be like.

Diane read hers. "I got Lenox, too. I have to climb every one of the animal statues in the whole mall, wearing a bikini, and have the monitor take my picture." Her dark brows drew together in consternation. Totally preppie Diane had a serious "outie" and wore only modest, gingham boy-leg one-pieces. Then her features cleared. "But I guess I'll have to skip the bikini part. I don't own one."

"You're not off the hook," Linda cautioned, ever the voice of reason. "I've got a feeling they're gonna provide you with one."

"Eeeeyew." We could almost see only-child Diane's skin crawl at the prospect of having to put on anything someone else had worn, much less something as intimate as a bikini. Fate had scored some major irony.

I opened mine. "All it says is FISH, downtown."

"You'll have to ask," Linda advised. She opened hers. "Uh-oh. Good news and bad news." She looked to us. "The good news is, I'm downtown, too. Maybe we can make it a foursome. The bad news is, I have to get a cop to autograph my butt with Magic Marker." She shook her head. "This might not be so easy. If I flash *my* ass, he'll probably arrest me."

"So round, so firm, so fully packed," we said in gleeful chorus as we always did when Linda complained about her womanly derriere.

"I'll trade you," Teeny offered, only half in jest.

"Sure." Without hesitation, Linda extended her strip of paper to swap. "No sweat."

Beanie saw them and piped up with an adamant, "Pledges, you are honor-bound to do the stunt you drew. If we find out you swapped, you'll be taken straight home with a big *adios*."

A chorus of groans revealed that we hadn't been the only ones who'd tampered with fate. Strips of paper reverted to their original owners all over the room.

Pam came over. "So. How fare the Six Musketeers?"

"Four to downtown, two to Lenox," Linda summarized.

Teeny just hiccupped.

Pam looked at her with genuine concern. "Honey, do you have those all the time?"

"Only when I'm"—Hic!—"scared or upset."

Pam hugged her shoulders, looking askance to make sure none of the big sisters was listening. "I've got news for you. There's nothing to be scared of. We're not cruel." I thought of Carolyn and disagreed. "This is all just a lark. Have fun with it, but don't be afraid."

Teeny nodded, suppressing another hic. Much as I wanted to believe what Pam had said, I wasn't convinced, either. But it must have helped Teeny some, at least, because the hiccups got lots farther between and less severe.

Imagine having your body betray your fears so publicly!

I handed Pam my stunt. "What does that mean?"

She laughed and waved the paper at Beanie. "Guess who got the fish?"

The big sisters laughed back, even Carolyn. Martha disappeared up the stairs with a devilish purpose in her face.

"Pam, can the four of us be a group?" Linda asked. She lowered her voice. "Teeny got the strip club, and we'd like to go along for moral support."

Pam didn't hesitate. "Sure. And I'll be your monitor."

That was a relief.

Martha came back down the stairs holding a huge fish by some paper towels wrapped around the small of its tail. The thing had to be at least thirty inches long, with bulging eyes and a pinkish tinge to its belly. I smelled it halfway across the room. She marched up to me. "Stand up, pube." She was one of Carolyn's toadies. "Take it. Your stunt is to get this cooked and bring it back. And it had better be good. It cost a mint." She took the paper towels with her when she handed it over.

The fish's scales were not as slimy as I had feared, but it weighed lots more than my purse! I breathed easier, though. It was a manageable assignment. Surely I could coax some chef down there to cook the thing.

"Who has the bikini stunt?" Beanie called out, holding a bulging plastic bag.

Diane raised her hand with a grimace.

Beanie came over, rummaging through the bag. "What are you? A ten?"

Diane waited until she was within confidential range to whisper, "No. A twelve."

"Okay." Beanie rummaged some more. "I know there's a twelve in here somewhere." Linda had been right, as usual. "Aha." Beanie produced a blue ruffled top of relatively conservative cut. "Now all I have to do is find the bottom that goes with it." That didn't take long. She handed it to Diane, who looked as if she'd just been sentenced to a leper colony. "You can wear it under your cutoffs and shirt," Beanie consoled, "and only strip down for the pictures."

"Lenox Square people, over here," a voice summoned from the far side of the room.

Pru gave Teeny a quick hug. "You'll do great. Just get in there and do it. Who knows?" she teased, "they just might hire you." She and Diane departed.

Pam held out her hand for Linda and SuSu's stunts. "Okay. We know what Teeny and Georgia have. Let's see what the rest of you drew." When she read them, she shook her head. "I do not believe this. Three of you got the worst ones in the whole bowl."

"Carolyn's, if I'm any judge of character," SuSu ventured.

"I really couldn't say," Pam replied, nodding in confirmation.

"A cosmic booby trap," Linda confirmed, anything but

daunted. She rubbed her hands together, all business. "Okay. Has anybody got a Magic Marker?"

Pam pointed her to a jumble of items on the pool table. "The props are all over there."

I looked at my fish. "I think I'll call him Fred."

Twenty minutes later, we arrived downtown via Marietta Street in Pam's mother's Cadillac, then parked at ground level in the Davisons lot. Pam unlocked the trunk and pulled out an instant camera. "For the scrapbook."

"Teeny's stunt is the worst, so let's get that over with first," Linda suggested, ever our organizer.

The resulting hiccup echoed in the concrete enclosure.

"Good idea." Pam put her arm around Teeny's quaking shoulders. "No sense prolonging your misery. Do the hard thing first, my mama always told me."

Teeny nodded, mute. All but catatonic between paroxysms, she chose not to participate in the selection of the strip club, so in the interest of time, we went into the first one we could find: The Pussycat Club, on a dingy side street near the bus terminal.

All but timid Teeny went inside with an invulnerable confidence born of privilege and safety. For obvious reasons, Fred and I brought up the rear. Talk about fish out of water. (Pun intended.)

We were greeted by a fog of stale-smelling smoke that pulsed to the blare of heavy metal rock. The place looked as seedy and sad on the inside as it did on the outside, except for two bored, caged beauties dancing in only their G-strings above either end of the long bar. Three patrons slumped over their drinks, more interested in us than the near-naked gyrations above them.

The place was *too* creepy.

But we—all except Teeny, who covered her eyes—stared at the cages in shock or morbid fascination. I'd expected to find some wrung-out rejects there, not these fit, attractive girls who couldn't have been much older than we were. The dancers' eyes

glazed over and avoided us, making me wonder if our middle-
class scrutiny put them ill at ease.

SuSu leaned over the bar and yelled above the music to the
indifferent bartender. "Who do we see about applying for a job?"

"Job? Who you kiddin'?" He sized us up with a jaded eye.
"We don't touch underage. You girlies got the wrong joint. Go
back to where you came from." He thrust a thumb in the direction
of home. "Country club's thataway."

SuSu bristled. "Where's the manager?" she challenged. "All
my friend wants is to apply for a job." Nothing had said it had
to be as a dancer. "Any job. We're not asking you to hire anybody. Just give us an application, she'll fill it out, and we'll be on
our way."

"Oh, Lord. She's only provoking him," Teeny wheezed out.
Her fright must have gone beyond beyond, because she stopped
hiccuping altogether.

"Job application?" the bartender scoffed, loud enough for
everybody to hear.

The customers laughed. I didn't see what was so funny, but
then one of them drawled, "Take it off, honey. Thass your job
application in a joint like this. Take . . . it . . . off," he finished with
a leer.

Linda snapped her John Romaine purse shut and stepped in,
brisk as a tidy little wren. She mounted a stool, motioning for the
bartender. "Look, sir, my friend here lost a bet, and she has to
apply for a job at a strip club. Could you help us out?" She
pushed a ten across the bar—big bucks in those days.

He scooped up the bribe, but relented only a little. "The one
with the fish? What's that? Part of the act?"

"No. He's just Fred," I responded, earning an elbow in the ribs
from SuSu.

Linda grinned at the coarse face below his shiny bald dome.
"Not her. She lost another bet." She pointed to Teeny, who looked
as if she might expire any second. "Her. All we need is proof she

applied for a job, then we'll get out of your hair," she said to the bald man.

Teeny and I quailed at the obvious gaffe, but Linda remained oblivious.

"For Christ's sake, Chug," one of the dancers hollered down from her cage, "give 'em what they want and get rid of 'em. They're distractin' all the customers."

All three of them.

Chug picked up the phone and hit a button. After a brief pause, he pressed his free hand to his ear and spoke into the receiver. "Hey, Eddie, we got some preppie cream out here who wants to apply for a job, only she don't really." We heard a faint explosion from the other end, even over the music. "Look, I'm just tellin' you what she told me. Could you come out here, okay, so's I can get rid of 'em? They're underage. God forbid Vice walks in." He winced, reddening. "Okay. I was just checkin'. After that time with the, you know, you told me to always check." He winced again, then slammed the phone back onto its cradle.

He pulled a napkin from the bar and scribbled on it with the pen from behind his ear. The napkin tore a little as he wrote, but he thrust it at Teeny when he was done. "Here. Ya got what ya needed. Now scram, alla youse. And don't come back till you're twenty-one."

"Thanks." I lifted Fred in a piscatorial salute.

Linda grabbed a pack of Pussycat Club matches from a bowl on the bar, then hustled me after the others. When all of us were safely back outside, Pam darted back in with her camera poised, then emerged seconds later at a dead run, Chug's "No cameras!" echoing across the sidewalk after her.

Electrified, we took off and didn't stop until we were safely around the corner and back in the sunshine.

The handwriting was surprisingly legible. "The preppie applied for a job. Charles Wilson, brtndr."

We all had a therapeutic laugh, even Teeny.

"Man," SuSu said to the rest of us as she gave Teeny a hug. "Did you see the boobs on that one girl? They hardly even moved."

"Fake," Linda decreed.

"And how would you know?" I challenged, as I always challenged everything, even though it drove people crazy.

" 'Cause they didn't move. Lots of Daddy's patients get 'em." He was a prominent gynecologist and surgeon. That was before boob jobs became the exclusive bailiwick of plastic surgeons. "He even did a *Playboy* bunny."

"I told you those centerfolds couldn't be real," I said to SuSu. We'd pored over my daddy's *Playboy*s for years. Blissfully unenlightened, I loved the jokes and the cartoons.

"Okay." Pam reined us in. "Time's awastin'. Who do we do next?"

"How 'bout SuSu?" I piped up. "The bus station's right here."

Linda spotted a fresh-faced beat cop coming our way. "Maybe we can kill two birds with one stone." She hurried toward him. "Oh, officer." We followed after.

He spotted my fish and stopped in his tracks.

"Officer," Linda explained as we advanced on the guy, "my friends and I have to do some harmless stunts for an initiation, and I was wondering if you might help us out."

He preened, thumbs in his gun belt, but remained noncommittal. "And just how could I do that, miss?"

SuSu poured on the charm. "I have to sing and dance in the bus station for five minutes. You know, entertain the weary travelers. Nothing illegal." Redolent of Canoe in the warm afternoon sun, she leaned close for a look at his badge, then came up inches from his face. "Officer Pelham. Do you think you could just keep an eye on things while I do, so nobody misunderstands?"

His chest inflated even more beneath his dark blue uniform. "Well, now, as long as you don't bother anybody."

"Oh, no. Just sing a little, dance a little." Bat, bat went her mascaraed lashes.

We were in. She'd hooked his ego along with his hormones.

"Sure. I needed to check out the station anyway," he said in an exaggerated bass.

"Oh, and there's just one more thing," Linda added. She tried batting her eyelashes, but it just looked silly. Rather than ask, she handed him her slip of paper, then proffered the Magic Marker. "Right or left. Officer's choice."

He read it, then burst out laughing. "The guys back at the station'll never believe this."

"Oh, yes, they will." Pam lifted the camera. "I'll take one picture for our scrapbook, and one for you."

"All right." He pointed to a large potted tree. "Let's do it over there. I wouldn't want to offend anybody."

"Left or right?" Linda asked again as she headed for the over-size planter.

"I'm a southpaw," he said, "so let's make it right."

We formed a protective shield around them, Pam's camera aimed.

"Okay. Marker ready?" Linda waited until there were no pedestrians to lower the right side of her cutoffs to half-mast. Officer Pelham blushed and scrawled, "You're under arrest. Ofcr. John Pelham."

"Okay. Keep the pen there, and hold for the camera," Pam instructed. She clicked the button, and the instant camera spit out a photo that she pulled free and then handed to SuSu. "One more for the boys back at the precinct." She repeated the procedure.

Linda pulled up her britches, grinning, then shook the cop's hand. "I'll have you know, sir, that you're the first man besides my doctor who has ever seen that portion of my real estate."

We all gathered around the developing pictures. Murder and mayhem could have broken out just behind us, and we never would have known it. When at last the black-and-white images were ready, Pam proudly presented them. They came out clear as a bell. Linda looked back with a devilish grin, and the cop was laughing, just as he'd been as he wrote on her fanny, but the inscription was the star. You could read it easily.

He tucked his photo into his shirt pocket and buttoned it closed. "Ladies, you have made my day."

We thanked him and headed for the terminal. "It ain't over yet," SuSu told him with a grin.

Frankly, it was the most fun I could remember having in a long, long time.

Inside, the terminal looked just plain weary. Everything had a battered, worn appearance, from the heavy, stained benches to the tiled floors to the forest of vending machines that took up most of the wall space. Hard-used and worn out, just like a lot of the people waiting on the benches. Just like most of the stuff at my house.

SuSu took a deep breath. "Okay. I can do this." She'd done skits at pep rallies for two years. "Okay. Mark the time."

We all noted the time on the huge wall clock—5:38.

SuSu chose the empty end of a bench and stood on the seat. "Ladies and gentlemen, for your entertainment, I would like to sing and dance for you a little, so please bear with me." She actually looked scared. "Okay." She closed her eyes and started to hum softly, searching for her song, but after several tries, leapt down to the floor and approached us. "Y'all, this is stupid, I know, but I've never had to do anything by myself in front of people. I've always had the squad with me. My throat just closes up, and I can't think of anything to sing."

Pam arched a brow. "Nothing says you have to do it alone."

We looked at each other. "Sounds like a job for the Supremes," Linda decreed.

"Oh, y'all, would you?" SuSu pleaded.

We'd been doing routines to their songs for years at slumber parties. "I will," I said, "if Pam'll hold Fred for me."

Pam shook her head. "Sorry, honey. I've gotta take the pictures."

"Here." Officer Pelham stuck out his hand. "I'll take him into protective custody."

In gratitude, we laughed at his little police joke.

The four of us mounted the bench together. Linda looked to Pam. "Time us." Then to us she said, "Baby Love." She hummed a note, and we broke into the routine we'd perfected at countless sleepovers.

"Baby love, ma baby love . . ." We always started with a chorus.

It sounded a little iffy at first, but by the time we got to the second chorus, people were clapping along and laughing. One lady stood up and went through the motions with us.

We did "Stop! In the Name of Love" next. By then, more people had stood up at their benches to sing along, and on the worn tile floor, a few were dancing among the shopping bags and boxes that served as their luggage. Pam took several photos of us and the dancers; then she and Officer Pelham—and Fred—did the Twist.

On a roll, we segued straight into "Come See about Me." By the time we finished, Pam came over and tugged SuSu's shirttail. "Show's over, guys. You've been up there more than fifteen minutes, and we've still gotta get Georgia's fish cooked."

So we took our bows to a very appreciative round of applause. Breathing hard from exertion, I bailed Fred out. "You wouldn't know where we could get this fish cooked, would you?" I asked our cop.

He shrugged. "Sorry." But as soon as he'd washed his hands in the water fountain (!), he lifted them and spoke. "Ladies and gentlemen, I'm sure we all enjoyed the entertainment our young ladies provided us. Now I'd like to ask y'all to return the favor. Does anybody here know where this young lady could get this fish cooked?"

I glanced at the clock—5:45! "In a hurry," I prompted.

"In a hurry!" he added.

After a muttering, shrugging interval among our audience, one of the ticket agents leaned forward to speak through the opening in the glass. "I do. Send 'em over here."

Delighted, we hurried over and crowded around the ticket

window. She pushed a piece of paper through the slot. "My husband's a chef at the Top of Peachtree. I wrote his name there, and the name of the hostess, Vickie. You tell her I said to take you back to the kitchens." She passed me another note that read, "This girl made me laugh, Thomas. Cook her fish for her, and do it quick. She's gotta get home before dark."

"Oh, thank you, thank you, thank you," I gushed. "I'd shake your hand, but mine smells like fish."

She laughed. "Wouldn't fit through the slot, anyhow." She motioned us away. "Now git. Kitchen gits busy by six. You girls better hustle."

"Come on," Pam urged. "I'll drive you to the building and double-park till you come back."

Only when we were in the car and on our way did she reach into her pocket and pull out the daring topless photo. "I can't believe none of you has asked to see this yet."

SuSu snatched it from her hand, then hooted. "Oooh! There they are, big as life. Major ta-tas." We all studied the slightly blurry image of boobs and body parts.

"Pretty good, for a 'run for your life' shot," Linda decreed.

When we reached the right building, Linda got out with me and Fred. "I'll go with you." She had the same deep-down happy look that I was feeling. It was the best time of our lives, and we both knew it.

"Race ya," I called, then sprinted for the elegant lobby.

Everything was a breeze from there on in. When we got up to the restaurant, Vickie spirited us back to the kitchen, where Thomas welcomed us like long-lost family and the busy staff acknowledged our presence from their stations with a nod or a spatula salute. I found a sink and scrubbed my hands with soap three times, but the smell of Fred still lingered.

Linda and I watched in amazement (and sometimes hygienic horror) as meal after meal was made to order. It was so fascinating, we scarcely noticed that twenty minutes had ticked by until Thomas returned with Fred—minus his head, bones, and tail—

laid out on industrial grade aluminum foil, resplendent in a crust of toasted almonds.

"Wow! You went all out, Thomas," I gushed. "That looks fabulous and smells divine!" I started to pinch off a piece, but Linda smacked my hand away.

"Remember where Fred's been," she whispered through a big smile, "and how long he's been out of the refrigerator."

"This is great," I told Thomas. "Thank you so much. Thank everybody."

He carefully rolled the aluminum foil to preserve Fred's presentation, then laid the parcel across my arms. "Hope the big sisters like him."

Linda brightened. "I think we should save him for Carolyn and her friends, don't you?"

"Perfect."

It was the word for our afternoon: *perfect.*

Back downstairs, we waited in the gathering dusk for Pam to circle the block and pick us up.

"This was the best," Linda said a little sadly. "Something we'll remember all our lives."

I understood her mood. We'd scribed something sweet and indelible in our young lives. "How could it ever be any better?" I said softly.

"Exactly." She put her arm around my shoulders, and we both cried happy, silent tears, then laughed, wiping them away before the others arrived.

The rest of initiation was what we'd expected. We all had to eat chocolate-covered ants (peppery) and canned rattlesnake meat (tough and greasy) and fried grasshoppers (mostly crunch instead of taste, but the little legs get caught between your teeth—*major* gross-out) and cold snails straight out of the can (like giant, rubbery blackeyed peas). Then we did a relay race from one block of ice to another with bubble gum clenched in our bare butts. Next we took turns being interrogated by the bio committee, and in the wee hours of the morning endured a demoralizing kangaroo court session that left us all thinking we'd been blackballed. But in the morning, our big sisters had taken us upstairs, one by one, where they had pinned our little black masks to our chests, and we were in, all of us—SuSu, too, thank God—candles burning as we took the oath and learned the sacred lore.

Yet even our solemn, triumphant celebration somehow paled next to that one, achingly bittersweet moment I had shared with Linda the day before when we both knew down to our bones that we'd just experienced the perfect afternoon.

It made us best friends forever.

13

Solidarity, at Last

Swan Coach House. Tuesday, March 12, 2002. 11:15 A.M.

IANE HALTED ABRUPTLY IN MIDSENTENCE DURING THE latest Harold report and stared past Linda and me, mouth slack, then recovered herself enough to say, "I hope y'all are prayed up, because the Lord is surely coming back this very day."

Knowing that something earthshaking was approaching from behind her, Linda lifted her eyes heavenward, hands clasped as if in prayer. "Ohmygod, please let it be Mel Gibson." We turned around in our seats to see what had gabberflasted Diane, and both of our mouths dropped open.

It was better than Mel Gibson.

SuSu had on a red hat!

Not a little one, but a gorgeous, supple fedora over her classic French twist, with a narrow ribbon of purple at the base of the red band. And she was grinning like she'd just snagged a gorgeous-kind-and-wonderful billionaire.

Dumbstruck, all three of us sat frozen for a heartbeat, then erupted into joyous celebration. Diane burst into happy tears. I hugged SuSu—carefully, lest my own red beaver pillbox disturb her new badge of sisterhood. Linda jumped up and down, clapping like the cheerleaders she and SuSu once had been.

Teeny arrived in the middle of everything, beautifully tanned from her fortnight at the cenacle, and let out an undignified cackle worthy of Bette Midler.

I hadn't gotten a surprise that happy since Mama won five thousand dollars in the lottery four years ago.

When we finally settled into our seats, we were all giddier than a flock of pheasants drunk on wild cherries.

"Well, now that we're all here"—Linda smiled at SuSu—"and fully red-hatted for the first time ever, who's got the joke?"

"I do," I said. They all settled back in anticipation, since I was the best joke-teller by far. Talk about pressure. As always, though, I dived right in. "Okay. Buckaroo Bob"—our nickname for the generic Buckhead professional—"comes home from the office early one afternoon and finds his wife lying naked and panting on the bed.

" 'Honey,' she gasps, 'I think I'm having a heart attack!'

"As he's rushing to dial 911, he almost stumbles over their crying five-year-old, who points to the closet and says, 'Daddy, there's a nekkid man in the there.'

"Buckaroo Bob runs to the closet, throws it open, and discovers his best friend without a stitch on. 'G.D.,' Bob screams at his friend. 'What the F. is going on here?'

" 'Dammit, Bob!' his best friend yells back, 'Nancy's having a heart attack, and here you are scaring the hell out of the kids!' "

There was a pulse of silence; then Linda, Diane, and SuSu laughed halfheartedly while Teeny frowned. "I don't get it." Teeny cocked her head at me. "There was just the one kid."

I had to shake my head. "Kid, kids—it doesn't really matter. What matters is, here's this guy, nekkid in the closet, and . . . I mean, Nancy's not *really* having a heart attack. . . ."

The others leaned forward, intent.

It was useless. "Look, dissecting a joke is like dissecting a frog. It kills it. You either get it or you don't."

Linda giggled. "I don't."

Diane laughed out loud. "Me, neither."

SuSu and Teeny joined in. "George, honey, face it," SuSu managed, "this is the dud of all duds."

The rest wholeheartedly agreed.

I puffed up to defend it, then realized they all couldn't be wrong. "Well," I grudgingly acknowledged, "not the worst, but maybe in the top ten." I had to smile. "You gotta admit, though, it got you laughing." That, after all, was the whole point.

As soon as we'd ordered—the usual all around, of course— SuSu laid her large, flat shoulder bag on the table and unlatched it. "Okay, y'all." Her green eyes danced. "I've come up with something else to flush Jackson out." She pulled out a slim stack of printed flyers that looked identical to the ads she'd run in Jackson's hometown paper and the national nursing home owners' publication, except for one thing: She'd upped the contingency reward to fifty thousand dollars!

She handed several to each of us. "Jason—you know, y'all met him at Diane's charity thing—showed me how to go on the Internet and get the addresses for everybody in Jackson's ZIP code. Then he modified the ad we'd done, and voilà! Straight off his printer. We made a thousand to mail out, first class."

A thousand! That was almost four hundred dollars in postage alone!

She beamed in anticipation. "They're going to every store and residence within miles of Jackson's house. What do you think?"

We all made polite noises. No way was I telling her the truth, that I thought she was stuck and sad and needed to move on; that she might as well burn the money this would cost her, for all the good it would do—money that she'd earned on tired, over-fifty feet waiting on cranky airline passengers in cramped quarters. But SuSu hadn't come to us for advice, despite her asking our opinions. She'd come for approval. So in keeping with Tradition Three (no lies), I looked at the flyer, smiled, and gave her *a* truth. "If this doesn't work, nothing will."

The others didn't jump in, but it was enough for SuSu. Glowing, she turned to Diane. "Well, that's my update. How about yours?"

Diane lowered her voice, and our five red hats huddled as close as the brims allowed. "I've finally got enough papers and tapes and diskettes to sort through, but I dare not do it at my house. There's so much stuff, I'll need half a football field to make sense of everything."

"How about the lake?" Linda suggested. "For real, this time. Brooks has to present a paper in Boston weekend after next. Does that work for y'all?"

"When's that? The date?" Teeny asked.

Linda flipped open her checkbook to the calendar. "That Friday's the twenty-second."

Diane shrugged. "I'm sure Harold will be delighted for me to go. We all know where he'll be heading."

Teeny looked like she was weighing some monumental commitment, then raised her eyebrows in resignation. "Sure. I'm in." As if she ever did anything besides take care of her house and do things for the boys, who were both still at school. Frankly, since they'd gone off to college, I often wondered how she managed to keep from being bored to insanity. Compared with that, no wonder a Catholic retreat seemed like fun.

"Betsy"—my eldest sister—"is having a family cookout," I remembered aloud, "but I'm sure she'll understand if I bow out."

"There's not a weekend from April till November when somebody in your family *isn't* having a family cookout," SuSu joked with more than a little jealousy over my big, close-knit clan.

"And who is always invited?" I reminded her. "Any time, last minute, date if you want, no RSVP required?"

She acknowledged with a nod. "I'd take my red hat off to you, but I'm afraid I'd mess up my hair."

"Can you come that weekend?" Linda prodded her.

SuSu consulted her day planner. "I can't make it till Saturday after lunch." Which probably meant three or four. "My flight doesn't get in until two that morning."

"That's fine. The rest of us can go up on Friday and get started." Linda rubbed her hands together in anticipation. "This'll be great, like Woodward and Bernstein sifting through White House memos, or Tom Cruise gettin' the goods on the mob in *The Firm*."

Diane laughed. "Not nearly so glamorous or dramatic, but between the five of us, I think we can make some sense of everything. I want to be ready and organized when I go to the lawyer. No sense havin' Harold pay exorbitant legal fees for stuff we can do ourselves. Every dollar that goes to the attorneys is fifty cents I won't get."

"Honey," Teeny said in awe, "I'd hire you in a minute to run one of my corporations." Assuming she ever had any.

It almost made me cry to see how much even that small vote of confidence meant to Diane. Her simple, "Thanks" was pregnant with gratitude.

"I could bring Jason to help with the computer stuff," SuSu volunteered, clueless as ever.

"No," we all answered in unison.

"So we're on for the weekend after this one," Linda confirmed.

After we'd all agreed, SuSu used a mini-muffin to point at Linda. "Now. What's the latest on your dear daughter, Abby?"

Linda squirmed.

I raised an eyebrow at her. "Might as well go ahead and tell 'em." When it came to my goddaughter, Linda never listened to me.

SuSu extended a dramatic palm forward. "Let me guess," she said, sparing Linda the need to tell on herself. "Abby's still living with the tattoo artist, and y'all are still paying her bills."

Her pushover parenting exposed, Linda suddenly became engrossed with a packet of sugar as she shrugged in wordless affirmation.

"So," Diane prodded, "any new developments?"

"None, thank God." Linda spread her perfectly manicured gel nails on the tablecloth and faced us. "She hasn't gotten any more tattoos. She's not on drugs. And she's first in her class at cosmetology school, with perfect attendance." She managed a wan smile. "She loves it. Keeps pestering me to let her color my hair."

"Let her!" we all said far too eagerly for diplomacy's sake.

"Thanks a lot, y'all." She pouted, well aware of how we all felt about her gray, football-helmet hair. We'd long ago given up invoking Tradition Two (makeover) with her. It was a waste of energy.

Half of me admired her for being so confident in the package God gave her, but the other half of me wanted her to look as good as she could for as long as she could, not just for Brooks's sake, but for her own, as well.

"Tradition Five," Linda decreed.

"Tradition Two," SuSu said in a futile countercoup.

"I think we have a stalemate here," Teeny intervened before their repartee got heated. "Oh, look. Here's our food." Saved by the dinner bell.

The rest of our lunch, we spoke of the myriad ordinary details of our lives and worlds—worlds that were about to shift on their axes, not just for tiny Diane, but for most of the rest of us.

Friday week after a dinner of quiche and salad at the lake house, the four of us sat lightly bundled and blessedly inert with our wine in the gathering dusk on Linda's deck overlooking the still waters of Six Mile Creek cove. We'd all had a difficult day trying to get out of town before the inevitable snarl of wrecks and traffic jams that ushered in every weekend of the world in Atlanta.

Linda had picked up Diane and all the evidence as soon as Harold was safely at the office, but Teeny and I hadn't gotten away until half past three. Big mistake. We'd found ourselves gridlocked on 400 North from Abernathy to way past Windward Parkway. I swear, the Friday afternoon rush starts before lunch these days, congealing into a massive outbound meltdown no matter where you're headed.

Diane took a sip of her wine, dropped her head back, and then breathed in the relative quiet. "Mmmmmm. It's almost worth the drive."

"It *is* worth the drive," Linda drawled without offense. "That's why we keep it."

Teeny yawned. "What time do y'all want to get to work?" she asked without enthusiasm. "The night is young."

Nobody answered. It was only seven thirty, but felt like midnight despite the faint, lingering glow behind us. Teeny's yawn was catching. All three of us indulged without restraint, allowing our faces to distort as gruesomely as they wished.

I wanted nothing more than to go to bed, but we'd promised to help Diane. "Any time," I forced myself to say. Maybe I could muster up a second wind. I dared not drink caffeine to wake myself up. One regular Coke or coffee, and I'd be jabbering and cranky until five in the morning, then crash so hard an air strike couldn't wake me up before noon.

Diane yawned again. "I never should have started this second glass. I'm afraid I'm not good for anything now except hitting the hay."

God love her. But my Protestant guilt forced me to ask, "Are you sure? Because we could get in several hours' worth, if you feel up to it." A blooming yawn distorted the last few words, making a liar of me.

"Thanks, sweetie," Diane said, "but why don't we all turn in and get a fresh start in the mornin'?"

"Amen, sister." Teeny rose to her full four feet eleven inches and stretched. "I'm off to my room." The house had six bedrooms, and Linda had designated one for each of us when they'd built it, complete with our names on the door, our favorite decors, and the exact firmness and size of mattress we preferred.

Money is a wonderful thing in the hands of a thoughtful friend.

The next day dawned foggy, so Linda let us sleep until ten, then wooed us into the kitchen with fabulous aromas of coffee, cinnamon rolls, and bacon, helped along by a few banging pots and oven doors. Always up at the crack of dawn, she'd made the cinnamon rolls from scratch, cubed Chilean honeydew and cantaloupe, scrambled eggs, and brewed a huge pot of full-bodied, mellow, almond-flavored coffee. Though she didn't keep kosher, she never ate the bacon, but always nuked tons of it to crisp perfection for us.

The rest of us stumbled in, as foggy as the cove beyond the wall of glass, and gave our hostess a hug of silent thanks, then helped ourselves to breakfast and settled to eat as the mist lifted, inside and out.

By the second cup of coffee, we were fit for conversation and started planning out our day.

"What should be first?" Linda looked at the three file boxes on the coffee table. "The tapes, the papers, or the computer files?"

"The papers," Diane said without hesitation. "They're the best evidence. As for the tapes, I labeled each one by date, then replayed them and indexed the subject matter, so those notes will be all we'll need to cross-reference."

Teeny's fingers were wrapped tight around her third cup of coffee. "I meant what I said about that corporation."

"Bless your heart, darlin'," Diane answered with a tired smile, "and I'd be happy to do it."

Deadpan, Teeny said gravely, "I just might take you up on that."

"Ha!" I couldn't believe it. "Teeny just made a joke."

An unfamiliar glint of warning tightened her azure eyes.

Damn. I'd hurt her feelings.

Linda stepped in with, "How 'bout y'all help me shove the sofas aside and set up my Hadassah tables?" The folding tables were enormous, but so was her pale peach airplane hangar of a great room. We'd have plenty of space for the documents.

"Okey-doke." I cringed inwardly when I heard the dorkey, *Howdy Doody* throwback come from my own lips.

Linda put a fabulous custom-mix of oldies on the surround sound, and we started working to an audio scrapbook of the Supremes, Martha and the Vandellas, Leslie Gore, the Four Tops, Otis, the Shirelles, the Beach Boys, the Stones, and other blasts from our pasts. It took us three hours, but eventually we had all the papers sorted into somewhat coherent piles. While we were finishing those up, Linda ran to Wal-Mart for an assortment of bright-hued yarn, which we used to connect pertinent files together in a colorful spider web of paper trails. She also picked up a huge sack of barbecue sandwiches and slaw from Pappy Red's. (She won't eat bacon, but she dearly loves nice, lean pulled-pork barbecue.)

After we'd eaten, we drafted a heading for each chunk of monkey business, then sorted the documents by date into individual accordion files. As soon as each file was completed, we used Teeny's copier to make duplicates for the lawyer. The master files would go to the safe deposit box. When all the evidence lay neatly alongside the duplicate files, it was growing dark.

I punched the remote to ignite the lifelike gas fire and collapsed onto one of the mama's-lap sofas, exhausted from all that thinking. For the first time that day, I looked at the clock. "Damn, y'all. SuSu has officially run out of afternoon and into suppertime."

Pouring herself a glass of wine, Linda paused at the sound of an approaching car. "Speak of the devil." She leaned for a look at the parking area, then tensed. "Wup. Whoever it is, it ain't SuSu's car."

The rest of us Chicken-Littled in anxious whispers.

But it was SuSu—and Jason, against all orders.

In the instant when we all reared back for battle, Linda raised a staying hand. "I'll handle this. Stay put."

Since it was her house, we had no choice but to watch through the blinds as she closed the door behind her and approached SuSu and Jason.

"SuSu, we were really getting worried." Linda arrested her progress with a concerned hug that blocked Jason from coming any farther. Then Linda turned to him and literally wrested the handle to SuSu's bulging rolly bag from his grip. "And wasn't Jason a dear to give you a ride all the way up here in the traffic?"

Frowning, SuSu tried to get a word in, "My car broke down, so I asked him to rescue me, and he did. After all that way, we can't just—"

"Goodness," Linda interrupted, turning to Jason. "We figured something must have happened. What was wrong with the car?"

Even by the subtle landscape lighting, we could see SuSu color. "I'd really rather not discuss that. About Jason—"

Linda ignored her. "Were you able to figure out what was wrong with the car?"

Jason chuckled. "Out of gas. Again."

We all rolled our eyes behind the blinds. Typical!

It never occurred to us that she might not have had enough money for a refill.

SuSu cocked a petulant frown, but Linda blinked at Jason in all innocence. "Well, aren't you her knight in shining armor. I can't begin to thank you enough for delivering her safe and sound." Before SuSu could get another word in, Linda went for the coup de grâce. "I'd ask you in, dear," she said with her most hospitable smile, "but I know you'll be wanting to get back to town before too late. The girls and I have already started our hen party." Here's your hat, Southern style—no debate, no voices raised, and oh so polite. "I do hope you'll come back some time when the men are here." She twiddled a dismissive wave.

"Yeah." Jason shrugged at SuSu, then retreated, gym bag in hand, with an, "I'll have to do that sometime," that none of us— least of all him—believed.

Only after he'd driven out of sight did SuSu turn on Linda. "I cain't believe you did that to him," she said as they started inside.

The rest of us hurried into the kitchen and tried to look busy fixing supper. The door opened to SuSu's whine. "Especially after the way he dropped everything to get me here. The least we could have done was give him a beer and some supper."

Linda didn't waste an iota of emotional energy on such flimsy tactics. And she admirably refrained from reminding SuSu that we expressly didn't want anybody to see the evidence. Instead, she just parked SuSu's carry-on inside and locked the door, then pushed up her sleeves and joined us in the kitchen.

"Hi, Suse." I waved the tomato knife I'd been using to halve grape tomatoes. "Where's your car?"

"You know perfectly well where it is," she grumped. "I saw y'all peepin' at the windows." She arched an eyebrow at Linda. "And so did Jason. *Too* rude." She popped a tomato into her mouth and plunked down, idle, on a stool.

Linda chuckled, then handed her three cukes and a peeler. "Here. Do these for the salad. We're having Fred." Almond-encrusted baked grouper with lemon butter sauce.

Teeny finished washing the romaine at the sink and started putting small batches into the salad spinner. Prompted by the mention of Fred (the sole significant Fred in our lives, fish or otherwise), Teeny waxed nostalgic. "How many years has it been since we got the original Fred fried at the Top of Peachtree?"

I hated head-math, especially with sixes subtracted from twos, but Linda whipped out an immediate, "Thirty-six years, this May."

We digested the hefty number in bittersweet silence. Emboldened by my status on the Mission Impossible team, I asked a question I hadn't even let myself consider until that moment. "Did you ever dream we would end up like this?"

Caught by my seriousness, they paused in the seamless rhythm of preparation we'd perfected over the years.

SuSu's eyes welled. "I was going to be Miss America, then marry a movie star and live happily ever after in the Hollywood Hills."

"I'm not talking about when we were little kids," I said, resuming the mindless chore of slicing the tiny tomatoes in two. "I'm talking about when we were starting out in life. What did you see for yourself when we got to this age?"

"That was it," SuSu confirmed. "Blissful in Bel Air."

Moans and rolling of eyes.

"How about you, Linda?" SuSu asked. "What did you see?"

"Exactly what I've got," Linda said without hesitation. "Except instead of shacking up with the Muslim tattoo artist, Abby would be married, no tattoos, to a nice, faithful Jewish executive—"

"Or plumber," Diane suggested.

"Plumber would be good. Better job security," Linda agreed. "And I'd have at least one grandchild to dote on."

"You'll get that grandchild," Teeny consoled her. "Abby will come around. She spent her entire childhood playing mommy with her dolls. That's still in there somewhere."

"I'll tell you one thing I didn't dream of, though," Linda said. "I never dreamed we would all still be best friends. What an unexpected blessing."

She gave Teeny a sideways hug. "How about you? What were Teeny's dreams?"

"I never thought this far ahead," Teeny said with quiet candor. "All I could think about was not letting my parents down." Her face eased with the glow of remembered youth. "And then Reid came along and paid attention to me. Reid, the most eligible bachelor in Atlanta, and he fell in love with me." The nostalgia cleared. "He did love me, you know. He just didn't know how a good husband was supposed to act." She pulled the salad spinner with force, and it whined and strained against her grip. "How could he, coming from a family like that? But I really believed I could teach him." Her expression was not that of a woman in denial. "But that was just my girlish fantasy."

She retrieved the dried romaine and stuffed in another batch. "Once I realized that and decided to make the best of the life I'd been given, we were all a lot happier." Another hard yank on the cord. She looked to Diane. "What about you?"

Diane sighed without self-pity. "Certainly not what I ended up with, although God knows I did my best to make Harold and me into a happily-ever-after."

"The real happily-ever-after is pending," Linda assured her. "A *lot* happier without Harold. Trust me. You've just got to get through the crap first."

"What about you, Georgia?" Diane asked. "Where did you think you'd be?"

I hesitated. If I told them the truth, they might pick up on my recent fantasies of Brad, and I'd never hear the end of it. If I didn't, I'd have to make up something convincing, fast, which I am no good at doing. And the longer I waited to respond, the sharper their expressions became. So I decided to tell only enough to satisfy them, but no more. "I thought I'd be Mrs. Brad Olson, with a son in med school and a future tycoon daughter at Wharton. Brad would come home every night at six to me at our vine-covered cottage by the lake, with two cats in the yard."

Where we would throw down, and I'd ride his forever-twenty body like a wild woman as he adored my middle-aged self—every night if I wanted—loving me to distraction with his mouth, then banging me half-unconscious—

A salacious explosion erupted in my underemployed privates, snatching me back to reality.

This fantasy business was getting completely out of control. I felt myself flush hugely.

What was I doing? I had a perfectly good husband, and I loved him. John was a good man. A very good man. He deserved better than this mental infidelity.

"With two cats in the ya-a-a-rd." SuSu sang a golden oldie from our youth. "Life used to be so ha-a-a-rd."

I chuckled, but it was edged with shame and a twinge of old grief for my long-lost love.

"Vine-covered cottage, my ass." Linda snorted, whisking her homemade salad dressing within an inch of its life. "The best thing Brad Olson ever did for you was disappear."

"Linda!" I glared at her. "It broke my heart. I anguished for years over what had happened to him." She'd always been so sympathetic until now, and suddenly, she pipes up with this? "If you felt that way, why in the world have you waited till now to attack me about it?"

"Attack?" Antennas went up all over the room.

"Okay," I admitted, "*attack* was too strong a word."

Laughing, Linda pointed the dripping whisk in my direction. "I tell you now because it's long past time for you to get over it, my dahling. Better a broken heart at seventeen than a sad, sordid saga with a drifter and a dreamer."

"Oooh," Diane admired. "Nice alliteration."

Linda resumed her task. "If you had tried to settle that boy down, he'd have left you with nothing but those two kids hanging onto your hem, and you know it. And no way do I see you happy as a surf slut or living in a commune."

She was right, but since my only entertainment of late had been my fantasies of Brad, I wasn't about to admit it. "And what makes you so sure he would have ended up on the beach or a commune? Especially if I had been with him."

Teeny studied us with an anxious frown. Emotions, emotions! Red alert!

Linda remained cheerful. "Damn, sweetie," she said to me, "don't even think about feeding me that 'love of a good woman' crap. Men don't get any better after we marry them, any more than we do when they marry us."

"Sad but true," Diane piped up while beating egg whites for the fish's almond crust.

"Yep." SuSu frowned. "They only clean up their acts until they've got us, then it's all downhill from there."

"Tut-tut, SuSu," Diane admonished lightly. "Can we say cynical? Bitter? These are not pretty thoughts. These are thoughts that put wrinkles in our faces."

SuSu and I exchanged a pregnant glance, then shared a laugh at the irony of that statement. Her spirits much improved, she added her single, peeled and sliced cucumber to the lettuce. At this rate, we'd be on dessert before she finished the other two. I dumped in the tomatoes, then grabbed the biggest cucumber, and started peeling and shaping it.

"Back to this Brad thing," Linda persisted. "We tried to warn you about him."

I bristled. "That is a blatant breach of Tradition Eleven." (No I-told-you-so's.) Though my intellect had to admit they were probably right, my heart—and my libido—rose up to defend my first-love illusions. "Brad was only twenty. It was the sixties. That was thirty-five years ago." Dark green strips of peel flew all over the counter. "People can change. Hell, if they didn't, we'd be surrounded by hippies." I straightened. "For all we know, he could be a doctor or a lawyer now."

"Brad?" Linda scoffed. "He was one damn-fine-lookin' boy, but flunking out of *four* colleges in two years doesn't bode well for graduate school."

"I wonder what really did happen to him," Teeny mused.

"He drew a twenty-five in the draft," Diane remembered. "Maybe he went to Canada to keep from getting sent to Vietnam."

"If he had, don't you think somebody would have heard something from him eventually?" This, from Linda. "Especially after amnesty." She was so annoyingly sure of herself. "No. Mark my words: Brad Olson shook the dust of this town from his shoes and never looked back."

"Maybe he's dead," SuSu proposed blithely.

"He's *not* dead," I declared with a force born of sheer physical conviction. No dead person could inspire the orgasms I'd been having. It didn't fit with my vision of the cosmos.

"Methinks the lady doth protest too much." SuSu waggled her eyebrows to the others. "Who'da thunk it? George is still carrying a torch for Brad Olson!"

Crepe. They were on to me. "That's the silliest thing I've heard in a long time." I traded the peeler for a paring knife and tried to feign indifference as I shaped the cuke. "Maybe he is dead. Let's talk about something else."

They weren't buying. "Georgia has a crush on Brad," Diane teased in singsong.

Teeny studied me. "Would you really want to know what happened to him?"

"Yes." Maybe then, I could get a grip on myself.

Or maybe it would be the same old magic!

My soul stuck its fingers into its metaphysical ears and squinched shut its eyes while my mother's voice harped, *Do not go there, do not go there, do not go there,* over the lascivious thoughts that babbled through my brain.

"George?" Linda's voice brought me back to myself. All three of them were staring at me in concern.

Good grief. I was losing it. "Are y'all just gonna stand there and make me fix supper all by myself?" My voice sounded brittle even to me. "Where's the Fred?"

"Fred!" Linda jumped as if the giant fillet on the plate before her a had suddenly come alive. "Bring the crust stuff, Diane," she instructed. "The oven's ready."

While they covered the fish in thin slices of lemon and then smoothed on the whipped egg whites with sliced almonds (we rarely ever bothered to arrange them like scales anymore) I concentrated on my cucumber art and tried diverting them with a joke, a male tactic I'd learned from my two big brothers. "Okay, joke time. Listen up, especially Linda. This is good shtick. I practiced it on all my brothers and sisters."

Our Red Hat Joke of the Month had trained them to pay attention, so they did.

"A young whippersnapper of an IRS auditor decides to make

a name for himself by auditing a synagogue," I began, very careful with the wording because you have to get it just right. "He goes over their books with a microscope, insisting that the rabbi explain every detail of running the synagogue, down to what they do with the wax drippings from the Shabbat, habdalah, and Hanukkah candles.

"The rabbi's more than happy to show the irritating little bureaucrat that nothing goes to waste, so he explains that all the wax drippings are saved, then shipped back to the candle factory, who sends the synagogue a little pack of free candles with their next order."

My diversion worked. Caught up in the joke, the Red Hats resumed their dinner duties.

I went on. " 'What about the matzo crumbs from the Passover?' the IRS auditor asks him.

" 'That's easy,' the rabbi answers with a twinkle in his eye. 'We send them to the kosher bakery, and they send us back a little extra matzo with our next order.'

"The obnoxious auditor is determined to get the best of the rabbi. 'I know you're a moyel as well as a rabbi,' he says. 'What do you do with the leftovers from the circumcisions?'

"The rabbi smiles. 'We send them off to Washington, D.C., and they send us back a little prick like you.' "

With that, I lifted the pale, anatomically correct cucumber penis I'd been sculpting and waggled it before them.

We all burst out laughing, including Teeny.

"Give me that!" Diane scolded, snatching it from me. Then she kicked us up another notch by biting off the end and chewing it with relish.

Half an hour later, when the last crumb of Fred had been eaten, we cleaned up, then wandered into the living area to survey our handiwork and put in a late shift.

"That doesn't look like much to me, for a whole day's work," SuSu commented with typical cluelessness.

The rest of us simply rolled our eyes. It would be a waste of breath to explain how many hours it had taken to accomplish that much.

Linda pushed up the sleeves of her sweater. "What next?" she asked Diane.

"We need to dub off a set of the tapes for my lawyer, and we also need to cross-reference the tape indexes and make a guide of all the pertinent sections for each hunk-a-monk."

"Hunk-a-monk?" SuSu asked.

"Short for hunk of monkey business," Linda explained, "which is what those of us who *worked* today call the files. Each file holds evidence of a separate act of wrongdoing by Harold or the bank."

"Oooh," SuSu's face lit up. "You got the goods on the bank, too?"

"Hope so," Diane said. "My lawyer brought in a consultant who used to be a senior auditor for the OCC. We can't be positive until she's reviewed everything, but I'm pretty sure we've nailed them."

"What's the OCC?" SuSu asked, never one to try to cover what she didn't know.

"The Office of the Comptroller of the Currency." Diane laid a protective hand on one of the precious files. "They're the government watchdogs over the banks."

Linda surveyed the fruits of our labors. "What I wouldn't give to be a fly on the wall when that consultant reports her results."

"Oh, you'll be there." Linda picked up a tablet and the tape indexes. "You all will, if you want to."

We all got our second wind in one breath. "What?"

Diane grinned. "What fun would it be to get Harold by the short hairs without y'all along to watch?" She clicked open a pen. "You're all invited, for anything and everything."

Talk about a gift! The rest of us clapped, cheered, and whistled, pumped up for the kill.

"Okay. Back to business." Diane pointed to the box of audio- and videotapes. "Linda, I see there's a high-speed tape dubber on that component system. Why don't you and SuSu copy and label the tapes?" Then she turned to me. "The floppy diskettes of Harold's computer files are in that red shoe box. Brooks has a CD burner on the desktop in his den." She handed me a package of blank CDs. "Think you can figure out how to put those files on these blank CDs? We'll need to archive two complete sets."

"I can try." Of all the jobs. I picked up the box of floppies. Maybe I'd get lucky and find the CD-burner's icon on the computer's desktop, and it would be self-explanatory. One can always hope.

We worked into the night, then got up with the dawn. SuSu spent as much time out on the deck smoking as she did helping inside, but that was par for the course.

It took a lot of brain-twisting thought to get and keep everything straight, but by Sunday evening when we all headed back to town, we had strong documentation to support Harold's recorded cocktail confessions. He'd taken huge kickbacks for churning some of the larger, less closely watched trust portfolios. (And I don't mean making butter. Diane had explained that *churning* was making unnecessary trades to milk commissions from an account.)

Even better, though, we'd found evidence that the bank was aware of it. Not to mention the fact that they'd been systematically holding trust client transfer funds far longer than the law allowed in order to artificially inflate their cash reserves.

Big-gun stuff. Criminal fraud. Jail-time, disbarment, sic-the-Feds-on-'em stuff.

Leverage on a Congressional scale.

We reveled in the delicious power of it, dancing along the edge of the dark side and loving it. Diane's arsenal was organized, duplicated, and ready to fire. And we were going to get to be there when she pulled the trigger.

14

Susan "SuSu" Virginia McIntyre Harris Cates

3278 College Circle. Saturday, August 22, 1953. 10:00 A.M.

STOOD IN THE SHADE OF MY PREGNANT MOTHER ON THE HOT August pavement of College Circle, oblivious of the mama-talk and cigarette smoke that surrounded me. I was far more fascinated by the shabby furniture being carried from the beat-up truck to the new little house three doors up from mine. At four years old, I had no way of knowing that the movers weren't the proper kind or that the house was tiny even by College Circle standards. A truck was a truck to me, and a new house was a new house, and I hoped that the family who'd built it had a little girl my same age.

There were so many kids on College Circle that in order to avoid fights over who got what friends, age was almost always the allocating factor—and sex, of course. Boys were tormentors, rarely friends, with the notable exception of Ed Gadunsen Johnson, who had shared my playpen from the age of two weeks and remained my ally.

I pulled against my mother's hand, craning for a better look through the open front door. The newcomers had already been there when we all got up, so the mothers were speculating about the family's composition.

"I saw dolls in one of those boxes," Ellen Beaumont's mama

said. "That means girls." Ellen was my big sister Betsy's age, and my younger sister Cathy had the twins across the street, so they didn't need another friend. But I had no girls to myself.

"Well," Mama said, her hand to the small of her back as her sandal crushed out her cigarette butt on the blacktop, "they can't have many, not with just two bedrooms." Spoken by a woman with three bedrooms and *five* children, plus one on the way.

Eavesdropping on the mamas and daddies in their evening front-yard circle of folding chairs, I had heard great discussions about how the two most recent houses—*prefabs* the mamas had called them with disdain—had "brought down the neighborhood." Not knowing what a prefab was, I had filed the information away for later clarification. But from where I stood, the house looked fine enough. True, it had two narrow, wrought-iron panels holding up the little roof over the front stoop, unlike the porch posts and square columns on all the other houses, but inside was the same knotty-pine paneling that we had in our living rooms and bedrooms.

Then a shift of movement drew my eyes to the open door and I saw her, a wide-eyed little redheaded girl clinging to the doorjamb, watching the people watching her house. She was wearing a white eyelet midriff and red shorts, just like me!

I tugged against Mama's hand with all my might. "Mama. Mama!" I tried to cut into her conversation. (I've always been bad to interrupt.) "There's a little girl my same age. Mama, can I go say hello?"

Mama assayed the situation. The movers had taken a break. "Okay, sugar." She finally let go of my hand, and I sprinted through the piled quilts and boxes at the top of the driveway. "Mind your manners, now," she called after me. "And watch out for those movers. Don't you go gettin' in their way. You might end up squushed." Which we all knew was far flatter than merely *squashed.*

I ran down the sloping yard, careful not to slip in my white leather Buster Brown sandals. I remember the concrete stoop seemed very high, level with my chest. I didn't go up the stairs. The redheaded girl seemed scared as a wild kitten, so I moved to the side of the stoop, my fingers twining in one of the wrought-iron supports, and looked up at her from a safe distance.

"Hey." I swung from the support. "My name's Georgia Peyton, and I live down there." I pointed to the gray brick cottage with a covered porch three houses away. "I have two big brothers and one big sister and one little sister, and my mama's gonna get another one pretty soon." I pointed to Mama in the crowd of neighbors congregated at the top of the driveway. "She's the really fat one, right there."

I vividly remember how she looked. She had on dark green sunglasses in flesh-colored frames, a long white skirt, and a peach maternity top embellished with black sketches of Paris—the Eiffel Tower was my favorite—and big, shiny black buttons.

The little redheaded girl nodded, her eyes alert, but she said nothing.

"You got any brothers and sisters?" I asked, trying to draw her out.

She nodded again, studying me as thoroughly as I was studying her. Long seconds elapsed before she said, "Just a big sister. She's mean."

Ah. Common ground. "So is mine." We both smiled. Since she apparently wasn't going to tell me on her own, I asked her, "What's your name?"

"SuSu." She said it as if she expected me to make fun of her for it.

"Lucky duck." I swung some more, my sandals braced on the brick side of the stoop. "That's a whole lot better name than *Georgia.* My brothers are always teasin' me about bein' a state."

She smiled, transforming her freckled face.

Encouraged, I invited, "You wanna play?"

She cast a frightened glance toward the kitchen, where I could hear her mama telling her daddy where to put things.

"I can't." she said in a wistful tone. "Mama said I hafta stay inside."

She talked kind of baby, but she was taller than me, with nary a hint of plumpness. "How old are you?" I came right out and asked, praying that I—not my one-year-younger sister, Cathy—could claim her.

"I'm four."

"Yesss!" Finally, I'd lucked up. "Can you play tomorrow, then?"

I fully expected her to ask her mama, but she only shot another worried look toward the kitchen. "I don't know."

"That's okay." I smiled, hoping to make her feel better about whatever it was she was afraid of. "I'll come back tomorrow. Mama lets me come to this whole side of the street all by myself."

SuSu's green eyes widened in awe.

"You'll like it here," I reassured her. "We have a dollhouse."

"I can do a cartwheel," she told me, her smile easier.

It was my turn to be impressed. I couldn't even manage a somersault.

"You can show me tomorrow." I smiled back. "You and me can be best friends." And we were, from that day on.

3258 College Circle. Tuesday, July 11, 1961.

"Oh, no." I flopped back onto my bed and moaned. "There she goes again." Betsy and Ellen were playing Elvis. I couldn't stand Elvis; as far as I was concerned, he was a low-rent. It never occurred to me that my big sister had realized the surest way to get rid of me and SuSu was to crank him up. "Let's go to your house."

"No, let's don't," SuSu responded, emphatic. She never wanted to go to her house, but then, it *was* pretty depressing.

While I was grateful to have found probably the one person in the world who actually preferred our chaos and clutter to the peace and quiet of her own place, I knew her reluctance was more than that.

"Listen, I told you before, there's nothing to be embarrassed about. It's not your mama's fault somebody robbed them."

SuSu's expression said otherwise. She didn't have to tell me that none of the other parents had ever been robbed and beaten, only hers. I knew her well enough to know she hated having the only mother for blocks who worked.

"It's not that," she grumbled. "Mama stayed home 'cause they're puttin' on burglar bars."

"Burglar bars?" On a street where nobody even locked their doors at night? "But College Circle is safe as my daddy's lap. They were robbed at the café, not here."

SuSu rolled up to hug her knees on Cathy's bed. "I told her and told her, but no. She said she'd never sleep safe again until the house was 'secure.' It's gonna look like Alcatraz." She'd always been ashamed that their house was smaller and shabbier than all the others. Now she'd have burglar bars to live down.

"Then let's go over and play hospital with Cathy and the twins." The twins had the whole upstairs of their house to themselves, with a big playroom, a bedroom, and their own bath, plus a huge fan to draw in cool, shaded air from outside. Little wonder Cathy spent every moment she could across the street instead of in the stuffy confusion of our house.

"No. The twins drive me nuts. They're so baby." Then she brightened. "I know. Let's spy on the boys."

Puh-leeze. Talk about boring. "I told you, I hate that." I tried another tack. "I know. Let's walk up to the dime store and see if they got any new Barbie clothes." Neither of us had a real Barbie, mind you, but we could dream, and our high-heel dolls had provided a wonderful outlet for our overactive imaginations. We'd created elaborate scenarios in which they—and we—became Russian princesses, Nancy Drew, Elizabeth Taylor in *Black Beauty*, Annette of the Mousketeers, and countless other exotic imaginings.

Until lately, that is, when SuSu had begun to lose interest. "Forget about Barbie," she griped. "We're too old for that."

What? I stared at her, my insides sinking.

Had puberty visited her and not me? I worried, appalled by the growing distance between our interests. (I knew all about puberty—which I pronounced *pooberty*—after reading about it in Betsy's *Now, You Are a Woman* booklet.) "Pick something else, then," I said, defensive. "Anything but spying on the boys."

I didn't have to remind her that the last time, Larry Bentley had hit me in the head with a big, green hickory nut and given me a concussion, prompting Daddy to go from house to house to put a stop to rock- (and hickory-nut-) throwing altogether.

But hickory nuts weren't the issue, here. The issue was that we hardly ever wanted to do the same thing anymore.

SuSu sulked, focused on the ceiling. Outside in the huge oaks of our backyard, cicadas sang their lilting summer song, and birds chirped in the canopy of the "woods" beyond, a narrow strip of old growth that separated our houses from the foreign territory of Pinetree Lane.

After several minutes passed, she sat up. "Well, I'm going to spy on the boys whether you want to come or not." She stood up and straightened her sleeveless blouse, accenting the presence of her budding nipples and the training bra that held them, then went to the mirror and used my brush to redo her thick, auburn ponytail.

I sensed something changing between us—already changed between us—and it made me more sad than angry, but I refused to let her be the boss of me. "Do what you want, but I'm not coming."

When I didn't relent, she arched a copper brow. "Maybe Joy Anderson is home. I'll bet she'd love to come."

Joy Anderson! She was a year older than us, plus, she lived on Pinetree! True, she could turn flips and cartwheels with SuSu and I couldn't, but aside from that, she was nothing special. SuSu was replacing me with an alien! "Fine," I said, hurt. "If you want to spy on the boys with Joy Anderson, go right ahead. As a matter of fact, why don't you just hang around with Joy all the time?

Maybe *she* can help you with your homework from now on!" I opened the door and held it. "Have fun."

Her jaw rolled slightly forward and her green eyes narrowed. "Fine," she snapped, stubborn as ever. "We will."

After she walked out, I slammed the door so hard, it cracked the full-length plate mirror on the back, which remains that way to this day. Then I hurled myself onto the bed and went through a long tirade of "I hope you get poison ivy. I hope you sprain both ankles. I hope you flunk all your tests and have to stay back," and other charitable thoughts, aching more with each one.

Half an hour later, purged, I decided to do some spying of my own—not on the boys, but on my ex-best friend and Joy Anderson. I had just scouted out College Circle and Pinetree, without results, when I heard distant shrieks from the park. They weren't the usual cries of kids playing a game or having fun. There was real terror in the sounds, and pain.

A tingle shot through me as I sprinted between the last two houses on Pinetree, then across the huge concrete culvert that was the shortcut to the bottom of the city tennis courts. There in the trees at the edge of the deserted lower parking lot, I saw SuSu and Joy tied, hugging the ivy-covered trees, while Larry Bentley and his toadies lashed them with tall weeds they'd picked from the verge of the pavement.

At thirteen, Larry was almost as big as a construction worker, with a top-heavy build and a mean streak a mile wide. The weeds he and his snot-nosed gang were using weren't little ones. They were six feet long, thicker than your thumb, and so strong that they'd left green welts across the backs of SuSu's and Joy's shirts.

"Stop that!" I roared over the girls' wails and the boys' feral shouts.

But instead of stopping, Larry Bentley turned his beady pig-eyes on me, pointed his lash, and bellowed, "Git 'er!"

Ricky Wallace and Tom Brewster, rope in hand, took off in my direction.

Running for my life, I sprinted back across the culvert, between the houses, and up Pinetree Lane, frantic to find help. The first person I came to was Patrick MacMahan, the most gorgeous lifeguard at Brookwood Hills pool, cutting the grass in all his tanned, muscular, high school senior splendor.

His back was to me, so I had to grab hold of his arm to get his attention. He jumped a mile.

"Help," I gasped out as he shut off the mower. "Larry Bentley and the boys tied SuSu and Joy to a tree, and they're whipping them." Tears exploded. "They're really hurting them, and now they're after me!"

His handsome face went dark. "Not anymore, they're not."

"There!" I pointed to Ricky and Tom, who had just run into the street, rope in hand.

"Go get your mama!" Patrick ordered me, then shot after the boys, who did an immediate about-face.

Loath to involve parents and confident that Patrick could handle the situation, I ran after him, but couldn't keep up. By the time I got to the knoll overlooking the scene of the crime, Patrick had Ricky and Tom by their collars in one fist, dancing on their toes, and had just begun to administer Larry a come-to-Jesus whipping with the same rope they'd intended to tie me up with. The rest of the boys had fled.

What a picture! It was better than *Superman* on TV.

Emboldened by Patrick's righteous judgment, I ran to free SuSu and Joy. Both of them were sobbing, limp, their faces buried in the mixture of trumpet vine and poison ivy that coated the tree trunks. As I struggled to untie the complicated knots (not what the Boy Scouts had intended when they taught them to the boys), I saw that there was blood mixed with the green stains across their backs, and SuSu's fragile skin was already red and swollen from exposure to the poison ivy.

Oh, Lord, I didn't mean it about the poison ivy, I prayed in silent remorse. *I'm sorry. So sorry. I really didn't mean it. Yes, you did*, a tiny inner voice chided.

By that point, Larry had turned on Patrick, so Patrick had to let the others go and was now circling Larry's wild haymakers with the precision of a prizefighter.

"Dammit," I cried in frustration as the knot, tightened by SuSu's efforts to escape, refused to budge. "Why won't you untie?"

Patrick moved on Larry with blinding speed and got him in a headlock, turning Larry's fat, freckled face crimson from lack of air. With his free hand, Patrick reached into Larry's pants pocket and wrested out a long, slender pocketknife, spilling money and gum in the process. Then he hurled Larry away from him so hard, Larry rolled on the hot pavement, badly scraping both arms.

Patrick scooped up the money and tossed it toward the bully. "Get out of here," he ordered hoarsely. "And if you ever so much as touch another girl, I'm comin' for you, with my friends, and I can promise you, you won't walk away from it then."

Neighborhood justice at its finest. I got goose bumps. He was a god.

Larry righted himself, sullen, then began to scoop up the wadded bills and coins. "They asked for it," he snarled, "always sneakin' around behind us. They asked for it."

Patrick stilled with deadly purpose. "I don't care what they do. You touch any of them, and you're dead meat. Now get out of here, before I lose my temper and *really* hurt you."

Shaken, Larry put his fat legs to record use. Patrick waited until he was halfway to the culvert before he flicked open the knife.

"A switchblade," I gasped out, my innards wrenching. "He had a switchblade." Those things were *illegal!*

Panting, Patrick turned to the exhausted victims. "Okay, y'all. It's almost over. Just hang on a little longer so I can get you loose." His voice was soothing and very gentle. He carefully slipped the blade between SuSu's wrist and the rope, then began to cut her free. "Hold on to her when it's almost through," he instructed me. "She's liable to need some help."

Sure enough, as soon as the rope gave way, SuSu sagged in a

fresh wail of tears. Poison ivy or not, I helped her to a safe, shady spot, then gathered her to me and rocked her like a baby.

Joy seemed to have fared better. She was still sniffing spasmodically from her ordeal, but she was able to walk to us unassisted beside Patrick.

He leaned over SuSu and shook his head. Her eyes were swollen almost shut, and not from crying. The poison ivy was beginning to erupt all over her face, arms, and the fronts of her legs. "We'd better get you to a hospital." He bent down and scooped her into his arms, the muscles rippling under his sweaty T-shirt. "I'm assuming you didn't tell your mama," he said to me.

I hung my head in guilt.

"Well, you can make it up by getting her now. And Mrs. McIntyre. Have them bring the car right away so we can get her to the emergency room."

SuSu cranked up again. "Oh, God, don't tell Mama. She'll never let me out of the house again!"

"Shhh, shh, shh, shh," He crooned into her hair. "It's gonna be all right."

It was *so* terrible, and *so* romantic!

He cut his head toward our street. "Scoot, now. And Joy, get home as fast as you can and scrub off three times with lots of soap in a warm shower. Not hot, warm. And don't stop for anything else. The sooner you scrub off, the less you'll break out."

Just like Dr. Kildare.

I sprinted for Mama, but this time, the adrenaline fading, I felt the uphill climb with every pounding step. When I finally reached home, I could scarcely speak. I must have been a sight, because Mama put down my old skirt she'd been hemming for Cathy and stood, her face pale.

"Mama, call Miz McIntyre. The boys whipped SuSu in the poison ivy, and she's swellin' up like a red blimp. Patrick saved us, and he said we need to take her to the emergency room."

Mama grabbed me by my upper arms. "Not my boys?"

"No, ma'am. Larry's gang."

Relieved but still grim, she raced for the phone. "What's SuSu's number?"

"Cedar three, four-oh-two-two."

"Sheila," Mama said into the receiver. "SuSu's gotten into some poison ivy, and we need to take her to the doctor. Can I pick you up right away? Patrick MacMahan is bringin' her up from the park."

I heard Miz McIntyre's voice buzzing. "No," Mama said, "I'm afraid it's more serious than that. We can talk in the car. I'll be right up." She hung up and grabbed her purse.

On her way out, she halted, taking me by the upper arms. "You, were you in the poison ivy?"

I hesitated. "Well, only sorta. I mean, maybe when I tried to untie SuSu—"

"Never a straight answer from this one." She shook her head. "Well, take a hot shower, anyway, and scrub and scrub and scrub with Ivory. And don't put those clothes in with the others. The last thing I need is everybody gettin' poison ivy." The screen door squeaked open. "Willie Mae's hanging wash in the basement. Tell her where I've gone."

"But, Mama," I argued after her. "I want to go. SuSu's my best friend."

"Go take a shower," she ordered through the driver's window, then backed our old Plymouth station wagon up the two concrete strips of our driveway in a squeal of rubber.

It was the next day before I got to see SuSu. I rang the bell, then waited for Miz McIntyre to unlock the new wrought-iron security door.

SuSu was in her bed, the blinds closed, swathed in threadbare towels and washcloths soaked in calamine and iced baking soda solution.

"Hey." For the first time ever, I was uncertain what to say to her.

She lifted a corner of the cloth covering her eyes and peered at me through swollen slits. "Hey." Even the one word came out thickened by drugs.

After a pause, she said, "Good thing you didn' go with me. There'd have been nobody to save us."

"I didn't save you," I protested. "I just went for help. Patrick saved you."

"How's Joy?" she asked, still slurred.

"She's okay," I said without the slightest twinge of jealousy. In atonement for calling down destruction on them, I'd resolved to include her in our group. "Some nasty places on her back, and a little poison ivy on her face and the insides of her arms, but that's it. Oh, yeah, and her wrists. They're pretty raw."

"And you?"

"I didn't even break out," I said with more than a touch of guilt.

I peered at the ice cubes floating in the basin beside her bed. "Mr. and Mrs. Anderson called the police. Two detectives came and took pictures of Joy's back. She had to let them see her with only a towel covering her front. How embarrassing."

"I know," SuSu said wearily. "They took pictures of me, too, at the emergency room."

"Oh." What can you say to that? "Then the detectives got Patrick's statement, and mine. And after that, they went and arrested Larry. Mama said they'll put him in reform school."

"A little late, if you ask me," SuSu said, then began to shake, scaring me, but when a soggy laugh escaped her, I relaxed. "What about the others?"

"Daddy told Mama they'd probably just get probation, but it'll go on their records." Most of the others were pretty decent when Larry wasn't around, so some perverse part of me felt bad about bringing such serious consequences on them. "Mama said they were all little hoodlums and deserved to be locked up."

"She's right," Miz McIntyre said as she carried in a glass of lemonade with a Flexi straw. "Look what they did to my SuSu.

Just look." There was a bitterness in her voice I hadn't heard in any of the other parents', but then, SuSu had gotten the worst of it by far. Not to mention the fact that Miz McIntyre was still purple and green and yellow from being robbed. "But would the police have been so eager to help if it had just been my SuSu, and not that Anderson girl? Don't you bet on it."

"Mama," SuSu chided weakly. "Don't."

Miz McIntyre pulled up a little stool beside the bed and sat, ignoring her daughter's request. "You didn't see cops swarming all around and arresting people when we were robbed and brutalized, did you? Oh, no. We don't belong to any Brookwood Hills Club. We're just honest, hardworking people, tryin' to make it from month to month. We don't count."

I squirmed in my chair, more uncomfortable for SuSu than for myself.

"And all the money this is gonna cost us," she ranted on. "Do you think those boys' parents will make good on all our emergency room bills and all these expensive drugs they've got her on? I'll believe *that* when I see it. Not to mention me missin' more work to take care of her. Abel can't run the café alone. We have to bring somebody in to help him. Who's gonna pay that, I ask you?"

Tears leaked out from under SuSu's compresses. "Please, Mama, don't. I feel bad enough already."

My heart broke for her. My mama might be strict and sassy, but she'd never fussed at me for my doctor bills, even when I'd broken my arm skating too fast after she'd warned me not to.

Her mother stuck the straw between SuSu's swollen lips. "Drink now. Doctor said you have to have lots of fluids, whether you want them or not." When SuSu obeyed, still leaking tears, Miz McIntyre looked at her in indictment. "Would you look at you. Why in this God's earth you let those boys tie you up, missy, is beyond me. Surely you could have gotten away. Always sniffin' around those boys. I told you no good would ever come of it.

You start with those boys this early, and you'll end up worse than your sister!"

I'd had enough. Outraged, I did something I had never done before in my life: I lashed out at a parent—not just any parent, my best friend's mother. "Don't you dare talk to her like that," I exclaimed, leaping to my feet. "This wasn't any more SuSu's fault than it was your fault that those robbers beat you up. How would you have liked it if your own mother had blamed you for that and said you could have gotten away?"

Stunned, Miz McIntyre went almost purple. "Listen here, missy, what I say to my daughter and what I don't is my private affair, and none of your damn business. Why don't you just go home to that holier-than-thou mama of yours and ask her why she can't keep her legs together. Y'all aren't even Catholic."

"Mama!" SuSu wailed, sitting up. Her back was striped with purple welts.

"I'm going," I said to Miz McIntyre, "but I'm coming back, as much as I want to, because I love SuSu." I reached out to my friend, knowing the wounds her mother inflicted were far worse than anything Larry Bentley had done to her. "I love you, SuSu, and it's not your fault." I glared at Miz McIntyre. "Your mama can say that, but it's not true. You never deserved any of this. It's not your fault."

I ran for the door, but couldn't get past the locked wrought iron. My eyes blurred by tears, I searched the living room for the key and found it on the dresser. I fumbled with the lock, then finally shoved the door open with a clang and ran all the way home.

I didn't tell anybody what had happened, not even Cathy. I just got out my copy of *The Count of Monte Cristo* and lost myself in a world where wrongs were all made right.

After that, Miz McIntyre and I never had much use for each other, but SuSu and I were closer than ever. We never mentioned that day again. It was a terrible secret that bound us in shame and sympathy. And it was the reason I always forgave her, no matter what.

15

A Picture's Worth a Thousand Words, but Videotapes Are Better

The law offices of Atchison, White, Bray, et al. Downtown Atlanta. Thursday, March 28, 2002. 10:00 A.M.

*I*N HONOR OF THE AUSPICIOUS OCCASION, WE ALL WORE OUR most dignified purple with our most tasteful red hats for moral support when we went with Diane to present The Evidence. She'd made us swear to bear mute witness only (Linda had pad and pen ready to take down the minutes), but it remained to be seen if we could make good on our promise of silence. My bet was against it, but we could always hope.

So there we sat in the elegant reception area's leather wing-backed chairs, perched like a flock of color-crazed peacocks, as taut with anticipation as I could ever remember being. Each of us held primly on our laps either files or boxes of audio- and video-tapes or neatly labeled computer diskettes. It was an impressive amount of ammunition, and we were feeling mighty full of ourselves. Until Teeny broke the atmosphere of grave resolution with a stifled hiccup.

"Oh, y'all," she murmured, stricken. "I can't believe this." She barely got her mouth closed before another one exploded inside her with the truncated sound of a distant cherry bomb in the bathroom pipes at high school.

"I thought you quit those when Reid . . ." I didn't need to add the "beat you up." Ironic, that her hiccups would come back here, of all places, the very spot where they'd left her. I couldn't help wondering if they'd lain dormant here all these years, just waiting to ambush her.

Another stifled explosion set her little body awrench.

"Oooh," SuSu whispered. "That was an eight, eight." With typical adolescent insensitivity, we used to rank Teeny's hiccups for decibel level and weirdness.

Teeny's big eyes went even wider. "Oh, no." She started to rise, handing me her box of evidence. "Maybe I should just leave."

"Don't be silly." Diane grabbed her arm and urged her back into her seat. "I want you here, even with the hiccups, and that's that."

Affection warred with embarrassment in Teeny's face. Just as she opened her lips to reply, another hiccup escaped with a loud pop, drawing amused glances from the three already curious men who shared the waiting room. Teeny clapped both hands over her mouth, mortified. She motioned for Linda's pen and pad.

Linda handed them over, doing her best to conceal her amusement, but not succeeding.

"Maybe it's this place," Teeny wrote in her perfect, elegant script. "The last time I was here was for all that mess with Reid."

"Oh, honey." Diane frowned with real concern. "I never even thought." She patted Teeny's leg. "Do you *want* to leave?" she asked softly, " 'cause if you do, I'll understand."

You could tell Teeny was torn, but she shook her head in denial as she wrote, "If y'all can stand it, I'd like to stay."

SuSu laughed. "Great. I'll get you some sugar packets from the receptionist"—our not-always-foolproof cure—"but if they don't work, we shall continue to rank you, just for old time's sake."

Teeny risked a brief grin, then clamped her lips tight just in time to stifle a prodigious *glurk*.

One of the businessmen, clearly dying to know what was up

with our outfits and boxes of evidence, tried to strike up a polite conversation so he could pump us, but we were too keyed up to suffer males at all, so we cut him off quicker than a debutante can say no to a half-carat engagement ring.

Teeny managed to swallow several more hiccups while SuSu was going for the sugar, but the process left her looking a little green around the gills. Once she got the sugar and left it to dissolve on her tongue, we didn't hear any more for a while and hoped she was cured.

When the receptionist opened the door to the back office and invited Diane in for her appointment, we all stood as one—our posture, even SuSu's, rigid as an honor guard's—and carried in the fruit of our hard work and devious minds.

On the way to Tom Atchison's office, a muffled *skreek* from Teeny told us the sugar hadn't worked.

Tom rose in obvious surprise when we crowded his office and deposited our sacred burdens on his enormous leather-topped desk. "Well, good mornin', ladies," he said in a gratingly condescending tone. "Diane didn't tell me she was bringing her whole bridge club with her."

Teeny hiccupped again, but we all ignored the interruption—except Tom, who cocked his head and frowned.

"We're not the bridge club," SuSu said sweetly. "We're the Red Hats, and the only game we play is kick-ass, for keeps."

"Ah-hah." His expression glazed. "Well, if we'd known you were coming, we'd have set up in the conference room." Can we say *territoriality?* "You caught us with our pants down," he said in a bizarrely ironic choice of words, considering our mission. It warmed the cockles of my heart to hear the likes of glib Tom Atchison stick his foot in his mouth as bad as I ever had.

He turned his best good ole boy charm on Diane. "We can still move. Simple enough."

Diane arched an eyebrow. "Oh, Tom, thanks so much, but I think we'll do better here than in the conference room." It was a subtle pissing contest, but she left no doubt who was in charge.

His unctuous expression congealed. He picked up the phone and punched a button. "Charlotte, we need three more chairs in here, please. Right away." He hung up. "While we're waiting, may I offer you ladies any diet drinks, sodas, coffee?" He looked at Teeny. "Bottled water?"

We all declined as the hapless Charlotte arrived lugging the first two chairs, which were clearly too heavy, but Tom made no move to help her. Linda and Diane relieved her of them, so we lacked only one. We all remained standing, though, and I could tell the others were enjoying keeping Tom on his feet as much as I was. I just love making self-important people uncomfortable.

Already, I couldn't stand the man, but Diane had picked him for his rottweiler reputation, not for his personality.

Teeny's next hiccup was so powerful, her eyes fluttered, and the sound of somebody strangling a rabbit escaped her nostrils.

"That was a double niner," SuSu whispered.

When the dutiful Charlotte returned with the last chair, we all sat. Always the gentleman, Tom made sure we were comfortable before he resumed his seat.

"All right, then." He craned his neck briefly, unconsciously adjusting the perfect knot in his tasteful tie as he scooted closer to his desk. Then he surveyed the boxes and accordion files we'd brought. "What have we here?"

"Evidence. We'll start with this." Diane handed him the thickest of the regular files she'd been holding. "The anonymous cover letter inside explains it all. Those are microfiche reproductions of all the checks and statements for Harold's secret bank accounts."

Tom shot her a look of surprise, then zeroed in on the contents of the file.

"As you'll see," she continued, "he has accumulated more than two million in cash. God knows how much more he has in non-liquid investments, but we didn't have the resources to search for those. Not a cent of that cash, by the way, has been reported to his Social Security number. He's listed the accounts under several numbers I don't recognize—none of them his mistress's; we checked. I would imagine he 'borrowed' them from some rich, comatose trust clients whose estates he's managing." A trace of bitterness had crept into her voice on the last, but she regained her control by reverting to the cold facts. "His secret assets are far larger than his salary or the meager returns from our retirement accounts. I'll explain where he got them in a minute." She paused for impact, and it was sweet.

Tom looked like somebody had just told him his wife was sleeping with another woman (which she was, by the way). His eyes widened, and his perfectly chiseled mouth dropped slightly open in amazement even as his lawyer's brain went into high gear. He started flipping through the pages, rapid-fire.

"I've made notations on all the checks he wrote that pertain to his mistress: clothes, gifts, appliances, entertainment, travel, hotels." All those "business trips" he'd taken while Diane was home eating soup and clipping coupons. It made my blood boil afresh. "Plus the expenses for the condo where he's keeping her. As you can see from the totals, he spent more than two hundred thousand last year alone."

Teeny squeaked, sending Linda and SuSu into silent paroxysms.

Diane remained composed. "He bought the condo through one of his so-called businesses four years ago, right before we moved back here from Nashville. There's a copy of the deed in there, too. We did a thorough title search, and there's no record of a lien, so I suspect he paid cash." She paused, cocking her head. "That was an interstate transaction. Could we get him on RICO?"

"Oh, that's good." Teeny said, in spite of the risk of opening her mouth. "Money laundering with his ill-gotten gains. Why didn't we think of that?"

Tom glanced up sharply. "We?"

"We," we all said in unison. Yummy, but this was fun!

He resumed scanning the pages. "Where did you get these, Diane?"

She lied with the calm believability of a cloistered nun. "I received them in the mail, in a plain envelope with no return address."

He shot her a streetwise, skeptical look, then continued assessing the orderly progression of the file. "Do you still have it?" he asked without looking up. "The envelope."

"No." And the only prints on the file's contents were Diane's. We'd made sure of that. "I was so shocked when I read the cover letter"—anonymous, printed out at a computer café on the other side of town—"that I inadvertently tossed the envelope in the trash."

He looked up, all legal eagle now. "How can you be sure these are actually his accounts? His name's not on them anywhere."

"No." She pushed a neat little box of labeled floppy diskettes to the center of his suede blotter. "But the records for all of them were in his private accounting files, which I copied onto these."

Arrogant Harold had been so confident of Diane's computer ignorance that he'd left his passwords on a slip of paper in his desk drawer, even the ones to his Palm Pilot. I couldn't wait to see his reaction when he discovered what underestimating his faithful wife was going to cost him.

"Oh, and I have the originals and copies of everything you see here in a safe place that only the Red Hats know," Diane concluded.

Tom leaned back in his chair, regarding her with a mixture of awe, shock, and admiration. "Christ. And I thought you were just another little housewife."

SuSu colored up and leaned forward to challenge his condescending remark, but Linda silenced her with hard pinch, a scowl, and an emphatic shake of her head.

Clearly, it jolted Tom to glimpse the goddess beneath Diane's innocuous exterior, so much so that he let down his guard and muttered, "Makes me wonder what *my* faithful little wife's been doing."

"As well you should," Diane replied in a masterpiece of understatement.

Teeny hiccupped, her eyes rolling upward in humiliation, but Diane got right back to business. "The computer itself is in my car. He purchased it with our joint credit card. Am I correct in assuming that makes it a joint marital asset that I can dispose of as I see fit?"

"You are," Tom confirmed with a new respect.

She handed him one of the two slim ring binders she'd been holding, marked AFFAIR: AUDIO, VIDEO LOGS, then pushed the smaller box of videotapes, audiotapes, and photographs forward. "As for the mistress, we've documented their illicit activities on dated video and audio tapes and photographs. The annotated logs for those are in that notebook."

He opened one of the captioned photo albums and scanned through our pictures of Harold being ravaged in plain view inside his secret condo. Tom tried to cover the fact that the explicit pictures turned him on, but when he continued to look them over far longer than necessary, we all knew he was getting a hard-on.

Typical.

At long last, he closed the album, then briefly inspected the tapes. "Who did these for you?"

"We did," we all answered again.

"Oh, and I've already transferred all our remaining joint assets into my name, so he can't do any more damage than he already has." Harold wasn't the only one who could play dirty. "Since it would put you, as an officer of the court, in an awkward position to know how I did it, I won't burden you with that information."

"That's sensible, but I have to tell you, it isn't strictly legal," he admonished.

"Oh, dear," she said without a drop of remorse. "I thought it was."

He poked through the evidence, then looked over the notebook entries. When he closed it, he leaned back in his chair. "Pardon my French, ladies, but damn." He shook his head, really seeing us for the first time. "You should work for the CIA. In thirty-eight years of practice, I've never had anybody walk in and hand me such a big stick."

"Actually," Diane said, "the documentation of the affair is of very little consequence." She laid a hand on the row of accordion files. "But these"—she smiled beatifically—"these are my ace in the hole."

"I'm almost afraid to ask," Tom said. "Y'all are pretty scary."

SuSu had set a world's record for keeping quiet, but that last little bit of male chauvinism was all it took to pop her cork. "That tears it! Would you listen to him? 'Little housewife,' 'little wife,' 'Y'all are pretty scary!' I told you to let us find you a woman lawyer. He clearly has a male bias!"

Tom puffed up like a quail. "See here, I have no such thing."

Teeny hiccupped, but we were all long past taking notice.

"Oh, hush up, SuSu," Diane said without heat. "Of course he has male bias—he's got a pecker, hasn't he? But that hasn't kept him from nailing an impressive number of errant Buckaroos. He's my choice. Tradition Five."

She turned to Tom, her hand still on the accordion files. "As I was saying, these files contain duplicates of the contents of Harold's briefcase for the last two months, compiled and cross-referenced by specific illegal acts both Harold and the bank committed. I made the copies every night after he went to sleep." She pushed the larger box of diskettes, audio-, and videotapes toward him. "And these are his related computer files, plus video- and audiotapes I recorded while we were sharing our evening cocktails."

She heaved a cleansing breath. "The only thing he ever talked about anymore was business—including professional monkey business—so I figured I might as well take advantage of that. All he needed was a couple of doubles and an adoring audience"— she batted her eyelashes—"and he couldn't wait to brag about what he and the bank were getting away with."

Her features hardened as she handed him the other notebook

she'd been holding. "Everything is logged and cross-referenced. He talks openly about the bank's illegally withholding trust funds to inflate their cash assets, as well as numerous other personal and institutional crimes. And you'll note that at the beginning of each tape, I ask him if he minds my turning on the tape, and he says no." She smiled. "Of course, he may have misinterpreted that to mean I was turning on the music, but that's his affair, pun intended."

Tom looked over The Evidence, practically hyperventilating. "If this is what you say it is, the man is nailed. Crucified. *And* the bank." He pinned her with a piercing stare. "What do you want from this? The way I see it, the sky's the limit."

She sobered. "Nothing so grand as that. I want the house, free and clear, and its contents; a top-of-the-line Buick of my choice, paid for"—she'd been patching up her old Mercedes since she'd inherited it from Harold ten years before—"a paid-up, million-dollar, twenty-year term policy on his life that I own, with me as the beneficiary; and five thousand a month alimony for life, whether I remarry or not." She rattled it off by heart, not missing a beat.

Sweet, sweet, sweet, sweet, sweet. I was tingling with righteous power from top to toe, as I know the others were. Even another hiccup couldn't wipe the smile off Teeny's face.

Diane went on, strength resonant in her voice. "As for the bank, all I want is for them to keep Harold on at whatever salary it takes to ensure that the judge will grant me the alimony. Plus an ironclad document guaranteeing that, should Harold leave the bank's employ for any reason, they will pay me the money direct, with a two-million-dollar bankruptcy-proof parachute if they fold."

Tom let out a low whistle.

"Oooh, Di, honey." SuSu spoke for us all. "We hadn't talked about those last little goodies. Too brilliant."

"I told you she could run a corporation," Teeny said with grinning admiration that let a giant chirp escape.

"Those terms are a stretch," Tom warned, "even under the circumstances. Will he fight this?"

"Not if he doesn't want to end up in prison," Diane answered with assurance. "Same for the bank."

Eyes glazed in thought, Tom spun his seat to stare unseeing past the pollen-hazed skyline. We all waited, hardly daring to breathe. Only a stifled *ga-lup* from Teeny broke the silence. When he swung back, he wore a sly, smug smile. "We'll walk a fine line on the sunny side of blackmail, but I can do it. Does he have an attorney?"

"Not yet."

"Would you prefer to enter into negotiations first or have him served, then work things out?"

"I want to serve him myself, as soon as possible," she said with grim resolution. "The Red Hats will be my witnesses."

Yesss! World Cup kick-ass!

"Works for me." Tom looked us over with almost as much respect as he'd accorded Diane. "I'll never think of a red hat the same again."

He rose, signaling that our time was up. "When you requested a contingency arrangement, I said we work only with a minimum pro-forma retainer of twenty thousand. But under the circumstances, I don't see why we couldn't make an exception. Shall we say twenty percent of the gross settlement, excluding the contents of the house? Harold pays, of course."

Diane met him eye to eye with a calm smile, fully aware that the more legal fees Harold had to pay, the more likely he was to balk at her settlement terms. "Tom, Tom, Tom. You said, yourself, we've given you the big stick. The mortgage on the house is almost three hundred thousand; ten percent of that alone is thirty thousand. For a few conferences and a little paperwork? You'll make out like a bandit. Do it for ten percent, and you've got a deal."

Tom tucked his chin, clearly taken aback at having a mere "little housewife" challenge his fee. Shark among sharks, he may be, but Diane was the Bargain Goddess, with thirty years of successful haggling under her belt. She wasn't about to pay retail, whether for bruised produce or nuclear-grade legal representation.

Fixing him with her warmest expression, she leaned over and started collecting the files and tape logs. "Of course, if that's not agreeable, I'll be forced to go elsewhere. No hard feelings, but I'd be disappointed." Her smile went wistful. "Everybody said you were the best, so naturally, you were my first choice. Still, I'm sure I can find someone quite competent who would be willing to meet my terms."

"A woman," SuSu couldn't resist, with a hostile glare at Tom.

Diane was right about the fees, and he couldn't deny it. We could see the wheels turning behind his eagle eyes. We'd already done all the hard part. The rest would be shootin' ducks in a barrel. Not to mention the fact that Tom would probably love to add this particular case to his résumé. It would make for great entertainment at the partners' meeting.

He spread his fingers, palms down, in a staying gesture. "Now, now. Nobody said we couldn't do it for ten." After another assessing pause, he offered to shake. "You've got a deal. Ten percent of the dollar value for the car, the house, and the premiums on the life insurance policy."

"Payable upon collection."

He conceded with a nod.

Victory!

Linda, scribbling away, noted the time on her watch.

"Done." Diane dried her hand discreetly on her skirt before she shook to seal the deal.

Teeny hiccupped.

Tom looked at his desk calendar. "I can have those papers ready by tomorrow afternoon. Say, three—three thirty?"

She turned to us. "Are y'all free tomorrow mornin' to pack Harold's stuff and deliver it to the condo after he leaves for work?"

Exhilarated, we all set our red hats bobbing in confirmation.

"If somebody else'll drive it," Linda offered, flapping her right hand to relieve the strain of writing furiously since we'd sat down, "we can use that honkin' big SUV of Brooks's."

Diane drew a stapled, folded set of papers from her purse and handed them to Tom. "Here's a complete inventory of Harold's personal belongings. The girls helped me go through everything. They can attest to the fact that I've held nothing back."

Tom shook his head. "Every *i* dotted, every *t* crossed. When this is all over, remind me to speak to you about a job with the firm," he said without a hint of sarcasm.

"I shall." Diane motioned us. "Come, ma girls. There's worlds yet to be beaten, and chocolate to be eaten. Éclairs are on me, and margaritas afterwards."

She walked out of that office a new woman. I wondered if Harold would even notice when he came home for the last night of his marriage. Probably not, but he'd notice tomorrow, boy oh boy.

Corporate offices of Harold's bank. Friday, March 29, 2002. 4:15 P.M.

We didn't wear our red hats to Judgment Day. Diane wisely decided we should keep a low profile at the bank, since she'd be needing their cooperation. So we dressed in discreet church outfits of shifts or slacks and blazers or two-piece silk ensembles.

When we got to the executive level of the parking garage downtown, Diane used her cell to call Harold's secretary, Shelley. "Hi, Shelley. Is Harold's Friday meeting on schedule?"

"Starts in thirty minutes," Shelley answered. "He's going over his report. Would you like to speak to him?"

"No. I'm on my way into the building. I'd like to surprise him, so don't say anything. Just make sure he doesn't go anywhere."

"Will do."

Diane hung up. "Shelley's a good egg. Too bad she has to put up with Harold."

For the second time in as many days, she swore us to silence, and we readily agreed. After all, this was her show, one she'd paid for with hard work and immeasurable heartache.

Harold was surprised to see us, all right, and more than a little annoyed. He rose from his desk. "Well, look who's here. What brings you ladies down?" Clearly it was a rhetorical question, because he barely paused before going on. "I'm afraid you caught me on my way out to an important weekly meeting, though. Bad timing. If you'd like to wait, we should be through by six thirty." He started for the door.

Smiling, Linda pushed it closed and leaned against it, blocking his way.

Harold's eyes sharpened.

"You have time," Diane said, taking his arm. "Shelley told me. But don't worry, this shouldn't take long." She steered him back to his chair. "Sit."

Wary now, he kept his eyes on Diane's triumphant face, lowering himself into the expensive executive chair as if he might find spikes in the seat.

"I have something I want to give you," she cooed. "A surprise. That's why we came down."

He eased, and I wanted to slap the smug expression off his face. "Now, I've told you," he patronized, "you don't have to give me presents."

"Oh, but I really, really want to give you this one. Close your eyes, and stick out your hand." Visibly impatient, he obliged.

We were loving this, savoring every second, as was Diane.

She reached into her purse and brought out the divorce papers. Then she laid them into his hand. "You can look now."

Linda aimed her digital camera to record the momentous occasion.

At first he frowned at it in confusion as the flash went off. But when he unfolded the document and read what it was, his usually pale complexion went ruddy. More flashes in rapid-fire succession. "And what the hell is this?"

"I've filed for divorce, Harold. The jig is up. I found out about your condo and your bimbo and all your dirty tricks, and I documented everything, including pictures of your mistress mounting you on the sofa. Pity, it looked like she had to do all the work."

Instantly, Harold's internal blast doors slammed, and every muscle in his body tensed.

"All those boozy conversations we had over cocktails?" she gloated, "I videotaped them. And I copied the contents of your briefcase for months. I also have your home computer. It sure was obliging of you to leave all your passwords where I could find them."

Bull's-eye. A shard of panic glinted in his hooded stare.

"And if you're thinking of hiding all your ill-gotten gains, I'd think again. My lawyer has all the account numbers, plus the bogus socials, and high-level connections with the IRS. A word from him or me, and everything's frozen. We're talking ruin. Prison. Which is not what either of us wants." Diane sat on the corner of his desk and smiled down at him.

Harold didn't move, just stared at her with soulless hatred.

She slid his gold letter opener behind his tie, then flicked it loose. "Actually, I'm not asking for much. Nothing inspired: just the house, a new car, decent alimony, a life insurance policy on you. It's only fair, considering that I put you through law school, not to mention all the money I made us on the renovation in Nashville, plus the money I saved pinching pennies all these years."

She paused to enjoy his reaction, but when it came, it was almost an anticlimax. We might have known he'd admit nothing, much less grovel. Harold tucked in his tie, then leaned back in his chair. "Di, I'm sure we can work this out. Nothing that's happened has changed the way I feel about you. You're my wife. I love you."

"Oh, but this *has* changed the way *I* feel about *you*," she said with quiet vehemence. "I don't love you anymore. And I never will, not after seeing you for who you really are."

"You're upset, deservedly so," he weaseled, "but this is no place to discuss it. Let's talk about it back at the house, after my meeting. Just the two of us."

She posed like a Kewpie doll, her fingertip pressing an imaginary dimple into her cheek. "Oh, I'm afraid that won't be possible. You see, you don't live there anymore. We moved all your stuff to the condo this morning, right down to your Sigma Chi shot glasses. And I had the locks changed."

Harold flared, his façade slipping. "That's illegal!"

"*You* want to talk to *me* about illegal?" She wagged her finger at him. "We got to the condo after eleven, but I'm afraid we woke your little friend Shae. I guess she sleeps late; all that night work." Diane crossed her legs and leaned forward. "She was a little upset at first, but when I explained that you were moving in with her and I was giving you a divorce so y'all could get married, she really brightened up." It had been glorious to behold. Diane's gracious solicitude had cooked Harold's goose with his mistress, big-time. "I wished you both all the luck in the world, now that you're free."

That tore it. Harold closed his eyes and dropped his forehead to the blotter. "Fuckin' goddamn hell."

Only then did Diane harden. She stood. "Look at me, Harold."

Seconds passed before he did, but he said nothing when he faced her, his expression shielded.

"I want to be very clear about this," she said coldly. "You can cut your losses and give me what I ask for, or we can go to war. But if you fight this, you're out of a job, the IRS and the DA are on to you, and the bank is in deep shit with the OCC."

Too sweet!

Hatred flared afresh in his eyes. "What if I tell you to go to hell?"

Diane sighed. "I'd take you with me, but I'm not the one on the hot seat. We're talking prison, here. Major fraud, you and the bank. Tax evasion. Hard evidence that's not only with my attorney, but also duplicated in a safe place so if anything happens to me, it goes to the DA and the press."

She shook her head. "You're slick, Harold, but not slick enough to slide out of this." Her tone went weary. "And you're nobody's fool. My way, we both win: You keep most of the loot, and I get what's fair. Fight it, and we both lose. It's as simple as that."

He gave the first sign of relenting. "Who's handling the negotiations?"

"Tom Atchison, of Atchison and White, et al. Who'll handle your end?"

"I don't know. Maybe just me." He twisted his chin defensively. "I am a lawyer, you know."

"I ought to," she responded coolly. "I put you through school."

We were all aware of what they say about a lawyer who represents himself, but it occurred to me, considering the nature of his crimes, that Harold might not want anybody else to find out about the bodies buried in his basement.

He stood. It was an excruciatingly awkward moment. Then he extended his hand to the woman he had defrauded and betrayed. "No hard feelings."

The monumental insensitivity of that gesture was all it took to reignite Diane's fire. She glared at his hand, then back to her soon-to-be ex-husband. "Oh, but there are hard feelings. Believe it."

Then she turned and led the way out of the office.

SuSu couldn't resist a parting shot. "Personally, I voted for putting your ass in prison."

Linda snapped another photo just as Harold hurled his desk set at us. "Get out!"

When we reached the deserted parking garage, Linda finally let loose. "Diane, you were a goddess. It was perfect. Absolutely perfect. Every jilted woman in the world wants to be you."

Diane sagged, the tension of the last two months breaking at last with tears. "It wasn't great. It was awful. Awful." She bent over, bracing her hands on her knees. "I think I'm gonna throw up."

"Oh, spare me," SuSu countered. "That's just your Southern brainwashin' talking! 'Be sweet, now, sugah,'" she aped in an exaggerated drawl. "We all know how far *that* got us!"

"Damn straight!" I said. "All those 'bad girl' feelin's are a lie from the pit of hell, perpetrated by men and passed on by women who didn't know any better. Don't you dare let them rob you of this triumph."

"Are we Miss Mellys?" SuSu challenged.

"No!" Teeny and Linda and I yelled, our voices echoing in the almost deserted concrete caverns.

Diane straightened, managing a lopsided smile through her tears.

"Do we feel bad about bringing that rotten snake to justice?" Linda hollered in her best cheerleader form.

"No!" we all, including Diane, answered.

"Are we Red Hat goddesses?" SuSu shouted, fist upthrust.

"Yes!"

"Can you give me a 'hell yes'?"

Diane straightened, wiping away her tears as the spunk returned to her expression, tempered by grief over the death of her happily-ever-after illusions.

"Hell, yes!" It came out *"hail*, yes" as we slipped back into our girlhood drawls.

"Let me hear ya say amen," Linda roared in classic Hosea Williams style, not caring who heard her.

"Amen, sister!" Teeny hollered. "Preach it!"

She pointed to Diane. "Are you gonna be better than ever without him?"

"Yes," Diane responded, her conviction softened by doubt.

Linda looked to us. "Did y'all hear anything?"

"No!"

She asked her again, louder. "Are you gonna be better than ever without him?"

"Yes!" Diane hollered back, releasing some of her pent-up anger.

Linda cupped her ear. "I can't *hear* you."

"Yes, dammit!" Diane exploded. "I'm gonna be great!"

"You're gonna have all the drawers and closets to yourself!" SuSu chimed in.

Teeny raised her hands to heaven. "Hallelujah!"

"And the toilet seat will always be down!" I added.

"And you can fart as loud as you like," Teeny hollered at surprising volume, "whenever and wherever!"

We all laughed, including Diane.

"And the remote is yours, baby!" SuSu crowed. "Yours! No more flippin' through a hundred channels at every commercial!"

"Amen!" Diane answered with a grin.

Linda bounced in her sensible Aerosoles. "And when you clean your house, it'll stay clean!"

"Yeah!" Diane got into the rhythm. "And I never have to stink up my kitchen with turnip greens or collards again!" She hated them both, but she'd cooked them for thirty years because they were Harold's favorites. "And I can eat what I like, when I like. Lamb chops every week!" Her favorite, which she never made because Harold couldn't stand them.

A disembodied female voice from the far side of the garage shouted over, "Yeah! And you'll never have to 'do it' unless you want to!"

We all applauded, cheered, whistled, and hopped.

Another woman chimed in from the level above us. "And you can skip supper and turn in at seven if you're tired!"

We cheered again.

"Bettah than evah," SuSu sang out in a dead-on imitation of Candice Bergen in *Starting Over*, one of our favorite movies.

Linda formed a chorus line with Teeny and me as we all joined in. "Yeah, I'm bettah than evah!" Diane sang out at the top of her tone-deaf lungs, and we made our way to Brooks's giant SUV with a progression of middle-aged knee-kicks.

It had definitely been a red-letter Red Hat couple of days. Make that months.

Rosy and exhilarated, we piled into the car. "Okay," Linda said. "Where to? And home is not an option."

"It's your call," Teeny told Diane.

"How 'bout some serious comfort food?" she answered. "And some luscious dessert?"

"Cheesecake Factory?" SuSu suggested.

I shook my head. "Buckhead Diner."

They all brightened.

"Perfect." Linda put the car in gear.

SuSu peered around the front seat at Diane as we headed for Peachtree. "And then?"

"And then, we wait," Diane said with quiet confidence. She frowned. "I have a big favor to ask y'all now."

Teeny took her hand. "Anything, honey."

"Can we not talk about the Harold thing anymore unless I bring it up?" The pain in her eyes was enough to convince us. "When I have something to tell y'all, I will. I'm just tired of thinking about it." She scanned us, her brow furrowed. "Understand?"

"Of course," Linda said, ever our fearless leader. "As long as you know that you can call on us, any time of the day or night."

"Deal." Diane's smile was bittersweet. "Now let's get some of those divine mashed potatoes and chicken."

And so, the big wait began.

Like it or not, the ball was in Harold's court.

16

T Minus Thirty-Six and Counting

Swan Coach House. Tuesday, April 9, 2002. 11:30 A.M.

ELEVEN DAYS LATER, WE MET AT THE COACH HOUSE FOR OUR regular April meeting. We were all dying to know how things were going with Harold, but we'd honored Diane's request and hadn't asked her a single question about it in the few times anyone had talked to her. Linda was worried that she'd holed up in a funk, spiraling down into depression, drinking too much, and gorging on junk food.

If it had been me, Linda's assessment would have been right on the money, but Diane was one of those people who ate to live, not the other way around, and she was way too much of a control freak to enjoy getting high, much less drunk.

Still, I told Linda that Diane would be well justified in taking to her bed for a while, junk food and alcoholic anesthesia included. As long as she came out eventually, which she'd promised she would.

Sure enough, she'd arrived at 11:08 in her red hat, tailored deep purple blouse, and rich purple paisley challis skirt. Her expression and manner were understandably subdued, but otherwise, she seemed as normal as you please—no extra weight or signs of hangover.

Curdling with curiosity while we waited for SuSu (she still hadn't perfected the punctuality thing), we honored our promise and didn't ask.

"Oh, yeah!" My memory jogged me. "Y'all will never guess what I found." I rooted in my purse for the tiny plastic bag that held my long-lost treasure. I located it between the Dentine Ice and a two-year-old gynecologist's appointment card. "Look!" I waved the tiny bag before them, then opened it and grasped the corners of the tiny black enameled harlequin's mask, the alpha pin hanging by its tiny chain.

"Ohmygod." Linda reached out to touch it with the reverence one would afford a religious relic. "Your Mademoiselle pin."

"It was in the bottom of my old jewelry box," I said, mellow with nostalgia. "I was cleaning it out to put in the neighborhood garage sale, and there it was. My senior ring, too. And John's."

Teeny took it from my hand. "Would you look at that."

"What about y'all?" I asked. "Do you still have yours?"

Diane and Linda shook their heads. "Half my old jewelry disappeared in that last move," Linda said. "Brooks and I were certain one of the movers took it, but the police didn't even bother to follow up."

Teeny passed the pin to Diane. "I still have mine. I've kept it close as a talisman of the happiest time of my life." Wheels were turning behind her bright blue eyes, but about what, I couldn't imagine.

Diane held the little mask with gentle fingers. "I lost mine at Vandy, freshman year. Somebody came into my room and hid my dresser drawers all over the dorm. At first, I thought it was just a prank. It was easy enough to find all the drawers but the one with my jewelry, and sure enough, when it turned up in the basement the next day, my eighteen-carat gold watch, my gold charm bracelet, my great-grandmother's lavaliere, and all my pins and earrings were missing."

She'd probably told us about it at least three or four times, but thanks to my middle-aged memory meltdown, it was news to me.

"Aaaanh!" Linda sounded a buzzer as the pleasant glow of nostalgia began to fade. "Sad memory alert. Bummer."

"Sorry, y'all." Diane colored. "I didn't mean to be a drag. Fifty lashes with a wet blanket for me."

Subdued, we made small talk until SuSu arrived at eleven twenty with great commotion, as usual.

As she settled into her designated spot, Diane sharpened. "Whose turn is it to tell the joke?" she asked with an eagerness I noted.

SuSu raised her hand. "Me." Without so much as a preliminary or a drop of caffeine, she jumped right in. "Okay. This guy has been marooned on a tropical island, all alone, for ten long years. Then one day, he sees something dark in the water, coming toward the beach. At first, he thinks it's only a dolphin or a shark, but as it nears the shore, lo and behold, he discovers that it's a scuba diver in a wetsuit. And when the diver finally rises to wade ashore and takes off the hood of the wetsuit, he sees that she's a gorgeous blonde, built like a brick shithouse."

Linda interrupted, fluffing up. "Wait a minute. We outlawed dumb-blonde jokes five years ago."

"This is not a dumb-blonde joke," SuSu said, exasperated. She paused, her continuity blown. (Fragmented as she was, it never took much to derail her.) "Now look what you made me do," she complained. "I lost my place."

Diane came to the rescue. "He sees that the diver is a gorgeous blonde."

"Oh, yeah." SuSu resumed her dramatic rendition. "Dumbstruck, he falls to his knees. The blonde comes over and drops her tanks beside him.

" 'Hi,' she says, eyeing his long hair and beard and ragged clothes. 'How long has it been since you've had a cigarette?'

" 'Ten years!' he says.

"She unzips a waterproof pocket in her sleeve and pulls out a pack of fresh cigarettes and a lighter, then hands them over.

"He lights one, takes a deep drag, and says, 'Man, oh man, is that good!'

"Then she asks him, 'How long has it been since you've had any whiskey?'

" 'Ten years!' he says.

"She reaches over to the other arm and unzips another water-proof pocket and pulls out a silver flask and gives it to him.

"The guy takes a long swig, then says, 'Wow! That's fantastic.'

"Then she starts to unzip the long zipper that goes all the way to the crotch of her wetsuit and asks, 'How long has it been since you've had any *real* fun?' "

" 'My God,' the man replies. 'Don't tell me you've got golf clubs in there, too!' "

There was a longer than usual pulse of silence, followed by laughter from me and Teeny. (Hold the presses! She actually got it, again!) Groans escaped from Linda and Diane.

"Boo." Linda signaled a thumbs-down. "We outlawed golf jokes, too."

"No, we didn't." SuSu held up three fingers and ticked them off as she reminded us, "We only outlawed woman-bashing jokes, which includes the blondes, man-bashing jokes—unless they're absolutely hysterical—and racial humor."

"She's right," I confirmed. "The golf jokes ban was proposed, but died for lack of a second." As a matter of fact, Linda the golf-hater had been the only one who'd wanted to exclude them, but discretion kept me from reminding her.

Killing two conversational birds with one stone, I shifted my attention to Diane. "So, now that the joke's out of the way, let's hear your big news."

We were all hoping the same thing.

She colored slightly, tucking her chin for a shy, Princess Di smile. "How could you tell?"

"You asked who had the joke," I explained. "Nobody ever asks who has the joke unless she's got something important to tell us afterwards."

"Yeah," SuSu agreed. "Why do you think I told it without so much as a sip of iced tea to wake me up and wet my whistle?"

Diane was clearly torn between triumph and tragedy as she announced, "Well, Harold signed day before yesterday, and so did the bank. All we asked for."

We clapped and cheered—politely, in deference to our surroundings.

"We need to have one hell of a celebration," SuSu declared. Her final decree party had been legendary. We'd had a long, elegant dinner at the Ritz Buckhead, followed by rafting in the Hooch (insanely reckless). Then we'd stayed up all night, swimming in Linda's pool, drinking Bloody Marys, and man-bashing. "When's the big day?"

"Tom got us on the docket for May fourteenth," Diane said. "Harold won't even be there, thank God." She exhaled heavily, a small, disbelieving smile on her lips. "May fourteenth, I will be a free woman, literally, figuratively, and financially."

"Harold didn't counter with a confidentiality clause?" Linda wondered aloud. We'd fully expected him to.

"No. He had a fool for a client," Diane joked, warming. "But the bank did, which I could understand perfectly. Once I agreed to that one thing, they couldn't settle fast enough. Tom was practically Snoopy-dancin'."

"May fourteenth . . ." Something about that date niggled in my brain. "Why does that ring a bell?"

Beneath the brims of our red straw hats, foreheads wrinkled and perfectly waxed brows lowered in concentration.

"I know!" True to form, it was our genius numbers person, Linda, who remembered. "Mademoiselle initiation. May fourteenth, 1965."

"Ohmygod," SuSu crowed well above the decibel level for ladylike communication. "That's it."

"Thirty-six years ago," Linda calculated instantly without even straining.

"Pure cosmic harmonic convergence," SuSu rhapsodized, "that it falls on that very day."

Teeny, eyes narrowed, laid her hand on Diane's. "I want to throw the party this time," she said. "We can do it instead of our regular meeting. We'll start out at the club." (The Piedmont Driving Club, of course.) "I have a very special theme in mind."

"How much fun could we have there?" SuSu was so ungracious as to gripe.

"Oh, I think you'll be surprised," Teeny said, delicious secrets dancing in her baby blues. "Wear red—no prints, just red. Dressy. You'll want to look your best. And afterwards, the five of us will adjourn to a very special place for a very special ceremony."

"Long as it's not a church," SuSu said, "I'm in."

A shockingly wicked laugh escaped Teeny. "Oh, it's definitely not a church." She took a sip of her water. "And that's all I'm gonna tell y'all, so don't even bother to ask me any more about it."

"That's thirty-six days from now," Linda whined. "Not even a hint?"

Teeny grinned with uncharacteristic malice. "Not even a hint. But I promise, you won't be disappointed."

17

Diane's D-Day Celebration: Surprise, Surprise, Surprise

Muscogee Drive. Tuesday, May 14, 2002. 8:00 P.M.

*B*ESIDE MYSELF WITH ANTICIPATION, I COULD NO LONGER SIT and wait. Girdled and gussied to the max, I paced our modest living room in my elegant new red Vera Wang–rip-off column dress. Its sheer, open tunic billowed, setting the pattern of exquisite opaque Chinese mums in motion. Even with 60 percent off, the two-piece silk ensemble had set me back three hundred dollars, but SuSu had assured me it was very slimming, and the usually sadistic mirrors at Saks had grudgingly admitted that it made me look better than I had since the early eighties. Who can resist timeless elegance that erases twenty pounds and sets the complexion aglow? Not me.

So I'd committed the guilty splurge, compounded by a ninety-dollar pair of gorgeous but dangerous stiletto heels. I'd be lucky to get through the evening without a broken ankle, but they looked so good and really showed off my still-shapely calves.

My overnight bag sat ready by the door.

I looked at my watch for the jillionth time, my punctuality fetish flivering inside me like cold water on a red-hot griddle—8:03 P.M. Not getting there too early was one thing; this was SuSu late.

Teeny had arranged for a stretch limo to pick us all up, insisting that we use it so we wouldn't "get there too early and spoil the surprise." When we'd protested the expense to her, she'd amazed us all by confessing that she'd charged it to Reid's corporate gold card, along with the entire cost of the party. (We're talking thousands; even small shindigs don't come cheap at the PDC.) Thrilled by such daring, we'd heartily congratulated her and accepted the limo.

I paused. Surely the driver wouldn't have been silly enough to pick SuSu up before they came for me . . . Nah. My deliberate stiletto-steps resumed in annoyance.

John lowered the *AJC* (*Atlanta Journal-Constitution* newspaper, for you nonnatives) with a scowl. "Good Lord, Georgia, calm down. You'd think you were a finalist waiting for the scores at Miss America."

A typically male-chauvinist scenario.

He set aside the paper and got up, clearly resentful of the break in his after-dinner routine. "Let me fix you a drink before you drive me nuts."

I glared at him, reminded that the term *hysterectomy* originated with male doctors who decided they could "cure" any woman who dared to complain about her life or get depressed by removing her "hysteria" along with her reproductive organs.

With John, it was always a drink or two "to settle my nerves," firmly offered and obediently accepted. Until that night of Diane's D-Day celebration.

"I do not want or need a drink," I snapped, taking him aback. "I want that bleemin' limousine to get here and take me to the party."

Visibly annoyed by my disruption in the way things were supposed to go, he went to the front windows and peered across our tiny front yard to the shaded street beyond. "Thank goodness." He let the blind drop. "They just turned the corner."

I checked my teeth for lipstick in the little mirror by the front door. None there, but with bright red lipstick, you can never let your guard down. I'd had quite a time finding a warm red shade that wasn't harshly bluish or brownish, but the subtly frosted long-lasting scarlet flattered my middle-aged lips and didn't bleed into the tiny cracks around them. "Do I look okay?" I asked him one more time, hating myself for doing it. Why wasn't what my own eyes told me ever enough?

Even my need for his approval got on his nerves; his frown deepened as he looked me over without really seeing me. "I told you, you look great." There was no sincerity in his words, only irritation, and suddenly I realized it had been that way for far too long. Since he'd turned fifty, he hadn't been the same. It was like his soul had sprung a leak, and all the life, the caring, had drained out of him.

I stared at him, trying to shake off the ominous sinking feeling that realization gave me.

The doorbell rang. Still frowning, John opened the door to a uniformed limo driver who looked like a Chippendales dancer, only taller.

The driver removed his cap and flashed me a grin of approval. "Wow. Don't you look gorgeous tonight, Miz Baker."

Puffing up like a toad-frog, John glared at the guy, then finally really looked at me with a satisfying glint of jealousy. "When are you going to be back?"

We went through this every time I left him alone, even for a few hours. Never mind that he was gone at least three nights a week; he pouted like a kid whenever the shoe was on the other foot. I'd accepted it as part of his nature for years, feeling guilty every time, but tonight, for some reason, it really got on my nerves. "Teeny didn't tell us," I said without a whiff of apology. "Tomorrow. Maybe the next day. I'll call."

The driver took my bag from John's hand. "My name is Drew, Miz Baker. I'm your driver for tonight." He granted John a brief, diffident smile. "Don't worry, sir. I'll take *real* good care of her."

John tucked his chin at the suggestive double entendre, but said nothing.

Good. Maybe seeing another man pay attention to me might wake him up a little.

"Bye." I stepped past my husband, deliberately omitting my faithful good-bye peck, and walked alongside muscular Drew. I didn't look back.

Tonight, I was gonna have *fun*. "Let's hit the road," I said to the stud-puppy driver. "The party's waitin'."

Drew grinned at me. "You ladies are gonna knock their socks off." He opened the limo door, releasing a heady combination of SuSu's Giorgio and Linda's custom-blended floral scent. They *had* picked SuSu up before me. I got in, adding my Chanel No. 5 to the mix, and started the long slide to the bar at the front.

Linda and SuSu looked fabulous, SuSu in an elegant orangey-red sequined sheath that showed off her still-gorgeous legs, and Linda in a flattering scarlet silk jacquard three-piece ensemble with an artfully draped swag of a jacket. Her impressive diamond suite set the whole thing sparkling.

I whistled. "Wow, the Red Hats are red hot tonight!" I employed my Billy Crystal–as–Fernando Lamas accent. "You look *mah*-velous."

"So do you!" Linda fingered the almost transparent silk between my tunic's chrysanthemums. "This is so you, classic, elegant, but with great cachet."

"Thanks for making me buy it." I glanced at my dress Timex. "I thought y'all would pick up Diane first. After all, she's the honoree."

Linda shrugged. "Teeny gave Drew specific instructions to get SuSu first, then me, then you, then Diane, last."

"Man, she *really* didn't want us getting there too soon." I helped myself to some phyllo triangles with Brie from the tempting fruit-and-cheese plate as I sized up the bar: all branded. "Wow. First-class."

SuSu opened the minifridge and pulled out three splits of Veuve Clicquot champagne. "Shall we?"

Linda got the flutes, and we ate and sipped our way to Diane's.

When we got there, we all crowded to the tinted windows for a glimpse of her outfit, but the woman who took Drew's arm and strode toward us was not our frumpy Diane.

Gone was her favorite baggy, back-belted dress style. Her stunning red dinner pantsuit fit like it had been custom made, showing off her tiny waist and camouflaging her heavy calves and ankles. But that wasn't the biggest transformation.

"Ohmygod!" SuSu shrieked. "She had a makeover!"

Even from a distance, Diane was radiant, her stride more confident than I had ever seen it.

Happy tears escaped as Linda took in the fabulous results. "Would you look at her hair!" Gone was her old dark brown—a harsh shade with nasty purplish undertones—replaced by a soft, golden-brown, subtly layered to give it volume. Even in the fading light, it shimmered when she moved.

"And her face!" I pointed out. Red was definitely her color, but her new, elegant, subtle makeup took years off her face and magnified her smallish eyes.

It was better than the best-ever makeover on *Oprah*.

When she got into the car, we gushed excessively, smothering her in hugs and compliments liberally salted with words like *goddess*, *queen*, and *gorgeous*.

"Who did this for you?" SuSu demanded.

Diane grinned, gingerly dabbing at her happy tears before they melted her wonderful new eyes. "Julia Davidson did my face. She does makeup for movies, but also for weddings and photo shoots and proms. Lee dated her for a while, more as a friend than a girlfriend." She let out a happy sigh. "So I decided to call her." She raised her eyebrows. "She recommended the hair guy. I had to go all the way down to Virginia Highlands. It was all *way* too expensive, though."

"How much?" SuSu demanded as she poured Diane a champagne. "Come on. Tell."

"A thousand dollars for the makeup and supplies," Diane confessed with a wince. "Two-fifty for the hair." She accepted the bubbly.

"Well, it was worth every penny," I said as the others agreed. "Get that chin back up, honey. You get what you pay for. You are a vision. A phoenix rising from the ashes."

We turned onto Piedmont, heading for the club. "What about this pantsuit?" Linda fingered the elegant summer-weight wool gabardine. "I never see fabric this good in the stores. Where'd you get it?"

Diane blushed to the roots of her gorgeous new hair. "I had it made—Hong Kong Tailors."

I raised my eyes toward heaven (or, more accurately, the moon roof) "Jesus is comin' again! Diane has finally gone from the bargain basement to the penthouse, in one swell foop." (I'm partial to spoonerisms.) We all laughed.

"Good for you," Linda congratulated. "You can afford to splurge."

Diane arched her left brow. "I'll say I can. As of Friday, all the financial deals are done—signed, sealed, and delivered. The house is paid off, the insurance policy is paid off, and there's fifty thousand cash in my new bank account."

"Fifty thousand?" SuSu's mouth dropped open. "Where did *that* come from?"

Diane smoothed the satin trim of her fitted jacket. "Ten thousand alimony for April and May, plus forty thousand for the car." She grinned. "I considered getting a low-mileage one- or two-year-old fleet car, but, dammit, I've never in my life had a new car. Since this might be my last chance for one, I decided to go for it. I was hopin' we could all go shopping for it together." She hugged herself. "Won't it be fun haggling with all the dealerships, then paying cash for two hundred over actual dealer cost?"

"Actual dealer cost?" SuSu made a face. "How the heck do you know what that is?"

Diane primped at her hair with youthfully endearing self-consciousness. "First, I checked out the features and model I wanted on the Internet. Then I e-mailed Lee, and he arranged for me to talk to one of his old fraternity brothers who works for GM Corporate. Such a nice young man. He gave me the straight skinny on actual dealer cost and factory rebates, so now I know the real, down-and-dirty, take-it-or-leave-it bottom line for the model I want." She added with alacrity, "Loaded."

"You e-mailed Lee?" I know I wasn't supposed to ask, but I couldn't help myself. "Did you tell him?"

Diane was amazingly casual. "Oh, yeah. I did that as soon as I got home from servin' Harold."

"Was he upset? I'm sure he was upset," Linda said with concern. "What did he say?"

Diane actually chuckled. "He said it was about time."

We all perked up. "You are kiddin' me," I said.

Diane took another swig of her champagne, then shook her head, still smiling. "Nope. He said he couldn't believe I'd put up with Harold as long as I had. Seems everybody, including Lee, knew about his daddy's carryin's on but me. Lee actually said he was proud of me for facing the truth and moving on. He loves his father, but he hated what Harold was doing to me. And I suspect he hated me, just a little, for letting Harold get away with it." She let out a relieved sigh. "So it's all okay. All my fears about breaking up the family were for nothing."

"Is this woman strong, or what?" SuSu praised.

"My, my, my, my, my," Linda said. "What have you done with the old Diane?"

The new Diane leaned back and crossed her custom-covered legs. "She disappeared completely a few weeks ago and, God willing, will never be seen again."

Linda stuck out her hand, palm down, for a pep rally group shake. "God willing."

SuSu added hers. "Amen."

I set down the grapes I'd been eating and added mine. "God willing."

Diane completed the hand sandwich, bracketing us. "And if she ever shows up again, you have my permission to point it out, posthaste." She bobbed our joined hands three times; then we broke, laughing.

It was going to be a great night. We hadn't been this full of ourselves since college.

With perfect timing, we were just finishing our champagne when the limo glided up to the Driving Club's main entrance. Drew lowered the window separating us. "We're here ladies, but I'm yours for the night. So if you want to go anywhere, just tell the valet, and your magic carpet is at your command." He parked, then headed around to collect us.

"Here we go," SuSu said, pulling her minidress down, none too soon, so you couldn't see her twat when she got out. (She wasn't wearing underpants with her sheer pantyhose, I'm sorry to have to tell you.)

Diane smoothed her jacket. "I can't wait to see what the big surprise is."

With that, four gorgeous men in tuxedos and black harlequin masks—two of them stud puppies (one dark and one honey blond) and two older and distinguished, but still built—stepped out of the lobby and waited, poised.

"Ohmygod." Linda gaped. "Are those for us?"

"Escorts?" I breathed out.

SuSu grinned. "She's gotten us escorts!"

"What a fabulous surprise," Diane declared, practically drooling.

"Teeny?" I couldn't imagine why she would do such a thing. Not only wasn't it Teeny's style, but this was independence night, Diane's rite of passage into singleness. Who were these guys? We didn't need men.

My eyes were drawn back to the older one on the end. He, alone, wasn't smiling, and his close-cropped, curly hair was a gorgeous shade of unabashed silver.

Something deep and distant stirred within me. Why did he

seem familiar? With the mask, I could hardly see anything of his face. But his broad shoulders and trim build were interesting enough. *Very* nice.

Odd. In all my years with John, I'd never so much as looked at another man, but there was something about this one. . . .

SuSu had already picked hers out. "Oooh, yum. Dibs on the tall one."

"They're all tall." I toyed with the prospect of any of those gorgeous hunks pampering and flattering me all night, even if he *was* paid to do it. Again, my eyes were drawn to the serious one on the end. "Which one was it you wanted?"

"The second from the right, with that sexy, sun-streaked mane of hair," SuSu clarified. A young one, of course. For some silly reason, I was relieved she hadn't picked Mr. Silver Hair.

I hastily applied fresh lipstick, then rubbed my front teeth with a cocktail napkin just to be safe.

"Do you think they're gigolos?" Linda whispered to us as Drew opened the door and extended his hand to help us out.

"Oh, I hope so," Diane said, setting us all off.

"Now, *that* would be some surprise!" SuSu wiggled down her hemline again, then took Drew's hand and elegantly extended her leg, emerging to her full height as sinuous as a snake goddess. She crooked her finger at the big, outdoorsy blond kid. "What's *your* name?"

"Jason." Grinning, he removed his mask to reveal a classic chiseled face, then drew from his pocket a large white name tag that said SUSU MCINTYRE in nice, big black-glittered letters that didn't require reading glasses.

Name tags? Curiouser and curiouser.

Poised, he hesitated over where to put it. Smart man. Sequins and stick-ons don't mix.

SuSu, who up to then had always hated name tags in any form, brazenly thrust forward her sequined bazooms. "Lay it on," she invited seductively, and he did.

"Now, you ladies don't let these guys make you forget about

me," Drew said as he reached in for Linda. She emerged to be greeted by the shortest escort—still almost six feet, a gorgeously dark-haired graduate-school type with snapping dark eyes. He took her hand and bowed over it, unmasking his sexy, Antonio Banderas face. "Good evening, *bella signora*," he said with a devastating hint of an Italian accent. "I am Marco." With a flourish, he produced her name tag. "May I have the pleasure of your company?"

"*Hail* yes." Silk be damned, Linda presented her own breast for the tagging, then latched on to his arm and sashayed into the club.

Two of us left, and two more men. I held back, suddenly intimidated. Etiquette said it was perfectly proper for a married woman to attend public activities with somebody besides her husband, but it didn't feel proper to me. "You go ahead," I told Diane. I leaned closer, dropping my voice. "I have a confession to make. I hope they're *not* real gigolos."

She smiled at me with what I can only describe as pity, then took a deep, leveling breath. "I think you're safe. That would hardly be Teeny's style."

"Yeah, well neither is charging this party to Reid without telling him."

"I know. Isn't it exciting?" When she got out with her usual briskness, the other older man, tanned and athletic, stepped forward. "Diane?"

Again, I felt a pulse of relief that "mine" was still there.

Diane blushed as her escort unmasked with one hand and drew a beautiful gardenia wrist corsage (her favorite flower) from behind his back with the other. He was dignified and gorgeous, just her type. "This is for you." He slipped the corsage onto her wrist, then drew out her name tag, the glittered letters red instead of black. After carefully applying it to her shoulder, he led her inside, leaving me alone in the limo and oddly insecure.

My "date" for the evening approached Drew, his face out of range above the open door when he spoke. "Thanks, but I can take it from here." So familiar, that voice. Low, but definitely familiar.

Drew walked away, which made me a little nervous.

Instead of offering his hand, my still-grim escort climbed inside, sending a tingle of fear through my chest. What was he up to?

He handed me a yellow rose, and then he smiled.

The sun exploded inside me. "Brad!"

I didn't have to see the rest of his face. I'd know that smile anywhere.

My first love, back from oblivion.

18

Fill in the Blanks

*B*RAD. ALL MY RECENT FANTASIES CLIMAXED AT ONCE, LEAVING me boneless with elation. He was alive! He was there!

The me who'd gone to sleep over the drift of years jolted back to life.

Brad, my quarterback with a big brain, the brave, bad boy I'd wanted with such fierce abandon that I'd dared to risk pregnancy and ruin to have him inside me.

A searing collage of urgent, delirious, deliciously forbidden couplings exploded, wonderful and terrible in their intensity. Memories that had been trying to surface for the last three months. Maybe they had been a premonition, after all.

All the unanswered questions evaporated. I felt only joy to find him alive, to find myself alive again, pungent, gliding, fearless, on the razor's edge.

Grinning, he pulled off the mask, and there it was: the face I had adored. Deep dimples, killer smile, piercing blue eyes, perfect skin—Paul Newman in his prime, only better—scarcely changed in all the years that had come between us.

"We thought you were dead!" Tears escaped me as I lunged into his arms.

He drew me close, and I reveled in his embrace as if we'd

never been apart. I was seventeen again, the darker voices over-whelmed by joy.

His unique smell was the same: and that elusive whiff of Jade East clean healthy male. I drank it in, along with the feel of his arms around me.

"Hey, don't cry, my lovely," he said, resurrecting my pet name. "You'll make me think you're not glad to see me."

I held on tight, irrationally afraid that if I didn't, I'd wake up, and this would be a dream. "We thought you were dead," I said, the anguish catching up with me.

"To tell the truth, so did I." My ear to his chest, I heard the emotion resonant in his deep voice.

A sudden splash of realization caused me to push away in outrage. "I thought you were dead!" I whacked him on the arm, hard. "Where were you?"

"That's my old Georgia," he said with pride, "Huggin' you one minute and beatin' on you the next."

"And that's my old Brad," I retorted, decades of suppressed fear and frustration spiking inside me, "always deflecting the hard questions. Why didn't you tell anyone where you were? Why didn't you tell *me?*" It sounded whiny, but I was beyond caring, wrenched from one emotional extreme to the other by his reappearance.

"I was a coward," he said, his tone low. "I couldn't face my parents, or you. Things had just gotten so . . . complicated. So I ran." He shot me a pleading glance. "It was years before my conscience caught up with me. When I finally found them and told them I'd dropped out, they were so angry, they disowned me," he said with calm finality.

No dire event had taken him from us.

Anguish doused the flame of anger I had felt. Fool. He hadn't even told his parents. "What do you mean, 'dropped out'?" Leak-ing tears, I dragged a cocktail napkin across my nose, then blotted away at the betrayal of my ancient pain.

He squeezed my hand so tightly, my diamond guard rings dug into my flesh. "God, Georgia, I am so, so sorry to have hurt you that way." I could see he meant it.

He may have been a coward then, but it had taken courage to come here now, to face me and the sins of his past.

What was left of my sanity chided me for fussing at him. What was done was done. Neither of us could change it. He hadn't come back into my life to get chewed out. "I expect a full accounting," I said, managing a lighter tone. "All the details."

Brad laughed, the old mischief returning to his gaze, and shot a glance to the club's entrance. "It'll have to keep until we've gotten to the party. The others are waiting for us. Teeny wanted you all to make a grand entrance together." He took my hand and pulled me closer to the door. "But before this night is over, I promise I'll answer each and every question with the truth, the whole truth, and nothing but the truth."

"I mean to hold you to that."

He got out, then reached inside to draw me to my feet close beside him on the driveway. I teetered precariously in my stilettos as he went on, "And then you can tell me all about what you've been up to, and how you stayed as beautiful as you were the last time I saw you." It wasn't glib. His blue eyes telegraphed sincerity—and desire. I could feel it in the possessive way he circled my waist.

He made no move toward the entry, just stood there, his arm around me. My fantasies started firing off out of control, and I fought to squelch them, but they kept popping up like the rubber moles in the Whack-A-Mole game at the arcade. My insides went aquiver, especially what was left of my private parts.

Brad leaned over and breathed in my scent, just as I had his. For an instant, I thought he might kiss me. Make that *hoped* he would. Then he pulled back. "We'd better go," he said at last, almost as if he had to convince himself. "They're waiting." Reluctantly, he drew me toward the club.

For a reckless moment, I seriously considered pulling a twenty-first-century Cinderella escape (*with* Prince Charming). Only Sacred Tradition Six (girls first) kept me walking toward the ballroom and Diane's emancipation celebration.

My mind raced. Teeny had to be behind this. She'd found Brad for me. But why? Nobody knew better than she how very married I was. Yet only she knew how deeply I had grieved for Brad. In a flash of insight, I wondered briefly if she'd done it so I could see him for who he really was, instead of my adolescent illusion blinded by first love.

Gorgeous was what he really was. And still very, very sexy.

The angel on my shoulder warned me to run away, back to the arms of my lawfully wedded husband, but I dismissed it with astonishing speed and conviction accompanied by a shocking mental image of me stuffing her into a gunnysack, bound and gagged, and hurling her into the infinite void.

Nothing had to happen, I rationalized above her ever-fainter protests. Brad and I were just going to talk. He was there, alive and gorgeous, but we were well chaperoned.

What harm could come from it?

Disaster, degradation, ruin, came the strident reply from the distant darkness.

Brad watched me walking beside him. "God, you're beautiful," he repeated.

And very married, but there was plenty of time to get to that.

"Oh, your name tag." He lurched to a halt, pulling it from his coat pocket.

Suddenly shy, I plucked it from his hand. "Here. I'll do it." The sheer jacket would never survive it, but my dress was sturdy enough.

We spotted the others waiting outside the ballroom doors. Teeny was luminous, tastefully gorgeous in rubies, diamonds, and a classic red crepe gown that showed off her figure without overwhelming her small stature.

The Red Hats were all grinning broadly but made no comment on Brad's presence. Teeny must have filled them in. Two extra escorts stood ready to admit us.

I blushed from the waist up.

"Dear Lord in heaven," I murmured to Brad as we approached. "I'm as self-conscious as I was that night we went back into the party after we 'did it' the first time."

He concealed a choked laugh by pretending to cough as we arrived. "Sorry we held y'all up," he told the others.

Teeny waved off his apology with a knowing smile. "I figured you might want a few minutes alone." She scanned everybody. "Okay. Ready for the big surprise?"

"I thought the dates were the big surprise," Diane said.

"Oh, no." Teeny rolled her eyes so the men couldn't see her. "You can thank Beanie for those. It was her idea." A diabolical glint sparked her expression. "*This* is my surprise." She nodded to the two men at the doors, and they opened up to reveal a harlequin wonderland of shiny black and crystalline white, where at least sixty red-clad, name-tagged women of all shapes and heights, each of them with her own escort, shouted "Surprise!"

A gaggle of photographers—regular and video—recorded the whole thing.

Swagged above a staggering buffet at one end, a banner declared, WELCOME, MADEMOISELLES, with a smaller PROCEEDS BENEFIT THE BUCKHEAD WOMEN'S SHELTER written underneath. At the other end of the room, the honest-to-God Shirelles cranked up with, "Mama said there'd be days like this," in perfect, undiminished form.

SuSu started jumping up and down and screaming, "Ohmygod, ohmygod, ohmygod!" then made a beeline for our waiting sorority sisters. Diane burst into happy tears, whereupon her "date" gallantly produced a spotless white handkerchief which she employed to minimize the damage to her makeover. "This is too perfect, Teeny. The best, the very ever best!"

Linda hugged Teeny. "Fabulous!"

Teeny pointed out a small table by the door with a sign that said, PLEASE REGISTER FOR OUR ALUMNAE DIRECTORY. "Y'all be sure to fill out the cards before you get too 'happy' to do it." As we obliged, the photographers asked each of us to pose for a portrait (without escorts), then dispersed to shoot candids.

"All right." Linda rubbed her hands together. "Let's get this show on the road." She went to see who was there, her date in attentive but unobtrusive tow.

My feet and I were happy to note that there were enough tables and chairs for everybody to sit, with plenty of room left to dance. "How on earth did you put something like this together in only a month?" I asked Teeny.

She grinned, straining to hear and be heard over the music of our youth. "Divine intervention. The room was available, and I found fifteen Mademoiselles in the metro area right off the bat. They all went nuts over the idea of a reunion, especially Beanie. She marshaled everybody like the marines. It was her idea to do the escorts—well, all of them but one"—she looked to Brad— "and she wouldn't take no for an answer." Teeny glanced around to make sure Beanie wasn't within earshot, then confided, "She's single again, and so are half the sisters."

That explained the escorts. But the band . . . "The *Shirelles?*"

She shrugged. "They had a cancellation."

I scanned the room, dead impressed. Maybe it was divine intervention. Fund-raisers like this one usually took at least six months to put together, but I doubted God had anything to do with the gigolo part.

Teeny squeezed my arm. "I need to go do my thing." She shot a pointed glance toward Brad. "Have fun. I'll catch up with you later."

If I hadn't known better, I could have sworn she was hoping I'd hook up with him.

Not!

Nervous as a rock star at a paternity hearing, I turned back to face him. "I can't believe Teeny did this. *Teeny!*" Trying to make small talk, I opened my mouth and inserted my foot up to the thigh. "A gigolo, divorce-party, Mademoiselle Reunion fund-raiser at the PDC. In only a month." I laughed. "God knows what all these men are costing Reid. I hope it's huge."

"I am not a gigolo," Brad said firmly, but without offense. "Neither are the others. And Teeny's not paying us. We're paying her."

My ears threatened to spontaneously combust from humiliation as my stomach plummeted to my pointy toes.

He went on, unfazed. "Most of these guys are Nine O'clocks or representatives from companies that still have money to donate to worthy causes. The only condition was that we be single. Beanie cashed in some serious chips."

Charitable bachelors, all, and I had accused them—and Brad—of being gigolos!

The band kicked up a notch, so he put his arm around my waist and turned his mouth to my ear, our spaces overlapping. "Your Mademoiselle alumnae were very persuasive."

His touch brought back the fantasies, so vivid I could barely form a coherent thought. Ashamed and embarrassed, I groaned out, "Oh, God! Could the floor please just open up and swallow me?"

Brad laughed, giving my shoulders a consoling hug. "No offense taken. That uncensored honesty was always one of the things I loved about you most. I'm glad to see you still have it."

"Well, I'm not." My ears would be red for six months, but I had to admit the humor in it. I couldn't wait to exorcise it later by telling the girls. They'd die.

I spotted SuSu, with Nature Boy in her wake, on her way toward us (probably to pump Brad), but she'd made it only halfway when I saw she was about to be intercepted by none other than Carolyn "the Bitch Woman" Watts. An older, harder Carolyn Watts, who by the look of her was already tipsy, with mayhem in mind.

"Damn!" Carolyn hollered, pointing, over the music. "If it idn't

SuSu McIntyre! I've been lookin' everywhere for you! We need to have a few *words*, pube." She closed in on a visibly panicked SuSu.

"Uh-oh," I told Brad. " 'Scuse me while I try to prevent a riot."

Linda had spotted them, too, and moved in for a rescue at the same time I approached from the other direction.

But before we could reach them, Carolyn had fallen on SuSu's neck and was all but blubbering, "I was way too hard on you, kid. Way harsh. I need to make some serious amends. Can you ever forgive me?"

Propping her up, SuSu smiled with surprised relief. "Sure, Carolyn. Sure."

"All righty, then." Carolyn brightened. "This calls for a drink. Let's suck a few down and bury the hatchet."

SuSu motioned us off, and we watched the two of them head for liquid refreshment. Once they'd gotten their drinks, they headed, thick as thieves, for the relative quiet of the club's main bar.

"Well, I'll be jiggered," Linda said beside me. "Maybe people do change, after all. I wonder what mellowed *her* out."

"Maybe she got religion," I guessed.

We looked at each other, then said in unison, "Nah!"

"More likely, drugs," I said, feeling a stab of shame at my cattiness even as the words were spoken. "Whatever it was, I'm just glad for SuSu's sake that *something* softened her up."

Brad reached us at almost the same time Linda's escort did. "Shall we dance?" he offered.

We'd always been magic on the dance floor, but my stilettos and arthritic knees made me hesitate to take him up on it.

Linda cocked a suspicious glance at him. "There'll be plenty of time to dance later. Why don't you two boys get some food while we catch up with a few old friends?"

Was she trying to protect me from Brad? I looked at her and realized she was. It made me laugh.

"Okay, we'll circulate," I conceded, not wanting to leave Brad, but not wanting anyone to know it. After so many years of being one of The Wives who functioned almost independently of The Husbands at affairs like this one, it felt odd to find myself worrying what Brad would do while I left him. But Linda was right: he and I could dance—and talk—later. "We'll be back, I promise," I said to him as Linda hustled me off toward the herd-of-birds roar where Diane and Teeny were already circulating.

I didn't worry about Brad for long. Linda and I were too busy trying to recognize friends we hadn't seen for years. Grateful for the big name tags, we found some sleek gone fluffy, some nipped and tucked to frightening tautness, some self-conscious, some high on booze, and others just high on old times. We spoke to born-agains, New Agers, and more than a few who worshiped at the altars of the latest diet craze, antidepressant, "in" salon, plastic surgery, or face-care regimen. They made me appreciate our Red Hat Sacred Traditions even more. SuSu and Carolyn, close as Siamese twins, returned from the bar with champagne cocktails, and dived head-first into the catch-up marathon.

Before I knew it, we were all having a ball. The cliques and subtle barriers that had separated us in our teens were gone—with a few notable, easily dismissed exceptions. All in all, the divorcées seemed to be doing the best. Go figure. And there were still a few successful, long-term marriages, but a nagging inner whisper wondered if they were truly happy like Brooks and Linda, or only happy on the surface, like John and me.

Then we heard SuSu squeal. Turning, we saw her rush with open arms, trailing a familiar litany of "ohmygods," toward the doorway to welcome a new arrival. Linda and I followed her line of progress and both blinked.

"This is Lazarus night, for sure," I breathed out.

There stood Pru Bonner in her mother's wide-hipped body—minus the beehive—her flashy red dress just a little too tight. But neither her body nor her badly streaked long shag nor her cheap clothes struck me most. It was her almost feral posture of fear, like a moonshiner making a delivery next door to the police station.

"Not Lazarus," Linda corrected. "It's the night of the prodigals."

We were already moving toward them. "Where's Diane? And Teeny?" I asked without taking my eyes off Pru as SuSu attacked her with a huge hug.

"I'll get 'em." Linda peeled off. "You go on."

When I reached Pru, I had to pull SuSu off her. "SuSu! The woman can't breathe. Let her go."

Pru's eyes telegraphed her gratitude. "I'm fine, really." Breathless, she straightened her dress. "Wow. Both of y'all look great. But I knew you would."

I hugged her, far more gently than SuSu had. She reeked of stale smoke and cheap cologne, but I didn't care. "God, it's good to see you." I drew back to look at her. "We were afraid we'd lost you forever."

Shame warred with self-defensive pride on a face that testified to hard living and too many cigarettes. "I've been over in Alabama. Livin' with this guy I used to work for—" Her features tightened further. "—well, not livin' with him exactly. It's his country place, but he comes real often. I look after things while he's gone."

It beat turning tricks for drug money, which was what we'd feared. I wanted so much to help her, but didn't know how to begin. "I'm sure you're real good at it." After a stiff little pause, I added, "Pru, you look a whole lot better than you did the last time I saw you."

Wrong, wrong, wrong! Don't bring up the past.

She became almost shy, some of the years falling away. "I've been clean and sober for eight months, now. I guess it shows."

I hugged her again to hide my tears. "I am *so* proud of you! And I'm *so* glad you came tonight."

She pulled away, her old sweet, sunny smile confirming that

the Pru we'd loved was still in there somewhere.

Diane, Linda, and Teeny arrived in a gust of welcomes and embraces.

We clustered six chairs in the corner, and all but Teeny spent the next twenty minutes bringing Pru up to speed with hilarious anecdotes about our last eighteen years, liberally sprinkled with references to how we'd missed her and tried to find her.

I noted that Pru looked long at Teeny when we did, her expression shuttered.

Then, after the third time SuSu mentioned trying to find her, Pru interrupted quietly but firmly. "It's no secret that I haven't 'turned out well,' as our mamas used to put it. Y'all couldn't find me because I didn't want you to." She glanced down, then raised her eyes again. You could see it took great courage. "Drugs'll make you do things y'all could never even imagine. I was in hell, and I had nobody to blame but myself. I wish I could say I've put all that behind me." Another pregnant glance at Teeny. "Thanks to the tough love of a wonderful old friend, I've been straight for the last eight months, but all I can think about is today. I'm clean and sober today." Her blue eyes welled. "And I wanted to see y'all more than I was ashamed to come here, so here I am."

All of us crying with her, we dissolved into a soggy lump of subdued hugs and renewed vows of friendship.

When we'd all regained our composure, SuSu insisted, "Pru, you've gotta come see us. We meet for lunch the second Tuesday of every month at the Coach House. You could come the night before and stay with me."

All of us added our own invitations to put her up, carte blanche.

Pru basked in the warmth of our good intentions, but shook her head. "Thanks, y'all. Really. But work and going to my meetings keep me pretty tied up." Her gaze slanted away. "It's not that I don't love ya'—I think about y'all all the time, but . . ." I could see she was holding on to her newfound self-control tighter

than an orphan clutching a new doll. "Maybe sometime soon . . . ,"
she said vaguely.

SuSu shoulder-hugged her. "Whenever you want, honey.
We're there for you."

"But no more of this dropping off the face of the earth," Linda
said briskly. She handed Pru one of the registration forms and a
pen. "We're not lettin' you go until you fill this out. Good, bad,
or indifferent, we want to know where you are. Regardless."

"Even if you're in jail," SuSu blurted out, superseding my own
gaffe by the power of ten. Oblivious, she beamed. "I've always
wanted to visit somebody in prison."

The Red Hats defused the hideous faux pas by attacking her
with shoves, halfhearted slaps, and mock anger.

Pru actually laughed. "Here's hoping you won't get the
chance." She handed Linda the form with only the phone number
and address filled out.

Just as we were lapsing into an awkward lull, Teeny stood.
"Come on, Pru. Your escort for the evening awaits you."

Escorts.

I'd almost forgotten about Brad. A glance at my watch showed
I'd left him sitting there for over an hour. *Too* rude.

My better instincts shot me a bright idea. Maybe the two prodigals could hook up. Then I'd be safe, from him and myself.

I took Pru's arm and tried to draw her toward our table. "Let
me have her first, Teens. Just for a few minutes."

Pru resisted, her fear returning.

"You'll never guess who else is here," I told her by way of
reassurance. "Brad Olson. He wasn't dead, after all," I said, in-
anely restating the obvious. "I know he'd love to see you." Which
was ridiculous, because they only knew each other in passing.

She pulled back in earnest, breaking contact. "That's great, but
maybe some other time." Her eyes flicked nervously over all the
curious alumnae who made no secret of watching the real action
in our corner. She paled, and I realized her courage didn't extend
past our little group. "As a matter of fact, I think I'll be running.

It's a pretty long drive back to Huntsville, and I'm an hour beyond that."

"Don't drive back tonight," I pleaded. "You just got here. You can stay with me." All but Teeny added their protests and invitations to stay.

Teeny waved us off with a firm but quiet, "Point of order. She wants to go home. Let her." She turned a warm, understanding smile on Pru. "Now that we've found you, there'll be lots of time to visit."

Pru covered Teeny's hand with her own. "Thanks, Teens." To us, "Sorry, but I can only handle so much at a time. I hope you'll understand."

We all hugged her with real respect, piling on reassurances that we did. And then she was gone.

As the door closed behind her, the five of us stood staring at it in pensive silence.

I don't know what the others were thinking, but I was overwhelmed by what it must have taken for Pru to come at all. So brave, so sad, so much of her life wasted. And yet she came. Ever since we'd met her, her uncomplaining struggles had provided our sheltered lives with perspective. Now, more than ever.

Suddenly I was very, very grateful for the tiny annoyances of my dull, privileged existence.

We were saved from descending into terminal wet-blanketdom when our escorts arrived en masse and took us back to our table to feed us.

"What was that all about?" Brad asked as he walked beside me, his arm again around my waist. But talking to Pru had put me back on the high ground, so my physical reaction to his presence had subsided to manageable limits.

For the moment.

"Who was that woman?" he pressed.

He hadn't even recognized her. "Pru Bonner."

He let out a low whistle. "Whoa. What's up with her?"

I had to fight to maintain my composure when I answered. Speaking of what had really happened would be a betrayal of Sacred Tradition Four (no telling), so I kept it brief and innocuous. "She was able to drop by for a few minutes. We had a lot of catching up to do. I only wish she could have stayed longer. I know she would have liked to see you."

Now why had I added that last, a pure whopper?

He took it in with an intensity that felt like X-ray vision of the soul. Then he broke the tension with a deliberate, and most perceptive, change of subject. "Have you eaten?"

I shook my head. "What about you?"

There was that grin. "While you were visiting, I was eating. And some very good eating it was." He took my hand and kissed it. Some of the spark returned. "Do you still like the same foods?"

Surely he couldn't remember, but I nodded with a smile.

"Okay, then. I'll be right back, my lovely. Food first, then those answers I promised you."

Minutes later, he returned with lobster, drawn butter, crab-stuffed mushrooms, shrimp with lots of cocktail sauce, and celery sticks mounded with ranch dip.

All my favorites. He had remembered. I almost cried.

After I'd polished it off with unladylike gusto, he led me outside near the pool, where we could talk at last.

We settled onto a bench in a quiet corner, sheltered by the plantings. After all the noise, it felt like a chapel.

"So." I took his perfect, Greek-statue hand in mine. "You promised to tell me: Where have you been the past third of a century? What happened to you?"

He exhaled, relaxing beside me. "As I'm sure you were aware, I had burned out drinking and partying in college. So when I found out my dad was going to be transferred to San Diego, I decided to drop out before the draft caught up with me. I went to LA to surf. My parents were crazed, of course. I left without a word to them or anybody." He stared out over the pool. "I told myself it was to protect them, if the government came after me. But now I realize I just couldn't face them or their expectations for me. Like I said, I was a coward."

What about me? my broken heart wailed. You could have told me!

"I changed my name and did my best to blend in. Everybody in LA was turning on, so I did, too. I got into the wrong crowd. I wasn't the man you thought I was, my lovely. Never had been, really."

"Did you ever think of me?" I hated myself for asking, but I couldn't help it.

"All the time." A loaded pause. "And I dreamed about you. It seemed so real, and you were so clean, so good. So uninhibited." He stared, sightless, at my feet. "I was bad news, Georgia. You deserved better."

"That's what Linda said," I mused aloud, my internal editor missing in action, as usual. "She said the best thing you ever did was leave me." Maybe it was the license that comes with age, but I wasn't sorry I'd said it.

Miraculously, he didn't take offense, just laughed instead. "Linda was right. That little brown biddy always did have my number." He lifted his eyes, dark with self-reproach, to mine. "You were way too good for a spoiled, hard-drinkin', ne'er-do-well like me."

For the first time, I was inclined to agree with him. He'd just run away, leaving me to pick up the pieces, kept me in the dark. No truth, no matter how hard, could have been worse than that. "I loved you, body and soul." I said it simply, with only a hint of indictment.

"I know. That's why I left."

The little girl inside me who'd read too many fairy tales swooned at the noble sacrifice of such a gesture, but my practical adult wasn't swayed.

He got an A+ for honesty on the past. But what about the

present? I didn't hesitate to ask him, "How about now? You seem fine enough."

"Thanks to Uncle Sam. I got busted one time too many, and the judge gave me a choice: prison, or the marines. Believe it or not, I chose the marines."

I sat up and looked at him in shock. He might as well have told me he'd had a sex change. Brad had been a vocal peacenik. "Uh-unh," I challenged. "You are makin' that up."

He rose without reply and seductively undid his tie, then removed his jacket and cuff links.

I knew perfectly well that no gentleman would strip at the Driving Club, but I sat transfixed, hopelessly titillated.

Slowly he removed the studs from his shirt, depositing them into a neat row on the arm of the bench beside his cuff links. When they were all out, he caressed open the remaining buttons, then slowly untucked his shirt.

A frisson of danger and desire made me squirm in my seat. I tried thinking about John, but my thinker had been overridden.

Grinning in the subtle landscape lighting, Brad eased down the shoulder of his shirt to expose a muscular bicep emblazoned with an expert, colorful United States Marine Corps emblem.

My aversion to tattoos immediately evaporated. It was the sexiest thing I'd ever seen. Drawn like a moth to flame (I know it's a cliché, but nothing else says it half as well), I stood. "May I touch it?" So much for the high road.

Sit down! my conscience wailed from distant oblivion. *Or run away. Yes, run away. That's even better.*

Instead, I moved in close to ease my palm over his smooth and fevered skin. My hand caught his heat and sent it racing through me. I let go, almost unable to breathe, but my eyes remained focused on his bare skin. His chest was marred by several faded, ragged scars. War wounds?

You never should have touched him! my conscience wailed, all but inaudible now. *This is not good! You are a good girl, Georgia. Don't do anything you'll regret!*

Believe me, I had no intention of regretting it. I always had been the kind of kid who was every mother's nightmare, weighing the punishment against the prize, then breaking the rules and taking my medicine without complaint.

Brad was going to kiss me. It was inevitable. And I was going to let him.

It was the wickedest thing I had done since he'd left me, but I didn't care.

His hungry eyes locked to my face, he shrugged his shoulder back into the shirt, then took my upper arms into his hands and drew me hard against the bare strip of his torso for a slow, aching kiss that gradually escalated into a five-alarmer. He tasted of seafood and stranger and, oddly, no booze.

John always tasted of bourbon.

Desperate to get a grip on myself, I conjured my husband there watching us. Maybe that would bring me to my senses. But when John materialized, he was too busy reading his paper to notice us, which introduced a disturbing element of exhibitionism to the whole thing, so I did an immediate mental husbandectomy and focused back on Brad.

Good thing he couldn't read minds. He'd have run screaming into the night.

The longer our kiss went on, the smaller the protesting part of me got, until it was muzzled completely. I finally let go and tumbled down the rabbit hole.

There was no guessing whether Brad enjoyed it or not. His body said he did.

And mine remembered the desire of my youth, keen and stinging as a razor-cut.

The angel on my shoulder returned, doing a jumping devil-dance. *You do not know where that mouth has been! He told you he was in jail! He might even have AIDS! This is not your husband!* But the blood pounding in my ears drowned her out.

When we finally broke, I was limp.

"Whoa." Brad caught my forearm and helped me to the bench. "Maybe you ought to sit down for a minute while I put my clothes back on."

His choice of words sent an embarrassed flush from my toes to my scalp.

"Uh-oh," I squeaked out, my lips pounding so strong with every heartbeat that I feared I must look like I'd just had collagen injections. "What now?"

Brad was far quicker fastening up than he'd been taking off, but he remained focused intently on me as he dressed. "I'd say that's up to you."

"I don't know anything about you." It was true. Who was he now? What did he do?

Once more impeccably attired, he sat facing me and took my hands. "I've been clean and sober for twenty years. Church every Sunday. Divorced twice, amicably. I was married to my work; you can call my exes and ask them. No kids."

"I'm married. Happily," I shot back, but the truth made a clumsy defensive weapon. It sounded hollow, even to me. "I have been for thirty years. He's a full professor at Tech. Two great kids. My older son's in graduate school at Duke"—why couldn't I remember his name?—"and my daughter's a senior at Georgia. I'm not about to do anything to dishonor my family."

He didn't say anything, but I could see he wasn't going to let this drop.

Damn. *Why* had Teeny done this to me?

Don't you dare blame Teeny, my conscience scolded. *All she did was ask him. You did the rest!*

I smoothed the neckline of my dress. "You still haven't told me what happened after you joined the marines."

"I served two tours in 'Nam. That'll either grow you up or break you, and it didn't break me. I came back determined to get an education and make something of myself."

Still trying to tamp out the ebb tide of euphoria from that kiss,

I pried further. "And what did you make of yourself?"

His mischievous twinkle returned. "I'm afraid to tell you. You might head for the hills."

Grateful that he'd lightened up, I said the first thing that came to mind. "Gawd. You're not a televangelist, are you?"

He laughed. "No. Not *that* bad."

Good. I was safe as long as he was laughing.

"I'm a lawyer."

"Zounds." I draped a dramatic wrist across my forehead. "Get thee behind me, Satan." Then I sobered. "Please don't tell me you get drug dealers or mobsters off. Then I really would have to head for the hills."

His handsome face drew into a mock scowl. "Heavens, no. I'm Robin Hood: a tax consultant. I've saved taxpayers millions of dollars. Most of them corporations, but still—"

"Tell me more." At last, I could relax a little. Work talk was safe.

"After I was wounded in 'Nam"—the scars?—"I got a commendation and a ticket out of hell. I used that second chance at life to get sober and stay that way. I patched things up with my parents, then moved back here, under my new name. It matched my service records, so—"

"Your new name! So *that's* why I never found you in the phone book! Or the ones in LA and San Diego." At his grin, I realized I'd said it aloud. *Damn! Stupid, stupid, stupid! When will you learn to keep your mouth shut?*

He inflated with masculine ego. "You looked for my name in the phone book? In all those places?"

"Go on," I ordered. "You moved back to Atlanta. Without telling anybody, I might add."

"How could I face you?" Shame darkened his eyes. "When I first ran away, I was too much of a coward. By the time I got back from the service, so much time had passed. You were married. I figured it would be kinder not to stir everything up." Seeing the hurt in my non–poker face, he admitted, "I guess I was still a coward."

It was an honest response to a hard question, and he'd answered it without my even having to ask. Definitely not the old Brad.

"It took me ten years," he went on, "but I worked my way through Emory and graduate school, then finally got a job downtown, where I've been gainfully employed ever since. Very gainfully." He waggled his eyebrows. "I go to three AA meetings a week, without fail, and I haven't been a selfish, spoiled, ne'er-do-well since I kissed the ground of the good old USA back in 1975."

His intensity returned. "Now I'm just a man who would like to see you again, on whatever terms you choose."

"Ahem." Linda rescued me from what might have happened next by appearing, arms akimbo. "So *there* y'all are." She glared at Brad. "I was afraid you'd lured her away to doom and degradation."

"And I love you, too," Brad teased.

She motioned us up. "Come on. Teeny's about to do her thing."

Brad shot me a last bittersweet look, then rose.

On the way inside, Linda leaned in close to me to whisper, "For goodness' sake, wipe your mouth." She shoved a paper napkin into my hand. "You've got lipstick halfway across your face."

That brought on the biggest blush of the evening. I licked the napkin and hastily made repairs.

"Okay. That's better," she whispered, "but put some more lipstick on as soon as you find your purse." She finished with a bang-on imitation of Olympia Dukakis's mother-moan from *Moonstruck.*

We had just gotten back to our table when the Shirelles reached the end of their song and paused. While everyone headed back to their seats, a microphone crackled, and a spotlight opened on Teeny standing at a raised dais behind the buffet line.

A drum roll and cymbal clash quieted the house.

"First," Teeny said into the mic, "I'd like to thank you all for coming, especially our gallant escorts."

Applause and cheers from the ladies.

"Gentlemen, one hundred percent of your contributions will go to the shelter and hot line in memory of Alice Hughes Witherspoon."

Reid's abused mother. Too deliciously ironic! The applause was underscored with a surge of whispered gossip and a few delighted hoots as those who knew explained it to those who didn't.

"Ohmygod," I unconsciously mimicked SuSu. "Reid is gonna crepe a brick. Not to mention his daddy."

Brad frowned in confusion. "Crepe a brick?"

"Our genteel equivalent for crap a brick," I whispered.

SuSu, Diane, and their escorts settled in around us. SuSu did her best to catch my eye, but I avoided her.

Teeny continued with her usual poise. "Thanks to you and your companies' exceptional generosity, and our Atlanta Mademoiselle Alumnae's tireless corporate solicitations"—another spotlight singled out Beanie at a nearby table—"under the inspired direction of Beanie Johnson Abercrombie"—Teeny paused so Beanie could wave—"we have raised seventy-five thousand dollars."

Enthusiastic applause and cheers were interspersed with a few masculine UGA grunts. (The sound effects are inevitable in Georgia wherever peckers and alcohol are present in any appreciable amount, regardless of caste.)

"I must also thank Witherspoon Development for this wonderful party, and for donating the services of Clayborn Security to help us locate our Mademoiselle Alumnae so quickly."

"Whoo," I confided to Brad amid the rampant applause, cheers, and whistles. "I can't wait to hear what Reid does when he finds out about all this."

Brad tucked his chin. "He doesn't know?"

"Not yet." We shared a warm, private laugh.

"And that's not all," Teeny went on. "Witherspoon Development will be matching the proceeds, dollar for dollar, which brings our grand total up to a hundred fifty thousand dollars."

Ooohs and *aaah*s punctuated the clapping.

I almost wet my pants. Teeny had stuck it to her husband and father-in-law, big-time. Now that they were on record for the contributions, they'd have to follow through.

What I wouldn't give to be a fly on the wall when the Messers. Witherspoon got the word.

"Now," she concluded, radiant with triumph. "Let's all eat some more lobster, drink more champagne, and dance to the Shirelles."

As the band struck back up with "Will You Love Me Tomorrow" all four of us headed for Teeny. I was prouder of her than I had ever been. We found her in the midst of a crowd of grateful Mademoiselles.

SuSu wriggled in and got hold of Teeny's arm. " 'Scuse me! 'Scuse me!" She waved to the well-wishers. "The honoree needs a moment with Teeny; then we'll give her back." Laughing and high on champagne and elegant revenge, we hijacked her to the bathroom.

Once there, we opened every stall to make sure we were alone, then stationed Linda in a chair blocking the door to keep anybody from coming in. Only then did SuSu break her big news. "Y'all, you are *not* going to believe this."

Grateful for something to divert their attention from me and Brad, I hunkered down. "What?"

She went up on her toes. "I know who the Dunwoody Dominatrix is!" she revealed in a dramatic stage whisper. "A Mademoiselle!"

It was gossip of the century, galvanizing us all. Okay, maybe only the gossip of the decade, but it was *big*.

"You are shittin' me," Linda lapsed, agog. "How the hell could you possibly know that?"

"She told me." SuSu was so full of herself, she almost exploded. She motioned us in close. "It's Carolyn Watts. We had a few drinks together in the bar, and I told her about Jackson, and then she just came right out and told me. Promised to try to lure him in Florida, then bring him back for prosecution, neatly trussed." Her train of thought took the inevitable sidetrack. "I doubt it'll work, though. He's such a wimp. S and M is definitely not his thing."

"She *told* you?" I asked in amazement.

SuSu nodded. "Maybe to make up for all the garbage she did to me when we were pledges. She swore me to secrecy, of course, but y'all don't count as telling."

"Well, I'll just be double-dog damned." Linda shook her head. "The Dunwoody Dominatrix, a Mademoiselle. Brooks will—"

We all rose up in protest. "No, no, no, no, no! Mustn't tell Brooks. Tradition Four!"

Linda colored. "Sorry. What was I thinking? Tradition One."

"Carolyn Watts," Teeny said with a sweet smile. "It fits. It definitely fits." She exhaled. "And to think, I almost didn't invite her because of the way she'd treated y'all."

Diane giggled. "What a perfect outlet for all that anger of hers. Playing sexual vigilante to all the Harolds out there."

I stood to attention, making the Girl Scout salute. "Long live the Dunwoody Dominatrix," I solemnly intoned.

They all joined me in solemn echo. Then we settled back down to SuSu's, "Okay. What's the scoop on Brad?" Palms up, she twiddled her bright red nails at me in a come-along gesture. "All the gory details, George. Come on."

I knew better than to tell them about The Kiss, much less my fantasies, so I confined my explanations to what Brad had told me. Omitting, of course, my stupid blunders.

"He changed his name!" Diane, perched on the marble counter, clapped her hands to her knees. "No wonder nobody could find him."

"What is it?" SuSu asked me.

"What is what?"

"Earth to George," she responded. "His *name*, darling."

I didn't think I had any blush left in me, but I did. "Oh. I forgot to ask him."

They jeered me good-naturedly for that. But just when I thought they had settled down, Teeny gave me that Bambi blink. "So? Are you gonna sleep with him?"

I all but choked. "Teeny!"

The others remained in suspended animation for a heartbeat, then burst into guffaws.

"Is *that* why you found him for me?" I demanded.

Teeny smiled, guileless as ever. "No. I found him because he was a big loose end for all of us, disappearing like that. I got him to come tonight because I thought it might do you good to see what you were missing and have a choice."

"Choice?" I blustered, the angel on my shoulder so prune-puckered in indignation that she all but caved in on herself. "There is no choice, here. I am married. End of story."

The others were watching us intently, back and forth, like the finals at Wimbledon.

Teeny remained undaunted. "It's only the end of the story if you really want it that way."

"Well, I do," I said, not convincing anyone, least of all myself.

She checked her hair in the mirror. "Okay, ladies. It's time to get back to the party. There's dancing to be done, and old friendships to be dug up, and new beginnings to be made." She shot me an amused glance before helping Linda move the chair away from the door.

"I do not need or want a new beginning, thank you very much," I said.

It didn't surprise me that none of us had mentioned Pru. It was still too fresh, too fragile.

Teeny hugged Diane. "I hope you don't mind sharing your D-Day celebration with a good cause."

"Of course not." I hadn't seen Diane this relaxed since I don't know when. "It was perfect," she told Teeny. "Everything you do is perfect."

"We thought the escorts were gigolos," Linda admitted, her voice thickening with amusement on the last.

Teeny did another Bambi-blink. "Gigolos?"

Diane nodded with her usual eager sincerity. "Male prostitutes."

Teeny cut loose and hooted, holding her sides just like she used to do back in high school when nobody but us was around. Lordy, but it was good to see.

Time for the exorcism. "Yeah, well, thinking it is one thing," I confessed. "I actually told Brad that I was amazed Teeny would give a gigolo-Mademoiselle-reunion-fund-raiser-divorce party for Diane."

"Ohmygod," SuSu wheezed out. "You didn't." Pot calls the kettle!

But I couldn't deny the humor in it, so I joined their laughter and was healed. "Yep. I did."

Teeny shook her head. "Brad probably loved it. You can do no wrong in his book."

"Is he dating anybody?" I heard my voice ask. Dear Lord, where had *that* come from?

A heartbeat of astonished silence was followed by guffaws.

"No," Teeny answered without reproach. "He rarely dates. Too much of a workaholic." She bobbled her eyebrows like Groucho Marx. "All the other escorts paid a thousand apiece. When I told Brad you were to be his date, he paid five."

"Aha! So he *is* still carrying a torch for you," SuSu goaded.

"Wooooo!" the others said.

"That's ridiculous," I defended. "He's been back in town for years without ever contacting me. Or anybody else."

"He knew you were married," Teeny calmly explained. "He didn't want to cause you any more trouble than he already had."

"Teeny, are you pimping me?" I shot back.

She grinned. "Absolutely not. What you do about Brad is

strictly up to you. I just told him you would rather know the truth than mourn the unknown for the rest of your life."

SuSu never could stand it when things got too deep. "Live a little, George; just sleep with the guy," she urged. "Husbands do it to wives all the time. Why shouldn't wives be able to do it, too? I'm not talkin' about leavin' John. Just addin' a little spice to your life for a while. From the look of things, you sure could use it."

I wrapped myself in the flag and fired back, "SuSu, you are totally degenerate, and I refuse to dignify that with an answer."

"Okay, y'all." Linda spread her arms like an umpire signaling "safe." "Tradition One, and that's all there is to it. Not another word, or we'll all regret it." She turned to Diane. "In case you've forgotten, this is Diane's night, not Brad's. So let's get back to that party and boogie down." She held open the door and motioned us out.

Properly chastised, we all followed.

"Remember, y'all," Teeny reminded us, "this is just the public party. The private one comes later, so pace yourselves." Teeny hustled us up. "And I still have surprises in store."

"Lord, Teeny," I said. "What next? We've already been surprised to smithereens."

"Something more personal," she said with a wink.

Little did we know that the A-bomb of surprises had yet to be revealed. The Big One. Front-page news that would dwarf everything else.

19

Teeny, We Never Knew Ye

PDC. *May 14, 2002. 2:00 A.M.*

THE LAST CHIT SIGNED AND THE GLAMOROUS LEFTOVERS ON their way to the shelter, things wound down to the final parting. Teeny stood beside the limo in the porte cochere with us—exhausted, shoeless, caught up to overflowing with old friends, sated with male attention, and way, way, *way* past our bedtimes—as we said good-bye to our "dates."

"Georgia." Brad drew me out of earshot from the others. Safely behind a pillar, he searched my face as if he might never see me again. "Please take this." He pressed his card into my palm—his cell phone number and e-mail handwritten in—then closed my fingers over it before taking my upper arms. "Now that I've found you, I don't want to let you go."

My resurrected teenager wanted to go home with him, then and there. Ditch the others and dive headlong into the past. Rip our clothes off and revel in his still-firm body. He wanted me—middle-aged, real woman me. The thrill of that drew me as if to a black hole.

But that middle-aged, grown-up me was more than wary, and deeply affronted by his long-ago abandonment. Regardless of how he might have changed, my sensible self reasoned, he hadn't been able to maintain his commitments. Two failed marriages.

But they weren't to me, my teenager cried. *I was the one he really loved!*

You were the one he left in the lurch, to grieve and wonder all these years! my sensible self countered.

Torn, I dropped the card into my little evening bag without looking at it and snapped it safely shut. "We'll talk. Soon," I reassured him, but the reservation in my voice was obvious even to me. Fantasies were one thing. Infidelity, though—mental or actual—was quite another. I laid my forehead against his shoulder to keep him from reading my thoughts in my anything-but-poker face.

True, Brad made me feel alive, but the thought of betraying John suddenly loomed larger than everything else. And in that moment, I realized something I hadn't let myself face: I loved John—not in a flashy, reckless infatuation, but with a bone-deep trust and gratitude that spanned the long, good years.

With that realization came a healthy dose of guilt. *When was the last time you really saw John, the way you want him to see you?* my conscience asked with poignant gentleness. *Or truly cared about him—not as a provider or your children's father, but just because you loved him?*

Spiritual javelin, straight to the heart.

Real love is more durable stuff than feelings. Even the most stable relationships cycle from closeness to distance and back again. Usually, it's a crisis that brings you back together, but I certainly wasn't wishing for that. And I knew better than to think an affair would be anything but destructive.

Brad sighed, his chin resting atop my head as he gently gathered me closer, as if I might break. "You're not going to call me, are you?" I heard both pain and resignation in his question.

A lingering teaspoonful of adolescent illusion kept me from saying no outright.

Shocking, how tempted I'd been to try a wild fling—nothing permanent, just a fling. It had appealed to me more than I ever would have imagined. To have that thrill of discovery, of being cherished, pampered, appreciated . . . Not to mention the possibility of hot, passionate sex.

But standing there in Brad's arms, I felt completely out of place. Bland though my sane, respectable couples' life might be, I couldn't turn my back on it any more than I could—or wanted to—erase the life I'd lived beyond Brad. More than that, I respected the woman who looked back at me in the mirror and wanted to keep it that way.

I knew who I was. "I'm very married, Brad. John's a good man, and I love him. Boredom doesn't justify my turning elsewhere."

"I have no intention of jeopardizing your marriage." he said. "We both know I'm not a good risk for the long term. All I want is some time with you, a corner of your life. I won't intrude on the rest."

Not intrude? What he didn't know about women was a lot.

Faced with the choice—not in some fantasy but then and there, complete with very real consequences—the temptation all but evaporated. Nothing I did or said could ever make me a fling kind of girl. "I need roots. And in spite of everything, I love my safe, decent life. And I do love John, even without the fireworks."

Odd, how the sound of those words in my own voice woke the feelings that went with them. Just like that, I wanted my husband. Longed for him, the feel of his arms around me, the smell of him.

Brad wasn't giving up so easily, though. "Of course you love him. But this doesn't have to have anything to do with John and you."

Oy!

I drew back. "That is so *male*, compartmentalizing it that way. It has *everything* to do with John and me." How could I make him understand? "Don't get me wrong; I'm attracted to you. God, am I attracted to you." I realized, too late, that it was a mixed signal when he tried to draw me closer. It got on my nerves, but I managed to maintain my composure. "Trust me, Brad, you're pretty irresistible, but an affair would jeopardize everything that really matters to me. I love my husband. I love my kids. Hell, I even love my in-laws. I can't do it. I won't do it."

Who was I trying to convince?

I should have been proud of myself. Why did I feel so rotten?

After a long pause, he shook his head. "If any of my wives had been half that loyal, I'd still be married." He gave me one, last, lingering hug, then released me. When he stepped back, the old mischief covered whatever he might have felt from my rejection. "You have my numbers, though. If anything ever changes, no matter when, call me." He cupped my cheek, his thumb smoothing away the single tear that had escaped. "I'll be waiting." A brief kiss, and he left me to watch him go.

After he'd driven away, I turned to find the Red Hats, arms linked, watching me. Linda was leaking happy tears. "Damn. That was better than *Casablanca*."

I exhaled a heavy, purging breath, then went to join them.

"Hah. I think you're nuts," SuSu rasped, her already scratchy smoker's voice destroyed from competing with the Shirelles. "Brad's a hunk. John would never have to know."

"That was his argument."

Diane regarded me with touching irony. "I'm glad to see somebody in this crazy world keep their commitments."

"Way to go, kid." Teeny's proud hug erased the imprint of Brad's arms around me. "I knew you'd do the right thing," she whispered in my ear.

"Yeah, well, for a while there, I wasn't so sure." The memory of Brad's hungry, possessive kiss sang through my body, and I surprised myself by bursting into sad, exhausted, relieved tears.

The Red Hats surrounded me with sympathy and gentle laughter, urging me into the limo.

Once inside, I was able to laugh with them, a floaty sense of the surreal buoying my spirits. "Why do I have to be so damned monogamous?" I asked rhetorically.

"You've always been a one-man woman," Linda said, "and

you always will, and thank God for it." She patted my knee. "John has no idea how lucky he is. I've half a mind to tell him."

I closed my eyes briefly, wishing she would on the off chance that it would wake him up. "Works for me."

"Drew," Teeny instructed as he started to close the door, "We need coffee. Pronto."

He touched his cap. "I know a great little all-night poetry bar just a few blocks from here. Be there in a jif." The door closed.

Coffee at that hour would keep me up till midnight tomorrow—today—but it was the only way I could make it more than a mile without falling dead asleep.

"Here, sweetie." Teeny handed me a bunch of cocktail napkins to mop up with. "You look like a raccoon."

I folded them and rubbed away until the paper came back clean of mascara.

Bald-eyed, I relaxed with the others in weary silence to the lulling motion of the limo as an inevitable letdown gathered like a pall.

"Crap, SuSu," Linda grumped. "A good-night kiss is one thing, but you practically raped that stud puppy standing up."

"He didn't mind it." SuSu preened. "Believe me, it was mutual." She stretched out on the banquette. "And anyway, it's two in the morning. Nobody saw."

"What about us? We don't count?" Diane challenged. "And poor Drew. He had to be embarrassed."

She yawned. "Di, contrary to your lifelong conviction, the rest of the world is way too busy with their own little red wagons to waste time worrying about ours."

The yawns were contagious. Linda let loose with one, ending with a protracted *skreek* as she stretched, then went limp.

"Don't y'all go to sleep now," Teeny admonished. "There are surprises still in store."

"Must we do it tonight, sweetie?" SuSu whined, eyes closed.

"It won't take long." Teeny laid her head back, too. After putting the party together, she had to be ten times more tired than we were.

"Once that's done," Teeny said, "we can all go to bed and sleep the clock around, if we want."

"Where?" SuSu croaked out.

"You'll see," Teeny answered, mysterious.

Diane laid her head in my lap. "God, tonight was wonderful." I started massaging her temples. It was a ritual we'd practiced since our husbands had lost interest in such solicitous attentions. "Everybody was there."

"I swear, Beanie must have made a deal with the devil," SuSu said. "She has not changed one whit."

"Great genes." This, from Diane. "There's no substitute. And she never could sun." We'd felt sorry for her in high school while we tanned ourselves black. Now we were paying the price, and she was home free. There wasn't an age spot or a sun freckle on her.

"She told me she planned to make good use of tonight's bachelor roster," I contributed.

Another yawn from SuSu. "More power to her."

"How about Catherine Nichols?" Teeny asked. "I never would have recognized her with that white hair and all that weight."

Linda set us straight. "It's from the steroids. She had a kidney transplant."

"Omygosh." Teeny raised up. "She never said a thing to me."

"She told me she was sick to death of being a walking disease, so she doesn't talk about it if she can help it," Linda clarified. "Maybe she told me because she was my big sister. Or because Brooks is a urologist."

"A transplant. Wow, you never know," I mused aloud. "You see people at something like this and think everything's fine, but all kinds of awful stuff could be goin' on underneath." I shook my head. "You never know."

"An oddly ironic observation comin' from you," Teeny said obliquely, but I was about as sharp as a Georgia mushmelon by that point, so I didn't pursue it. Later I realized she'd been referring to my legendary inability to keep my troubles to myself. If I have a problem, the whole world hears about it—a fact that annoys oh-so-private John to no end.

I resolved to turn over a new leaf and keep our family business to myself, just because I loved him.

It felt wonderful, loving him. I wrapped myself in it like it was a pashmina stole.

Drew parked the limo at the tiny midtown hole in the wall, then took our orders and returned in record time with double-caf lattes all around.

"Home, James," Teeny said when he cranked the engine.

Home?

We never went to Teeny's. We all perked up, curious.

"I thought Reid didn't like having us over," Linda said.

"Cool your jets." Teeny sipped her latte. "All will be revealed."

So we stuffed our curiosity and passed the leisurely trip up a deserted Peachtree, recapping the evening's events—and blessedly sidestepping the subject of Brad.

Fifteen minutes later, the Cathedral of Saint Philip rose golden and majestic in its night illumination ahead of us. Just before we reached Park Place (Elton John had a couple of penthouses there), Drew turned right into the Plaza Towers. It was an older development, but still a great address—if you like high-rise living, which Teeny absotively, posilutely didn't.

Verrrrry interesting . . .

The limo swung wide and glided to a stop by the front doors of the southeast tower.

"Here we are." Teeny stretched.

"Where is here?" I challenged, but she didn't answer, only smiled.

Drew helped us out, then held the doors as we entered the two-story lobby. "I'll get that luggage right away."

The night attendant rose with a deferential, "Good morning, Mrs. Witherspoon."

Teeny nodded. "Hi, Thomas. Drew will be bringing our luggage. And please make a note to send these ladies up anytime they come to visit."

He scanned our faces. "Absolutely."

Bold as you please, she led the way past the soaring dark-paneled wall to a short side hall that hid the elevator. A punch of the button, and the doors opened immediately. Teeny herded us in, then pressed 20 without the slightest hesitation.

"Teeny," Linda said, "what happened to your elevator phobia?"

She smiled. "I decided it was silly to let something other people did without thinking terrorize me anymore. Same with heights, but that's taking me a little longer to iron out completely."

"How'd you do it?" I asked. "Desensitization therapy?"

Teeny laughed. "Well, sort of, but nothing formal. I just prayed to the Virgin for help, made up my mind, and kept on ridin' up and down. Every time, it got a little easier."

She shot a wry glance at the floor indicator. "But if this thing should get stuck, I'd appreciate it if one of you would be merciful and cold-cock me. I'm not *that* cured."

As if on cue, the doors opened on the twentieth floor. Teeny crossed the elegant, muted hallway and placed her hand on a lighted panel beside two impressive doors. The doors clicked open, then automatically swung inward, revealing an amazing, Zen-like interior in soft whites and subtle grays, accented by muted blacks and sparse flashes of color. A wall of glass gave out onto a flower-laden terrace and the distant city skyline. The spacious great room looked like some wonderful, futuristic movie set, but it wasn't cold. Lush plants, tranquil abstract paintings, and carefully chosen accessories made it peaceful and inviting.

SuSu let out a low whistle. "Whose place *is* this?

Teeny smiled. "It's mine. I combined two units and decorated it myself."

An electric current couldn't have zapped us to attention any better. Shock combined with caffeine to bring us wide awake. We stood transfixed.

Our timid Teeny faced us, world-wise and assertive. "I live here now. I left Reid three days ago, but he didn't even realize it until I served him divorce papers this morning—yesterday morning—at his office. The Church will annul us later."

SuSu exploded first, of course. "Ohmygod, ohmygod, ohmygod!" She hugged Teeny so hard, I feared our newest liberee would asphyxiate before she had a chance to try her wings. "At long last!"

The whole gigolo-reunion-fund-raiser evening paled to oblivion.

"My God, Teeny," Diane breathed. "Did you charge this place to him, too?"

Half-smothered in SuSu's embrace, Teeny laughed. "No."

The doorbell rang, so I tore myself away to admit Drew and our luggage.

"SuSu, honey," Teeny gasped out, "you gotta let go of me. I need to give Drew his tip; then I promise I'll explain everything."

SuSu did as ordered, but she was still half-berserk with excitement. "Oh, Teens, this is the best surprise ever."

The sentiment was unanimous.

Teeny opened the doors to the most gorgeous all-white, fabric-draped bedroom I had ever seen. She pulled three hundred-dollar bills from the bedside table drawer, then returned to the foyer. "Here you go, sugar." She extended the humongous tip toward Drew. "You were wonderful."

Three hundred dollars! Bargain Queen Diane looked like she might faint dead away.

Instead of accepting the money, Drew took Teeny's hand and bowed to kiss it first. "It was my pleasure." Only then did he pocket the proceeds. Another devastating smile for all of us. "Please ask for me the next time, ladies." He pivoted smartly, giving us a lovely view of his gorgeous, tight ass. "I'll close the door on my way out."

"A three-hundred-dollar cash *tip?*" Diane exclaimed when the lock clicked shut.

"I can afford it," Teeny said calm as you please. Gone was any trace of her waiflike naivety. This was a woman in charge of her life at last.

"You can afford it?" I couldn't help challenging. (It's one of my worst faults, one I inherited from my mother—asking somebody a question, then arguing with them about the answer.) "But Reid's the biggest tightwad since Scrooge. We all know what a tight financial leash he's kept you on."

Teeny led the way into the living room, where she subsided into a silk tuxedo chair perfectly scaled to her petite dimensions. "He didn't keep me on a tight leash. As a matter of fact, he was quite generous with the household budget and never once questioned my figures." Now *there* was a news flash.

Rapt, we piled onto the sofas to hear the rest.

"After he hit me," she went on, "I kept *myself* on that tight leash so I could invest every spare penny for me and my children in case we ever needed to escape."

We stilled in astonishment.

Teeny kicked off her shoes and we followed suit. "It was so easy. At first, I saved half and put the rest into the market. I made good choices, Home Depot on the ground floor, stuff like that. I bought a nice chunk of Chrysler at seven dollars and sold at fifty-six. I also started paying close attention to Reid and Big Dalton's drunken renditions of the inside scoop. When they made money, so did I, and it didn't take long to amass a tidy nest egg. Once I had enough to spare for some high-risk ventures, I tried my hand at commodities and penny stocks."

"Oh, Teeny, but those are so dangerous," sensible Linda fussed. "Everybody I know who tried that ended up losing big-time. Us included."

"Well, you'll have to change that story now, because I didn't."

"You didn't?" SuSu said in breathless anticipation.

Diane cut to the bottom line. "How much did you make?"

"Two million in eight months," Teeny said as calmly as if she were discussing the price of pork chops at the Publix.

"Two million?" we shrieked in unison.

Timid Teeny, with all that money? And all this time, we'd thought she was scraping along!

"When was this?" Linda demanded.

"Early eighties." Teeny stretched. "Then I had this weird feeling, so I put the money in a Swiss bank account and risked only the interest from then on."

Two *million* dollars! We gaped at each other.

Small potatoes to Reid, but a helluva sugar bowl for Teeny.

I'll say she could afford a three-hundred-dollar tip! She could have afforded to throw tonight's party, but I loved it that she'd stuck it to Reid and Big Dalton, instead. "You are a goddess, a true, angel goddess."

"Trust me," she said with absolute conviction, "I am no angel."

"So what are you worth now, if you don't mind telling us?" Of course, it was SuSu who crossed the crass line.

"I don't mind, truly, but it's really hard to say. I took a bad hit with the market lately, just like everybody else." Teeny wiggled her toes. "Fortunately, I never had any money in telecoms. Or dot coms: it didn't make sense to me how they could be so great without showing a profit, and as it turned out, I was right."

"You're avoiding the question," Linda scolded.

"No, I truly can't say exactly." We could see Teeny meant it. "Everything's been so volatile lately."

"Ballpark," I wailed.

"Ballpark, counting the condo and real estate investments . . ." Her eyes narrowed in concentration; then she shrugged. "About twenty million."

And the rich get richer.

We sat stunned, unable to wrap our brains around such a figure.

"This can't be real," I said, doubting my sanity. Teeny, a secret tycoon? Surely we would have known, sensed something. If this was true, none of us had really known her for a long, long time. I peered at her. "Who *are* you?"

"I'm still me." Her eyes begged us to understand. "At first, I was afraid to tell y'all. What if I failed?" She colored. "Or what if you let something slip? I couldn't risk Reid's finding out."

It stung that she hadn't thought it safe to tell us, but I forgave her, as I knew the others would, too.

"But then," she went on, "I got good at it. Really good. And it made my life bearable to have something that was just mine, not anybody else's—not only the money, but a part of me I didn't have to share with anybody, not even y'all."

I tried to understand but couldn't help feeling betrayed that she'd been living a double life without trusting us to know.

"Da-yum," SuSu wheezed. "And all this time, I felt guilty whenever you broke Tradition Nine or Eleven and had to pick up the check." We could see SuSu's brain take a small right turn. "Give me the name of your broker!"

Teeny shook her head, recovering her smile. "Unless it's something exotic, I trade direct on-line or use a true discount broker, whoever offers the lowest cost. But once you reach a certain bracket, it gets much easier. I'm very diversified and heavily sheltered."

I couldn't absorb what I was hearing. "And I used to wonder how you kept from being bored silly with your circumspect life."

"Oh, I've never been bored." She smiled her same shy smile. "Trust me."

"Teeny, we never knew ye," I stated on behalf of us all. (As I said earlier, stating the obvious is one of my official Red Hat functions.)

Linda scanned the gorgeous condo. "This place is fabulous, but I thought Williamsburg was your favorite decor."

"It was," Teeny said. "Loved it to death in 1970. My tastes have changed."

"My God, I'll say," Diane said in awe. "Stock trades, Swiss bank accounts, this."

"How long have you had this place?" Linda asked.

"I got the two units in ninety-eight, had them gutted, and only finished up last week. Perfect timing, because it coincided with my lawyers' finally sheltering the last of my assets so it would be hard for Reid to find them." Her eyebrows lifted. "I had deliberately gotten them to draw up the divorce agreement in broad, simple terms. No legalese. I served the papers on Reid myself this morning"—she amended—"yesterday morning."

"And?" Diane leaned forward, rapt as the rest of us.

"Total shock. At first, he didn't believe I was serious. Then he balked, which was understandable."

"Little wonder," Linda said. "He'd gotten away with murder so long, he probably thought it would go on that way forever."

Teeny didn't take offense. She seemed almost wistful as she related the final release of the devil she knew. "I had to do some serious talking to make him realize this was best for both of us. I think it was my lack of anger or blaming that finally convinced him. Men like Reid are so predictable," she said with quiet assurance. "No matter how horrible they've been, they want to come out feeling like a good guy."

Diane leaned forward. "So what did he do?"

"Once he started to relent, I went straight to the financial part of the agreement. He was so amazed that I hadn't asked for anything, it never occurred to him to wonder why. I told him my lawyer had advised against my letting him off the hook financially, but I just wanted out. No house, no alimony, no stocks, no pension, no nothing. As I'd hoped, he was stunned by his good fortune."

"Little wonder!" SuSu sat up and propped a fist on her hip. "Getting away scot-free. It's the errant husband's wet dream."

"That's exactly what I wanted him to think," Teeny said. "I just kept reassuring him that it was best for us to go our separate ways, no hard feelings." She chuckled. "He read the settlement over six times to make sure it really said what he thought it said. I counted. He points like a first-grader at what he's reading." Only then did she betray the first sign of smugness. "Then he called over his in-house attorney, who reviewed the wording and reassured him there were no catches. Ironclad, I would get nothing."

"And the bastard never even asked how you planned to manage?" Linda asked.

"Of course not." Teeny calmly took responsibility for her part in his self-centeredness. "I'd trained him not to give me a thought."

"Joke's on him." Diane hugged herself with glee.

Teeny nodded. "It went even better than I'd hoped for. Reid was so ecstatic, he summoned his secretary and had her notarize his signature with the lawyer looking on. So now I have two very credible witnesses to the fact that he never even asked about my assets." She laced her fingers and pushed her palms outward. "Reid always has been too impulsive for his own good."

She was the one who'd gotten off scot-free. With a signed agreement, Teeny would be divorced within thirty days.

I gathered enough wits to ask the question we all wanted answered. "What finally made you decide to do this?"

She looked to Diane. "Diane. When I saw her courage in facing the truth about Harold and her life, I realized that I had been a coward all these years." Tears welled in her eyes. "I've known for a long, long time that Reid wasn't capable of being the husband or father I had hoped for," she admitted. "But it took Diane to make me see that living a lie was no substitute for a real life.

Even all my money couldn't change that; it gave me far more options than most women have, though." She drew up her knees and wrapped her arms around them. "Everybody, including me, thought I stayed for the boys' sake, but Diane's honesty made me admit that was just an excuse for my fear of leaving our couples' world to face life on my own."

Her self-assessment was so serene that I felt only pride in her, not pity.

"I didn't think I could survive without a husband. And it never occurred to me that there might be something better out there. Either way, my faith forbids divorce." She sighed. "Then, suddenly, I'd had enough. I got on my knees and before God. I told Him I know He only allowed divorce because of the hardness of our hearts, but I couldn't do it anymore. And you know what happened?"

Certain that I wasn't the only one who was wondering how she'd reconciled this radical step, I shook my head with the rest of them, afraid to answer aloud lest we shatter Teeny's fragile aura of hope.

"That still, small little voice inside me said, 'It's not your heart that's hard.' " She glowed with absolution. "So I knew it was okay. Father Paul said so, too. He said Reid had never intended to be faithful to me, so there would be no problem with an annulment."

It never ceased to amaze me, the lengths the Catholic Church would go to to bend its own rules, but in Teeny's case, I was heartily glad it did.

She got up and hugged Diane. "You did it for me, honey. You made me strong enough to realize I deserved a life."

Never comfortable when the sentiment got too deep, SuSu rubbed her hands together. "Well, good for you, and none too soon," she said brightly. "Now that that's all settled, Teens, can I have $750,000?"

Teeny burst out laughing even as the rest of us threw sofa pillows and insults at SuSu to protest her crudeness.

"Shit, y'all," SuSu defended. "She can spare it! And we all know I'm never gonna get a cent out of Jackson!"

"An awfully convenient time for you to finally admit that particular fact of life!" I scolded.

"Leave her alone," Teeny managed between laughs. "Of course you can have $750,000!" No strings, no reservation, just yes. "What good is money if I can't share it with my best friends?"

Suddenly, the whole huge, unbelievable, exhilarating truth seemed hilarious to all of us.

"Twenty fricken million dollars!" Linda's tickle box tumped over, triggering ours.

When finally we subsided, chuffing and still a little giddy, Teeny stood up. "Okay. If I don't get out of these pantyhose this instant, I'm gonna die. We can do my surprise in our pajamas."

"Lord, Teeny," I gasped out, "if your next surprise is anything like the last one, I'm not sure my heart can stand it."

"It's an easy one. Trust me."

Teeny waved toward the back of the condo. "There are enough beds for all of y'all. Take your picks, but be back in five minutes."

We all knew perfectly well it would be at least fifteen. Looking like Tammy Faye on a bad day, we grabbed our gear and retired to relieve ourselves, liberate our boobs and waistlines, and get ready for another round.

"The honoree is hereby officially turning into a pumpkin," Diane groaned out as she followed SuSu into the far guest room.

The clock in the second guest room said 3:58, well past the point of no return. (If I'm ever still awake past three, I always force myself to pull an all-nighter so I won't get my days and nights turned around.) But even though I didn't plan to go to bed, I dropped my stuff onto the luxurious twin bed opposite Linda's, then traded my svelte gown in for fuzzy slippers and a pink cotton knit sleep-shirt embroidered with little white hearts from Talbots. The poster child for letting yourself go, I topped it with a pink seersucker wrap from Kohl's.

While Linda was in the bathroom, I gathered my scarlet finery to hang it up. Sassy as a rebellious thirteen-year-old, my little red evening bag popped open and spit out Brad's card on the gray bedspread. The mere sight of it was enough to make my stomach do a traitorous flip.

I picked it up and smoothed a finger across his neat, masculine print. My first love still wanted me, married or not. The power of that swelled to a bittersweet crescendo in my chest. I was still desirable, and I could take that with me from this day forward.

Her midlife prom dress draped over her arm, Linda emerged wearing plaid pajama pants and a slightly faded oversize T-shirt that said, IF YOU LOVE SOMETHING, LET IT GO on the front and IF IT DOESN'T RETURN TO YOU, HUNT IT DOWN AND KILL IT on the back.

I slipped Brad's card back into the purse, a talisman of my youth. Then I scrubbed my face—proud of the woman who looked back at me—splashed it with cold water, brushed my teeth, and returned to the great room while Linda finished stowing her things.

Teeny, clad in an elegant, long, black satin gown and matching robe, was putting the final touches on five places at the glass-topped dining table. A centerpiece of assorted heavy red candles illuminated the settings, each place with a unique, outrageously overdone red hat, an exquisitely wrapped little gift no larger than a pack of cards, and a crystal goblet of what turned out to be iced water. Dozens more tapers glowed in sconces and candelabra around the room, reminding me of the final stage of Mademoiselle initiation.

"There." Teeny positioned the last of the little gifts at the side places, then donned her hat—a turned-up brim crammed with rose blossoms and dripping "rubies," beads, and crystals—and took her seat at the head of the table.

I surveyed the hats. "These are priceless. Where in the world did you find them?"

"Find them? Honey, I made these," she said with pride. "Every last flounce, jewel, and cherub."

I sat down at the one I liked best, a tightly woven red straw with a wide picture brim. Red-glittered tulips interspersed with little red cherubs massed at the base of the crown. I tied the satin ribbons to one side under my chin. "How do I look?"

"Katie Scarlett, eat your heart out." Teeny straightened hers. "I knew you'd pick that one."

No mystery there. All my hats were broad-brimmed or fedoras.

Linda arrived, brisk with her second wind. "Oh, Teeny. How great." She went straight for the oversize pillbox encrusted with assorted jeweled, sequined, and beaded red appliqués. It was definitely her style and looked adorable when she put it on and sat. "*Too* cute! And I can't wait to see what's in my present."

"No presents until everybody's here," Teeny admonished.

"Teeny made our hats," I informed Linda.

"They're perfect." Linda peered at Teens yet again in wonder. "I had no idea you were crafty." She pointed her schoolteacher finger. "But then, we're finding out all kinds of things about you this night, ma girl."

"Are the hats the surprise?" I asked.

"Nope." Teeny lifted her chin. "And that's all I'm saying until everybody's here."

Diane came out small-eyed without her makeup, barefooted, in bright green nylon pajamas like the ones my mother wears. "Ha! Y'all are priceless." She went straight for the red-sequined baseball cap whose crown was adorned with a small white dove, wings spread in flight, below FREE AT LAST spelled out in fake diamonds. She donned it squarely, then gulped down a deep swig of iced water. "Thank goodness. Cotton mouth has set in."

The power of suggestion sent us for our waters.

SuSu, of course, arrived last. "I'm coming. I'm coming." Still fully made up, she minced out in high-heeled, red satin marabou slides, wearing a transparent red wrap over a satin tap set slit halfway to the waist on the sides.

I found myself wishing the tabletop were opaque.

There was only one place—and red hat—left. She sat down (revealing *way* too much hip) and put on the red fedora with a flashy iridescent red plastic band. Only when she moved could you see the holographic LAYOVER QUEEN LAYOVER QUEEN LAYOVER QUEEN wink in the band.

When we all laughed, she took it off and saw for herself. "Damn straight!" she said with a grin.

After we'd complimented her sufficiently on her millinery genius, Teeny brought us to order with a tap of her nails on the rim of her crystal goblet. "Okay. Time for a serious moment."

We dutifully sobered.

"This is Diane's night, not mine, and I wanted to commemorate it with something tangible, something that would represent not only her new start, but also all the victories, big and small, we've shared in the past thirty-six years."

Thirty-six years. Seeing our fellow Mademoiselles at the reunion had really brought home the passage of time.

My mind could accept it, but not my heart. How could it? Memories of high school were still so vivid. Of our weddings. Our pregnancies. It seemed only last week when we'd all been driven by the urgency of youth, when everything was a big deal.

And there were still so many things I'd meant to have done by now: spent a summer in England and Scotland, built the perfect house, seen the gardens in Victoria, learned to touch type, experienced Paris, written a book, taken a cruise, sung a solo in choir.

"The Red Hats will officially come to order." Teeny raised her glass. "Here's to sisterhood, stronger than blood."

Solemn, we repeated the toast, then drank.

"And to surprises," Diane said. "May we welcome them with joy."

"With joy," we repeated, then sealed with a sip.

SuSu put her glass aside. "Okay. No more toasts. I'm opening my present." Careless of the exquisite wrappings, she ripped hers open to reveal a hinged red velvet box. "Oooh. Lookin' good."

As we dived into ours, she flipped open the box and promptly melted into tears. "Ohmygod," she said with uncharacteristic reverence. She looked to Teeny. "Oh . . . my . . . god."

Inside the boxes were identical jewel-pavéed black harlequin masks patterned after our old Mademoiselle pins, only a bit larger, complete with tiny gold chains with *alphas* in white diamonds.

Basking in our reactions, Teeny hugged herself. "I'm so glad you like them." She grinned. "After y'all mentioned losing your pins, I thought of these. We can't always wear our red hats."

Diane dabbed at happy tears with her black damask napkin. "Where's yours, Teens? You did one for you, too, didn't you?"

"Sure." Teeny retrieved hers from under her place mat and pinned it to her gown.

"Honey," Diane decreed, "this night is the be-all and end-all of surprises."

We admired each other until SuSu set off a wave of yawns.

On emotional overload, all of us but SuSu flagged. Still brittle, she popped to her feet. "You party-poopers can veg out if you want to, but I'm checking this place out."

We looked at her as if she were an alien, but Teeny didn't protest, just yawned deeply and waved her on. Behind her, SuSu made straight for Teeny's gorgeous master suite.

We chatted for a few minutes; then Diane rose and hugged Teeny. "All of this has been the best surprise anybody has ever given me. Thank you, honey."

Linda yawned hugely and half rolled out of her chair. "The best, babes." She shuffled toward the bedroom, but stopped short at SuSu's scream of excitement.

"Aaaaaaah! Get in here! Teeny has a rogues' gallery!"

Teeny rolled her eyes, blushing furiously, then dropped her forehead to the table. "Shit."

Linda and Diane rushed into the bedroom, but I lagged behind. "Teens?"

"That armoire was locked." She rose with a sigh. "I never should have let her loose in there."

I followed her into the little salon off her bedroom to find the others poring over photos from the armoire in question.

"Look!" SuSu brandished three photos of Teeny, each with a different man I didn't recognize. On boats, at romantic restaurants, dancing. The only thing they had in common was that the backgrounds looked tropical, and Teeny was clearly enjoying herself, happier than we ever saw her.

Diane and Linda stood speechless.

The top of the armoire was full of tastefully framed photos crowding the shelves. There must have been thirty, at least, as far as I could see, all different men, some gorgeous, some ordinary, some plump, some old, some young.

I stared at her in astonishment. "Teeny?" This double life thing went deeper than I could fathom.

"Well," SuSu decreed, "all I can say is way to go, honey. What's good for the gander is good for the goose. Reid had his share of affairs. Why shouldn't you?"

Irked, Teeny pulled the photos from her hands. "That cabinet was locked."

Unrepentant, SuSu dangled a key on a red ribbon. "I found this in your jewelry box. Had to find out what it fit." When Teeny snatched the key, SuSu got in her face. "And good thing I did. Tradition Seven, big-time!" (No secret affairs.)

"And who said I broke Tradition Seven?" Teeny replaced the pictures, then turned on SuSu. "These men are my friends. Nothing more."

"Hah!" SuSu retorted. "And if you believe that, I've got some swamp land in Valdosta I'd like to sell you."

"How?" Linda asked her. *"When?"*

"The only time you were ever gone was to those retreats," Diane added.

"You met them at a Catholic Women's retreat?" Linda exclaimed. "Man. That's enough to make me consider converting."

Keeping the money from us was one thing. I could forgive that. But this . . . "Were you lying about the retreats?" I challenged, chopped off at the knees.

"No." Teeny closed the cabinet and locked it, then pocketed the key. "I did go to the cenacle, at first. But when I got enough money to buy a condo at Sanibel and started going there instead, y'all assumed I was still going to the cenacle, and I let you, for all our sakes." She scanned us. "I didn't want you to be compromised or have to cover for me. And it was the only time that I could escape and have some fun."

"I'll say, some fun." SuSu grinned, smug.

"I mean it, Suse," Teeny said. "They were just friends. All single, and no two ever the same. No complications. No commitments. And no sex."

"Which explains why no two were ever the same," SuSu observed wryly.

I stared at Teeny, wondering if I had ever really known her. Yet even after all the lies, I felt inclined to believe her. And the last thing I wanted to do was begrudge her the little happiness she'd managed to hide away.

Diane embraced her. "I'm glad for you, but you deserve so much more happiness than that. Maybe now you can find it."

Teeny held on tight for a moment, then looked to each of us in turn, her eyes pleading. "This is the biggest thing I've ever asked of y'all, but can I call a Tradition One about all this?"

She'd done so much for us, been so much to us. How could we deny her?

One by one, we nodded, Linda with quiet tears, me with weary relief, and SuSu with a tactless, "Well, I still think you should have slept with at least a few. After all, what's confession for?"

Depleted, we stood there in a rare moment of awkwardness.

"Well," Diane offered, "I'm going to bed. Don't wake me up till dinner." She trundled toward the guest rooms.

Linda yawned. "Me, too." She followed after, pulling SuSu. "Come on. You've done enough damage for one night."

"Damage?" SuSu protested as they retreated. "What damage? All I did was have a good time and say what everybody else was thinking."

"How about breaking into Teeny's private stuff?" Linda retorted, but the door closed on SuSu's response.

Teeny rose, the peace in her face made haggard by fatigue. "I need to put out the candles."

"I'll help you."

We walked into the dining area, where she handed me a snuffer. "Thanks." She picked up another snuffer and one by one, we smothered the flames, releasing the smoky tang of burned wax and wick. "Are you going to sleep late like the others?"

My watch said 5:40. "Not me. I'm gonna tough it out and go home to bed early tonight." With John. Would he sense the difference? Pick up on the change in me?

She stretched. "Do you mind if I stay up with you? I don't think I could sleep just now."

"Sure." The sky outside was beginning to lighten. "Why don't we sit on the terrace? I could use some fresh air."

"Good idea."

We settled in silence on the comfortable cushioned chairs. In that quiet moment alone with her, I suddenly wasn't sleepy, just content. Never one to suffer long silences easily, I told her softly, "I am so proud of you. Of all you've accomplished. Of your finally standing up for your life."

"I was afraid y'all would hate me for lying to you all these years. It was a big reason I never told you."

"Oh, Teens. We could never hate you." I smiled. "Especially not SuSu, now that you've given her three-quarters of a million dollars." I paused, wondering what would come next for SuSu now that she had enough money to buy a nice little house and finally stop chasing men who could help her chase Jackson. "I hope she really can move on."

"She will. It's more of a gift to *me*, now that everything's in the open and I can offer her a second chance."

Teeny's answer eased the niggling fear that her money might have put us in very different worlds.

She peered at me, hesitant. "We all face the truth when we're ready."

I nodded. "Thanks for tonight. Specially for Brad."

"It was a risk, but I had faith in you."

I arched an eyebrow. "What would you have done if I'd gone home with him?"

"Covered your ass," she said without a blink, "and waited for you to come to your senses."

"Who says I would have come to my senses?"

Teeny grinned. "You couldn't help it. You've got a double helping of the sensible gene." She rose and brought us some water, handed me mine, then took hers to the exposed aggregate half-wall to gaze across Buckhead as it started to stir. The sounds of the waking city brought new energy on the cool morning air.

I rose to join her, impressed by her relaxed confidence. "Look at you. Twenty stories up and cool as a cucumber."

She chuckled. "I'm fine as long as nobody makes any sudden moves toward the edge."

"No sudden moves toward danger for me," I said in one of those double entendres my subconscious excels at.

The sun would be up soon. And the Original Pancake House would be open at 6:30 A.M.

Suddenly, I was hungry enough to eat an apple pancake all by myself.

I raised my glass. "Here's to starting over."

She touched her goblet to mine. "For both of us."

"We can start over, can't we, John and I?" It was more of a statement than a question.

"Damn straight. It'll take some time, but he'll wake up. The best thing you can do for both of you is make the most of your own life. How about finally getting that degree, just for yourself? I can totally see you as a student." She shot me a grin. "I just happen to know where you can get a full scholarship. Emory, if you want."

I'd never seriously considered going back to school until that moment, but the idea was intriguing. Learning, simply for the joy of knowing. Getting a degree in something that interested me because *I* wanted to.

Once I started to think that way, I began to see other possibilities I'd been too afraid to consider while I'd guarded the safety and security of my predictable existence. I wasn't bored; I was boring. But not anymore, I resolved, remembering at last how it felt to believe I could do anything I set my mind to. It was exhilarating.

I lifted my glass. "Here's to possibilities."

We drank again, leaving only one more sip in our goblets.

"And last but not least, here's to the Red Hats," Teeny proposed. "Long may we reign."

A chorus of "Hear, hear" erupted behind us, and we turned to find Linda, Diane, and SuSu red-hatted, dressed in their sweats, and ready to go.

"We were too tired to sleep," Linda explained. "Come on. Last one to the Original Pancake House is a rotten egg."

"Hah! You read my mind."

"Mine, too," Teeny said. "I've got plenty of room in my minivan for all of us."

"Minivan?" SuSu turned on her. "You've got twenty million dollars, and you drive a minivan?"

"Among others. I love it."

"You can take the little woman out of the house," Linda bemoaned, "but you can't take the housewife out of the little woman."

Teeny swatted her. "Hush up, you." Then we both hurried to throw on some clothes.

Ten minutes later as we headed down Peachtree toward Lindbergh, I surveyed the five of us, our faces au naturel under our red hats. "Do you think the Pancake House is ready for this?"

SuSu was emphatic. "Honey, *nobody's* ready for us. But we'll break 'em in."

A new tradition was born that day. From then on, the milestones in our lives were commemorated by vast infusions of refined carbohydrate in the form of apple pancakes and fresh-squeezed orange juice. And there would be many, many milestones.

Our red hats might change over the years, but not the love and loyalty beneath them. Nor the Twelve Sacred Traditions that guard our friendship.

SuSu thinks Congress should add our Traditions to the Bill of Rights. I do, too, but they'd probably ruin everything trying to make them politically correct.

And if there's one thing these particular Red Hats are not, it's politically correct.

We're too busy savoring the joys in life, and it's always worked just fine—even better now that there's twenty million to play with.

We're starting with a week at this fabulous Fiji spa Teeny saw on the *Today Show*. We plan to be unabashedly ourselves. They'll love us.

Acknowledgments

Atlanta in the 1960s was a magical place to be a white, middle-class teenager. Still aglow with the illusions of our *Father Knows Best* childhoods, we reveled in pep rallies and paper drives and school dances and breakups and makeups. Our biggest sins were sneaking out, drinking at parties, and—for the few truly daring—discreetly surrendering our virginities. The only violence at school was an annual drubbing between a few of the "hoods" on campus. Oh, we suffered the usual teenaged angst, epitomized by *Rebel Without a Cause*, but for the most part, our biggest worries had to do with grades, clothes, boyfriends, popularity, and parents who "didn't understand."

If I'd had any idea what was coming just around the decade, I would've worried less and enjoyed it more, but youth is wasted on the young.

The Mademoiselles really existed, a rare and golden circle of Southern maidenhood that was quite ecumenical for its time. While I was good enough for our Northside sorority of Theta Alpha, I got passed over for Mademoiselle. Happily, I took it in stride, but several of my friends did join. So when I decided to write this story, I called on them to share their Mademoiselle memories. Alas, their middle-aged brains were as Swiss-cheesy as my own. They couldn't have betrayed the Mademoiselle secret lore if their lives had depended upon it, much less the details of initiations, and the like. So I was forced to appropriate what I could remember of my own Theta Alpha experiences and fabricate the rest. There are probably plenty of Mademoiselle alumnae out there who have every accurate detail recorded in diaries, scrapbooks, or memory, but I couldn't find them. So I hereby issue a humble apology to all of them and beg their indulgence for the liberties I have taken.

As always, I must thank my perceptive editor, Jennifer Enderlin; my agent, Mel Berger; and my indispensable critique partner, Betty Cothran. Thanks, too, to one of the most personally and professionally generous organizations I've ever been privileged to participate in, Georgia Romance Writers.

And to the real people whose stories provided a jumping-off point for my overactive imagination. You know who you are.

For moral support, I would be remiss if I didn't mention my good friends Kris and Tom Olson, who have helped me so much. Thanks to Maggie and Charlie Garriott for the sunshine they bring to my life. Thanks, too, to my personal Red Hats Carla Fredd and Carmen Green, most excellent Christian playmates who like good, clean fun as much as I do. Kudos go to Mavis Stevens for her sunny inspiration and precious spirit, to Judy Surowiec for her hugs and smiles, her amazing paintings, and my wonderful, one-of-a-kind bug box. And to my great Shadowbrook Singles Sunday School class—Gary, Mike, Sharon, Ralph, Robin, Kathryn, Steve, Pam, and Jean—who not only supported me in prayer, but also brought pizza to the hospital. I am so blessed by you all.

To my mom and all the Pritchett clan, thanks so much for all your patience with me and your practical help, not just when I had my hip replacement, but all the time. What would I do without you? And to dear Dr. R. Marvin Royster of the Peachtree Orthopedic Group, the best orthopedic surgeon in the whole, wide world and a fine Christian gentleman, and his able assistants, Judy and Deborah. The hip replacement went so well, I can't wait to get my new knees and the other hip done.

All my love and thanks to my stepmother, Fancy, who has been such a beacon of strength and heart in my life. And to my wonderful stepfamily, the Hinton clan, who were so kind and helpful during my dad's illness and passing: Doug and Sharon, Katie Rose, Stuart, Will, and Madison; David and Kathy and Clint; Dan and Angie, Logan, and Gray; and Dana and Richard Pharr. Daddy loved you all so much, and now I know why. I'm proud to call you kin.

Thanks, too, to a friendly local banker, T.B., for the inside scoop on the banking poop. And to Jim Noel and Jeff Robel with NOAA at the National Weather Service. And Reid Yates, wine expert extraordinaire at Green's Package Store in Atlanta, for the info about champagne splits.

Thanks also to all the female authors who have taken advantage of my writers' retreats. I have been so blessed to know you, and I've learned much from working together on your manuscripts. And sometimes I find a real diamond like Lynn Frost; Lynn, it will happen for you. Keep polishing your craft, and never let go of the dream.

DISCUSSION QUESTIONS

1) Why do you think the Red Hats have stayed friends for so long? Give at least three specific reasons. What's different about their relationships compared to friendships that don't last?

2) Discuss the role that loyalty and acceptance have played in the interactions between the characters.

3) Which of the Red Hats is your favorite, and why? Which woman is your least favorite, and why?

4) Many women choose to "look the other way" in troubled marriages. Do you think there were signs of Diane's husband's affair before the incident with the note? If so, why do you think she chose to overlook them? And why do you think she finally made the choice to confront the truth?

5) How do you feel about Georgia's expectations (or lack of them) for her marriage? At the end of the book, how do you feel about her chances for real happiness with John?

6) One of the main themes of the book is that it's never too late to make positive choices in our lives as women. What positive choices do the Red Hats make? Would you have chosen differently?

7) Another main theme of the book is the power women have when they choose to accept and support one another without qualification in a culture that conditions women to tear each other down both personally and professionally. Are there any positive examples of that support in your life? Share those as a group.

· ·

Haywood loves to hear from readers who have enjoyed her books. You may write her care of St. Martin's Press at 175 Fifth Avenue, NY, NY 10010, or e-mail her at haywood100@aol.com (please reference THE RED HAT CLUB in the subject line).

She also enjoys speaking to women's organizations. For information concerning bookings, e-mail her at haywood100@aol.com and reference PERSONAL APPEARANCES in the subject line.